Saving

Rain

A Novel

By Kelsey Kingsley

For Daddy & Mike—

Because above all else,

You are good men.

Two of the best

A Letter from the Author

Dear Reader,

This is my favorite book I've ever written—at this point, anyway.

I'm jealous of you—genuinely and horribly jealous. Because you get to meet Soldier for the first time. And let me tell you, I have read through this story time and time again, and unlike every other book I've written, I still haven't reached a point of being tired of it. I think maybe that says a lot—or at least, it should.

I do have to give you a bit of warning, though. This isn't an easy story. It'll likely bring a tear or a thousand to your eye. Some topics addressed within these pages might be difficult to handle, and if heavy angst isn't your thing, you might want to turn around. But if none of this has scared you off, I strongly urge you to continue.

Because his name is Soldier, and he was never meant to be a hero.

But ...

PROLOGUE

A BOY NAMED SOLDIER

"All right, Diane," the obstetrician said to the young woman in the bed as she moved to stand between her parted knees. "I'm gonna need you to push."

Diane—barely eighteen—exhausted and dripping with sweat, lolled her head from side to side in protest. "I can't," she wheezed between sobs. "I can't do it. I can't. I don't want to."

God, what the hell had she been thinking? She wasn't in any position to have a baby. She could barely take care of herself, let alone a brand-new little life. One that would depend on her and only her.

"Come on, honey. Just one more push," the doctor encouraged with a kind, sympathetic smile. "Your baby is almost here."

My baby, Diane thought, hardly believing that someone like her could—or *should*—have a baby at all.

What the fuck was she going to do with a baby? She didn't have a job; she had no money. For fuck's sake, she couldn't even get through those first few contractions without knocking back the bottle of Grey Goose she had snatched out of her dad's liquor cabinet—the one he had kept locked ever since she had moved back home, as if she didn't know how to pick it.

Come to think of it now, she should've just gotten rid of the damn thing growing inside of her while she had the chance months and months ago. Her mother had been the first to suggest an abortion. Even she knew Diane would never have it in her to be a mother, let alone a passable, decent one.

I can prove them wrong, she thought, staring up at the bright light overhead. *Maybe I can even prove myself wrong. Maybe it's not too late for me, and this baby is what's gonna save me.*

She nodded to the light, like it was some kind of heavenly being looking down at her from the ceiling of this cold and sterile hospital room. With a deep breath and the resolution to get that damn kid out into the world, she lifted onto her elbows and squeezed her eyes shut, and with every drop of determination left in her tired body, she pushed and pushed and pushed until she heard the frantic squawking of something tiny and new.

Diane fell back against the pillow, gasping for the same stale air her baby was desperate for.

"What's the time?" someone asked.

"Eleven eleven p.m.," someone replied.

"We have a boy!" someone called out.

3

So many voices, but all Diane could focus on was the shrill sound of a tiny, innocent newborn, rising above everyone else in the room.

Her mother squeezed her hand.

"Diane, open your eyes and meet your son," she instructed in a voice so full of astonishment and pride that Diane couldn't help but do as she'd asked.

There, in the hands of a nurse she couldn't remember the name of, was an angry, shaking, crying, red-faced baby. He was the ugliest, noisiest, dirtiest thing she had ever seen in her life, and yet her heart reached for something she still wasn't sure she was capable of feeling.

"Can I hold him?" she asked the nurse.

The older lady smiled and nodded. Coming to stand beside the sweaty girl, who was barely an adult, she passed the little bundle down to her. "Just for a minute. He still needs to be cleaned up."

Diane had never held a baby before. Nobody she knew had ever let her hold theirs, and who could really blame them? She was almost always drunk or high, and when she wasn't, she was wishing she were instead of being hungover. These months of pregnancy had been the only sober months since … God, she didn't even know how long. For all intents and purposes, no baby had any business being near her.

But this one … this one was hers.

And he was going to save her.

"He's beautiful, honey," her dad said, peering over her shoulder.

He isn't beautiful, Diane thought.

4

His face looked like a prune with a gaping hole in the middle, all gums and no teeth, and he sounded like an outraged cat in heat. But she supposed that, one day, maybe he *could* be beautiful, so she forced a smile onto her face and willed her head to nod.

"Yeah, he is," she replied because that was what she was supposed to say, right?

"What are you going to name him?" her mom asked, brushing the damp hair from off her daughter's forehead. "Have you thought about it?"

In truth, Diane hadn't thought about it at all. She had been too busy these past thirty-seven weeks talking herself out of sneaking sips from the locked-away bottles in the liquor cabinet while cursing the parasite in her belly for keeping her awake and making her puke and squeezing her bladder down to the size of a poppy seed. But now that she looked at him, now that she knew he was in fact a he—the little ray of sunshine sent to brighten her gloomy world and save her life—she could only think of one name, one word, worthy of someone brave enough to be born to a wreck like her.

"Soldier," she replied as he cracked his tiny eyes open to look at her for the first time. "His name is Soldier."

CHAPTER

ONE

HEARTS OF HOPE

Age Five

"Mommy?"

I peered through the crack in the open door. The room was dark.

I wasn't scared of the dark, but I was scared of what it meant.

Mommy only liked it dark when she was sleeping or did the Bad Stuff, and since it wasn't morning time anymore, it probably meant she had done the Bad Stuff.

But maybe not. Maybe she was sick. Billy's tummy hadn't felt good when I saw him a couple days ago, so maybe her tummy didn't feel good too.

"Mommy?"

I walked slowly inside to see her on the bed and giggled because she looked so silly. Her jammie shirt was on backward, and she had forgotten to put on her pants.

"Mommy, I see your undies," I whispered, still giggling wildly. "I can see your *butt*."

She snorted against her pillow. She sounded like a piggy, and I giggled again before making a piggy sound too.

"Soldier?"

Uh-oh.

Gramma was coming up the stairs, and she was going to be mad if she saw Mommy sleeping when it wasn't morning time anymore.

I hurried out of the room and saw Gramma. She smiled big at me and raced for me super fast to pick me up and swing me around.

"What are you doing up here? Did you find Mommy?" she asked.

I nodded and wrapped my arms around Gramma's neck. "Mommy's sleeping."

Gramma didn't like that. Her face got liney and mad, like the time when I had dropped *The Lion King* into her fishbowl.

"Mommy's sleeping, huh? Maybe we should wake her up, don't you think?"

I thought real hard about that.

If Mommy was sleeping because she had done the Bad Stuff, then Gramma would yell. She would tell Grampa, and he would yell, too, and Mommy would yell back, and I would have to hide because I didn't like it when they yelled.

But if Mommy was sleeping because her tummy didn't feel good, she should stay sleeping because sleep made you better when you didn't feel good.

So, I shook my head.

"No," I said, tapping Gramma's nose. "Mommy's tummy doesn't feel good."

"Oh, it doesn't, huh?"

I bobbed my head real fast. "Uh-huh. Billy's tummy didn't feel good when I was at his house. His mommy said he maybe caught a bug, so I think Mommy caught Billy's bug too."

Gramma's face wasn't liney anymore. Now, she looked sad, like she wanted to cry, and I didn't think I liked that.

I poked at her lips and tried to make her smile again.

"Mommy caught a bug all right," Gramma muttered in a quiet voice, and I was happy because I was right.

Then, she really did smile, and I felt good again. Because I'd made it happen.

"Come on, my little man," she said, carrying me back to the stairs. "Let's go make some cookies, okay?"

"Yeah!" I threw my fists in the air like Superman.

"Chocolate chip?"

I shook my head.

Gramma looked surprised.

"No?! But you love chocolate chip!"

"I wanna make oatmeal today."

"Really?"

She couldn't believe it. Gramma knew I didn't like oatmeal.

"Yeah." I stuck my bottom lip out because, now, I was sad even though I didn't really know why. "They're Mommy's favorite."

Then, Gramma was sad again, too, but she nodded. "Okay, little Soldier. We'll make oatmeal cookies for Mommy."

***

Age Six

Grampa zoomed around the living room and made the plane noises. My arms stretched out real wide, and Gramma laughed as she put another sparkly ornament onto the Christmas tree.

It was the biggest, glitteriest tree I'd ever seen, and I knew Santa was gonna love it and leave me tons and tons of presents.

"I know being an airplane is fun, but I think someone needs to get some sleep," Gramma said, and I knew she was talking about me.

"No!" I yelled, trying real hard not to yawn. "I gotta stay up for Santa!"

Grampa put me down and bent over to tap my chin. "Oh, but if you stay up, Santa won't come."

I couldn't help it. I yawned big, stretching my mouth out like a lion, and Gramma laughed again.

"How about Grampa flies you up to your room and gives you a nice, soft landing in your bed?"

I looked at the tree and felt a little sad. If I went to bed, I wouldn't get to see if Santa liked it or the tinsel I'd helped put on the branches. But I really was getting sleepy, and what if he didn't come if I was awake anyway?

So, I stuck my lip out and nodded, and Grampa chuckled, picking me up once again and zooming all the way up the stairs and down the hall to my room.

Mommy's door was open, and she wasn't inside.

She hadn't been inside in a long time.

Grampa swooped me down onto my Mickey blanket and knelt at the side of the bed. He smiled, and I told him I thought he looked a lot like Santa. That made him happy, and he smiled even bigger.

"You think so, huh?"

I nodded. "Yeah. 'Cause you have a big white beard and glasses."

"Do you think"—Grampa came real close and made his eyes big—"*I* could be Santa?"

I couldn't stop laughing. "Nooo!"

"Oh, no? And why not?"

"Because you're not fat!"

Grampa laughed. I loved Grampa's laugh. He didn't sound like Santa, but it made me just as happy.

"You know, if you and Gramma keep baking all those cookies, I *will* get fat. And *then* can I be Santa?"

I thought about that, but then shook my head. "You don't have reindeer."

"Maybe Sully wants to be my reindeer."

"Grampa," I groaned, smacking my hands against my fluffy Mickey Mouse blanket. "Sully can't be a reindeer. He's a dog."

"Hmm ..." Grampa cupped his chin and closed one eye. "I guess you're right. I don't really fit the criteria."

I didn't know what that meant, but I agreed anyway.

Then, I asked, "Is Mommy coming home soon?"

It had been a long time since I had seen Mommy. I'd heard Gramma say something to Grampa about picking her up in a few weeks, but how long ago was that? When did a few weeks end? And where had she gone anyway? Nobody would tell me, and it made me sad.

Grampa sighed and said, "Soon, buddy."

"Where is she?"

"She went on a little trip, but she'll be back soon."

"But not for Christmas?"

He sighed again and shook his head. "No, not for Christmas. Not this year."

Mommy was going to miss Santa and the tree and Christmas, and now, I wanted to cry. What if Santa didn't know where she was? What if she didn't have presents? What if she didn't get me anything after she said she was going to?

"Hey, hey, hey." Grampa wiped away a tear as it rolled down my cheek. "Mommy will be here before you know it. She just needed to go on a trip for a little while, but I promise she's coming back good as new, okay?"

"B-but what if Santa can't find her?"

"Ah, buddy ..." Now, Grampa looked sad as he put his hand on top of my head. "He always knows, and I bet

11

he's gonna bring Mommy the best present in the whole world."

I didn't know what that was, but I fell asleep, thinking about it. Maybe it would be a fire truck or a castle or a gigantic pirate ship. Those were things I'd like, and maybe Mommy would like them too.

When I woke up, I ran down the stairs with Sully before Gramma and Grampa were even awake to see if Santa had come, and he had. A great big pile of presents was stacked under the tree in colorful, sparkly wrapping paper, and I bounced against the bottom step at the sight. Even the stockings above the fireplace were full— Mommy's too!

"Look, Sully. Presents," I whispered loudly. "Let's see if Gramma and Grampa are up."

We turned around and ran back up the stairs to burst through Gramma and Grampa's door. They grumbled and growled as I jumped onto the bed and crawled between them.

"Santa came!" I cheered, jumping up and down.

"Did you hear that, Gramma?" Grampa mumbled, sounding too sleepy to be excited. "Santa came."

"I heard," Gramma replied, her eyes still closed.

"Let's go open them!" I jumped some more.

"Soldier, why don't we—"

"Ah, come on, Gramma. We can sleep later," Grampa said, already climbing out of bed and pulling his red-and-green robe on. "Want a piggyback ride, Soldier?"

I never said no to piggyback rides.

We went downstairs with Gramma shuffling slowly behind us and Sully hopping around our feet, and we opened hundreds and hundreds of presents. I got lots of cool stuff, almost every single thing I had asked Santa for. But when everything was opened and there was wrapping paper all over the floor, I looked at all of my new toys, and my eyes felt like they could cry.

"Hey, what's wrong, buddy?" Grampa asked.

I lied to Gramma and Grampa sometimes. I knew it was wrong, but sometimes, it felt right. But today, I didn't lie when I said, "I miss Mommy."

Gramma looked at Grampa, and I thought maybe they'd cry too. But they didn't.

Instead, Gramma said, "You know what, my little man? I think it's time you gave Mommy your present."

I sat up real straight and asked, "What?" Because the only present I had gotten for Mommy was a new pencil at the school Christmas fair, and how was I supposed to give it to her if she wasn't here?

She grabbed the phone from the table next to her chair and pressed some buttons. I still didn't know what she was doing or how I was supposed to give Mommy the sparkly pink pencil in my backpack when she wasn't here, but then she said some stuff into the phone and asked if she could talk to Diane Mason. Diane Mason was Mommy's name, and all of a sudden, I was really, really happy. Happier than I had been when I opened hundreds and hundreds of presents.

"Hey, honey. Merry Christmas," Gramma said, a smile growing on her liney face. "Yeah, he's right here. You ready to talk to him? Okay."

Then, she passed the phone to me and said, "Mommy wants to talk to you."

My legs couldn't stop moving around as I took the phone and pressed it to my ear. "Hi, Mommy!"

"Hey, sunshine!" She sounded different than she had the last time I'd seen her. She sounded good and happy and like a million Lucky Charms marshmallows. "Merry Christmas!"

"Did Santa know how to find you?"

"Oh, yeah, baby. He sure did. *Of course* he did."

That made me so, so happy. Because even if I couldn't find her, Santa had still known where to go. I guessed Grampa was right—hey, you know what? Maybe he could be Santa after all.

"What did he get you?!"

"Oh, baby," she said, and I thought maybe she was crying. I didn't like when Mommy cried. "He got me the best present ever."

That didn't make any sense at all. If it was the best present ever, why was she crying?

"What was it?"

"He got me a phone call from you!"

"But ... but ..." I bit my fingernail and turned around so Gramma and Grampa couldn't see me because I thought I might cry too. Then, I asked, "Why are you sad?"

"Oh, no, Soldier," Mommy said. "I'm not sad. I'm happy. I'm so, so happy. I love you, and I promise when I get home, things are going to be better. *I'm* going to be better. You'll see. I'll be the best mommy in the world

14

because that's what you deserve for being the best little boy. Okay?"

As she sang her sunshine song to me, I wondered what all of that meant. She already was the best mommy, and if she was so happy, why was she crying?

But if she had said she was happy and that things would be good when she got home, then I believed her.

Because that was what I always did.

I believed her.

***

Age Eight

There was still a little snow on the ground, but the birds were singing in the trees, and the sun was warm. Grampa said it was a good sign that spring was coming soon, and that was cool. Spring meant spending more time in the backyard with Sully. It meant bike rides and sleepovers in Billy's tent and going for walks with Gramma. Plus, once spring was here, it wasn't long before summer was, too, and I loved summer. Well, I didn't like how hot it was, but summer meant I didn't have to go to school, and I got to go fishing with Grampa.

I really, really loved summer.

But it wasn't summer yet. It was February, and it was cold. But it was my birthday, and that meant it was a good day. Even if there was still a little snow on the ground.

"Soldier!" Gramma hurried past the front door, carrying a tray of cupcakes she had spent all morning baking. "What did I say about cleaning up the Legos in the living room? Your friends are going to be here any minute."

Oops.

I had gotten distracted, staring out at the snow through the big window in the front door and thinking about everything I wanted to do once summer got here, and I'd forgotten to put my toys away.

"Sorry, Gramma," I said, hurrying to throw the little plastic pieces into the bucket she let me keep in the living room.

"It's okay," she said with a chuckle, stopping me with a clasp of her hand against my forehead. She wrapped her arm around me and kissed the top of my head. "You're pretty excited, huh?"

"Duh!"

I couldn't remember the last time I had gotten to invite friends over to the house—actually, had I ever? I usually went to one of my friend's houses, or we met up at the park or arcade or library or something. Gramma said she didn't like to entertain, Grampa said he didn't wanna listen to Gramma complain about entertaining, and Mom didn't say much of anything about it at all.

Besides, she was usually working or out with her friends or going on another trip.

I guessed she was just too busy to care about entertaining.

So, anyway, when Gramma had asked if I wanted to have a birthday party at our house, I was so, so, *so* excited. I couldn't wait to show Billy and Matt and Robbie my room and video games and Legos. And they were gonna think Sully was the coolest dog ever; I just knew it.

Knock! Knock!

"I'll get it!" I shouted, scrambling up from the floor so fast that my socks slid against the wooden planks.

Grampa entered the room and laughed at the sight of me tripping over my own dumb feet. "Easy there, buddy!"

Billy's mom had picked Matt and Robbie up on the way over. She stood behind them on the stoop, holding a stack of wrapped packages, and she smiled down at me.

"Hey, Soldier! Happy birthday!" she said, her face bright and happy.

"You wanna see my room?!" I exclaimed to my friends, ignoring Billy's mom and the presents in her arms.

Gramma came up behind me, laid her hands on my shoulders, and kept me from leaving. "Wait a second there, birthday boy. What do you say?"

Excitement was zipping wildly through every one of my fingers and toes, and I could barely stand still. But I sighed and remembered I was supposed to be polite, so I looked up at Billy's mom and muttered, "Thank you."

"You're very welcome," she said with the prettiest smile I had ever seen.

Billy's mom wasn't like mine. She was more like Gramma. She baked cookies and cooked dinners and did the laundry. She brought snacks to school and went on class trips. Sometimes, I wondered what it was like to have a mom more like her, but I never really thought about it for too long.

17

Not until now anyway.

"Laura, would you like to stay?" Gramma asked Billy's mom. "We're having pizza and cupcakes, if you're interested."

Billy's mom shook her head and passed the gifts to Gramma's wrinkly hands. "I have some errands to run," she said as I noted that Mom never ran errands. That was Gramma's job. "But I'll be back in a few hours to pick these guys up for a sleepover at my house, if Soldier wants to come."

I turned to look up at Gramma with hopeful eyes. "Can I, Gramma?"

"We'll talk about it, okay?" she answered before looking back at Billy's mom. "I'll let you know."

Billy's mom nodded and gave Billy a kiss on the top of his head. He rolled his eyes and told her to leave already. I wondered if he'd want her to leave so bad if she regularly left on her own, like my mom did.

Gramma closed the door as Billy's mom went back to her car, and my friends and Sully and I ran like a herd of elephants up the stairs to my bedroom. And I was right; they liked my room. They liked my room a lot, and we took turns playing video games until the pizza was delivered.

Gramma called us to the dining room, so down we went like a herd of elephants again. Grampa told us all to wash up before we ate, and while my friends made a line at the kitchen sink, I announced I needed to pee anyway.

I went upstairs to the bathroom with the good-smelling soap—the downstairs bathroom soap smelled like baby powder, and I hated baby powder. The door

18

was closed, which was kinda weird because Gramma and Grampa always said to leave it open unless someone was inside. And if Gramma and Grampa were downstairs and Mom was at work, then who was in there?

Maybe someone forgot to leave it open.

So, I turned the knob, finding it wasn't locked, and gasped when I saw Mom standing at the sink with a bottle of medicine in her hand. She turned on her heel as she tossed something into her mouth and swallowed quickly.

"S-Soldier!" she shouted angrily, her eyes squinty and her cheeks red as she stuffed the medicine bottle into her pocket. "Goddammit! You're *supposed* to knock!"

I hurried backward a couple of steps. "S-sorry. I'm sorry."

My heart was beating so, so hard and fast. What was she doing home? She was supposed to be at work; that was why she couldn't be at my party. That was what she had said, so ... what was she doing here now?

"Hey, buddy, don't leave your friends hang—" Grampa stopped talking when he saw Mom in the bathroom. "Diane, what are you doing here? Aren't you supposed to be at work?"

Mom's eyes moved rapidly from me to Grampa. "I, um ... I-I got off early."

"O-kay." Grampa used the same voice on her that he had used when I told him I ate all my broccoli at dinner the other night when he knew I had given it all to Sully.

I hated broccoli, but Gramma kept giving it to me.

I was never ever, ever going to eat it.

19

"What's that in there?" He pointed at the white cap of the bottle sticking out of her pocket.

Mom shook her head and crossed her arms over her chest. "I have a headache."

"Oh, yeah? So, what are you taking for it?"

"Something for a headache."

"Let me see." Grampa held out a hand and waited for Mom to give the bottle to him.

I didn't like this. I didn't feel good. My heart was going to blow up, and Mom was going to yell. I could see it in her frowny mouth and tomato-red face.

"How about you just mind your own fucking business?" she shouted, proving me right once again.

Grampa squeezed my shoulder. "Soldier, go downstairs and eat your pizza with your friends. Tell Gramma to come up here."

"B-but ... but I have to pee," I said, suddenly feeling like I was five again, not eight. Eight-year-olds weren't supposed to sound like they were going to cry.

"Go pee downstairs," Grampa ordered.

My bottom lip began to wriggle like a stupid baby. "B-but, but, but—"

"Fucking hell, Soldier! Why the hell are you like this?! Get the fuck out of here!" Mom yelled at me, pointing her finger toward the stairs.

I took one look at her angry eyes, and then I ran.

I ran down the stairs to the bathroom with the baby-powder soap, slammed the door behind me, and wished so, so, so hard that my friends hadn't heard my mom yell at me. I bet their moms didn't yell at them. I bet their moms didn't fight with their grammas and grampas.

I peed and washed my hands with the gross soap and hoped my friends didn't ask me why my mom had yelled at me on my birthday. Mostly because I was embarrassed, but also because I didn't know why she had yelled in the first place.

"Why the hell are you like this?!"

Like what? What did I do? All I said was that I had to pee.

I wiped my eyes, opened the bathroom door, and almost ran right into Gramma.

"Go eat your pizza, Soldier," she said in a hurry as she ran up the stairs.

Grampa and Mom were still yelling at each other up there, and I wished my friends weren't here at all.

But I ate my pizza and talked with my friends, and they didn't treat me weird or anything. Even though Grampa and Gramma had been upstairs for a long time and I knew they were all mad at each other for some reason. But Billy, Matt, and Robbie didn't seem to notice or care. And when Gramma finally came back down, she announced that it was time to sing "Happy Birthday" and have cupcakes.

Mom didn't come downstairs.

Mom didn't sing.

Mom didn't have a cupcake.

I bet Billy's mom sang and had a cupcake on his birthday. I bet Billy's mom didn't yell at him for having to pee. And then I was sad as I opened my presents and watched as my friends left. Gramma had asked if I wanted to sleep at Billy's house. She'd said she wanted me to because it was my birthday and I deserved to have fun with my friends, but I didn't want to.

Instead, I went to bed with Sully, feeling like a five-year-old instead of an eight-year-old because I cried into my pillow until I fell asleep and dreamed of walks with Gramma and fishing with Grampa.

"Soldier? Soldier, wake up, sunshine."

My eyelids opened a crack to see Mom kneeling beside my bed and humming her sunshine song. She was crying, but she was also smiling, and in her hand, she held a cupcake with one lit candle standing in the center.

"You didn't think I'd let you go to bed without singing 'Happy Birthday,' did you?"

I sat up slowly, rubbed the sleep from my eyes, and asked, "Why did you fight with Gramma and Grampa?"

She sighed and shook her head. "Because I screwed up again, baby. I … I have to get a new job, and I had a headache and took something I shouldn't have to make it better. The Bad Stuff, you know. But I'm gonna clean myself up, okay? I promised them I would, and I'm promising you too. Everything's going to get better."

She always promised. But unlike Gramma's and Grampa's, Mom's promises broke easily.

"Okay, Mom."

"Now"—she checked her watch and smiled—"it's eleven eleven, baby. You changed my life at this time eight years ago. I told you then you were gonna save me, and I still believe that. I really, really do. You're gonna save me, right, baby?"

I didn't know what she was talking about. I was only eight years old. I was just a kid, and I wasn't Superman.

22

How was I supposed to save anybody? What did she mean?

But I didn't bother asking because, sometimes, it was better to just let her talk, so I did.

"Sure, Mom."

"Now, make a wish, sunshine. Make it a good one, okay?"

So, I squeezed my eyes shut, made a wish that this promise wouldn't break, and blew out the candle, then watched a spiral of lingering smoke reach for the ceiling before it disappeared into the dark.

***

Age Eleven

Grampa's tackle box creaked open to reveal his treasured collection of bobbers and hooks. Last year and every year before it, he never let me touch them myself. I was too young, he'd said. I could hurt myself, he'd said. But now, he was showing me how to attach the hook to a line and bait it without his help.

"Look at you go," he said, watching with a glimmer of pride reflecting in his tired eyes as I hooked the wriggling worm with ease.

I didn't poke myself once.

"Cool." I grinned, holding the line up to smile at my handiwork.

Grampa laid a hand against my shoulder and squeezed. "Soon, you won't need me anymore."

All at once, my pride was wiped away by an unfamiliar, unexplained sadness and dread. Billy's grandfather had died a couple of years ago, and ever since then, I'd been acutely aware of Grampa's wrinkled skin and white hair. He wasn't as fast as he used to be, and he couldn't go up and down the stairs without complaining about his knees. I was doing more of the chores around the house because Gramma had insisted Grampa couldn't do them anymore, and I didn't like it.

I didn't like that dead meant gone, and with every chore that Grampa couldn't do, I knew he was closer to being gone.

What am I going to do without him?

Maybe if I do all the chores, he'll never be gone at all.

"Hey, buddy. Are you gonna cast that line or what?"

I cleared my throat and threw away all thoughts about death and growing old. Grampa wasn't dying. He was fine. He was here right now on the lake, like every other summer, and we were fishing, like we always had. Nothing was ever going to change that.

So, I stood on the dock and sent my line out into the water, refusing to pay attention to how he needed to sit instead of stand.

We fished for hours, collecting enough bass to be frozen and eaten for the rest of July. We collected our things and trudged back to his truck in the gravel parking lot. On the way back to the house, we listened to Grateful Dead and George Harrison and stopped at McDonald's for a soda and a burger. Grampa glanced at me across the truck and lifted one side of his mouth in a smile that made me feel weird and confused.

"What?" I asked before taking a bite of my Big Mac.

He stretched his arm out to lay it across the back of my seat. "I don't think I've ever told you how proud I am of the young man you're becoming."

"Oh …" I looked at the burger in my hands and shrugged. "Thanks … I think."

Grampa laughed and gripped the back of my neck, giving me a little shake. "I mean it, Soldier. Gramma and I … we have tried so hard to do right by you and your mother. And I know we've made mistakes—of course we have. *God*, we've made a lot of them. And sometimes, I'm not even sure we've done the right thing at all. I mean, there were a couple of times, I—you know what? Never mind."

I stared at the gooey mess of cheese and meat and lettuce, even more confused than I'd been before. "What?"

"Nothing. It doesn't matter. I'm just saying, all things considered, life could've been worse—*so* much worse. And the fact that you are such a smart, kind, *good* kid tells me that, even if we haven't always made the right choices, we never ever went wrong with you. There's gotta be something to be said for that."

I turned my head to look at him then, forgetting entirely about the burger in my hands, even as shreds of lettuce fell out and onto my lap. I knew what he was talking about now—Mom's drinking; the parties she went to and the people she hung out with; the trips Gramma and Grampa sent her on; the jobs she got, only to lose

25

them shortly after; and the pills she took from Gramma's medicine bottles and others she'd get her hands on from I didn't know where. They did what they could to stop it, they did what they could to fix it, but more than that, they did what they could to protect me and keep me with them and out of the system—as I'd heard them put it when they thought I wasn't listening. I didn't know exactly what that all meant, but if it meant living with them and not with a stranger, I was glad for whatever they did to keep that from happening too.

"I love you, Soldier," Grampa said, squeezing the back of my neck gently. "I love you as my grandson, but even more than that, I love you as my son. You have always been—and always will be—my *son*. And … anyway, I …" He cleared his throat and turned away, removing his hand from my neck to put it back on the wheel. "I just wanted you to know that."

My emotions were a fuzzy, confused mess. I didn't know why he was saying this now, or why his words made me want to cry, or why a sick feeling swelled in my stomach like I was going to throw up. I crumpled up the wrapper around the other half of my Big Mac and tossed it into the McDonald's bag as we drove home, and I tried to piece together the reason for all these feelings battling inside my head. But it was pointless. I couldn't do it. There was too much to figure out, too much to sort, like my big mess of a sock drawer—Gramma had called it a lost cause, and she was right.

So, I left it alone, focusing on Bruce Springsteen on the radio and sipping on my Coke until we pulled into the driveway. I helped Grampa get the cooler of bass out of the trunk and grabbed his tackle box from the backseat.

And then, as we walked up the concrete path to the stoop, he clutched his hand to his chest and collapsed at my feet.

"Grampa!" I screamed, tossing the tackle box aside and dropping to my knees beside him. "Gramma! Gramma, help!"

But no amount of screaming, no amount of dialing 911, no amount of pleading or incessant *I love you*s could stop him from dying in front of me before the ambulance arrived and took him away. Making his death the first real and horrible tragedy to strike my life.

At least I wasn't foolish enough then, even at eleven, to believe it'd be the last.

CHAPTER

TWO

TWISTED INTENTIONS

Age Thirteen

"Soldier Mason!"

I lifted my head from the puddle of drool on my desk and opened my bleary eyes. "Huh?"

The classroom full of students broke out in a hushed round of laughter.

Mrs. Henderson didn't look as amused as all of them. With her hand on her hip and her lips pursed, she asked, "Did you enjoy your nap?"

I leaned back in my creaky seat, stretching my arms overhead. "It was okay, I guess. Wish I had a pillow though."

Another round of laughter. Another unamused sigh from my English teacher.

The bell rang, and the scraping of chair legs against beige linoleum resounded throughout the room. I was quick to follow suit, but Mrs. Henderson stopped me with a light grip of her hand around my arm.

"Soldier, wait," she said gently, preventing me from leaving, and I turned to face her with a tired nonchalance.

Last year, I had been shorter than her.

This year, I could see the top of her head.

"What?"

She removed her hand from my arm and sat at the edge of my desk, a look of deep concern creasing a line between her brows. "Is everything okay?"

I shrugged and hoisted my heavy backpack onto my shoulder. "Sure. Why?"

She didn't look like she believed me. Not at all. And she had every right not to.

"Well"—she wet her lips with her tongue, and the act stirred that stupid thing in my pants—"I know things have been difficult … *different* at home, what with your grandmother passing away earlier this year and you and your mom having to move and all. So … I just wanted to make sure that you were okay."

My fingers tapped erratically against the strap of my backpack at the mention of Gramma dying of cancer. Of moving from the house I'd grown up in to live in the nasty apartment building across from the train tracks. She hadn't mentioned Sully dying or Mom losing another handful of jobs, but I guessed she wouldn't have. She didn't know about that stuff, and I definitely didn't talk about it. But I thought about it now, tacking that stuff onto the long list of heartache I'd been dealt since

Grampa had had a heart attack in front of me over two years ago.

So, no, I wasn't okay. Far from it. But I wasn't going to tell her that in the event that my *not* okayness could lead her back to Mom.

Mom had enough problems. She didn't need my teacher to be one of them.

"Really, I'm okay," I lied.

She tipped her head and pulled her lips between her teeth. Mrs. Henderson was the prettiest teacher I'd ever had. I thought about her a lot, especially at night and in the shower. But when she pulled her lips into her mouth like that, she looked like the Crypt-Keeper, and I smirked and made a mental note to tell Billy.

"You'd tell me if things weren't okay, wouldn't you?"

No. "Yeah, sure."

She didn't look like she believed me, but she relented with a nod anyway. "Okay. I'll see you tomorrow." I hurried to the door, relieved to be released, but she wasn't finished. "Oh, and, Soldier?"

Come. On.

I noisily huffed out my agitation before glancing over my shoulder. "Huh?"

"If you ever need a break, if you can't handle the work and you just need to focus on yourself and how you're feeling, let me know, and we'll figure something out. Okay? Just … just let me know."

An overwhelming rush to tell her everything whooshed through me like the trains that passed across the street from our crappy apartment. My eyes met hers as a painful ache pressed against my chest, making it hard to breathe, and I thought maybe she could see every truth I tried to hide behind my lies. I hoped she could. I hoped she'd help and rescue me in any way she knew how. But she didn't. She just offered a sad smile and wished me a good night, and I turned away and hurried down the hallway while I thought about how not okay I was.

***

"She did *not* give you a free pass from doing homework 'cause your frickin' grandma died," Billy said as we pushed our bikes down the dirt path, paved between the thick brush of trees.

I cracked a grin, thinking about Mrs. Henderson's pretty lips and sad smile. "She definitely did."

Billy scoffed. "Nobody gave a crap when my grandpa died."

"You jerk," I grumbled, shoving against his shoulder. "*I* cared."

"Yeah, okay, but my teachers didn't care."

I didn't say it, but Billy had also gotten two weeks off of school after the death of his grandfather. Mom hadn't even had a funeral or anything after Gramma died, and she had seen no reason why I should have to take off from school if she didn't get to take off from work.

Maybe I do need a break. Maybe Mom does too.

I fantasized for a minute about taking a vacation. A real one, like the ones kids at school took. I had never been to Disney World or the Grand Canyon or New York

City or anything like that, but maybe that was exactly what Mom and I needed. Maybe that was why everything sucked so much—we had never gone somewhere. We had never gotten away from this crappy town and had fun. But I also knew vacations and trips cost a lot of money, and Mom barely made enough to pay our rent. She'd laugh at me if I suggested going on a vacation.

Besides, Mom didn't even like getting up from the couch. How would I get her to the friggin' Magic Kingdom?

Billy and I continued our walk down the path, coming closer to The Pit—a clearing in the center of the unkempt woods near our high school. It was where a lot of the kids came to chill, make out, and whatever else they wanted to do without their parents hovering over them.

Not mine, of course, but everyone else's.

Teenage chatter broke through the trees, and we stepped into the flood of sunlight. There weren't a lot of kids there today. It was only Thursday. Come Friday or Saturday, the place would be crawling with half of the student body. But, like most nights, I just needed somewhere to hang for a while before heading back to the apartment, and other than Billy's house, this was the only place to go.

"Hey, look, it's Levi," Billy said, dropping his bike at the edge of The Pit.

I left mine beside his. "Yeah, so?"

"Got any money?"

I couldn't help but laugh at that. I hardly ever had money. "I spent all of my money on lunch."

"Okay"—he shrugged and dug out a ten-dollar bill from his pocket—"no biggie."

I followed Billy to where Levi—a guy too old to be hanging out with us—stood with his arm around a hot blonde girl I didn't recognize. The guy was nineteen, six years older than me, and I stood eye-level with him.

Gramma had always said I was big for my age. Or maybe it was just that everyone else was small.

"Hey, Levi," Billy said, talking to him like they were pals but I knew better. "Do you have any of those … you know …"

Levi looked me over, his gaze meeting mine with a hardened edge I didn't understand. What was his problem? I barely knew him, and we never spoke, so I couldn't figure out why the hell he'd be looking at me like he couldn't trust me. But then, he pulled his eyes away from me to give the girl a kiss on the temple. She didn't seem to notice though. Her gaze was on me, just as his had been, but hers lacked the judgment his held. Instead, she looked hungry as she bit her lip.

I didn't think I liked it, but then again … I found I maybe liked it a lot.

She raked her eyes over me as she asked, "What's your name?"

I watched Billy hand his ten dollars over to Levi with a heavy dose of confusion as I replied, "Uh … Soldier."

She laughed like she thought I was kidding. "No. Are you serious?"

That was when I decided I didn't like her at all as I glowered at her and her sarcastic grin. "Yeah. Why?"

"Just making sure."

She looked over me from head to toe as she licked her lips—in a different way than Mrs. Henderson had—and there came that stirring again between my legs.

"How old are you, Soldier?" she asked me.

"Thirteen."

"Hmm, too bad," she replied with a pout of her pink lips. "You're a really big boy."

No. I definitely didn't like her.

I dragged my scrutinizing glare from her and back to my friend, who was now waiting as Levi removed a plastic baggie of little pink pills from his jacket pocket.

Wait, wait, wait, wait. What's happening here?

"Ten bucks only gets you one oxy," Levi said, opening the bag.

Oxy …

There had to be fifty pills in that bag. Fifty pills that looked an awful lot like the ones Mom liked to take. The kind that made her drop onto the couch and stare at the TV until she passed out.

Where was Levi getting them from?

And why did Billy want one?

"That's okay," Billy said. "We can split it."

Split it? Wait … what? Split it with who?

Billy shot a grin in my direction.

Is he talking about me? *No way. He wouldn't be …* *right?*

Levi dropped a pill into Billy's hand. Billy thanked him and told me to follow. I did, uncomfortable and stunned, feeling like everything was suddenly even more messed up and wrong than before.

34

What did Billy want with that pill? Why had he spent money on it?

I had known him since preschool. He didn't do that type of crap. Kids like him had nice moms and nice houses and no reason to want the pills my mom took.

Yet he had one.

"Dude, she was *into you*," Billy whispered, both disbelieving and excited. "You should've—"

"Why do you have that?" I cut him off, my voice urgent and hushed against the voices around us.

"Because I saw Robbie take one last week and it looked like fun."

Last week, I hadn't gone to The Pit with Billy and Robbie when they asked me to. Last week, I had been too scared to leave Mom alone.

I had wondered what my friends were doing without me. I had felt jealous and left out, worried I was missing something crucial while I was too busy cleaning up Mom's puke and making sure she didn't die. But now, I knew, and I wasn't jealous anymore. I was disgusted and disappointed instead, and I stared at my best friend for a moment, feeling suddenly like I didn't recognize him anymore.

"*Fun?*" I lifted my bewildered gaze to the sky and shook my head. "It's not—"

"Okay," Billy said, plopping himself onto the ground next to our bikes, "I'm gonna break it in half, and you can take one side, and I'll—"

"I don't want it."

"What?" Billy was incredulous as he painstakingly broke the little pill in half with a barely audible snap. "Come on. It's fine. It's not gonna even do anything."

I imagined Mom passed out on the beat-up couch that had come with the apartment. I imagined the countless times I'd shaken her, making sure she was still breathing. That never looked like *nothing* to me. But I wouldn't tell Billy about that. I wouldn't tell anybody.

"I don't care. I don't want it."

"Fine. Be a baby. More for me." Billy dug into his backpack for a water bottle and dropped one half of the pill onto his tongue. Then, with a quick sip of water, he swallowed it. "See? No big deal."

Billy was wrong though. It *was* a big deal because just a half hour later, his head was lolled heavily against my shoulder, and he was barely able to keep his blackened eyes open. He laughed at the dumbest stuff, could hardly speak in full sentences, and every time I asked if he was okay, he'd tell me to relax.

But how was I supposed to relax when my heart was racing so fast?

***

It wasn't until a couple of painful hours later, when the sun had set and the moon dropped silvery beams of light into The Pit, that Billy finally announced that he was ready to go home. He said his mom would start to worry about him if he didn't get back. He said she'd be mad, so we collected our stuff and left, although I doubted his mom could be mad about anything at all.

I insisted on walking him home, making sure he got there safely, even though he'd sworn he was fine.

Mom said she was fine all the time, too, but I knew better than to ever believe her.

"Hi, Soldier!" Billy's mom called from the door, waving in my direction as her son slowly trudged his way up the path. "Do you wanna come inside for something to eat? I made a spiral ham!"

God, when was the last time I'd eaten ham? When was the last time I'd eaten anything that hadn't come from the school cafeteria or out of a can at home? I couldn't say for sure, but it had to be before Gramma had gotten really sick and couldn't cook anymore. What I did know was, ham sounded great. Billy's mom was a good cook, and I knew there'd probably be a couple of excellent side dishes to accompany the ham as well.

But I smiled and shook my head. "No, thanks, Mrs. Porter," I replied. "I gotta get home and do my homework."

"Oh." She looked disappointed. Billy's mom was always so nice to me; she always seemed like she genuinely enjoyed my presence in her house. "Well, okay then. Maybe another time. Get home safe, okay? Tell your mother I said hi."

"I will." I smiled and waved, all too aware of the painful ache that struck my heart as I began to walk away. "Bye!"

The journey home was long as my feet dragged along the sidewalk. I could've ridden my bike, but I didn't feel like it. I couldn't stop thinking about Billy. I couldn't stop thinking about the half circle he'd swallowed and the other that was still in his pocket. I should've said something to his mom. I should've taken her up on her offer for a nice ham dinner. I should've done a lot of things, none of which I'd ended up doing, and that was my fault. That was my neglect, and even though I didn't know it then, I would pay for it forever.

What wasn't my fault though was walking into our crappy little apartment to find all the lights off, including the one Mom always kept on in the kitchen—*always*.

I flipped the switch beside the front door a few times, up and down, and with every flick, the same thing happened—absolutely nothing.

With my blood whooshing loudly past my eardrums, I dropped my backpack onto one of the two dining chairs and headed through the doorway into the living room, where I found Mom lying on the couch in the dark when she was supposed to be at work.

"Mom?"

She didn't move, and I immediately thought she had died.

What am I going to do? Where will I go? Would Billy's mom let me live with her?

God, I hope I can live with Billy's mom.

Guilt settled cold in my gut as I carefully took a step closer, scared that she was dead. Scared that she wasn't.

"Mom?" I asked again, and this time, she rolled her head against the cushion.

"Hmm," she murmured.

I couldn't tell if her eyes were open, but she was awake, and a tiny part of me was disappointed.

"What happened to the lights?"

She slowly sat up, lifting a hand and dropping it onto her lap with a dismissive attitude. "The choice was pay the rent or the electric."

I sighed and sat on a folding chair I sometimes used to watch TV if Mom was sleeping on the couch. "We always had lights at Gramma and Grampa's house."

"Well, we're not at Gramma and Grampa's house anymore, so fucking deal with it."

"How am I supposed to do my homework?"

"Guess you're gonna have to do your homework in the dark."

Mom stood up and shuffled past me to enter the kitchen. I looked over my shoulder to watch her open the fridge and reach into the darkness, and she pulled out the bottle of milk.

"You're having cereal for dinner, so don't even think about asking for anything else," she mumbled, dropping the bottle on the table. "Use the milk. It's gonna go bad if you don't."

I thought about the ham Billy was eating with his family as I asked, "Why aren't you at work?"

Mom sighed and touched her fingers to her temples. "They, um … they let me go."

"So, we don't have any money?" If Mom couldn't pay to keep the lights on, how were we gonna pay for anything else? What were we going to eat? What if we didn't have a place to live? "Mom … what are we going to do?"

"God, Soldier, it's *fine*," Mom said, throwing my worry away with a roll of her eyes. "I'll go on some more interviews, find another job … you know how it goes."

I did know. Mom had been through probably a million jobs as far as I could remember. But back then, I hadn't worried. I had Gramma. I had Grampa. They didn't let us go without lights. They had made sure we had food and lights and TV and whatever else we needed. But now, without them, things were bad, and they were getting worse, and what if Mom couldn't find another job? What if she'd been through all of them and there were no other jobs to lose?

"Soldier," Mom interrupted my thoughts and walked into the living room, "it'll be *fine*, okay? Now, stop worrying about it."

I didn't say anything because I didn't believe her. Then, she announced she had a headache and was going to bed. I stayed in my uncomfortable folding chair and watched as she opened her purse and took out her bottle of pills, popped it open, and dropped two little pink pills into her mouth. She swallowed without water, put the bottle back into her bag, then went to her room without saying good night.

My eyes remained on her bag as I thought of everything that could happen if Mom couldn't find another job. If we couldn't get the lights back on. If we couldn't buy food or pay the rent or find anywhere to go. We'd be homeless and hungry, and where would we go? What would happen to us?

But if I could make some money …

I slowly got up from the chair and tiptoed to Mom's bag, thinking about the ten dollars Billy had spent on one of those pink pills. *One.* If Billy was paying Levi for them, other kids probably were too.

I quietly opened her bag, gritting my teeth as the cheap zipper resounded loudly through the dark, hushed apartment. The bottle was right there on top of everything else, and I picked it up in my shaking hand, careful to not let the pills rattle against the plastic. There were tons of them inside the orange bottle.

Would Mom notice if I took five or six?

Hell, what about ten?

I wasn't the best at math, but my mind raced with equations and possibilities. Ten pills would equate to a hundred dollars. A hundred dollars could feed us for a couple of weeks. A hundred dollars was worth the risk of Mom finding out and yelling at me. She was going to yell anyway. She always did.

But above all else, what made me open that bottle and count out ten of those little pink pills was the thought that, if I took them and stuffed them into my backpack, Mom would have ten less pills to take. And that was worth it—even if my thirteen-year-old brain couldn't compute that she would always, always, always find the money for more … regardless of if the lights were on or not.

CHAPTER

THREE

ROTTEN APPLES

Age Sixteen

"Thanks so much, Soldier," Billy's mom said after I finished loading a dozen bags of groceries into her trunk. "Am I allowed to tip you?"

My boss, Gordon, had told me I wasn't supposed to accept tips. Sweeping the floor, bagging groceries, and helping people load them into their cars were what I was paid to do, he had said on more than one occasion, and accepting extra money for it was strictly prohibited.

Still, I hesitated for a moment as I watched her dig a ten out of her purse. I stared at the bill in her hand as the very end of the green paper flapped gently in the breeze, tempting me with every flutter. I heard the sound of it like an alcoholic heard a cap pop off a beer—amplified ten times over, resounding louder than the rest of the world around me. I wanted to reach for it, grasp it in my greedy hand, and spend it on something. A nice, juicy burger or maybe a new pair of jeans down at the thrift store. Something I needed more than I wanted.

But I didn't.

"Oh, I can't accept tips," I finally told her, peeling my eyes away from the bill after too many seconds went by. "Gordon doesn't let us."

Billy's mom eyed me with more sympathy than I preferred. Then, she whispered, "You can take it, Soldier. I won't tell anyone. You know that."

She was tempting me too much. If she'd pushed just a little harder, I probably would've taken it and blamed it on her insistence and not on how badly I needed some new socks. But I shook my head profusely and thanked her anyway with a forced grin, and she sighed and tucked the money back in her purse.

"What about dinner?" she asked hopefully. "Can you at least come over for dinner? You haven't been by in such a long time, and we'd love to have you."

It wasn't an exaggeration. I couldn't actually remember the last time I'd been to Billy's house for anything, let alone a meal. Hell, I only ever saw Billy at The Pit these days, when he wanted to get high after school or over the weekend. Sometimes, I walked him home if there wasn't anybody else hanging around, but usually, I hung back to mingle and watch for the hungry eyes that always came my way.

No point in leaving if business was good.

But now, I wanted to eat dinner at his house. I wanted to remember what life used to be like before Gramma and Grampa died, back when I could afford to have a life outside of work, The Pit, and making sure Mom was still alive after she passed out on the couch. I wanted to remember, just for once, that I was still just a sixteen-year-old kid, and I wanted desperately to simply *have fun*.

So, I lifted one side of my mouth in a smile and said, "I'd really like that."

And later that night, I did like it. No, scratch that—I loved it.

God, I loved everything.

I loved the meatloaf she had made. I loved the mashed potatoes and buttery green beans and gravy. I loved the fresh iced tea and cornbread. I loved how Billy's mom didn't care if I ate seconds or thirds. I loved hearing his dad talk casually about his workday. I loved that Billy's mom asked her son how school had been that day and how Billy answered in a bored kind of way, as if she asked him that question all the time and he was sick of hearing it. I loved that they all listened to each other and cared, and most of all, I loved that his parents had no idea what their kid was up to after school and on Saturdays.

I loved that they couldn't fathom the idea that he'd ever want to do shit like get high on little pink pills.

But I also hated it just as much because I knew the truth.

Billy was messed up, and I wished I knew how to stop it. I wished I could say something to his mom, I wished she knew the same things I did, but …

To tell her about him would be to tell her about me—and I couldn't afford to do that. I couldn't afford the lack of money or the way I knew her disapproval and disgust would pierce my heart and make me bleed out on her living room floor.

So, I said nothing about that. In fact, I said so very little about myself all night, afraid Billy's mom might see between the lines and discover every dirty truth I tried to hide. Then, when it was time for me to leave, I thanked her repeatedly for dinner. She wrapped the rest of the meatloaf up and sent me home with it, insisting that I could stop by whenever I wanted, and then I wished for something else. Something I hadn't wished for since I had been eight years old and in the middle of my one and only birthday party.

I wish she were my mom instead.

***

"Where the hell have you been?" Mom demanded angrily the second I walked through the door. She said it like she'd been waiting for me, like she gave a crap where I'd been.

But I knew better than to think wonderful things like that about my mother.

She didn't care where I'd been.

She cared about nothing but herself and those stupid fucking pills.

45

I dropped my keys on the cluttered table. "Out."

"I asked you *where*."

My lips remained sealed as I opened the fridge and put the foil-covered meatloaf inside. Mom would probably eat it later, but that was okay. She needed it more than I did.

"Excuse me." She got up abruptly from the couch and stomped into the kitchen, swaying a little as she moved. "I asked you where the hell you've been. And don't you dare say school because you know who I ran into today?"

I grunted a reply as I pulled out the milk and then grabbed a glass from the drying rack—the same one I'd washed that morning; my mother couldn't be bothered to wash dishes or put them away.

"Mrs. Henderson. Remember her? She told me she heard your teachers talking in the faculty room. They said they haven't seen you at school in *weeks*. So, you tell me where you've been right now or—"

I slammed the glass down on the counter hard enough to make an audible sound, but not enough to break it. "Or what, Mom? What the hell are you gonna do to me?"

"Or you'll be in deep shit—that's what."

Oh God, I wanted to believe her. I wanted to believe she gave a fuck about me and would actually do something motherly. Ground me. Load my schedule with more chores than I could handle for the next week. *Something!* But I knew better, and still, I answered honestly … just in case.

"I've been working at the grocery store," I told her, pouring the milk.

"*And?*"

I looked up from the glass to meet her accusing glare, my eyes narrowed with irritation. "And what?"

"What the hell else have you been up to? Because I know damn well you're not spending all your time at the fucking grocery store, and if you're not at school, you must be doing something else."

She was right about that. But I wouldn't tell her what exactly I was doing. Her wrath wasn't worth it, and I needed the money.

We needed the money.

"I just hang out with the guys."

"Bullshit," she spat, snatching the milk carton from my hand and stuffing it back into the fridge. "I bet you're out there, knocking some of those slutty girls up. Aren't you?"

"Yeah, Mom, that's exactly what I'm doing," I muttered, shaking my head.

Little did she know, I was still a virgin. When the hell was I going to find the time to have sex when I was too busy making enough money to make sure I could keep the lights on between her thousands of lost and found jobs?

"Well, I know for a fact that you're popping pills."

Now, *that* got my attention.

"What?" I snapped, neglecting the glass of milk on the counter. "What are you talking about?"

She hurried for her purse, hidden among the piles of mail and oddities on the table. She pulled out the orange bottle I was all too familiar with and shook its contents in my face.

"Look familiar?" she accused snidely, and of course it did. I'd only been watching her shake that thing around since I had been old enough to use the potty by myself. "You've been taking them, haven't you? Don't think I don't notice them missing, Soldier. I'm a fuck-up—I know it; I *admit* it. But don't you fucking think for a second that I'm stupid because I'm *not*, and the apple doesn't fall far from the fucking tree."

I shook my head slowly. "You have absolutely *no* idea what you're talking about."

"Oh"—she snickered, tossing the bottle back into her bag—"I know *exactly* what I'm talking about. You're a damn junkie, just like your old mom."

"I am nothing like you, Mom." It made my skin crawl, just thinking she could even accuse me of being anything like her. "And you know why?"

She squared her shoulders and looked up at me, like her skinny, bird-like five-foot-two frame had any chance of intimidating me at six foot five and a half. "Why?"

"Because *I*"—I jabbed a finger at my chest, making sure to hit the grocery store logo on my T-shirt—"keep the freakin' lights on, Mom. And, hey, have you ever wondered why Mr. Purcell doesn't ask for the rent when you forget?"

I didn't give her the chance to reply. I snatched my glass of milk off the counter and stormed away toward my room, where I slammed the door behind me and flopped onto my unmade bed. Then, I read a chapter of the book I had been reading and listened as Mom microwaved something—probably the meatloaf Billy's mom had made—and went to her own room. I waited fifteen minutes, ensuring she wasn't coming out anytime soon, and then I tiptoed out to the kitchen, went into her bag, and restocked my inventory.

The weekend was coming, and we needed the cash.

***

Age Eighteen

"Hey, Soldier, you got something for me?"

"Maybe." I slipped my arm from around the shoulders of Tammi, a girl I was getting used to calling mine. At least for the moment. "Do *you* have something for *me*?"

The Pit was crowded, but that was typical for a Saturday night in late spring. I led the kid who I knew to be a senior away from watchful eyes and let my hand drop to my side. He slipped a folded bill between my fingers. I looked down to see that it was a twenty and proceeded to produce two little pink pills from my pocket.

"You know the deal," I said to him, keeping my voice low with a cool warning. "You don't come back to me for at least a couple of weeks. And I'd better not catch you asking anybody else to buy for you. I have eyes all over this place. You understand me?"

It was a rule I stupidly believed would do some good. They could pop a pill, maybe share it with a friend, and have a good time, but that was it for a while. I figured if these kids weren't coming to me constantly for a fix, they were less likely to become dependent on the shit—or so I told myself.

I guessed, deep down, I knew they were just going to someone else. I mean, there was always Levi Stratton—who had in recent years become something of a rival—and that creepy asshole he always hung out with, Seth. Neither of them had gone elsewhere since I'd started swiping Mom's pills and selling them to my peers, so I knew business had to be worth it for them still. But … I dunno. I supposed I liked to think it at least wouldn't be my fault if they got hooked, never stopping to realize that I was also holding their hand on the dark, filthy road to addiction and dependency.

The guy insisted he understood, thanked me, and wandered off like a kid who'd just gotten done raiding a candy store as I headed back to Tammi.

I'd known her for years—from the moment she'd asked me for my name and age five years ago. I knew she'd been interested ever since—she didn't keep it a secret with her frisking eyes and bottom lip clamped salaciously between her teeth—but she had never made her move until I was legal. Now, at twenty-three, she loved teasing that she was a cradle-robber.

Me? Well … honestly, I just liked getting laid.

"You wanna give me one of those?" she asked, holding out a hand and waggling her fingers.

"No," I said, perching myself on an old, rusty bench someone had dragged into The Pit way before my time.

"Come on, baby." She climbed onto my lap and straddled my thighs. "I'll suck your dick."

I rolled my eyes. "I'm not letting you suck me off for pills, Tammi."

"Why? I'm your whore, aren't I? Treat me like one."

Okay, can I be honest?

I didn't like Tammi a whole lot. We had nothing in common. Kissing her was akin to licking an ashtray, she wore enough cheap perfume to make the strongest lungs asthmatic, and the way she spoke made me cringe.

Still, I was also eighteen, feeling a little too much like hot shit with the cash lining my pockets, and it was nice to have someone as sexy as her hanging from my arm and sitting on my lap.

It also felt nice when we fucked.

But I always respected her and treated her right, and I'd never give her pills in exchange for sex.

"You're not a whore," I told her flatly, tipping my head back to catch her eye and wrapping my arms around her waist.

Tammi pouted. "Levi liked when I was his whore."

I hated it when she talked about Levi.

Hell, I thought I just hated Levi altogether. Him, that guy he hung out with, and every one of their friends.

"Well, he's right over there if you wanna go suck *his* dick." I nudged my chin in his direction.

The guy was twenty-four and *way* too old to be hanging out with high school kids. But I saw him now for what he was—a predator—and I often wondered if I'd be like him when I was his age. The thought scared me, but what I did now scared me, too, and yet I couldn't see an end in sight. I was in too deep, and I—*we*, Mom and me—depended on this too much.

Tammi glanced over her shoulder and stared at her ex-boyfriend like maybe she was considering it. But she made a contemplative sound before saying, "Nah, I don't feel like it right now. Yours is bigger anyway."

I wanted to grumble a sardonic *thanks* because I didn't doubt for a second that, if my dick had in fact been smaller, she would have sauntered her way back into Levi's arms without a second thought. But before I could say anything, my thoughts were blown apart by a bloodcurdling scream not twenty feet away from where I sat.

Tammi turned her head abruptly in the direction of where the sound had come from. "Wha—"

She couldn't get her sentence out before I shoved her off my lap.

I bolted from the bench and ran toward the scream that had now turned into a girl's pleading voice, saying, "Stop it! *Please*, get off of me! Get off!"

Her frantic, desperate words crushed my soul, and what I found made my blood boil.

A young girl I had never seen before was pinned against a tree by the body of Levi's buddy, Seth. One of his hands was on her chest while the other was working at getting his fly undone. She was writhing, struggling to get away from him, as she cried and gasped and begged for someone to help her in a field of dozens of people who were ignoring her.

But not me.

Without a moment of hesitation, I grabbed Seth from behind, gripping his shirt in my fists and pulling him off her with such force that we both fell backward into a couple of other kids.

"What the hell, man?!" one of them asked, as if they hadn't been aware of the girl being violated against her will mere feet away from them.

Seth rolled away and out of my grasp. "Get the fuck—"

My fist stopped his words from coming out, and a spray of blood hit my face as I broke his nose.

"Motherfucker!" he cried in agony, cupping his hands over his face. "You piece of fucking shit!"

I began to get to my feet as I turned to the girl, still standing there with her back against the tree, watching the scene unfold in front of her.

"Are you okay?" I asked, panting and trying to catch my breath from the tussle.

She began to nod when her already-frightened eyes widened further.

"Look out!" she screamed, but I was too slow to react.

The broken bottle came down, slicing my face, just below my left eye. I cursed and hissed at the sting as a fiery heat throbbed and the blood began to pour. It hurt like a bitch, and I expected a trip to the emergency room was in my near future.

Someone—some guy I didn't recognize—grabbed Seth, holding him back and forcing the broken bottle from his hand.

"You wanna take care of him, Soldier?" the guy asked, and it made my skin crawl that he knew my name and I barely even recognized his face.

I laid a hand over my cheek and pulled it away to stare at my blood-soaked palm. "Holy shit," I muttered, shaking my head before looking at Seth and asking, "What the fuck is wrong with you, man?"

His eyes reflected a rage that threatened to pierce my soul as he snarled, "With *me*?! You fuckin' attacked me out of nowhere, you asshole!"

I thrust my hand toward the girl, frozen and terrified of what was happening in front of her. Terrified of what had almost happened.

"You expect me to just stand back like all of these other pieces of shit while you fucking rape someone?"

"Rape?" Seth snickered, rolling his eyes. "I wasn't fucking *raping* her. She *wanted* it."

I looked at the girl, noting now that her hair was the softest shade of brown I'd ever seen. Like a teddy bear. Warm. Comforting. Almost familiar in the way it begged to be touched.

Like Sully.

"Did you want it?" I asked gently.

She shook her head rapidly, and I looked back at Seth, scowling.

"She's fucking lying!" he spat, his eyes now on her.

I knew a liar when I saw one, and she wasn't it. I walked over to the girl with the soft brown hair, noticing the way she stiffened as I approached.

"How old are you?" I asked quietly, too hushed for the others to hear, while my eyes fell upon hers.

God, they were so green and vivid, and my soul jerked restlessly, as if trying to rid itself of the confines of this body in this fucked up life. Desperate for

54

something better. Something more vibrant and alive, like the emerald sparks glittering in this girl's eyes.

"F-fifteen," she answered in a small voice, yanking her gaze from mine to study her hands, clinging to her skirt.

"Fifteen," I repeated slowly, allowing the word to sour against my tongue before I looked over my shoulder at Seth, still being held by the guy I didn't know, who apparently knew me. "She's a fucking *kid*, you asshole."

Then, I took her carefully by the wrist and instructed her to come with me. She trembled under my touch, and goose bumps broke out along her skin, but she didn't protest or pull away. She did as I'd asked, and it irked me to the bone that she did it all so easily.

***

"W-what are you going to do to me?" was the first question she asked after I had her in my car.

It was a ten-year-old piece of junk, held together by rust molecules holding hands. But it was mine, and it always took me where I needed to go.

I didn't immediately answer. Instead, I asked a question of my own. "What is your name?"

"Rain," she replied without hesitation.

I looked across the car at her, dubious, while holding a handful of blood-soaked napkins to my face. "*Rain*? Your name is *Rain*?"

"Yes."

I snorted, turning my eyes back on the road. "Wow. Okay. What, are your parents hippies or something?"

"Uh, I don't think you should be the one making fun of *my* name," she fired back with more confidence than before. "Like, hello? Your parents named you Soldier."

One side of my mouth quirked into a smile. I saw no reason to tell her I only had one parent, and I winced at the pain in my cheek. "Touché."

"I mean, is that *really* your name?"

"Yep." I glanced at her again, noticing her reluctant smile, and I was glad to see her relax in my presence.

She was pretty. Maybe the prettiest girl I had ever seen.

"And by the way, *I'm* not doing *anything* with you. I'm just taking you home. So, where do you live?"

"Really?"

She sat up straighter, and I darted my eyes toward hers, startled to find a heartbreaking amount of hope glimmering within those mosaic shards of green.

I didn't know her. She meant nothing to me, yet the thought that she could lump me in with those other guys in The Pit crushed my spirit. But what hurt even more was knowing I couldn't blame her.

"Yes," I replied firmly, looking back to the road before flicking my gaze back to hers for a split second to add, "Really."

So, she gave me the address and told me how to get there from where we were, and I steered the car in that direction.

The ride was spent mostly in complete silence with my eyes on the road and hers on her hands, nestled over the black fabric of her skirt covering her lap. I couldn't tell what she was thinking; I didn't even know if she was truly okay. All I knew was, I felt better, knowing she wasn't in The Pit anymore. It was no place for a kid her age, and it wasn't lost on me that I'd started going when I was even younger.

"You shouldn't go back there," I finally said as we neared her street. "Those guys want to hurt you. Stay the hell away from them."

"Do *you* want to hurt me?"

Shocked, I looked at her. "I don't want to hurt anyone," I replied honestly.

"But you hurt him."

I shook my head. "I hurt him because he was hurting you. Protecting someone is different. I'll always pick protecting over making someone my victim."

I pulled up to the curb a couple of houses down from hers. The last thing I needed was for her parents to see her getting out of a car driven by an eighteen-year-old guy with a bloody face.

"Thank you for the ride," Rain said quietly. "And thanks for being so nice to me."

"Yeah, no problem," I replied, turning to rest my elbow against the back of the passenger seat. "But please swear to me you'll never go back there or be around that guy again."

She didn't even hesitate. "I swear."

"Good."

She got out of the car, and I waited the two minutes it took for her to run to her house and get inside the door. Then, I drove myself to the ER, all while cursing Seth and his inability to understand the word *no*.

***

"Soldier!"

The doctor, who'd just checked my face for any signs of infection, stopped my panicked mother from entering the emergency room bay. "Ma'am, I need you to—"

"Don't you tell me what to fucking do. That's my *son*!" She said the word like she'd spent the past eighteen years playing the part of Doting Mother. She pushed past him and grasped my chin in her hand. "Oh my God, look at your *face*! What the hell happened?!"

There was panic and affection in her eyes, one I hadn't seen since I had been small enough to hold her hand when we crossed the street. An unexpected surge of emotion barreled straight through my hardened muscle and into my weary, wounded heart, and I suppressed the need to wrap my arms around her and cry for no other reason than to simply be held by my mom.

"I got into a fight," I answered plainly, like it was nothing.

Because, well, it was.

I was no stranger to fights these days. But most of them didn't leave me needing anything more than a few Advil.

She looked horrified, like she couldn't believe I'd do such a thing. Diane Mason had always been a good actress.

"A fight?!"

I shrugged. "He got me with a broken beer bottle."

"Did they check for rabies? Or tetanus?"

58

The gray-haired nurse setting up the metal tray with the supplies to do my stitches smiled reassuringly without making Mom feel stupid. "It's unlikely that he contracted rabies from a broken bottle. But we did give him a tetanus shot, just in case."

Mom sighed and sat beside me on the bed. Her hand reached out to grip mine, lacing our fingers together and squeezing tightly. I reminded my heart it meant nothing, that she'd go back to being her usual self the moment we got back home, but, man ... I hoped she'd hold on for a while.

"How does the other guy look?"

"Well, his nose isn't ever gonna look the same— that's for damn sure," I muttered while thinking Seth had deserved worse for what he'd almost done to that girl.

Rain. With the pretty eyes and soft hair.

The nurse tried to bite back a laugh as Mom nodded. "Good."

It was funny that she hadn't asked what the fight was about or if the cops had been involved. And I couldn't tell if it was that she just didn't care or simply didn't think to ask, and honestly, I didn't care or think to divulge the fact that I'd stopped an adult man from forcing himself on an underage girl. I wasn't looking for credit or brownie points from my mom or anybody because knowing Rain had gotten home safe was good enough for me.

No. All I cared about in that moment was that, as the nurse pieced my face back together with fifteen stitches, my mom was there, holding my hand. Humming a song in a voice that was only vaguely familiar, worn and faded, like an old baby blanket.

"You are my sunshine, my only sunshine ..."

With my eyes squeezed shut, I imagined how nice life would've been if moments like this weren't a fluke. If every single day of my life since birth had been filled with so much love and affection that there'd have been no chance in hell that things would've ended up the way they had. I wouldn't be selling pink pills to school kids in the hopes that I wouldn't find Mom on the couch one day, dead or in a coma. I wouldn't be a high school dropout, spending my days at the grocery store or spending my nights in The Pit with other delinquents like me, just trying to make enough money to keep the lights on.

I guessed Mom was right. The apple really didn't fall far from the tree.

But then ... I thought about Billy.

His mom was perfect. She was everything a mom should be, and his dad was as cool as they came. They had done nothing to push him to do what he did, and yet he did it anyway.

And that was when I realized that it didn't always matter what tree the apple fell from.

Sometimes, it was just rotten.

CHAPTER

FOUR

THE LAST PILL

Age Twenty-One

The rent and electric bill were both due, and it wouldn't be long before the cable bill was late. There was nothing to eat in the kitchen. And Mom had, of course, forgotten to do anything but buy her precious pills and booze with the little money she'd gotten at the new salon in town.

She had worked there for a promising two months before Gordon asked me to open the grocery store for a week. Apparently, Mom needed me to wake her up in the morning, and she had failed to show up for work that entire week.

"Mom, you *need* to get another job," I said with a sigh, holding my head in my hands at the kitchen table we could no longer use for eating.

I hadn't seen the surface of that table in years.

I had six hundred expendable dollars in my wallet. That could cover the electric, groceries, and part of the rent, but it wasn't enough for everything. And while I could maybe beg the landlord for a couple more weeks to get the rest of the money together, that would only solve the problem this month. What about the next or the one after that?

"Maybe you can pick up more hours at the grocery store," she suggested, slumped in her chair.

She was taking more pills than usual these days. She could barely keep her eyes open on a good day—and today wasn't one of them.

"I can't work more hours. They have laws against that."

"Since when do we care about laws?"

She might not care about laws, but I did. Maybe I didn't always do the right thing, maybe I didn't live my life by the book, but that didn't mean I didn't *care*. And all I wanted was to get myself to the point where I could afford to live life by the rules.

Unbeknownst to her, I had been working on it. I just needed to stuff a little more money into the envelope I kept taped to the underside of my bed, and I'd be good to get the hell out of this shithole. All I needed was to convince her to come with me. Life would be better elsewhere; *we* would be better. We just needed to get away.

"Don't you have any more money?" Mom asked, her unsteady voice teetering toward begging.

She didn't want to be homeless any more than I did. She just didn't have the willpower to look beyond her next high to do anything about it.

"No," I lied.

If we absolutely needed it, I could tap into my escape fund. I wouldn't let us starve. But I would sell some more pills before I did that.

I was already thinking about maybe heading over to The Pit. It was cold outside—a dreary Friday in February—but I knew there'd always be the usual suspects, not wanting to go home after school even if the ground was frozen and the air was bitter. They'd be looking for me. And while I never pushed anything on them, they knew who I was and what I did, and I hated every bit of the reputation I'd built for myself.

But, man, when you dug a hole that deep, how the hell were you supposed to climb your way back out if you hadn't thought to bring a ladder down with you?

It's never too late to turn shit around though.

Just dip into your savings. Take out enough to pay what you gotta pay.

Don't go down there. Don't go to The Pit. You can change.

I blew out a breath and nodded to myself, suddenly ready on my twenty-first birthday to turn to a fresh, new page in the story of my life. I wouldn't go to The Pit. I wouldn't fill my former classmates and the current wave of high school students with my peddled poison. I would do better.

Standing abruptly, I barreled toward my room with determination, then dropped down beside my bed and felt around the underside of the bedframe until I found the envelope.

A pitiful, strained sound squeezed its way from my lungs before I uttered, "What the hell?"

As if my brain needed a few seconds to catch up, I stared at the flat envelope—too flat to have as much money as I'd had in there—turning it over in my shaking hands while my heart rapidly climbed to an anxious, irregular beat.

"Oh no. Oh fuck." I tore the paper open, revealing what I'd already known. "No, no, no, no ... *no!* Where is it?!"

I dropped the envelope, thrust my hands into my hair, and pulled tightly at the strands as I tried to think over the hammering of my heart.

"It was *right here*. Where the hell did it go?!"

I had just put away a hundred bucks last night, and now, nearly nine thousand dollars I'd saved throughout the years was gone. My mind tripped over itself, scrambling to make sense of what was happening.

You know *where it went.*

I didn't want to believe what I knew to be the truth.

But you know it's true.

"Fuck."

My throat tightened as I slumped against the rickety bedframe, holding the back of my hand over my mouth. My eyes watered, and my nose burned, but I couldn't afford to give in to the tears I desperately wanted to unleash.

"Mom!" I stood up from the side of my bed to storm through the door and into the musty living room to find her in her usual spot, draped over the couch. "Mom, have you been in my room?"

"Huh?" She opened her eyes a crack to peer up at me.

"Have you been in my room?" I enunciated every word through my throat, clenched with panic and despair.

"I ... I don't know, Soldier. Probably. Why?"

"Did you take anything?" My hands were shaking uncontrollably. My teeth were chattering, as if I were freezing, despite the fire licking away at my veins and cheeks.

She turned away to face the ripped cushion beside her head.

"Mom! Did you look under my bed?! Did you take something from me?!"

Her silence told me everything I needed to know.

"Oh my God." My eyes flooded as I lifted my hands to my hair. I stared down at her limp form, shaking my head and taking one, two, three steps backward.

What the fuck am I going to do now?

How the fuck are we ever going to get out of here?

I gasped, choked by a blinding panic I'd never felt before in my life. I knew we needed to get the fuck out of this hellhole. We needed to leave if there was any hope of us getting better and turning shit around for ourselves, and she had taken every last shred of hope for that from me—from *us*. She had taken every last penny I'd saved—and for *what*? More drugs?

Jesus fucking Christ, didn't she have *enough*?

Angry and upset, I spun on my heel and headed straight for her bag on the floor beside the buried table. I knelt and opened it up for the first time without a care if she saw or not.

"What are you doing?!" she shrieked, sounding like a scared little animal as she tripped from the couch. "Get out of there! What are you doing?!"

There were four full bottles of pills. Four whole, large bottles. I shook my head as I pulled them all out and stood slowly, staring at the little pink pills through the translucent orange plastic.

"Give those to me!" She grappled with my arm, but I was too strong, too tall, and she couldn't get the bottles away from me. "You fucking bastard! Give them back!"

Feeling simultaneously powerful and helpless, I brushed her off of me easily and barreled for the door as I said, "No."

"Soldier! Stop! Those are mine, you piece of shit! They're *mine*!" She was crying, begging, and pleading. "Where are you going?! What are you going to do?!"

"*What am I gonna do*?!" I looked over my shoulder, seething at the woman who'd had the nerve to bring me into this fucking world twenty-one years ago to the day, and shook my head. "I'm gonna go save your ass. Like I always fucking do. And maybe, just *maybe*, you'll thank me for it one day."

***

"Hey, man, I'm heading to The Pit. Just thought you might wanna come," I said over the phone, steering my piece-of-shit car through the darkened streets, barely lit by the dim streetlamps in need of new bulbs.

"Ah, jeez, I don't know … Jessica wanted me to head over to her place tonight, and Mom was saying she has some shit for me to do around here tomorrow morning."

Billy liked his drugs—he liked them a whole lot—but he at least still had a handle on his responsibilities. That was one thing I could give him—more than I could say for my mother.

For now.

"Tell Jessica to meet us over there."

"Dude, you know she hates The Pit. She doesn't like it when I'm high."

Neither did I, but I never pushed the point the way his on-and-off girlfriend did. "All right. It's fine. I just—"

"You know," Billy cut me off, already talking himself out of being the responsible one, "maybe I can go for a little bit. Then, I can just swing by her place afterward."

I smiled despite the gross feeling in my gut. I was grateful I wouldn't have to do business alone. Ever since Tammi had gotten back with Levi, I'd been flying solo a lot of the time, and most days, it sucked. It got lonely, and if I was being real, I was starting to feel like a creepy piece of shit, surrounded by a new batch of high school kids with so much potential and hope—if only there weren't guys like me and Levi around to take it all away.

Hell, if we were being *really* real here, I hated myself.

So much.

But what could I do?

After I pulled up to the curb outside of Billy's parents' place, his mom waved out the window as he climbed into the passenger side. Both of us were losers, still living at home, but we both had reasonable excuses. He was in school, too busy with classes and drugs to get a job, and me?

Well, you know what I was doing.

I forced a smile and waved back to Billy's mom as the little boy living in my heart cried and screamed, pressing his hands against the frosty window and begging her to rescue him from a life he'd had little choice of living.

Then, we drove away, and Billy reached for the orange bottles in the center console.

"Holy shit! What did you do, hit the fuckin' jackpot?!"

"We're not selling them all," I warned him, flashing him a pair of narrowed eyes. "But I need to get rid of them. I dunno … maybe I'll, uh … I dunno. Maybe I'll throw them in the lake or something."

"Fuck, no, don't waste them! I'll take whatever you don't get rid of tonight." He popped one of the tops off the bottles. "God, how much did she buy?!"

Billy was the only person on the planet who knew where I got my supply from—and who the hell knew who Mom bought them from? It was a question I never asked because I knew she'd never say. But I had my suspicions.

"I'd say nine thousand dollars' worth," I grumbled as I begged the anger nagging at my nerves to settle just a little. Nobody wanted to buy from a guy who sounded like he was two seconds away from choking the life out of someone.

"Get the hell out." He shook his head with disbelief, then plucked one pill from the top. "Well, don't mind if I do."

He swallowed it in one quick gulp and sighed with satisfaction. I shook my head, the disappointment in my soul never ending as I drove toward the high school parking lot. The snow had melted, the night was a little warmer, and I was hopeful that enough young people wanted a Friday night out of the house. I wouldn't sell enough to replenish my savings—of course not—but with any luck, I'd make enough to pay the rent and keep a roof over our heads for another month.

Why I still cared, I couldn't tell you.

Maybe it was just the hope that we could one day be better.

"So, it's your birthday, isn't it?" Billy asked, tipping his head back and deflating with another sigh.

The high was already taking over. I always hated watching the decline of his energy and spirit as a little voice in my head whispered I needed to do something before it was too late.

"Yep," I croaked through a throat so tight and choked with unease and worry.

"Remember that time you had a birthday party?"

And I caught Mom doing the Bad Stuff for the first time.

A muscle in my jaw pulsed at the thought. "Yeah."

"That was a good day."

I smiled weakly at the sentiment. It *had* been a good day; Gramma and Grampa had made sure of it. And then I felt sad. All of a sudden, I struggled to swallow down the rise of sadness and tears and emotion as it clotted heavily in my chest, piling higher and higher until I struggled for a gasp of air.

Oh *God*, why had they had to die? Why couldn't they be here now? Why couldn't they have stopped this shit before it got this bad? I was immediately desperate for the salvation they'd always provided, their affection and love, and I pulled at the collar of my coat, unable to breathe past the heart-wrenching despair.

Then, in need of a distraction, I glanced at Billy.

His head was lolled to the side, bouncing off the window, his neck limp.

"Billy?"

It never happened like this. His high never hit quite like this. He never blacked out. He never breathed like he was trying to suck bubbles through a straw.

"Billy!" The tires squealed as I pulled the car over, just outside the high school parking lot. I reached over and gave his shoulder a violent shake. "Billy!"

He didn't wake up.

I threw my door open and got out to race around to the other side. I opened the passenger door, unbuckled his seat belt, and pulled him from the car. He was limp, every breath shallow and slow—but he *was* breathing. And I held tight to every one of those puffs of air with more hope than I'd ever thought I could muster as I got down on my knees and called 911.

"Fuck!" I cried, releasing the torrent of emotion I'd been suppressing. "Fucking hell, Billy. Don't do this to me. *Please*. Don't do this."

The operator answered and asked for my location and what the emergency was.

"My friend just took an oxy and won't wake up," I told her after telling her where I was, wiping the tears from my cold, wind-bitten face.

"Okay, sir. An ambulance is on the way. Can you describe to me what's happening to him right now?"

I did as she'd said, and I realized that what little breath had been passing through his lungs had stopped.

"F-f-fuck, no ... h-he's not breathing. He's—he's n-not breathing. Oh *God*! What do I do?! W-what the fuck do I do?!"

A few stragglers from the parking lot had wandered over to see what was happening. I heard their whispers. I heard my name. I heard Billy's.

"Sir, I need you to calm down. Do you know how to perform CPR?"

"Yes." I had learned in school and had never been more grateful for those few hours I'd actually paid attention.

"Good. I'm going to talk you through it, okay? I need you to do what I say. Hang on. The ambulance will be there in two minutes ..."

***

Two minutes was a long time.

It had been too long.

I was surrounded by flashing lights on the side of the road, watching through wide, bewildered eyes as a handful of cops searched my car—Stone Temple Pilots' "Big Empty" playing on the radio—and the paramedics zipped up a body bag.

Billy was inside.

"It's not him anymore," I could hear Gramma saying as the paramedics took Grampa away. *"It's just his body."*

But it had looked like Grampa then, and it had looked like Billy now. Just … different.

Empty.

Cold.

"Soldier Mason?"

I looked up at the man in a police uniform through eyes that couldn't stop tearing up. "Y-yeah?"

Maybe it would've been more respectful to stand. But I didn't have the strength in me. Not after I'd watched my closest, longest, oldest friend die beneath my pressing hands.

So, the cop sat beside me instead.

"I'm sorry about your friend," he said quietly, folding his arms over his knees.

I just nodded, unsure of how I would ever look at Billy's mom again.

God, who's going to tell his mom?

I imagined her receiving the news, imagined her pain and screams and tears, and I started to cry again, unable to find it in me to care that this cop and all of those people against the fence behind me were staring.

"My name is Officer Sam Lewis. But you can call me Sam if you'd like."

I didn't call him anything as I pulled my knees to my chest and pressed my forehead against them.

Fucking hell, Billy. You fucking idiot.

"Look ..." Officer Sam laid a hand against my back. "I know the last thing you want to do is answer my stupid questions. But you know I have to ask them."

Somewhere beyond my realm of thinking, a little voice told me to run and to not stop until every person in this shitty town forgot my name. But there was no forgetting a guy named Soldier, and that was just another thing to blame my mother for.

"So, do you think you could answer a couple of questions for me, Soldier?"

I lifted my head and watched as the ambulance, void of its siren, drove away with Billy in a body bag. A second cop car drove closely behind it, and I presumed they were on their way to deliver the heartbreaking, life-changing news to Billy's oblivious parents. They would blame me, and they would hate me, and they wouldn't be wrong in doing either.

It was all my fault.

And it seemed that Officer Sam agreed.

"Don't you have to take me down to the station or something?" I asked quietly, sniffling.

"Nah, not yet. We can chat here for a couple of minutes ... as long as you're cooperating."

I pulled in a shaky breath and nodded. "Okay."

"So, you have a lot of pills in your car," he said. "Are they yours?"

My brain worked quicker than it ever had before. If I said no, he'd ask whose they were. I could tell him they were Billy's, but Billy was dead. I had killed him, and whether he was here to fight for himself or not, I couldn't do that to him. I refused. No, I'd have to be honest and tell him they were Mom's. She'd be arrested—*oh my God, they're going to arrest me*—and she'd go to prison. But Mom wouldn't survive jail ... but *I* could. I was younger, stronger, more resilient. Mom would let it break, destroy, kill her, and I couldn't live with that.

I was supposed to save her after all. It was all I knew how to do.

So, with a shaky breath, I closed my eyes and nodded. "Yes."

"What were you doing with all that stuff, Soldier?"

"I was going to The Pit." It wasn't a lie. That was exactly where I'd intended to go. But I wasn't going to sell them all. I'd wanted to get rid of most of them. All I'd wanted was to make enough money to pay the stupid fucking rent, and the rest would be gone. Thrown in the lake, flushed down the toilet—*gone*.

But Officer Sam didn't know that.

"That's where the high school kids hang out, isn't it?"

"Yeah."

"You sell to high school kids?"

"N-no ..." *But that's exactly what you've been doing, Soldier. It doesn't matter how careful you've been. It doesn't matter how good your intentions are. It*

74

doesn't matter. *Don't be a fucking idiot.* "Yes," I gasped, breathless, like the word had been pressed from my heart with every life I'd been helping to destroy.

The life I had ended.

"Okay." Officer Sam sighed, disappointed. "And what happened? You sold one of those to your friend and …"

"No. I didn't sell anything to Billy. H-he … he just took one, and I don't know. I was talking to him, and … he p-passed out or something."

"But he took one of *your* pills," Officer Sam confirmed, speaking slowly, and I nodded. "All right."

He stood up and said some shit into the transmitter on his jacket. Shit I didn't understand, shit I barely heard. I was too busy staring at the dirty shoulder of the road, where I'd laid Billy's lifeless body. Where I had pounded on his chest and tried to make him breathe, *begged* for him to take a fucking breath. God … he should've fucking breathed because it was my birthday, and it wasn't fair, and none of this was supposed to happen to me or anyone, and yet …

It had.

Dammit, you should run, my mind told my legs. *Officer Sam is over there, talking to whoever the fuck, getting ready to slap the cuffs on you, and you have an opportunity to book it. Just run, run, RUN until you can't run anymore, and even then, keep running.*

Yet I didn't. Because beneath all the shit I'd gotten myself into, beneath the mess I'd made of my life, I was still a good person. I would always be a good person.

And I had killed my best friend, and I knew I had to pay for it.

"All right, Soldier Mason," Officer Sam said with a sigh, like he regretted what he was about to do, and I thought, *Maybe he knows I'm a good person too.* "On your feet, man. Hands behind your back."

I had seen enough of those cop shows where the perpetrator fought their arrest and the cop had to throw them against the car and slap the cuffs on.

This wasn't one of those moments.

Officer Sam read me my rights as I stood there with my eyes on the patch of dirt where Billy had died. He cuffed my wrists and asked if they hurt and apologized when I said they did a little.

He loosened them slightly, enough to keep the circulation moving in my hands, and I muttered, "Thank you."

Then, he walked me to his car, asked me to crouch down, placed a hand on my head, and assisted me in getting inside.

"All right, buddy," he said as if he were my friend, and hell, maybe under different circumstances, we could've been.

As he shut the door, I looked out the window toward the parking lot adjacent to the high school and woods. The Pit wasn't far from here, just a quarter of a mile through those woods. The kids there must've heard the sirens, and a bigger crowd had gathered to watch as one of their suppliers was hauled away like the criminal he was.

And there, in the middle of them all, pressed up against the chain-link fence with his arms slung over the top, was Levi, wearing a sinister, triumphant grin. And suddenly, as my eyes met his, I was so acutely aware of the vile animosity I hadn't known existed, and as Officer Sam drove me away, Levi lifted his hand and waved goodbye.

CHAPTER

FIVE

APOLOGIES & GOOD MEN

Age Twenty-Two

"In my twenty-six years as a judge, I have unfortunately had a number of these cases pass my desk. I will say, most have been colored in stark contrasts of black and white, and an appropriate punishment has nearly always been easy to decide.

"Mr. Mason, your case has not been one of those.

"I have thoroughly reviewed the charges against you over these last few days, and while I wholeheartedly agree with your plea of guilty on every account, I don't hold the same opinion as you that you are, as you have repeatedly put it, a *bad person*.

"Mr. Mason, I believe that, while, yes, you committed these crimes, you unwittingly did so with curiously good intent and without a genuine desire to harm. And your outward displays of emotion and your cooperation with law enforcement, along with your excellent behavior since your arrest, have been greatly taken into consideration in determining your fate.

"And so, with all the aforementioned in mind, I have decided to sentence you to a total of twelve years of imprisonment at Wayward Correctional Facility, taking into account the year you've already spent in custody, with the possibility of early release on good behavior. Do you understand this?"

Eleven more years.

It felt like an eternity—a death sentence—and yet it still didn't feel like enough when all I could think about was Billy and the life I had stolen from him.

"Yes, Your Honor," I answered, my voice hoarse and my heart thundering.

Somewhere in the courtroom, someone began to cry.

Billy's mom.

"Additionally," the judge went on, "for the crimes of involuntary manslaughter and possession of a controlled substance with the intent to sell, a fine of fifty thousand dollars is required. On top of that, you will be required to serve two years of probation upon your release, in which you must report to an assigned officer as well as remain within the state of Connecticut for the remainder of your sentence. Do you understand this?"

"Yes, Your Honor."

The judge nodded, then leaned forward and folded his arms against the bench. His eyes met mine with a touch of sympathy, and then he spoke. "Mr. Mason, as I mentioned before, I do wholeheartedly believe that you are, regardless of the unfortunate circumstances in which

79

you were born into, a good man because it is my personal opinion that a truly terrible man doesn't believe he is in fact terrible. It is my deepest hope that you will somehow find peace in spite of the crimes you have committed and the tragedies you have faced during your short life and that, at the end of your sentence, you are able to begin the second chapter of your life with the brightest of lights guiding your way—the way the first *should have* begun—coupled with a predisposition to act in a way worthy of your character."

I heard the words he spoke; I saw the honesty in his heavy, wrinkled eyes. And yet I couldn't allow either to touch my heart. Not when Billy's mom sat somewhere behind me, her cries of anguish escalating as her husband tried desperately to console her.

She hated me. Everyone did, including my own mother—who hadn't bothered to see me in the year I spent locked up, let alone attend my sentencing. And for that reason alone, how could I not hate myself?

Still, I stared ahead, as I'd been told to do by my assigned lawyer, and said, "Thank you, Your Honor."

His lips barely twitched into a forlorn smile. "And with that, Mr. Mason, I wish you a good life." The gavel hit the bench. "Court is adjourned."

I stood as the cop came to collect me and take me away. I kept my eyes trained forward, not wanting to so much as glance over my shoulder at the people who had come on Billy's behalf. But there was a commotion, a shuffling of chairs and loud voices, and then there was Billy's mom, shouting above the rest.

"Soldier! I opened my heart and my home to you. I *fed* you, and I *loved* you, and you repaid me by taking away the thing I loved most in this world."

"Okay, Laura," Billy's dad said quietly, his voice choked with anguish. "Let's go."

The guard gripped my shoulder, silently urging me not to engage, and led me toward the door where I'd entered the courtroom.

"How am I supposed to live with that?!" she yelled after me. "How am I supposed to go on with my life, knowing you get to live yours?!"

I stopped walking despite the guard's insistence. I glanced quickly over my shoulder, keeping my gaze diverted, unable to look at the woman I'd always wished had raised me instead.

I wanted to ask her to let me know if she ever found the answer to her question. I wanted to beg her to never stop loving me despite it all because if she did, there wouldn't be a single shred of love for me left in this entire world. I wanted to thank her for everything she'd ever done for me over the years, especially during the ones in which I had nobody else.

But I didn't. Whether for a lack of time or courage, I didn't know. Hell, maybe it was both.

Instead, I whispered, "I'm so sorry," hoping she heard me. Hoping she knew I meant it.

"Let's go, Mason," the guard said, nudging me along.

So, without another word, without looking back, I went.

CHAPTER

SIX

LETTERS TO RAIN

Age Twenty-Seven

This is the part where you probably expect me to say that prison was a slice of hell, served to me on a shit-stained platter. You probably expect a harrowing tale of endless fights, shower seduction, and enough misdemeanors to tack another fifteen years onto my sentence.

Am I right?

Well, I wouldn't lie to you.

For those first five years, I actually hadn't hated prison.

I didn't love it; don't get me wrong. It was far from a walk in the park. But for all intents and purposes, it was better than how I'd lived the first half of my life.

I had a guaranteed roof over my head and three meals a day.

I landed a janitorial job and started working shifts in the cafeteria, cooking and serving breakfast a couple of times a week.

After accepting the fate handed to me, I'd spent the first two years working toward taking the GED exam, and by the time I was twenty-four, I had passed with flying colors. And once I was done doing that, I spent three years taking some online college courses and got a bachelor's degree in business. In my downtime—and there was a lot of it—I decided to finally take up something I hadn't had much time for since I had been a kid—hobbies. I quickly found that when I wasn't swiping shit from Mom, selling in The Pit, or working my ass to exhaustion, I could devour about four books a week. I genuinely enjoyed running and strength training. I had a knack for carpentry, and gardening was something I found a lot of pride in.

So, all things considered, I was doing okay. I wasn't making enemies, and I was finding plenty of stuff to pass the time.

But, man, I was fucking lonely.

It was easy to be lonely in prison. And I wasn't talking about finding someone to chat with during mealtimes or while working whatever job you were assigned to. No, that part was a piece of cake, and if we were talking about casual acquaintances, I had plenty of those, and all of them were just like me. Good-hearted guys who had ended up in shitty situations.

But what I was talking about was, when everyone else was having visitors or weekly phone conversations or receiving regular letters and packages in the mail, I had none. And that honestly blew my mind a little. To know that these guys—and I mean dudes convicted of worse crimes than me—had parents, wives, kids, and friends out there who loved them and cared for them after everything they'd done and I had no one. Not a single fucking person. And that sucked. A lot.

So, one day, out of desperation, I took up writing letters to the one person I could think of who I'd never wronged. The only person who I'd truly saved.

I wrote letters to a girl named Rain. A girl with the prettiest, softest brown hair I'd ever seen.

I knew, even when I'd started writing them, that it was stupid. I also knew I'd never send them and she'd never read them. But it was cathartic, in a way, to write to this person I'd built up around a girl I had known for all of fifteen minutes. And while I knew what had happened to me—up to this point in my life anyway—I often wondered what had happened to her after I dropped her off at her house.

She'd be twenty-four now.

Where had life taken her after that night? Had she heeded my warning to stay away from those assholes? Had she gotten the hell out of that town and run far away, just as I'd always dreamed of doing?

Every week, I filled my letters with those questions, my confessions, and the things that had been happening inside the prison walls. The initial struggles. The acceptance. The hard work I put into being the good, decent person I'd always insisted I was. They served as a diary of sorts, and it was better to get it all out and down on the paper than keep it locked inside. Then, I tucked them away beneath my mattress, for nobody to read, ready to face another week of loneliness.

Until, one week, five years into my incarceration, Mom showed up.

***

Mopping the bathroom floor was dirty, disgusting labor, and I was sure it was understandable when I said I didn't care much for it. But it was quiet work—monotonous and relaxing—and it gave me a lot of time to think. To remember a life I'd once had and fantasize about the one I probably would never have at all.

I thought about Gramma and Grampa. How disappointed they might've been to see where I'd been living all these years and the things I'd done to put me there. But sometimes, I thought, *You know what? Maybe they wouldn't be all that disappointed after all. Maybe they'd even be proud of me.* Not for the things I'd done— of course not—but for what I'd done since I had gotten there.

I thought about Billy's mom and the grief and pain she lived with every day. The broken heart I'd single-handedly stuffed inside her aching chest. Every now and then, I considered the possibility that, *Hey, maybe she doesn't hate me as much today as she did yesterday,* and that pipe dream filled me with the smallest amount of hope. But the reality was, I knew she wouldn't ever care about me again. Not until the day I was also dead.

But mostly, I thought about Billy. Where he had gone wrong and how he was also to blame for the choices he'd made in his life.

And, no, I couldn't say I was mad at him, even given the situation I was in because—let's be real—I would've ended up behind bars eventually, whether or not he had died. But I was sad. Sad he wasn't still around. Sad that my friend was gone. Sad that he'd swallowed that damn pill, laced with enough fentanyl to kill three men. Sad that there hadn't been anything I could do to save him.

I was sad about Billy a lot, and as I scrubbed the bathroom floor, I tried to imagine what he'd look like now. Six years older than twenty-one, maybe with a little more hair on his face and a little more bulk on his body.

Probably not, I thought as I stared into the murky water in the bucket. *He was always a scrawny fuck.*

"Soldier."

I looked up to see Harry, the only prison guard who called me by my first name, standing in the doorway. I pushed Billy out of my mind and smiled at the older man in the silver-framed glasses I liked to consider my friend.

"Hey, Harry. How's it going?"

He returned the smile and walked casually into the bathroom, his hands stuffed into his pants pockets. "Ah, can't complain. The wife and I went to visit our daughter over the weekend. It was nice to see her. Been a little while."

"Good for you guys," I replied, leaning my weight against the mop handle.

"Yeah, we had a good time." He nodded, meeting my gaze. His eyes twinkled, and he reminded me of my grandfather. There was just something about him. Familiar and comfortable. "Hey, so, listen, you have a visitor today."

My smile was quick to turn into a frown. "A visitor?"

The words felt strange in my mouth. Nobody visited me. I hadn't seen a person from my life outside of this place since my sentencing, and I couldn't even begin to imagine who'd wanna see me now after all this time.

Harry nodded with the same suspicion in his eyes, seeming to read my mind. "Yeah. Someone named Diane."

I dropped my gaze to the bucket and held on tightly to the handle of the mop. "Holy shit. That's my mom."

"I know." He reached to lay a hand on my shoulder, the way Grampa used to. "You don't have to see her if you don't want. I'll tell them you're not interested."

Harry was a good guy. Always looking out for me.

But I shook my head. "No, I'm good. I'll see what she wants."

The curiosity would kill me if I didn't.

I left the mop and bucket in the bathroom and headed through the halls to the visitor center. I'd never been in there before, but I knew exactly where it was, and when I crossed the threshold into a crowded room, guarded by several officers at every entrance, I spotted her right away.

Mom.

She was thinner than I remembered, and her hair was as dry as straw, piled on top of her head in a sloppy bun. Her eyes were fixed on the table in front of her, her hands fidgeting like crazy. She was nervous or doped up—hell, probably both—and I wasn't sure that I cared anymore to know what she wanted. Maybe I'd be better off leaving her stranded until she got the hint and left.

Honestly, I probably would be.

But I approached anyway.

Slowly, I walked toward her, trying to think of something to say, when she looked up at me, startled and looking as though she'd seen a ghost.

From her perspective, that was probably exactly what it was like.

"Soldier?"

"Mom."

She dropped her gaze to my hands and said, "Are you allowed to be in here without handcuffs?"

I stepped over the bench across from her and sat, staring at her with narrowed eyes. "Do you think I *need* to be in cuffs?"

"Well, what if you hurt someone?"

I snickered and looked off toward the window, secured by chain links and a lone spiderweb. "I'm not a psychopathic killer, Mom. Frankly, if I were, they probably wouldn't let me in here at all."

"Some people think you are."

My eyes met hers then for the first time in … God, I didn't even know how long. "Oh, yeah? Is that what *you* think?"

She shrugged, not a hint of regret on her bony, sallow face. "I haven't decided yet."

I couldn't help but laugh as I raked a hand through my hair. It was getting longer. I'd have to start pulling it back if I didn't want to get it cut, and I wasn't sure I did. It was nice to have a change for once. It was nice to become a new version of myself ... or someone else entirely.

"What are you doing here, Mom?" My voice sounded exhausted to my ears. Like the two minutes in her presence had already been too much.

She seemed taken aback by the question. "I'm not allowed to see my son?"

"Nobody said you're not allowed. But considering you haven't come to see me in fucking *years* ..." I lifted my hands in a shrug. "I mean, sorry, but you gotta understand why I'm a little confused."

She blew out a breath, then nodded. "I guess maybe I've missed you. And maybe I've been a little nervous about seeing you like this ... in here."

It was a shit excuse, but I guessed it was also a valid one. I'd never visited someone in prison before, and I supposed if I hadn't already been here, I would've been a little nervous about it too. But I wouldn't have let six fucking years go by without seeing my only kid—I knew that for certain—and it was for that reason I remained void of emotion as I stared across the table at her.

"So, this is it." She looked around the visitor center. "This is where you've been this whole time."

"Yep."

"What do you do here?"

"Work. Sleep. Eat. That's about it."

She gestured toward my arms. "Looks like you've been working out too. You look good."

"Thanks."

She shifted on the bench she sat on. "I've, uh … I've been working too. And I have a boyfriend."

I snorted at the thought of my mom working or being in a relationship, and then I noticed her confused expression and realized she was serious. My interest was certainly piqued.

"How long have you been working?"

"Uh, about six months now," she said with a smile that looked an awful lot like pride. "I'm a secretary at a doctor's office."

"That's good. I'm happy for you."

Her smile broadened. "It's been … a nice change."

"I bet."

Was it possible Mom had turned things around for herself? Six months wasn't a long time, and it didn't account for all the years she'd spent without me in her life. But she seemed happy. She seemed to hold her head a little higher, her back a little straighter, and I felt a little more hopeful that, hey, maybe this was a good thing.

"And this boyfriend? What's he like?"

Her lips twitched as her face tipped downward and—wait, was she blushing? Holy crap. I couldn't help it; I smiled back.

"He's amazing," she said with a sigh. "He's a little younger than me, but … he treats me pretty well. He treats me like … like I'm a-a-a princess or something."

"That's good, Mom."

"Yeah, so, uh ..."

She glanced around the room at the other inmates meeting with their loved ones. They behaved differently than we did. They spoke with affection and hope. They hugged until the guards told them to stop. Mom though ... she looked at me like she wanted to run away.

Maybe she really does think I'm a psychopath.

Then, she asked, "How long do you have in here?"

I shifted on the hard bench. "Right now, to have a visitor? Or do you mean, how long do I have left to be locked up?"

She looked uncomfortable. "The, uh ... the second one."

"I have another six years, max, as long as I don't screw up." And I had no intention of screwing up.

Her lips pursed as she nodded, like she was considering what to say next, and then she replied, "People in town ... they don't want you getting out."

"Well, that's too fucking bad," I said, lowering my brows and scowling at her.

"Yeah, well ... that's not for a long time anyway." She sighed and seemed to relax, and a part of me wondered if she was one of those people who didn't want me getting out of this place ... and why.

I cleared my throat and decided to change the subject because it *was* a long time and I didn't like to think about that. "So, how's—"

"I guess I'll get going," she cut me off, beginning to stand.

"What?" I asked, taken aback. "But you just freakin' got here."

"Yeah, but I have stuff to do, and I'm sure you're busy, so ..." She hoisted her bag onto her shoulder—that same bag I had taken those last bottles of pills out of—and forced a smile. "I'll come back soon though."

"In another six years, right?" I challenged, standing up and reminding her of the seventeen inches I had on her modest five foot two.

She looked embarrassed as her cheeks burned bright red. "I'll see you soon," she insisted.

"Yeah, okay."

Then, she turned and left. No hug. No attempt at affection. She just scurried away like a rat, attempting to get away with something, and I had to wonder ...

What the hell are you really up to, Mom?

And why don't you want me coming home?

CHAPTER

SEVEN

TASTE OF FREEDOM

Age Thirty

"It's my birthday, boys," I announced to the kitchen crew the moment I burst through the swinging doors. "So, we're not eating any of this shit. I wanna make something good." I grabbed the trays of burger patties and turned to stuff them back into the freezer.

"So, you wanna trade this shit for other shit—that's what you're saying?" Chuck—serving seven years after being caught snorting coke outside his daughter's day care after nine years of being clean—asked, crossing his beefy arms over his chest and smirking.

"Ah, come on. We gotta have something good in here." I dug through the shelves of various frozen foods. The selection was worse than an elementary school cafeteria, but I was determined to not eat another crappy burger for my thirtieth birthday.

It was a new decade, baby, and I had a good feeling in my bones.

I pulled a few boxes of bland French fries and something that sort of passed as chicken breast aside to uncover a stack of thirty frozen pizzas. My face lit up like a freakin' Christmas tree at the thought of eating pizza on my birthday—something I hadn't done since I had been eight years old.

"Hey, check it out," I said, pulling one out of the freezer and holding it up for the other guys to see. "Anyone want pizza?"

"Dude, that shit's gonna give us salmonella or E. coli or somethin'," Jag—serving three years for stealing his ex-wife's car, following an ugly divorce that had granted her both vehicles—replied. "Like, I dunno how long that's even been in there."

"Definitely long enough that I don't remember loading it off the truck," Chuck muttered, looking both skeptical and grossed out.

I turned it over in my hands, looking for a clue of its age or if it would kill us if consumed. "I don't see a date on it or anything."

"That's 'cause they don't give a fuck if we die of food poisoning," Jag said. "They probably hope for it. One less mouth for tax payers to feed."

"But, hey, man, if you wanna risk it, go for it. Happy birthday. Have a lovely case of diarrhea," Chuck muttered with a snort, nudging an elbow at Jag's ribs.

Jag laughed and grabbed for a bag of potatoes to peel for dinner. "Nothin' better than kickin' off a new year with the runs."

Harry wandered in, his hands stuffed into his pockets, and greeted us with a, "Good evening, fellas. How's it going?"

"Same shit, different day," Chuck grumbled, opening the freezer to grab the patties I'd just put away.

I turned on the stove, getting it ready to fry up the mystery meat. It had been stupid of me to expect I could eat something other than what I'd been choking down the past nine years of my life. And why? Because it was my thirtieth birthday?

I hadn't been special to anyone since I had been twelve when Gramma was still alive. What the hell had made me believe something would suddenly change now, especially as a convicted felon?

So, we cooked while Harry supervised, and then I ate my dinner with a little less enthusiasm than usual. Chuck and Jag did me the solid of rounding up a couple of other guys to sing a rousing chorus of "Happy Birthday," and they gifted me with a Twinkie someone had grabbed from the commissary. It was nice—more than anybody had done for me in years—and I enjoyed my Twinkie with the stupidest smile on my face. Because when I closed my eyes, sitting with my back against the library wall, I almost felt normal.

I had come in to find a new book to read, hoping there'd be something I hadn't read yet, and thought I'd enjoy a few quiet minutes alone, surrounded by the warm scent of musty, old books. And now, I sat on the floor, finishing my birthday present with my arm wrapped around my knees, as I breathed deeply and imagined I wasn't here, trapped within these stone walls. I was on the outside, free to come and go as I pleased. Free to breathe the fresh air or buy a pizza whenever I damn well felt like it without worrying if it would give me salmonella.

The years were somehow passing slower now, and the monotony of life behind bars was taking its toll. The more time I spent at Wayward, the more I began to wonder when I'd ever see the outside again. It had been nine years since I'd been arrested, eight since I'd begun my sentence, and I knew it could be any day when they decided to release me back into the wild. I mean, why not? For the most part, I hadn't done a fucking thing wrong since being locked up, apart from a few minor misdemeanors that hadn't earned me anything but a little bit of time in solitary. I worked hard, I mostly stayed to myself or was otherwise friendly, and I never gave a guard or the warden shit.

God, when I really thought about it, why had it already been nine years of model citizenship without a single mention of what a good job I was doing?

I groaned, flopping my head forward against my arms, as my heart started a war with my head.

I was comfortable here. I liked the routine of it, the safety of it. And there was a reason I was here—a damn good one. I never forgot that. Not once. But, man, I missed freedom. And right now, I really missed pizza.

"Hey."

I opened my eyes with a jolt to see Harry standing before me, and I said, "Man, you'd make an awesome thief, you know that? Nobody would know you were coming."

He chuckled and offered a kind smile. "I think I'll stick to my day job, thanks."

Then, he handed me what looked like a piece of paper. "Here. I came to give you this."

"What is it?" I asked skeptically before accepting the white bundle that turned out to be a folded-up paper towel.

Inside was a slice of pizza.

"Oh, man, Harry …" It was stupid, the way my eyes teared up at the sight of the melted mozzarella and sliced pepperoni.

"We had pizza for dinner in the break room. So, I saved you a slice." He nudged the toe of my beat-up canvas slip-on sneaker with the toe of his shiny shoe. "Happy birthday, Soldier."

"Don't ever let anyone say you're not my favorite," I said before taking a big bite.

It wasn't the freshest, and it was a little cold, but, holy God, nothing had ever tasted better, and I groaned like I'd just received the best blowjob of my life.

Fuck. I missed that too. Women. Blowjobs. Sex. The guys and I talked about it sometimes, remembering the people we'd had at one point or another, but most of the time, I preferred not to think about it at all. It didn't suck so much that way. But right now, with the pizza and pepperoni mingling joyously in my mouth, I recalled other things I wouldn't mind tasting, and it left an ache so dull in my chest.

Harry chuckled. "Good?"

"You have no fucking idea."

I took another bite, and as I chewed, I left behind the memory of women and instead thought about a time from even longer ago. A whole other fucking life really, and I said, "The last time I had pizza on my birthday was the only time I had a party. My grandparents—I told you they raised me in the beginning, right?"

Harry nodded, a hint of melancholy touching his eyes. "You've mentioned it a few times."

I'd known Harry for eight years, and there were only so many things to tell.

Hell, it was likely he'd heard this story before too. But he didn't stop me from telling it.

"Right. Anyway, my gramma wanted me to have a normal birthday, I guess, and had me invite a couple of friends over. Billy was one of them. We ordered pizza, and right before I sat down to eat, I went to the bathroom to take a piss and walked in on my mom popping pills." I studied the pizza crust. The hardened bubbles of sauce. The crispy edges and softer middle. "All my grandparents had ever wanted was to give me a normal childhood while still protecting my mom. She was their only kid. I always got that they genuinely thought they were doing the right thing, and I don't blame them for anything ever, but …"

"All we can do is our best," Harry said, injecting a bit of wisdom into my moment of reflection. "Even if our best isn't all that good at all."

I nodded thoughtfully, turning the piece of crust over in my fingers. "It's crazy. Like ... sometimes, we have these moments, you know, that are so profound in our lives, but we have no clue they're happening when they're actually happening. And all Gramma wanted that day was for me to be a normal kid, but there was Mom, fucking it up again. Gramma could never stop the inevitable. The only way she could've done that was to stop protecting her own daughter, and no matter how bad shit got, she could never abandon her."

Just like me.

"You know, Soldier ... the thing about the past is, it isn't always up for speculation. Sometimes, the best thing you can do is to simply accept that what's happened has already happened and move on."

I laughed and took a bite of the crispy crust. "You say that shit like the very nature of my situation isn't because my past is under speculation."

"True," Harry said, nodding reflectively. "But rumor has it, your present has been looked at quite a bit as well. And what I hear is, you might be getting out of here soon."

I nearly dropped the rest of the crust as I looked up at him and gawked, so fucking scared of letting hope take control. "Wait. You heard that?"

Harry shrugged, but the little smile tugging at his lips was unmistakable. "Like I said, rumors. But I thought you'd like to know. Anyway, it's almost lights out. So, grab a book and head back, all right?"

I could barely nod as I considered the possibility that I could maybe get the hell out of this place sooner rather than later. "All right," I replied, staring off toward nothing at all but a potential future I could almost see, taste, and smell. "'Night, Harry. Thanks for the pizza."

CHAPTER

EIGHT

SOMEWHERE TO GO

Six months after my thirtieth birthday, nine and a half years after my time behind bars had begun, I was officially up for parole. I'd been given the notice that my hearing was coming, and I had a pretty good feeling what the outcome was going to be. And, hey, maybe that was a little cocky of me. Maybe I should've expected the worst—hell, I'd only been doing that my entire life. But like I'd already said, I had woken up on my thirtieth birthday with a good feeling settled deep in my bones. Maybe it was safe to believe it had something to do with getting out of here.

I mean, it sure as fuck had nothing to do with my mother's second visit in over nine years.

I didn't know how it was possible for someone to age fifteen years in only three. But somehow, Diane Mason had done it. She looked like a witch from one of those old kids movies. An ancient hag, settled deep in the woods. Her eyes were sunken in, her cheeks hollowed out. Her hair as dry as a scarecrow's straw. I sat across from her, wondering how the hell this could've been the woman who'd given birth to me when I looked absolutely nothing like this sack of paper-thin skin and bones.

And just like that, for one of the first times in over thirty years, I wondered about my father and who he might have been.

"So, you still popping pills, or have you moved on to harder shit?" I accused, guarding my heart with my arms folded over my chest.

"Well, I see you're still a wiseass."

I inconspicuously diverted my gaze to the table beside me. Evan—a really great dude, serving twenty-five years for shooting a man in the back as he fled from Evan's home, after the guy had broken in and brutally raped his wife—was sitting with his kids, crying unabashedly over his wife not coming. He'd said she had a hard time seeing him here, knowing she'd eventually have to leave without him, and I guessed she just couldn't find it in her to come at all.

I wished she had, for his sake.

I also wished Mom had never shown up for my own.

Glancing back at her, I drawled, "No. I'm just wondering what bullshit I'll have to deal with once I get out of here."

Her demeanor shifted subtly. Like a storm cloud passing quietly through an otherwise clear sky. "So, it's true. You're up for parole."

I nodded. "Yeah. My hearing is in a week."

Her jaw shifted as her eyes dropped to the table. She picked at her frayed cuticles, at her brittle nails, before saying, "I don't want you coming home."

Off to my right, Coop—a guy who'd attempted a bank robbery after finding out he was gonna lose his house—must've just told his wife he had a good shot at getting out of here, too, because she was jumping out of her seat to throw herself at him. The guard allowed the hug for a few seconds before asking them to break it up.

And there was my mom, telling me she didn't want me coming home.

It must've been nice to have someone who wanted you out, where they could hug you without someone telling you to stop.

A muscle in my jaw twitched. "Why not?"

"Because …" She squeezed her hands into white-knuckled fists, like she was suddenly angry. She leaned forward and dropped her voice to a whisper. "Do you even know what you have done to my life since you murdered Billy?"

The air was sucked out of the room as I stared at her skeleton face. Those words—*murdered Billy*—sliced deep, cutting through bone and muscle, until they pierced what was left of my heart. Except she had it wrong.

I hadn't murdered Billy.

I hadn't wanted him to die; I hadn't asked him to take her poisoned drugs. But he had done it anyway, and I would live with that for the rest of my life.

The fact that she thought I'd murdered him though … that hurt when I knew it shouldn't. Her opinion shouldn't have mattered. Yet it did. It always would.

"I didn't *murder* anyone," I replied, my voice low.

"Bullshit," she hissed, sneering. "And *I'm* not the only one who thinks so. Billy's mother? You ever wonder what it's gonna be like for her, seeing you wandering around like nothing happened? You think anybody is gonna wanna see your face, knowing what you did? You *embarrassed* me, Soldier. You disgraced our entire family. God …" She sucked at her teeth as she looked away, shaking her head. "I can't even imagine what your grandparents would say right now if they were alive."

I could've sat there and taken everything she gave me without even moving a muscle. But the moment she brought Gramma and Grampa into it, everything I saw before me turned red.

"Shut the hell up," I said through a jaw clenched too tight.

But she just wrinkled her nose and stared right into my eyes as she continued, "Grampa wouldn't have been able to even look at you. You disgraced his name. You tainted it and everything he'd taught you. He would've regretted ever talking me out of aborting—"

I smacked my palms against the table, allowing the sound to echo through the room. A heavy hush settled over the inmates and visitors alike as a nearby guard warned me to settle down, but you know what? Fuck that.

I leaned forward, nearly touching my nose to hers, and said, "I should've let you die."

Her eyes widened. Fear ignited in her tiny, pencil-dot pupils as her mouth fell open. "What ... what are you—"

"Everything ... *everything* I have ever done, everything I did to *myself* ... the reason I am here is because of *you*. To save your ass. To *protect* you. That's what Gramma and Grampa taught me to do—to protect *you*." I jabbed a finger at her bony chest.

"Mason, this is your last warning," the guard said, edging closer to where we sat.

"That's fine. I'm finished," I said, standing up from the bench. But before I could walk away, I leaned over my mother, purposely intimidating her with my size and height and whatever the fuck she thought of me. "Just remember, you are alive right now because of me. Billy is dead because of you. And I've been the one paying for it for the past nine and a half years, and you thank me by telling me I'm not welcome in the home I fucking helped pay for? *You're* the fucking disgrace, Diane. Not me."

The guard was beside me now, his hand on his billy club, just in case. But I'd never give him a reason to use it. I quickly offered an apology for my misconduct and hurried away from the woman I'd once believed cared about me. And you know what? Maybe there had been one point when she did. Maybe that time in the hospital, when I'd had my face cut open, was the last. But she didn't give a fuck about me now—that was for damn sure—so why did I even attempt to give one about her?

Except I did. And what she had said, I couldn't shake it off as I slumped to the floor of the library and held my head in my hands.

My parole hearing was in a week. I'd likely get out of here, unless they really just liked my company that much.

Where was I supposed to go? If I couldn't move back home, what the hell was going to happen to me? Did the entire town truly hate me as much as she'd said they did? What the hell future did I have in a place where nobody wanted me—not even my own mother?

Unless I never left.

I had a life here.

I had shelter, food, friends.

Why the hell would I ever want to leave?

I listened to the shuffle of sneakered feet entering the library. I dropped my hands to watch Gene—an older guy who had thought it'd be a good idea to break into a string of houses after losing his job—walk toward a shelf not far from where I sat. Without thinking, I stood up, grabbed the heaviest book I could reach—sorry, Stephen King—and made my fast approach.

I was going to bring that book down onto his head. I prayed I wouldn't kill him, but if I did, my apologies to Gene, but at least I would ensure my spot here for the rest of my shitty life.

The book was high, ready to drop, when Gene turned to find me looming over him like the angel of fucking death. His eyes were immediately huge, his hands raised to shield his face.

"Soldier, what the—"

"Hey, hey, hey!" Harry hurried into the library. "All right, Soldier, put down the book."

I stared right at my friend, barely able to focus on his silver glasses, and shook my head. "Harry, I have to. I-I don't—"

"Soldier, give me the book. We'll talk, okay? You don't want to do anything to Gene."

He was right. I didn't want to do anything to Gene. I didn't want to do anything to anybody—never had. My resolve crumbled quickly, and I dropped *The Stand* to the floor. Harry told Gene to get the hell out of there as I turned and rested my forehead against a shelf, and then I felt Harry's warm hand against my back.

"What happened, son?"

Son.

Nobody but Grampa had ever called me son. Nobody else had ever treated me like one. I didn't know what it was like to have a biological dad, but I did know what it had been like to look up to Grampa for the first twelve years of my life. And for the last eight years, I knew what it had been like to turn to Harry. And I turned to him then, not caring that I was supposed to be this big, tough guy, and I let him hug me as I bent at the waist and shed a few silent tears against his shoulder.

"What happened?" he repeated in a hushed whisper. "You can tell me."

I collected my damn emotions and took a step away from him, hastily wiping my eyes against my arm. "She doesn't want me coming home," I told him, knowing he'd know exactly who I was talking about. "She said I'm the fucking embarrassment, that I ruined her life."

Harry's expression hardened to stone as he shook his head. But Harry was also one to give people the benefit of the doubt, just as he'd done for me when we first met all those years ago. And he said, "Well, sometimes, people need time to process their emotions. Your mother has had a long time without you at home now, so maybe … maybe she just needs a little more time to get used to you being back."

"Oh, you have a lot more faith in her than I do, man," I grumbled, shaking my head and stuffing my hands into the pockets of my pants. "You don't know my mom."

"No," he agreed, nodding. "But I do know you, and I know your mom would be a fuckin' lunatic to not want you in her life. So, give her a little time, all right? Your hearing is, what, next week?"

I nodded.

"Okay. So, that gives her a whole week to think. You're gonna get out, Soldier; I know it. You *deserve* it. And when you do, you go home, and I bet she'll be singing a very different tune."

My eyes lifted to the fluorescent lights running the length of the library ceiling, and I chewed at my bottom lip for a moment before replying, "Well, Harry, I hope you're right. But forgive me for being realistic."

***

A week later, I had my hearing, and I waited like a kid on Christmas to hear the news.

Two months after that, the board made the decision to release me back into the world, and two more months went by before I was receiving fist bumps, handshakes, and even hugs from the friends I'd made inside. I promised to write them letters, and I made them promise to come see me if and when they got out themselves.

And then, there at the end of the line, on his day off, was Harry.

In an instant, a flash of memory came rushing in from nearly ten years ago. I had been much younger and scrawnier and way, way, way more scared then but just as tall when I walked through those gates and made reluctant eye contact with this same man before he ushered me through to Receiving and Discharge. I had noted then that, while the rest of the guards manhandled us and spoke in condescending tones, Harry never did. And although I never thought of the others as bad men for looking down on us, I always considered Harry better because he never did.

Now, I stood before him—not in prison garb, but jeans and a plain black sweatshirt—and for the first time, we felt like equals even if Harry never treated me as anything but.

"I'm not saying goodbye to you," I warned him, defiant as I hoisted the duffel bag higher on my shoulder.

He scoffed despite the heavy swallow of his throat. "I'm not saying goodbye to you either," he insisted, grinning before pulling me in for a tight bear hug. "It's been a pleasure getting to know you, son. You're a good man."

"And you're the best."

He released me from his hold and patted my shoulder. "I'm gonna miss you."

I couldn't say the words back, not without choking up, but I nodded. Because I was going to miss him too. More than he could possibly know.

I was getting really fucking tired of missing people.

"Oh, hold on a sec." He held up a finger and dug a hand into the bag he'd brought with him. He pulled out a wrapped box a bit smaller than my hand and gave it to me. "Merry Christmas, Soldier."

"Harry, what the fuck?" I turned the box over in my hands. "You're not supposed to get me shit."

He shrugged casually. "You're a free man now. I can do whatever the hell I want. But, hey, don't open it now, okay? Wait until you're in the car or home or whatever."

Home. Fuck, I couldn't believe I was actually going *home.*

I hated the way my limbs and hands shook as I pulled the duffel bag off my shoulder and put the present inside. Harry didn't get it … or, hell, maybe he did—what the hell did I know? But the thing was, I hadn't received a present—a real, honest-to-God *present*, all wrapped up and shit—since I had been twelve years old. Mom hadn't given enough of a shit to get us a tree, let alone buy me a present and wrap it up. With this thing in my bag, I hardly knew what to do with my emotions as I pulled the duffel back up my shoulder and bit at my inner cheek until the urge to cry or jump around like a little kid subsided.

I cleared my throat and glanced toward the door. The car was here and waiting, sitting idle in the parking lot.

Harry followed my gaze and pulled in a deep breath before saying, "Anyway, I'll see you around, okay?"

I nodded, not knowing if I'd ever see him again. Not knowing what I was going to do without him. "Yeah."

"I'm proud of you, son," he said as another officer told me what we already knew—that the cab had arrived to pick me up. "You have a good life, okay?"

I reached out to grip his arm, squeezing to ensure he knew I meant it when I said, "Thank you, Harry."

Then, because I wasn't going to say another goodbye, not to him, I turned and walked through the doors and gates and everything that had kept me separated from the outside world for nearly ten years. I got into a car for the first time since I had been a much younger man and gave the driver the address to the shitty apartment building I had once lived in with my mother.

I watched Wayward Correctional Facility disappear from view, and as the distance grew, a strange, crushing sense of homesickness settled deep into my gut. I knew I should've been happy to be out, to be driving away, and I guessed, in a way, I was. But I couldn't help that I was also sad and more than a little scared of what I'd face on the outside. The world had never been very kind to me, and I didn't expect it was about to start now. Especially when I had a big, fat sign taped to my back that read **CONVICTED FELON** in bold red font.

But I wasn't going to think about that now. Not when I had a present in my bag and I was too excited to not open it.

So, I tore away the paper to find a small envelope taped to a white box. When I pulled the envelope away, I

gasped to see I was holding the box for a freakin'
iPhone—something I'd never held in my hand before, let
alone owned.

"What the fuck, Harry?" I muttered, furrowing my
brow as I opened the envelope with hands that hadn't
shaken this much since the first time a guard had told me
to bend over and spread 'em.

Soldier,

*So, before you start thinking that this is way too
extravagant of a gift for me to be giving you, let me
remind you that you're a __free man__ now and I can give
you whatever the hell I want. So, accept it and move on.*

*Also, it's activated and paid for. So, don't worry
about that either.*

*My number is the only one currently on it. Use it. I
told you I wasn't saying goodbye, and I meant it.
Whenever you need me, I'm there, day or night—don't
hesitate.*

*You are cared for, Soldier, and as long as I'm
around, you will never ever be alone in this world. You
will __always__ have somewhere to go. Remember that.*

Harry

CHAPTER

NINE

AN UNWELCOME SURPRISE

Wayward Correctional Facility was two hours away from where I'd grown up on the south shore of Connecticut, and I spent the ride checking out my new phone while the cab driver made invasive small talk.

"You were a prisoner, huh?" he asked.

"Yeah," I replied, turning the phone on and marveling at the smooth, bright screen.

"How long were you locked up?"

"Uh … nine years and some months."

"Wow, man. What'd you do?" His eyes flicked to the rearview mirror to meet mine.

"Killed my best friend," I muttered while pressing my pointer finger to the icon that looked like a phone. It took me to a list of Favorites, and the only name on that list was Harry.

The cab driver grumbled a shaken, "Shit," as I fumbled my way through sending a text to my only living friend.

I just got myself out of two awkward hours of small talk, I typed with a triumphant smirk as the driver turned the radio up. *Thanks for the phone, by the way. I know you don't want me to say you shouldn't have, but, man, you shouldn't have.*

And I told you not to worry about it, Harry replied almost immediately. *Hope you didn't scare the driver too much. Tell me when you make it home.*

I smiled at his message, feeling for the first time since I had been a child what it was like to check in with someone.

Man, it felt nice.

The cab pulled up to the curb outside the apartment building I used to recognize. But it didn't look the same now.

That was what was funny about the passing of time. Things were constantly changing around us, but when we were actively witnessing that change, it was subtle. We didn't notice until we sat back years later and thought, *Huh, what the hell happened to this place?* But if you went away for a while, our minds were tricked into believing that change happened all at once, with the snap of a finger, overnight, because for us, it did. And that type of shock, man … it really fucked you up.

"Holy shit," I muttered under my breath at the sight of the trash and overgrown grass and graffiti splattered across the front of the building.

"You need anything else, man?" the driver asked, not bothering to look at the building.

"No," I replied, opening the door slowly, unable to tear my eyes from the place I used to call home. "Thanks."

The cold December air encircled me with a crushing sense of foreboding as I stepped out onto the crumbled sidewalk. A gust of wind lifted the hair off my neck, almost as though the universe were sending a message— a *warning*—and I wondered for a moment if I should listen.

But I'd never been one to pay attention to caution and alarm bells, and I walked up to the door like I was about to step through the mouth of madness.

And I soon found out that was exactly what it was.

***

The scream came instantly the second I opened the apartment door, and I almost thought about running away, thinking I'd had a lapse in memory and unknowingly broken into the wrong place. Until I peered inside, past the kitchen and into the living room to see my mother, naked from the waist up and hurrying to cover herself up.

Then, I remembered she'd told me once that she had a boyfriend. Silly me for believing it wouldn't have lasted this long—unless, of course, it was a different guy.

I clapped a hand over my eyes, giving her the privacy to hide what I didn't want to see. "Hey, sorry. I should've knocked but—"

"What the *fuck* are you doing here?!" she shrieked.

I dropped my bag on the kitchen floor. "I don't have anywhere else—"

"Hey, Soldier."

After almost ten years of being away, there were voices I was sure I wouldn't recognize if I heard them again. I knew I wouldn't be able to pick out my old boss from the grocery store out of a lineup, and if you asked me to recognize my first-grade teacher by voice alone, I wouldn't be able to.

But there were some voices I'd always remember, and when I dropped my hand, not caring about my mother's nudity anymore, I was faced with the wicked grin time wouldn't let me forget.

"Levi."

Levi Stratton stood in my mother's living room, zipping his pants up. He was missing his shirt and shoes, and given the casual way he moved around, it didn't take a genius to figure out he was comfortable here.

I wanted to throw up.

He walked over, every shitty tattoo on full display, and looked me over. "God, how long has it been? Oh"— he tapped his temple—"that's right. Just short of ten years, isn't it?"

Mom had turned her back to me and hurried to pull a shirt on as I managed to ask without wincing, "You're fucking my mom?"

He grinned and offered a nonchalant shrug while Mom hurried, barefoot, to thrust her hands against my ungiving chest.

"I told you not to come back!" she shouted, frantic.

117

"And where would you like me to go, Diane?" I asked, turning my narrowed glare from Levi to look at her. The woman who hadn't changed her mind the way Harry had said she might. "I have nowhere else to go."

"You think I give a fuck where you go? I don't fucking care as long as you're not *here*." She smacked my chest. "Now, get the fuck out. Go!"

"Better listen to your mother, Soldier," Levi said, passing us to head to the refrigerator.

I ignored him and brushed her hands away, unwilling to show any of the hurt and anguish I was feeling. I didn't know where I was going. I didn't know what I would do. But wherever it was, she wouldn't know, and she'd never be aware that she was breaking my heart with every hateful word.

"I have to get my stuff," I said, my tone as cold as the world outside.

She crossed her arms over her chest. "Make it fast."

It had been a long time since I'd been inside the apartment, and most people in my position would presume that their belongings would've been moved, put away, or even thrown out. But I knew better than to think my mother would lift a finger to do anything productive regardless of how much time had passed, and when I pushed past her and Levi and headed to my old room, I found that I'd been right.

My room had remained frozen in time. It was as neat as it'd always been, save for the empty envelope where my savings once had been, still lying beside the bed where I had left it almost ten years ago. Nothing else appeared to have been touched or moved, and I slammed the door behind me to quickly collect everything worth taking.

A pair of boots in better shape than the shoes I was wearing. Some clothes that I thought might still fit. A smaller stash of money I'd taped beneath my dresser—a couple hundred bucks maybe—surprised that the thieves in the next room hadn't found it first. A picture of my grandparents and me, another picture of Billy and me from when we had been young and untouched by death and the loss of innocence.

Then, I opened the closet and grabbed Grampa's tackle box from the top shelf. I hadn't opened it since the day he had died, hadn't even cared to. But there was no way in hell I was letting Diane keep it. And who knew? Maybe I'd even pick up fishing again, wherever the hell I ended up.

I left everything else and didn't bother turning off the light or closing the door behind me as I reentered the living room. I ignored Levi and stared my mother down, who was now, once again, sitting on the couch.

That was the only thing that had changed about this place. The fucking couch.

I guessed she only gave a shit about the things she needed the most—drugs and a place to crash after the high.

"You're never seeing me again," I warned her, keeping my voice even. Unmoved as my heart ached incredibly. "The second I walk through that door, I am gone, and you will never see me again for the rest of your miserable fucking life. Do you understand that?"

She said nothing.

"You won't know where I go. You won't have any way to contact me. This is it. Tell me you understand that, tell me you're good with it, and I'm gone forever."

That was when she looked right into my hardened glare, her pupils missing from her eyes, and she said, "I should've aborted you."

Levi laughed, grinning like she'd just told the funniest joke he had ever heard. "Man, our lives would've been easier. Think of everyone who'd still be alive. Imagine that."

I could kill him. I wanted to, and you know what? Maybe I should. I could be thrown back into Wayward. I would have a place to live, eat, sleep …

But it was what he wanted.

He wanted the reaction, and I wasn't going to give it to him. Because he might've chosen this piece-of-shit life for himself, but I was going to be better. I *was* better.

So, without another word, without looking back, I walked through the door and slammed it behind me.

***

"Harry?"

My voice cracked on his name, but I didn't think Harry had noticed because he said, "Hey! I didn't expect you to call me so soon. How's it going?"

I wiped the snot pooling beneath my nose with the back of my frozen hand and said, "She didn't change her tune."

"What? Soldier—"

"Sh-she didn't want me there, so I left."

"Ah, man …" He sighed, sounding so far away now. Farther than I needed him to be. "I'm sorry, son."

I sat on the side of the road, staring across at a patch of dirt. My ass was freezing, I couldn't feel my fingers, and my teeth were chattering against the cold. But I couldn't stop staring. I hadn't stopped since leaving my mom's apartment over an hour ago.

"Where are you?" Harry asked.

"I let him die for her," I said as another round of tears began to soak my wind-stung face. "He'd still be alive if I hadn't been so fucking busy saving her goddamn life."

"Soldier, tell me where you are. I'm coming, okay? Just tell me where to go, and I'll be there."

So, I did, and he came. It had taken an hour for him to drive to me, but he had. It was more than I'd expected when I called. I could've walked down to the motel outside of town and gotten a room with the little bit of money in my pocket. But I had called Harry to have someone to talk to, and instead, he'd given me warmth.

But before he did anything else, he sat beside me on the side of the road and stared across at the last place I'd been in this shitty town before spending a third of my life behind bars.

"He died right there," I said, pointing toward the patch of dirt that looked so much the same. Not like everything else around here.

Hell, even the woods had been plowed down. The Pit was gone, thank God.

Where do the kids pop their pills these days?
How is Levi doing business?

I cringed at the thought, and then I cringed at the idea that he, a guy only a handful of years older than me, was fucking my mom.

And why?

Harry nodded solemnly. "It's an unfortunate thing that happened," he said, his breath creating puffs of silvery clouds against the black sky.

"They were her pills." It was a truth I hadn't uttered to a single soul outside of my letters to a girl named Rain. And now, Harry knew too. "I had been swiping them from her for years to make some money to pay our bills and so she'd have fewer pills to take." I laughed at that now, shaking my head and rolling my eyes. "I was such a fucking idiot for not realizing she'd just buy more. I just … I thought I was doing a *good thing*, you know? Like, the lesser of two evils or some stupid shit."

Harry had turned to look at me, his mouth frozen with parted lips.

"We needed the money for rent and electric, and I was going to pull from my savings to pay it off. But she had stolen it all. Nine thousand dollars gone"—I snapped my aching fingers—"just like that. God, I hadn't known she even *knew* about that fucking money, and she'd taken every last penny. I was going to use it to leave, to get us the hell out of here, and she had taken it."

Harry released another silvery breath, closed his eyes, and hung his head, letting it shake a little.

"She had bought four fucking bottles, *full* of pills, and I took them from her. I was only going to sell enough to pay our rent—that's all. I could've lived without lights—I'd done it before—but we needed the roof over our heads. That's all I was gonna do, but f-fucking Billy …" I choked on a sob I thought I'd been holding for nearly ten years as my stomach clenched and heaved. "Fucking *Billy* had to go ahead and take one. Because fucking Billy had a problem. He'd been popping pills since we had been kids, but I never told anyone. I did *nothing* because I thought it was *fine*. I thought, as long as I was in control, it was okay. But it wasn't okay, and I wasn't in control. I couldn't save him. I tried, and I tried, and I fucking *tried*, but I couldn't save his stupid fucking life."

I wrapped my arms tighter around myself and gritted my teeth against the winter chill, staring at the patch of dirt across the road. I imagined that Billy's ghost was there, forever tethered to the last place he'd been alive. I imagined he could see me, angry and hateful and so fucking pissed. I wondered what he'd say to me now, knowing he'd never uttered anything worth saying while he was alive, and I shook my head.

"Billy Porter was such a fucking asshole," I muttered, dropping my chin to my chest. "He was an idiot and a loser, and if I'm being real with myself, he probably would've been dead by now anyway. I just wish I hadn't been the one who killed him. That's all. I wish that weren't a part of my shitty story."

With another sigh, Harry wrapped an arm around my shoulders and pulled my body against his. Then, he said, "Soldier, do you know how many other people would've died had Billy not taken that pill?"

I swallowed and blinked away the tears. "I never thought about that."

"Your heart is so good, and your intentions were as well—as twisted as they might've been. But if you had taken those bottles and sold even just *ten* pills to ten kids, that would've been the blood of ten people on your hands. And while it still wouldn't have been your *fault* they were laced, you would still be in prison, maybe even for the rest of your life. And there is more to your story than that, Soldier. I promise you. There is a reason Billy took that pill before you had the chance to sell any—*he* saved *you*."

Holy shit.

I had never thought of it like that before. I had never looked outside of what had happened to imagine what could've happened had things gone just a little differently.

It didn't take away from everything I'd done to save my mother, only for her to continue being an ungrateful bitch. It didn't take away the fact that I was still here and my best friend wasn't. But maybe, by unwittingly sacrificing his own life, Billy had truly saved mine. Because of his carelessness, I'd been given a second chance. I'd gotten a taste of what it was like to be out of this hellhole. And for that, I could find it in me to be grateful.

"Come on," Harry said, squeezing his arm tighter around my shoulders before letting go. "Let's get you warmed up."

So, I got up, collected my few belongings, and headed toward Harry's Mazda.

But before I could get in, I looked back toward the patch of dirt and offered a small lift of my hand, a little inconspicuous wave, as I muttered, "Later, Billy."

CHAPTER

TEN

GOOD THINGS FOR A GOOD MAN

Harry's house was small but welcoming in the way every house should be. I felt all the love contained within those walls the moment I stepped through the door that night, and it never stopped, even after Harry announced to his wife, Sarah, that I'd be staying for the foreseeable future.

Initially, I could tell she wasn't sold on the idea of letting an ex-con sleep under her roof. Her stony gaze and tight grip on her husband's arm had given her understandable nerves and fear away.

But Harry explained my predicament to her, and when he finally introduced me by name, the fear and anxiety vanished as her face lit up with instant recognition, and she asked, "*This* is Soldier?"

Harry had been talking about me for years, apparently, and I guessed he'd put in a good word because it was then that she rushed off to make up the guest room and told me I could stay as long as I needed to.

So, that was what I did.

I stayed there for a week, feeling like I'd tripped and fallen into the lap of hospitable luxury, and then, just like that, it was Christmas.

Now, Christmas with Gramma and Grampa had always been nice—whether Diane decided to show up or not. There were always presents, and Gramma always made a nice dinner. But the thing about Christmas with Gramma and Grampa was, it was always just us. Which was still fine and forever appreciated, especially because after they were gone, I didn't have Christmas at all really. But it had been small, quiet, and low-key, much like everything else during my life with my grandparents. So, anytime one of the kids in school had mentioned how crazy their holiday had been, I'd fantasize about what that might've been like while never really knowing what to imagine. I'd seen big family get-togethers on TV plenty of times, but was that really what it was like? Or was it exaggerated for the sake of entertainment? I had never really known—that was, until I spent Christmas with Harry's family.

Harry was one of four kids, and each of them was married with children, and several of those children had children of their own. Now, somehow, they'd planned to squeeze all forty-six of those people into their little house, and although I couldn't begin to fathom what kind of miracle they needed to pull off to make that happen, I also couldn't wait as I helped Sarah cook dinner just hours before the guests were supposed to arrive.

"It's definitely handy, having you around," she commented as I easily reached a baking dish from the top shelf of a cabinet.

"Hey, it's the least I can do." I then brought down the ingredients for what she'd said was her famous cornbread casserole. "I gotta do something to feel useful when you're feeding me and giving me a place to sleep."

"Oh, don't be silly, sweetie. You're our guest. You don't have to feel obligated to do anything. Now"—she took the last cans from my hands—"your clothes are in your room. Go get dressed."

I was getting tired of saying, *"You didn't have to do that,"* but I meant it.

All of this—the room, the food, the company, and now, the clothes, apparently—she didn't have to do any of it. And to insist that I didn't need to repay her in any way at all, even by helping in any way I could, was absurd. Especially after I'd spent my entire life working and doing things for other people—I didn't know how to turn that off.

But I did go back to the guest room to find a brand-new pair of black dress pants and a navy-blue button-down on the bed, both in my size—and at six foot seven, that wasn't always an easy thing to just stumble upon. I was touched and grateful to have a new set of clothes to wear on the first Christmas of the rest of my life, and I got dressed to find that Sarah had a good eye for what would make a guy like me look nice.

After tying my hair back in a low tail at the nape of my neck, I left the room and heard the voices of people I didn't know coming from the kitchen.

"Daddy, you let a *criminal* stay in your house?"

"Mom, how could you let him do that?!"

The first voice scoffed. "Oh my God, what if he kills you in your sleep and takes everything you own?"

The second said, "Wait. Has he killed anybody? Why was he in prison in the first place?"

Harry sighed. "Okay, first of all, he's not going to kill anybody. He was in prison for manslaughter and—"

"So, wait. He *has* killed someone," the second voice interrupted. "Oh my God, Pamela. Daddy invited a *murderer* to Christmas. Isn't that awesome?"

I pulled in a deep breath and decided it was time to stop eavesdropping and get the introductions with Harry's daughters over with and out of the way. I couldn't force anyone to feel comfortable in my presence, but the least I could do was be polite and hopefully prove to them I wasn't a threat. So, I cleared my throat and entered the kitchen to find two blonde women. They looked nearly identical to their mother, and they turned at the sound of my footsteps.

"Girls, I'd like you to meet Soldier. Soldier, these are my daughters—"

"Wait," one of the two cut in, holding her hands out. "Soldier. I knew a kid named Soldier. He was one of my students, and he …" Her voice trailed off as something dawned on her, and she laid a palm over her chest. "Oh my God, are you Soldier Mason?"

"Um ..." I swallowed as it dawned on *me* that she had heard of my case. "Yeah, I—"

"Soldier, oh my God." She walked toward me, her eyes instantly misting with nostalgic recollection and sympathy. "Do you remember me? Mrs. Henderson?"

My jaw dropped at the name as I nodded. A tidal wave of memories flooded back, filled with school-day moments and after-class meetings. "Oh, wow, yeah. You ..." I actually laughed, bewildered and completely blown away. "You were my only favorite teacher. You—" I didn't think it was appropriate to mention that she'd been my first real crush on a person I knew outside of TV. So, I smiled and chose to tell her a different, less embarrassing truth. "You made school decent."

That hand remained on her chest as she shook her head. "I had asked if you were okay. And you weren't."

I smiled apologetically, like it had been my fault. "No, I wasn't okay."

"I'm so sorry. When I heard what happened, I felt like I'd failed in some way, which"—she laughed, her cheeks pinking a bit beneath the kitchen light—"I knew was ridiculous. There was nothing I could've done, I don't think, but ..." She sighed and reached her hand out to touch my wrist. "I'm just really sorry."

Harry, his wife, and their other daughter had remained silent as they watched this unlikely reunion take place.

I mean, come on. What were the chances that Harry's daughter would just so happen to be the only teacher who had ever truly given a shit about me when I was a kid?

130

But then, when I really thought about it, I guessed it made sense.

It was fitting for her to be the child of the only man since my grandfather to care about what happened to me. And now, standing within both of their presence, I realized something for certain in a way I'd never known it before.

I was going to be okay.

One way or another, that was how it was going to be.

Finally.

***

Harry's brother Howard owned a grocery store—The Fisch Market, it was called—in a town nearby, River Canyon, and on Christmas Day, Harry asked him if there were any positions to be filled.

"Actually," Howard said, eyeing me with a hint of scrutiny, "our janitor just left us, and I've been having to do all the cleaning myself. If you don't mind pushing a broom, mopping the floor, and scrubbing bathrooms, you've got yourself a job."

I couldn't help but chuckle. "It just so happens I'm overqualified for the job, and I'll take it."

Howard's wife, Connie, was the mayor of River Canyon as well as the local real estate agent, and while she was a little hesitant to allow a convict to live within her apparently prestigious little hamlet, she agreed to set me up in a place just within the town limits.

"We have a reputation to uphold, you see," she said in a voice that was unintentionally snooty, waving around a wineglass that was just a little too full. "And to clarify, it isn't that *I* mind you being there or think you're a threat to our little town. But it's the others, you understand?"

Actually, I could tell she did very much mind and was only going along with the plan for the time being to keep the peace among her husband and brother-in-law. It wouldn't surprise me if she immediately demanded that Howard revoke the job offer as soon as they got home. But still, I was grateful she was at least being kind of nice to my face. Judging from the way she pinched her lips and sucked at her teeth, it wasn't easy for her to do.

I shrugged and lifted one side of my mouth in a lopsided smile. "I'm just grateful to have a place to go."

"Then, you won't mind that it's in a trailer park?" She observed me with a heavy dose of doubt and the tiniest hint of hope. I bet she would've crossed her fingers, too, if she hadn't been holding that wineglass with both hands.

But I could only laugh. She wasn't going to scare me away that easily.

"Ma'am, I just spent the greater part of my adulthood sharing a room with sixty other guys. I could move into a freakin' box, and I'd be grateful just to not have a roommate."

Harry and Howard both chuckled, but Connie didn't find it very funny. Instead, she downed her wine in two big gulps as she eyed her brother-in-law with a stony glare.

You owe me big, the look said, and Harry smiled as if to say, *Yes, I do.*

And so did I.

***

I knew the next chapter of my life would officially begin in River Canyon the moment I crossed town lines. It was a feeling I didn't even necessarily want—because, let's be real, it was a little too quaint and pedigree for a mutt like me—but there it was, warm and comfortable, building up from somewhere deep in my gut.

It was so different from what I was used to and where I'd been. Every lawn we passed was mowed to perfection, and every bush was trimmed and meticulously shaped. There wasn't a piece of trash in sight, and all the lamp posts looked to be straight from one of those Norman Rockwell paintings Gramma used to love.

I'd fallen into some small-town twilight zone, and I was beginning to second-guess my decision to give this a shot despite my heart telling me I was in the right place.

"I dunno about this, Harry," I muttered as a cop waved at the car, wearing a friendly smile. "You know, maybe I should find something somewhere else."

"Soldier, this is your best chance at starting over while still remaining within the state lines," Harry replied, but what he meant was, *There is nothing else.* "Honestly, if it wasn't for your probation, I'd tell you to just get the hell out of Connecticut altogether. Move to Alabama and start over."

"Why Alabama?"

Every single house was decorated for Christmas, decked out to the nines. I wondered if it was a part of the agreement when buying a place here.

Connie looked like the kinda lady to pass some crazy rule like that. *Thou shalt not leave a shingle untouched by a twinkling light.*

I snorted at my own joke.

Harry shrugged. "I dunno. First state I thought of."

"You think I'd cut it in Alabama?" I asked, glancing at him with a raised brow.

"Dunno. Never been there."

"Then, why'd you think of it?"

Harry sighed as we pulled up to a Stop sign. "Soldier, you're worse than my grandkids."

"Sorry," I said, raking both hands through my hair. "I'm fuckin' nervous."

"Don't be. We're gonna check out your new place, then go to the grocery store and get things set up there. No big deal."

I glanced at the older guy beside me and said, "Harry, I dunno why the hell you're doing all this for me, but ... thank you. I know I've said it already, but really, I mean it. Thank you."

He peered at me from over his silver frames, then smiled. "Good people deserve good things, Soldier, and it's about time someone showed you that."

It wasn't that I disagreed. Good people did deserve good things—karma and all that. But, for one, I hadn't exactly been a saint prior to prison. And for another, I knew that the world was full of good people who were regularly shit on by the circumstances they found themselves in, whether by birth or otherwise. Hell, I'd been locked up with many of them. Guys who were inherently good but had gotten fucked over in one way or another. What made me more deserving than them? What had made Harry tuck *me* under his wing and not Drake— a young guy serving two years because he had stolen food from the grocery store too many times, needing to feed his sisters?

I couldn't make sense of it, and as we pulled into the trailer park on the outskirts of town, I still didn't get it. Because this wasn't the type of trailer park you thought of in your mind—you know, some trashy, beat-up-looking place, where some shirtless guy named Buck sat on a busted lawn chair all day, scratching his hairy gut, drinking a beer, while he waited for the unemployment check to roll in. No, this place was a bright, cheery community of tiny houses, all close together, with gardens and itty-bitty porches. Sure, as we drove through the narrow streets, I found not all of them were as taken care of as others, but, man, it was *nice*. Nicer than any place I'd lived before.

"All right," Harry announced, "here we are—1111 Daffodil Lane."

Eleven eleven.

Make a wish.

My palms were coated in a sheen of sweat as I remembered a cupcake and a flameless, smoking candle from a long time ago. I cleared my throat and made an attempt at a joke to hide my nerves.

"Harry, do I look like the kinda guy who would live on *Daffodil Lane*?"

His gaze traveled over my face, as if he were really considering the question. "You look like the kind of guy who's getting a second chance at life. Now, come on. Let's check it out."

We got out of his Mazda, and Harry opened the mailbox, where Connie had told him the key would be waiting.

She had said the place was a little run-down and could use some TLC. The former owners had walked away from it after no longer being able to afford the bills, and because Connie decided it was better to let someone fix it up rather than have it go to hell in a handbasket, she offered it to me at a monthly cost of two weeks' pay at her husband's grocery store.

"I can't go any lower than that," she had said. "So, if you find you can't afford that and the utilities—"

"I'll make it work," I'd promised her, just happy to have somewhere to go. Somewhere to call mine.

And now, looking at 1111 Daffodil Lane, I was filled with even more of a determination to make it work. Because this place—with its peeling siding, warped little stoop, and broken front window—needed me as much as I needed it.

The three steps creaked and bowed beneath my feet, and the door needed a good push after being unlocked. The interior wasn't much better than the outside. Stained carpet, flaking paint, dirty appliances, and a bathroom I would've gotten written up for at Wayward greeted us.

Harry stood at the crusty kitchen counter as I finished my tour of the bleak-looking place. His face was locked in a permanent grimace, like even he was ready to drop the Mr. Positivity act.

"So, uh …" He rubbed a hand over his chin as his eyes frisked the living room-slash-dining room once again and the questionable brown stains on the carpet. "Listen … if you wanna say screw it, I wouldn't—"

"I like it."

He closed his eyes and pressed his fingers to his forehead, sighing exhaustedly. I was wearing the poor guy out.

"Soldier, you don't have to say that just because—"

"Listen, is it the lap of luxury? No. Does it need some serious cleaning and work? Yeah. Could they use this place as the set for the next *Texas Chain Saw Massacre* movie? Absolutely. But what else do I have going on, Harry? I mean, apart from sweeping some floors and scrubbing a toilet at a grocery store, my schedule is pretty clear." I looked around the grimy kitchen and nodded. "And honestly … even as is, it's better than living with Diane."

Harry wasn't convinced. He released a long breath that left his shoulders drooping and his head shaking. "Look, if you wanna give it a shot, that's fine. I'm just saying—"

"Harry"—I held up a hand, already thinking about what I could do to spruce up that shitty living room—"I'm good. Now, let's go check out that grocery store."

***

For Christmas, Harry had not only given me the phone, but also his old bike.

"If I got on that thing now, I'd probably break a hip," he'd said even though I knew it was bullshit.

Harry might've been well into his sixties, but the man could hold his own in a fistfight.

I would know; I'd seen it happen.

So, as we drove the two minutes from the trailer park to The Fisch Market, Harry was sure to point out that the bike ride would be an easy one.

"It'll be a pretty easy walk too, if you want to take the bike back," I mentioned with a smirk.

"You don't wanna walk during a blizzard. Don't be stupid."

I snorted. "Harry, I don't wanna ride a damn bike in a blizzard either, but I'll do what I gotta do."

We parked the car and got out, and that was when the light shining over River Canyon dimmed, casting shadows where I'd once thought there were none. As we walked to the entrance, a blonde woman with a few young girls in tow took one look at me and shielded her kids with an arm, steering them out of my way. At first, I thought maybe she was just maneuvering them, instructing them to watch for others and whatever. But then I heard the whispers.

"That's the guy Mayor Fischer told us about," the woman whispered to another nearby lady, this one with black hair.

"The guy who was in prison? How do you know?"

The blonde nodded. "She said he was big and hard to miss."

"Didn't she say he killed someone? Does Officer Kinney know he's here?"

"Yeah. He said he'd keep an eye on him, but we should probably watch out for the kids. Just in case."

I wasn't an inconspicuous guy by any means. At six foot seven, it was hard for me to blend in, and I sure as hell wasn't going to win any games of hide-and-seek anytime soon. The height and size had their advantages sometimes—I could always reach the highest shelf, and nobody had dared to fuck with me at Wayward—but now, I felt like I stood out like a giant, throbbing sore thumb.

Harry patted my back reassuringly. "Hey, don't worry about it. They'll learn."

"It's fine," I muttered, pushing the door open and walking into the store.

"They just don't know you yet."

"I get it."

And I did. Once upon a time, if I'd heard that some guy moved into town who'd been locked up for ending someone's life, I'd have jumped right on that rumor train with everyone else. But that didn't mean being on the other side of the rumors didn't suck. In fact, it hurt. It hurt a lot. But what was I going to do about it, other than to be patient and hope they gave me a chance?

"Hey there!" Howard called, wearing an apron and a pin-striped shirt.

He looked like he belonged in an old-timey painting of a general store, and so did The Fisch Market with its wooden fruit displays, two mechanical cash registers, and antique gumball machine. He ran over to us and shook each of our hands before leading us to a room toward the back of the store.

"All right, Soldier," he said, then chuckled. "I'm sorry. It's just hard to get used to calling a man Soldier who isn't … well, a soldier."

I shrugged, sweeping my gaze around the small frozen food section. "I probably would've been better off if I were, to be honest with you. The military would've done me some good before I had the chance to *really* screw things up."

Howard twisted his face with immediate discomfort. "I think you should keep talk about your past to a minimum, if you catch my drift."

Before I had the chance to reply, he cleared his throat as he opened the door to reveal a closet full of cleaning supplies. He began to point them out, but I stopped him to say I'd spent most of my life cleaning and that I knew my way around a broom closet.

He nodded with approval before saying, "Now, I don't expect you to wear much of a uniform. All I ask is that you make sure to cover your tattoos with long-sleeved shirts and wear one of the store aprons."

I swallowed and made a mental note to buy some more clothes as soon as I was able.

And as if he were reading my mind, Howard said, "If you don't have any long-sleeved shirts—"

"I think I might have a couple," I said, cutting him off. "I'll just have to wash them often. It's all good."

He nodded with satisfaction. "All right. So, when do you want to start?"

I looked between him and Harry and said, "Uh, today?"

Howard clapped Harry on the back. "I think we're going to get along just fine."

CHAPTER

ELEVEN

11:11

So, I began my life in River Canyon.

And like many things worth having, it didn't come easily at first.

My first day of work was going well enough. There was nothing difficult about pushing a broom and making sure the toilet flushed properly. But if anything got under my skin, it was the whispers.

Not even the curious and accusing looks could compete with the whispers.

"What happened to his face?"

"How many people do you think he killed?"

"What the hell was Mayor Fischer thinking?"

I thought what got to me the most was, I knew my name was public knowledge, and so was my record. I was sure every one of them had a phone they could use to look me up and find out exactly what had happened and what I'd done. But no. People preferred to speculate; they preferred to talk. All because it was more interesting than the truth.

I got through it though, and because I hadn't expected to work that day, Harry had left me without a ride back home.

Home.

1111 Daffodil Lane.

So, I walked the short ten minutes it took to get from The Fisch Market to my run-down trailer, where I made a can of soup I'd bought at the store and went to sleep on the air mattress Harry was letting me borrow until I got my hands on a bed.

And that was more or less how things went the first week or so with only work on my little house to break up the monotony. One day, I came home and went to town, scrubbing the bathroom until it was suitable to shower in. Another day, I came home and pulled up the matted, stained carpets in the living room and bedrooms. Little by little, it was looking cleaner, at the very least, and I was starting to see the potential underneath the grime.

But the whispers hadn't stopped.

It was the start of my second week when I walked into McKenna's Delicatessen to grab some lunch. The only cop I ever saw wandering around town watched me with a blend of curiosity and suspicion as I walked up to the counter and asked the woman at the register—the same woman who'd shielded her kids from me that first day—for a chicken salad sandwich.

"Of course," she replied and set to work, risking a cautious glance in my direction. "So, um … you work at The Fisch Market, don't you?"

She knew I did. She'd seen me there several times, just as I'd seen her. But she was making friendly small talk, or so it seemed, while that cop observed the exchange from the row of refrigerators behind me.

"Yeah," I replied, nodding. "I just started last week."

"How are you liking it so far?" She laid out the bread and pulled out the container of chicken salad.

I shrugged and stuffed my hands into my pockets. "It's okay. Honestly, I'm just grateful to have the job. I owe Howard and Connie a lot for setting me up like this."

The cop took a step closer. "They're good people," he said, and I turned to look at him.

"They are," I agreed.

"Everyone here is." He met my eye with what I perceived as a warning of sorts. As if to say, *This is my flock, and if you fuck with them, I will fuck with you.*

But he wasn't going to intimidate me that easily. His job was to protect—I got that. But my job was to move on and make something of myself, and I had no intention of fucking with anyone.

"I'm sure they are."

The woman behind the counter turned with my sandwich wrapped up and smiled as she rang me up. I paid, accepted my change, wished her a good day, and turned to leave without another look at that cop.

He followed.

"Hey, wait," he called, and I stopped to glance over my shoulder. "I think we're gettin' off on the wrong foot," he said, then offered his hand to shake. "Officer Patrick Kinney."

I eyed his palm for a moment before accepting the gesture. "Soldier Mason."

"Ya have to forgive us, Soldier," Officer Kinney said with an apologetic glint in his blue eyes. "We live in a quiet small town, and just the thought of someone comin' in and upsettin' the balance shakes us up."

I allowed the tension in my spine to loosen a bit as I nodded understandingly. "I don't blame anyone for being suspicious."

"Give us time," he said, and I agreed with a smile and a nod.

It was the first act of kindness I was shown.

The second came later that day in the form of a prepubescent boy.

While I sat on a chair at the back of the store, eating my sandwich and trying to figure out how to send Harry a picture in a text message on that damn phone, I spotted movement out of the corner of my eye. I turned to see a boy of maybe ten or eleven watching me. I was sure he thought he was hiding effectively behind the rack of bananas, but the kid hid worse than I would behind a flagpole.

But I pretended not to see him.

I wondered where his mom or dad was. If they knew he was missing or if they knew their kid was doing a bang-up job of snooping on the new guy in town. And I

145

bit back a laugh when he leaned too far to the left and tripped over his own feet.

"Shit," he muttered under his breath, realizing he had blown his cover, only to turn right into the banana rack and knock several bunches off their hooks. "Ah, man ..."

I stood up, dusting the sandwich crumbs off the bib of my apron. "Don't worry about it. I got it."

"What? N-no, it's—" He looked over his shoulder, and his eyes raked over my body before widening with awe. "Wow. You're, like, *really* tall."

"Huh." I made a show of pressing my hands to my head and looking down at the floor. "Look at that. I guess I am."

"How tall *are* you?"

"Last time I checked"—I pointed to the glowing Produce sign I was regularly having to duck under in order to mop the floor between the apples and oranges— "as tall as it takes to smack my head on that."

The kid stared at the sign, his mouth open in shock. "Whoa."

"Yeah. I keep asking Howard to move it, but"—I shrugged—"what can ya do?"

I knelt to pick up the scattered bananas, and the kid mimicked the motion to help.

He never stopped staring at my face.

"My mom said you were in jail," he blurted out, and I couldn't help but chuckle.

Man, I loved kids. They didn't fuck around. They asked what they wanted to ask, said what they wanted to say. There was no beating around the bush with them,

146

and I appreciated it so much more than the scrutinizing glances and whispers behind my back.

"I was," I answered with a nod.

"Is that where you got that scar?"

I shook my head as I returned the bananas to their rightful hooks. "No. I got this scar before—"

"Noah!"

The kid turned at the sudden sound of a woman barking what was apparently his name.

That would be Mom, I thought, turning to face a woman in a baggy sweater, tight jeans, and black boots, carrying a handbasket full of groceries.

Her wavy light-brown hair might've been drab in color to some, but to me, it reminded me of Sully's coat. Soft. Irresistible. Comforting.

Like Rain's hair.

The sudden thought brought with it an odd sense of relief I hadn't felt in a long time, along with the most curious taste of déjà vu.

And I probably shouldn't have been staring as much as I was. Especially considering how much it was annoying me to have this entire town staring at me. But I couldn't seem to help myself when the last time I'd laid my eyes on someone so beautiful was when I saved a fifteen-year-old girl years ago.

Noah's mom hurried to stand beside him, tugging at his sleeve as she readjusted the basket on her arm, while I took the bananas from his outstretched hand.

"Noah, I've been looking all over for you."

"Sorry. I was just—"

"We have to get home and make dinner. You still have home—"

As I stood, she gasped before clearing her throat, like she was embarrassed to have gasped at all.

"I-I'm sorry he was bothering you," she said, diverting her gaze to stare at the things in her basket. "Come on, Noah. Let's go."

"He's fine," I replied as I busied my hands by wiping them on my apron. "It was nice to actually talk to someone."

She swallowed, taking a moment to look me over. Then, she forced her lips into a tight smile. "Um … well, have a good day."

"Yeah, you too." I waved at her son, already being dragged away by his mom. "Bye, Noah. Thanks for the chat."

"Bye." He looked over his shoulder and waved back with a slight curve to one side of his mouth. "I'll see you around."

I laughed to myself as I turned and cleaned up the wrapper for my sandwich. I dropped it in the trash and got back to work, making sure to smack my head against the Produce sign as I went. And all the while, up until I got onto my bike and rode home, I thought about Noah and the first honestly friendly, albeit brief, conversation I'd had since I'd arrived.

And I thought about Rain.

***

148

If prison had taught me anything, it was how to keep a strict schedule, thanks to the rigid regimen they'd kept us inmates on. So, almost immediately after I ate a dinner of canned soup and crackers, I spent an hour pulling down the wood paneling in the second bedroom. Then, I took a shower and got into bed with the book I'd recently started reading—a collection of Edgar Allan Poe's stories and poems.

Harry's wife had an entire library of books I hadn't read yet, and I was grateful she had passed a bunch on to me to keep me busy during the hours I wasn't working or sleeping.

Then, at nine p.m. on the dot, I closed the book, turned off the light, and went to sleep.

It was a restless slumber, one that kept me tossing and turning, haunted by the past, the silence, and a foreboding that sometimes weaseled into my veins, one I couldn't shake or explain. One that said the demons from my life before this place were never too far behind.

But just a little before eleven o'clock, an echoing crack through the night sent me bolting upright in my bed.

"What the fuck was that?" I asked nobody, breathless and shaken.

I couldn't discern what the sound might've been. I had been half asleep when it happened. It could've been anything. A branch breaking. Thunder. A gunshot. Who the hell knew? But I knew I couldn't go back to sleep until I investigated and ensured a bogeyman wasn't out there, lurking in the skeletal shadows of the trees overhead.

So, I rolled out of bed, wearing nothing but my sweatpants and socks, and pulled back the sheet I was using for a curtain. I peered into the road and saw nothing to raise suspicion. And maybe, at that point, I should've just gone back to sleep, but something told me not to, the same something that said to go outside and make sure it was in fact nothing.

I opened the door and stepped out onto the steps I was convinced were going to snap under my weight one of these days. The night was cold. Snow was beginning to fall. Little flecks of white drifted through the sky, landing in my hair and on my bare shoulders.

Fuck, it's freezing out here.

I rubbed my arms vigorously with my palms as I swept my gaze over the small area in front of my house, and then they landed on the toppled-over metal garbage can. I sighed and rolled my eyes, feeling like an idiot for being so spooked by something so stupid, and I went to pick it up when a sound—much smaller and quieter than the crash before—came from beneath my rotten steps.

I turned on my heel to find my eyes meeting the yellow gaze of a tiny gray kitten.

"Hey," I said softly, kneeling and extending a hand. "Come here, little guy."

I'd never had a cat before, but I knew they were selective in who they would trust. But this kitten seemed to have a good feeling about me because he came right to me without hesitation—or maybe he was just cold. His little nose bumped against my fingers, as if he were saying, *Hello,* before running his scrawny back beneath my hand.

150

"Where's your mom, huh?" I asked, knowing he'd never answer.

Except he did. He mewed with anguish, and I felt I understood.

"You don't have anybody either," I guessed, letting him use my hand to get all the affection he'd been missing in his short life. "You hungry?"

His eyes met mine, and I took that as a yes. So, I scooped him up, holding him tightly to my chest as I stood the garbage can up once again, then went inside.

I pulled out the remaining tuna fish I'd had for lunch the day before and dumped it onto a paper plate. It probably wasn't what he should've been eating at his age—I doubted he was more than a month or two old—but it was better than nothing, and he seemed to agree as he scarfed it down like he hadn't eaten in days.

"All right, buddy," I said, using the nickname Grampa had given me, as I headed back to the living room, where my air mattress was waiting, "I'm going back to bed. Feel free to join me. Or don't. Whatever you wanna do."

I got under the covers, making myself comfortable again, and the little kitten hurried to curl up in the warmth of my armpit. I smiled, grateful to actually share this space with someone else, as I glanced at the clock.

It was eleven eleven, and it had been my first good day in River Canyon.

CHAPTER

TWELVE

THE FIRST VERY, VERY GOOD DAY

It was a Sunday, a month after I'd arrived in River Canyon, and I had a day off. It was the beginning of February, close to my birthday, and it shouldn't have been as warm as it was. So, I found myself outside, assessing the beat-up steps leading up to my door.

I had helped Grampa with quite a few projects in my youth, and I'd done some woodworking at Wayward. I was confident I could do something with those steps if I had the supplies, but that was another issue entirely. For now, I was only checking them out. Seeing if there was anything I could do to keep them from collapsing before I got the chance to get to Home Depot.

"Hey!"

I turned to the familiar voice, and there was Noah. Standing on the little porch of the trailer next to mine.

"Hi, Noah," I replied, offering a small, friendly wave.

"Can I come over?"

"Uh …" I rubbed my bearded chin, unsure of how to answer. "You know, I'm not sure your mom—"

"Okay, hold on. I'll ask her!"

He ran inside before I could stop him, and I sighed, listening to him bellow for his mother.

There's no way that lady is going to be okay with him coming over here. She seems too overprotective. No freakin'—

"She said it's fine!" Noah shouted, running out of his house and down the steps.

"Oh. Uh, okay." I watched as he ran to stand at the bottom of my stairs. "Watch out for this, okay?" I pointed to the loose and rotted boards. "I don't want you getting hurt."

He nodded. "Okay."

This wasn't how I'd planned to spend my day. Sitting outside, entertaining a kid I didn't know. Yet something about it felt good. Normal even.

I turned to face him, pulling off my gloves and stuffing them into my back pocket. It was too warm to be wearing them now with the sun set high above us.

I gestured toward the house next door. "So, you live over there, huh?" I asked him, making conversation.

"Yep." He kicked at the dirt. "Just me and my mom. Well, sometimes, my dad is here, but most of the time, it's just us."

"Oh, cool. I haven't seen you guys around."

Noah shrugged. "Mom said I couldn't talk to you before. She gets kinda worried about people. But"—he kicked at a rock this time—"I guess she changed her mind."

I twisted my lips and nodded slowly. I wondered if seeing me at the grocery store had altered her opinion of the ex-con who had infiltrated their cozy little River Canyon bubble, and I took it as a good thing.

"But she did say I can't go in your house," he added, lifting a hand to gesture at my door. "She said she hasn't decided if you're a creep or not yet."

I laughed at that. "You have a smart mom."

"So, like, *are* you a creep?"

I tipped my head back to squint toward the blinding sun. "I mean, *I* don't think so, but I guess that depends on who you ask."

Noah inhaled deeply and nodded, studying my unfortunate-looking house. "Well, I don't think you're a creep. I can usually tell that kinda stuff."

"Oh, well, thanks," I said, stifling a chuckle. "I don't think you're a creep either."

Next door, a window opened, and I glanced over my shoulder to see his mom peering outside. I lifted a hand in a small wave, and she lifted hers to wave back.

Then, she mouthed, *Sorry,* and pointed at Noah, standing there, kicking at the same rock with determination, and I shrugged and smiled.

Of all the things I minded in the world, I decided that Noah wasn't one of them.

"So, why were you in jail?" he asked, looking up with innocent curiosity.

I took a deep breath and once again glanced toward the open window next door. "Uh, you know, I'm not sure your mom would want me talking to you about that."

"My dad went to jail once."

"Oh my God, Noah." The woman rushed out of the neighboring trailer, hugging a sweater around her slender frame as she hurried down the steps. "We can't just go around, telling people everything about our lives, okay?"

"Well, maybe he knew Dad in jail," Noah reasoned with his mother.

"It isn't … your dad didn't …" She sighed, pressing a hand over her eyes. "Your dad was only held at the police station for a few days. He didn't go away to, you know …" She looked up and met my gaze as she quietly added, "Prison." Then, she contorted her features into the cutest grimace I'd ever seen, as if she was truly worried she'd offended me. "Sorry."

I shook my head, tilting my lips in a crooked smile I knew was probably stupid. "It's fine."

She surprised me then by extending her hand. "I'm Ray."

I offered mine, and we shook lightly, briefly. "Soldier."

Her lips parted at the sound of my name, her emerald eyes narrowing just a little. "That's … an interesting name."

"My mom was an interesting lady," I replied.

That's putting it gently.

"Are you a real soldier?" Noah asked, studying me with the same green gaze as his mom.

I shook my head and gripped the back of my neck. "Nah, not really. Although, sometimes, I feel like one with all the crap I've been through."

"Like what?"

Noah asked more questions than anybody I'd ever met.

"Uh, you know, just—"

"Hey! You have a cat?" Noah abruptly cut me off, changing the subject as he hurried up the steps to crouch in front of the screen door.

"Uh … yeah … well"—I scratched at the back of my head—"I guess, kind of."

"You guess?" Ray asked, amused. "How do you not know if you own a cat?"

"He kinda adopted me," I replied sheepishly. "I brought him in about a week ago after finding him out here when it was snowing, and he just sorta decided not to leave."

She smiled, and my stomach stumbled over itself, mid-somersault.

"He's cute," she said, never diverting her gaze from mine.

"He's a good guy," I replied, unsure in the moment if I was still talking about the cat or not.

"What's his name?" Noah asked, letting the kitten sniff his fingers through the screen.

"Uh … I'm calling him Eleven for now."

Ray hummed contemplatively, and I raised an inquisitive brow.

"The guy with the interesting name *would* call his cat something equally interesting," she said, studying me with the most curious glint in her eyes.

"Guess I like to, uh … keep things interesting," I replied awkwardly, followed by a chuckle that was just as, if not more, awkward.

What the hell is going on?

Are we … flirting?

It'd been a while since I had flirted with anyone. Hell, it had been a while since I'd had much contact with the opposite sex at all, particularly one seemingly in my age bracket. One who was beautiful, wearing a smattering of freckles across her nose and a sweater as soft-looking as her hair.

But the kid had a dad, and I could only assume that dad was in a relationship with this woman. So, whatever might've been going on needed to stop.

"Anyway …" Ray tipped her face downward, concealing a smile and—was she blushing? "Um … Noah, we should get lunch ready and let Soldier get back to whatever he was doing."

Noah was quick to hop to his feet, startling Eleven into scurrying farther away. "Can Soldier have lunch with us?"

Ray's eyes darted to mine with a blend of panic and hesitation. "Uh, well—"

"I should get back to this," I said, gesturing toward the stairs. "But thanks, Noah. Maybe another day."

"Oh. Okay."

The kid looked absolutely crushed, and I felt bad. But his mom looked relieved as she began walking backward toward her house.

"Come on, kiddo," she said. "It was nice to, um, meet you, Soldier."

"Yeah, you too." I offered her a friendly, hopeful smile. "I'll see you around, Ray."

***

And I did.

I noticed that every Tuesday, Ray and Noah came to The Fisch Market to do their grocery shopping. And every Tuesday, Noah stopped by to chat with me wherever I was cleaning or stocking the shelves while his mom did the shopping. She never seemed thrilled that he was neglecting to help her to while he was talking with me, but she never seemed bothered by it either. Not the way everyone else seemed to be.

"I can't believe you're letting your son talk to him," I overheard one woman say. "You know he's a criminal, right?"

"Lots of people are criminals, Sheila," Ray replied, unamused. "Doesn't make all of them bad."

"I'm not talking about a couple of nights in jail, Ray. He was in prison for a *decade*."

Actually, it was just short of ten years, Sheila, but who's counting?

What stood out to me though was that Ray hadn't just replied to that woman—she had *defended* me. And while Noah followed me as I swept and his mom let him while not allowing others to talk shit about me to her, it almost seemed like I had two more people on my side. It was nice, and Tuesdays became my favorite day.

That was until the Tuesday when I turned thirty-one. My first birthday back in society and the ten-year anniversary of the day I'd been arrested. Harry had called to wish me a good one and asked if I'd like to come by that weekend for dinner at his place. I appreciated the sentiment, but I couldn't say I was really in the mood to celebrate. Because all I could do was think about Billy. When I woke up, as I ate breakfast, and when I got dressed for work … I thought about Billy.

And I continued to think about him on the brisk bike ride to work, and I continued thinking about him as I smacked my head against the Produce sign not once, but three times throughout the day.

"You always duck," Noah observed on the third hit as I rubbed my forehead and cursed under my breath.

I glanced over my shoulder at him. "Huh?"

"The sign." He pointed at the damn thing, taunting me with its bright, colorful light. "You always duck."

"Yeah, I usually do," I agreed with a sigh, resuming the push of the mop through a puddle of spilled apple juice.

"So, why not today?"

"Because it's …" I stopped and leaned against the mop handle, deciding if I should be honest or not. But I always found it was usually better to tell the truth, so I said, "It's not a great day for me."

"Oh." Noah frowned. "Why not?"

"Well, it's my birthday, and—"

159

Ray gasped, and I turned to see her standing near the pyramid of potatoes. "Wait. It's your birthday?" Her mouth remained frozen in a wide O, like she should've realized this.

I brushed her shock away with a shrug. "It's no big—"

"Oh my God, happy birthday!"

"No"—I shook my head adamantly—"you don't have to do that. It's, uh … it's not a happy day. I …" *What? Killed my best friend on this day? Was arrested on this day? Was born on this fucking day?* "A lot of stuff happened today that I don't like thinking about, so …"

"But you *are* thinking about it," Noah pointed out, gesturing toward the sign I was bound to suffer a concussion from eventually.

I inhaled deeply, feeling all at once ridiculously defeated. "Yeah, I know. It's hard not to."

"You should come over," Ray decided out of nowhere. "I'll make you dinner."

Mayor Connie Fischer had entered the store at that moment, her curious eyes immediately on the felon talking to the nice mom and her preteen son. I waved at her, and she waved back, but that look of suspicion never left her face, even as she walked away.

Ray followed my gaze. "So, you actually know the mayor, huh?"

"She's my friend's sister-in-law," I replied.

Ray nodded slowly, as if it was all starting to make sense. "*That's* why she let you live here." Then, she tittered with a nervous laugh, her cheeks immediately

160

bright pink with shame. "Sorry. It's just ... everybody's been wondering. Connie is so strict about everything. I mean, she won't even let them open a Starbucks in town because she doesn't like chains."

"Hey, I get it. You wouldn't want anything competing with that place." I nudged my chin toward the window in the direction of Black & Brewed, the town's quintessential coffee shop. "I mean, I've never been to a Starbucks, but I can tell you right now, they don't hold a candle to what they have going on over there."

Ray bit her bottom lip for a moment, looking up at me with those gorgeous, sparkling green eyes, and I wished I knew what she was thinking—what she thought of *me*. But she looked away just as quickly, pulled her purse higher onto her shoulder, and declared very affirmatively that I should be at her place by six for dinner.

Then, she told Noah it was time to check out, and he left with an enthusiastic, "See you later, Soldier!"

What the hell just happened?

I wasn't sure it was a good idea to go over there. I wanted it to be. I wanted to believe that building this friendship with Ray and her son was one of those good things I apparently deserved, according to Harry. But that foreboding I couldn't quite figure out was back, nagging in my gut with these little pangs and punches as I finished mopping the floor between the apples and oranges. I didn't know what it meant. I wished I knew. I wished it were obvious and that I could figure out what it all meant. But I couldn't.

Yet I didn't bump my head on that sign for the rest of the day, and that had to mean something too.

***

Ray had made a pot of spaghetti and some of the best meatballs I'd ever eaten in my life. I even told her they were better than my grandmother's, which was one of the greatest compliments I could ever give anyone.

"You were close with your grandmother?" she asked, making conversation as she spooned another meatball onto my dish.

"I was."

I cut the meatball in half with my fork and popped one side into my mouth, eating like I hadn't consumed good food in a really, really long fucking time. Which wasn't entirely true. The weeks I'd spent with Harry's family were filled with excellent food. But it'd been over a month since then, and Ray's cooking, I'd found, was even better.

Ray studied me with a soft, albeit intense, stare, a slight curve to her lips as she watched me stuff the other half of the meatball into my mouth. I met her eyes mid-chew, and she didn't look away. We held each other captive for a few thundering beats of my heart as the questions mounted between us, piling high on the table and cluttering the bowl of spaghetti and incredible meatballs.

Why is she looking at me like that?
How is she so fucking pretty?
Where is Noah's dad?

162

Would a woman already involved with a man stare at another like this?

Noah sighed and shifted in his chair, breaking the spell between his mother and me. I diverted my gaze to the sauce smeared across my otherwise empty plate while Ray cleared her throat and addressed her son.

"Excuse me, are we boring you?" she teased, reaching over to nudge his arm.

"No," he grumbled against a heavy breath, but he was lying, and I laughed.

"Go ahead," Ray said, dismissing him. "I'll let you know when we have cake."

Noah didn't need to be told twice, and we both laughed as he ran to drop his plate in the sink before throwing himself onto the couch and grabbing his Nintendo Switch.

Ray met my gaze with a smile and a glint in her eyes as she stood with her own plate in hand. I wouldn't let her take mine and instead helped her clear the rest of the table.

"You didn't need to do all this," I said, leaving the bowl of food on the counter. "I haven't really done anything for my birthday in a long time, so …"

"You know, Soldier"—she turned from the sink to lean her back against the counter, crossing her arms over her chest—"you could just say thank you."

I sniffed a short laugh and nodded. "Thank you."

"Do you mind me asking why today is so bad?"

I was quickly finding that Ray shared that same no-filters-allowed quality with her son, and I liked it. It was a breath of fresh air when everyone else around me

163

seemed to walk on eggshells. Nobody ever knew how to act or what to say while Ray and Noah simply didn't care. They just said whatever was on their minds, and, man, it was nice.

I chewed at my lip, wondering if I even wanted to say it aloud when tonight had already been so nice. Would I ruin it all by allowing that persistent black cloud to hang over us? But Ray was so insistent with those soft, big green eyes, watching my every move, and I felt I couldn't run away from this. I felt I didn't want to.

"My best friend died today," I admitted. "The same night I was arrested. Ten years ago."

She held my gaze for a moment, not at all surprised by the admission, before letting her head hang as she nodded in a way that said she had already known and had somehow forgotten. "I'm sorry," she said quietly. "That must suck, having to share your birthday with such a horrible memory."

"Honestly"—I laughed, beside myself—"it's not the first. But it's definitely the worst, and yeah, it does suck."

Her hands clenched at her sides before she blurted out, "Did you actually kill him?" She shook her head immediately after and spun quickly on her heel, facing the sink again. "You know what? No, never mind. Don't answer that."

I swallowed, allowing a war to begin in my head. I had only known Ray and Noah for a few weeks now. They were my only friends in town, and I liked the bond we had seemed to build on honesty and a lack of judgment. But an admission like this was a heavy one. It could be simultaneously destructive and freeing, and what would I do if the only friends I'd made decided they no longer wanted to know me? What was I supposed to do then?

I can't expect her—or anyone—not to care, but what if she simply accepts it?

Or she could just look up my damn name and find out for herself.

But wouldn't it be better to hear it from me?

And with that thought, I let a breath whoosh from my lungs and was sure to keep my voice low—too low for Noah to hear—as I said, "His death was the result of something I'd done, but, no, I didn't intentionally kill him."

Ray turned from the sink, bringing her green gaze to mine. Her eyes were so kind, so bright, and I swore I recognized them from somewhere I couldn't quite put my finger on.

"So, you're not really a murderer?"

I shook my head. "Despite what some people might want to believe, no, I'm not a murderer."

She exhaled deeply, her cheeks deepening in color with a hint of embarrassment as she nodded. "I actually kinda knew that. I had googled you a while back. I knew you were convicted of manslaughter, but … you know … people cover stuff up, and—"

"Not in this case," I told her, offering a reassuring smile.

"Still, kinda weird that a guy who killed someone is standing in my kitchen." She swept her gaze around the small room before letting her eyes fall back on me. "Feels like it should be scarier."

I crossed my arms over my chest and smirked. "Are you saying I don't scare you?"

"Well, do you want to hurt me?" she asked, almost as a challenge.

I shook my head. "No. I don't want to hurt anyone."

"So, then, no, you don't scare me."

My eyes narrowed as I tried to peer into my past while déjà vu barreled through me like a freakin' freight train. Where had I had a similar exchange before? And why couldn't I remember, if the moment felt so familiar?

Ray pulled a box from the refrigerator and opened it, revealing a cake that was the perfect size for three. The sight of it brought on the same emotions I had felt a year ago, when Harry gave me a slice of pizza on my thirtieth birthday.

God, how was that only one year ago?

It hit me all at once, all of a sudden, that it was possible for guys like me to be surrounded by good people. People unrelated by blood. People who'd made the choice to know me and like me, simply for being myself, despite the shit I'd been convicted of.

"Are you okay?" Ray asked, eyeing me with concern.

Realizing my eyes had begun to tear up, I cleared my throat and blinked them away. "Yeah," I said, nodding. "All good."

"Okay," she said with a smile before calling Noah back to the table.

They sang "Happy Birthday," and we ate the cake, which was delicious. After, it was Noah's bedtime and mine, and I had a cat to feed. So, I wished them both a good night and counted the thirteen steps between her place and mine, knowing that it undoubtedly was a very, very good night.

CHAPTER

THIRTEEN

A MONSTER NEXT DOOR

L ittle by little, the trailer started to look more like a home and less like a condemned wreck.

With every paycheck, I bought something else to help the renovation along—a can of paint here, an area rug there. I snagged a hand-me-down couch from Mrs. Henderson and an old coffee table from Harry's other daughter, Pamela. On my way home one day, I found a few perfectly good lamps on the side of the road, and on another occasion, I uncovered a decent dining table that just needed some sanding and a fresh coat of paint.

After a couple of months of working at The Fisch Market, I'd saved enough money to get myself an actual mattress. And just like that, the bedroom looked more like what it was intended to be and less like a dungeon.

Needless to say, of everything I'd accomplished in my life—the good stuff, I mean—I was the proudest of this.

By March, the interior was looking decent. It wasn't done—the kitchen was still in desperate need of an overhaul with its shit-brown cabinets and peeling Formica countertop—but it was passable as a home. And with the snow starting to melt and the days beginning to warm, I figured it was time to start planning what I was gonna do outside.

Noah had ideas too.

"You should have a garden," he declared as we stood outside together, assessing the exterior and what little land I had to work with. "Mom's always wanted a garden, but she doesn't have time."

"So, why should *I* have one?" I challenged despite agreeing with him.

I had loved gardening when I was at Wayward, and the idea of growing my own food sounded better than paying for it.

Howard liked to jack up the prices on produce—likely to fund his wife's addiction to fancy clothes and purses—and I wasn't making enough money to regularly cover my desire for fresh veggies.

"Because I like tomatoes," Noah replied simply.

I crossed my arms over my chest and eyed him with a raised brow. "So, let me get this straight. You want *me* to have a garden because *you* like tomatoes."

He nodded and stuffed his hands into the pockets of his jeans. "Yep."

"And what do I get out of this deal?"

"I guess you can have some, too, if you want."

"Oh, okay," I said with an amused snort. "Sure. Sounds like a plan."

The day was quiet for a Saturday, especially one this beautiful. The sun was warm, and the birds were singing joyously from the trees surrounding our houses. Spring was quickly approaching, and we were the only people outside in our part of the community. So, when the sound of an enormous vehicle rumbled down Daffodil Lane, shattering the peace and silence, Noah and I both jumped with a start.

"Oh, that's my dad," he mumbled, sounding less than enthusiastic.

It was odd to me that, from the beginning, the kid had mentioned that he had a father on a couple of occasions, but not once had I seen him. Why had months passed of me living in this town before I finally witnessed any evidence of a father?

"You should go inside," Noah said hurriedly, like he was on the verge of panicking.

"Why?" I peered down the road, eager to catch a glimpse of this guy who never seemed to check on his family.

"Because ..." His breath escalated, and his hands fidgeted at his sides. "Because my dad doesn't like me talking to people he doesn't know, so ... go ... please."

I knew desperation when I heard it, and I listened out of respect for Noah. But I didn't like the small, frightened tone of his voice, and it was for that reason that I stayed directly on the other side of my front door, watching through the flimsy curtain as the silver pickup

170

truck came into view and parked sloppily outside of Ray and Noah's house with its front tire up on the bricks surrounding her small front yard.

I didn't like that truck almost as much as Noah's panicked voice.

It was big with tinted windows and a bumping sound system that rattled the few dishes I kept in the kitchen cabinets. It reminded me of the types of cars guys at The Pit would drive—the ones with money anyway. Guys who needed to overcompensate for the things they lacked. Cash. Street cred. A big, noteworthy dick.

I was intrigued now, wondering what this guy looked like. I mean, who was Noah's father anyway? Why had I heard nothing about him in nearly three months? Why hadn't I ever seen him or this truck before in all this time? A barrage of questions was pelted at me all at once as I watched, peeking through the window and waiting to catch a glimpse of this elusive dude with the obnoxious truck.

But he never got out, never showed his face. Instead, he bellowed from beneath the cover of his shitty music for Noah to "get in this goddamn truck right now," and Noah did as he had been told, hanging his head as he climbed in.

And you know what?

I liked that least of all.

***

"Hey, Patrick," I said, walking into McKenna's that following Monday, not surprised to see him hanging around.

Officer Kinney's wife, Kinsey, worked the counter at the deli. So, naturally, the guy spent a good deal of his time busting her chops while she worked.

He offered a friendly smile at my greeting. "Hey, Soldier. How's it goin'?"

"All right. Can't complain." I stopped to lean against the counter beside him. "Actually, I have a question for you."

"Yeah? What's up?"

"You know a lot about the people around here, right?"

He puckered his lips with contemplation before saying, "Sure, I'd say so. Why do you ask?"

"So, what do you know about Ray's boyfriend?"

Patrick wrinkled his brow as he turned to Kinsey, waiting behind the counter for me to give her my order.

"Does Ray have a boyfriend?" he asked her, and she shrugged and replied, "No, I don't think so."

Well, that's an interesting turn of events.

"Okay," I hummed and tapped my fingers against the glass case housing the deli meats and prepared salads. "What about Noah's dad then? What do you know about him?"

"Well, I know he has one … obviously," Patrick replied, still deep in thought. "We don't see him often around here though. As far as I know, he's never lived with Ray. Honestly, I'm not sure they've ever been *together*—or at least not in the time she's lived here."

"And how long has that been?"

Kinsey twisted her lips to the side before saying, "Um … maybe five, six, seven years, give or take? Noah wasn't a baby when she bought her place. He was at least a few years old."

"Hmm …" I nodded slowly, growing more and more curious by the second.

Patrick bumped his shoulder against mine. "Why don't ya just ask her? Don't you two hang out sometimes?"

It wasn't a lie. Ray had become a good friend in the weeks since we'd started spending time together. We chatted regularly, saw each other every Tuesday at the store, and ever since I had learned that she worked at the library, I'd made it a point to visit her weekly when I needed some new books to pass my time with. But that didn't mean I wanted her to know that I was digging for information about her or her kid.

"Yeah, I might," I half fibbed because who knew? I might find a reason to ask eventually.

But now wasn't the time.

***

That time did come, however, when, a couple of days later, that same truck was parked outside Ray's place late into the evening.

Noah was sitting on the curb in the quiet dark.

"Hey," I said, poking my head out my door. "What are you doing out so late?"

173

It was nine o'clock on a school night. Noah was never outside this late on a school night.

He looked in my direction, but didn't say anything. So, I brushed Eleven out of the way with a sweep of my foot—that damn cat was always trying to sneak back outside into the same world I'd rescued him from—and walked out the door and onto the steps I still hadn't fixed.

At the sight of my approach, Noah began to shake his head, his eyes widening with a warning.

"Noah, why are you outside?" I asked again, sterner than before. "Is everything okay?"

"I can't talk right now," he hissed quietly.

A loud sound came from inside Ray's house. It could've been a piece of furniture being thrown. A door being slammed. Whatever it was, warning bells rang loudly in my head, clanging with every beat of my heart, and I took a step further toward Noah.

"No, no, no. Please, Soldier," he begged in a frantic, hushed voice, just as a man's voice shouted something incoherent from inside the house.

I didn't want to go back into my place. I didn't want to pretend that the kid wasn't scared or that something wasn't happening inside the house he shared with his mom. Everything told me to do the opposite, and so I did.

I marched right past Noah on the curb, who was still begging and pleading for me to stop and go back home, and I walked up the porch steps and knocked loudly on the door.

"Who the fuck is that?" I heard a man's voice shout.

"I-I don't know." That was Ray, and she sounded small and terrified. Her voice … so, so different from the woman I knew and so, so familiar from somewhere far away.

"Well then, *maybe* you should answer the fucking door." He was angry, condescending.

I knew without meeting the man that I hated him.

Ray did as she had been told and slowly opened the door to reveal her tear-streaked face and giant, baggy sweater wrapped tightly around her body. Her eyes widened at the sight of me standing on her porch, her cheeks reddened with embarrassment, and she shook her head, just as Noah had done.

"You have to go—"

"No." I stopped her, placing my palm against the door as she tried to close it. "What's going on in there?"

"It's nothing. You have to go now."

"It doesn't sound like nothing, Ray." I kept my voice quiet.

I didn't want the monster inside to hear me. I didn't want to get her into more trouble by simply being there—for *caring*. But if she was in danger—and it sure as hell seemed like she was—I wasn't going to sit back and listen to it happen.

"Just blink twice if you need me to do something, and I'll do something right now."

She made a show of keeping her eyes open, void of any emotion but sincere warning. "What I *need* is for you to go. *Please*."

Her tone was flat and tense, and my face remained just as expressionless as I took one, two steps back. She had to know I was serious. If she had given me the word, I would've barged through that door and physically removed whoever the fuck was terrorizing her and her son. But I didn't know the facts. I didn't know what was going on, so I resigned with a single nod despite the fiery urge to do the opposite, and she closed the door in my face.

I didn't want to get Noah into any trouble for talking to me either, so I didn't stop on my way back to my place. Instead, as I passed, I said, "If you need me, you know where to find me. Bang on my door, yell for me—whatever you have to do—and I will protect you."

He didn't reply, but I knew he'd heard me, and I lied to myself, thinking that it was good enough.

***

Noah didn't go back inside until Ray opened the door an hour later, and I never stopped watching through the faded cloth hanging over the window. Once he was inside, Ray stepped onto the porch and cried. She held her arm against her chest, and I narrowed my eyes.

What the fuck is going on over there?

I wanted to walk over and demand an explanation. But I figured now wasn't the time, so I continued to watch until the shadowed figure of the monster next door left without a glance at the woman on the porch and drove away in his big, obnoxious truck, and I didn't stop watching until Ray went back inside.

The next day, bright and early in the morning before work, I wandered over to the house next door and knocked until Ray opened the door.

There was a brace on her wrist and a forced smile on her face.

"H-hey, Soldier. What can I—"

"What the hell happened here last night?"

She shook her head indifferently. "Nothing. Really. Noah's dad and I just got into an argument, and things got a little heated. I told Noah to go outside so he didn't have to hear us yelling."

"I could hear the yelling from inside my house," I countered, crossing my arms and eyeing her studiously. "What happened to your arm?"

She glanced at the black brace Velcroed to her wrist. She must've acquired it sometime in the night after I'd somehow gotten to sleep, and she swallowed at the sight of it now. Then, she waved a dismissive hand, sending the question away with a lighthearted laugh.

"I was putting some stuff away and fell. I think I sprained it or something. It was so dumb."

"Is it broken?"

She rolled her eyes and shook her head, like the sheer thought that it might be was ridiculous. "No," she said with a scoff. "Probably just a little sprained. I'm just wearing the brace until it doesn't hurt anymore."

I narrowed my eyes skeptically. "And you said you … fell?"

"Yep."

Since the moment we'd become friends, Ray had never bullshitted me. She had always been up front, honest, and real, never holding back or filtering herself. This new side of her was bothersome and concerning, and I didn't fucking like it. Not one bit.

I stepped closer to her, encouraging her to tip her head back to look up at me. "If you wanna lie to me, you should learn how to act better than that," I said in a low, hushed, concerned voice so Noah couldn't hear, if he happened to be awake. "I have to go to work, but I hope you'll tell me what's going on. You can trust me, Ray— you know that—and whatever's going on, I can help. I *want* to help."

She said nothing in reply as I turned around to leave her porch and grab my bike. But I hoped she would take me seriously. I hoped she would tell me sooner rather than later, and I did eventually get my wish … just two weeks later, when another new, coincidental development touched both of our lives.

CHAPTER

FOURTEEN

LETTERS: DELIVERED

Once the list of things to do in the trailer started getting shorter and more expensive, I was flying through books closer to my prison rate. Two or three books a week was my average, depending on the length of the story, and thankfully, the library was just a short walk from work.

And thankfully, I had an in with the prettiest librarian.

One day a week, my work schedule coincided with Ray's, and on that day, we would go home together. Sometimes, if the weather was nice enough, we walked. On other days, we took her car and shoved my bike into the backseat.

I always preferred the days we walked. The air in River Canyon was different from anywhere else I'd been. It was sweeter, lighter, like cotton candy without the stomachache. I couldn't understand how, when it wasn't far from larger cities or highways and the traffic wasn't much unlike other towns. But maybe all I was smelling was hope.

Or maybe it was just the pretty lady at my side.

Whatever it was, on this particular night, it had never been sweeter as we walked slowly through the town—a bundle of new books under my arm and a small bag of groceries in the other. Ray carried her purse as well as a book of her own, one I hadn't read before—*A Scarcity of Condors* by Suanne Laqueur. I said that I should read it, and she said I wouldn't like it, that it was probably too mushy and romantic for my taste. But ever since the moment I'd met her, I had been pretty certain I would like anything she did, for the simple opportunity of getting to know her—her heart and soul—just a little better.

So, we walked along, beneath a sky with more stars than I'd seen in any other town with this many lights, and I made sure to keep my steps in time with hers, never wanting to leave her side. During a lull in conversation, I decided to ask something I'd never thought to ask before, something silly. Something that I didn't know was about to change our world forever.

"So, is Ray short for anything? Like Rachel or something?"

She didn't respond right away, hugging her bruised wrist to her chest. Even weeks later, I couldn't look at her with that brace without the prickle of anger edging its way beneath my skin.

"I thought it was an innocent question," I muttered, my feelings mildly hurt as I led the way, turning off Main Street and toward our neighborhood.

"It is, but ..." She huffed irritably and tipped her head back to look up at the overhead trees that were beginning to bud with new leaves. "Rain."

I looked up, squinting at a clear, star-filled sky. "What? I don't see any—"

"No. I mean, that's my name. Ray is short for Rain."

My gait slowed as, all at once, I remembered a girl with soft brown hair and a scream I could still hear to this day. The only girl—the only *person*—from my time before Wayward whom I had never wronged, whom I had simply saved. The girl who had kept me sane during a time I might've otherwise gone crazy.

"That's weird," I said quietly, hardly seeing the road in front of me when I could only see that face. Those big green eyes, full of fear and suspicion.

"What is?"

"I met a girl named Rain once."

Ray hugged her book even tighter. "And I once met a guy named Soldier."

There's no way. There's no possible way ...

But ... what if ...

I swallowed at a lump in my throat, but to no avail. It wouldn't budge, just as my heart wouldn't slow and my hands wouldn't stop shaking. "When ... when did you meet him?"

We took our time turning the corner into our shared community as my pounding heart drowned out the sound of nearby cars. We were hanging on to something life-altering, and I wished she would just say what I had a feeling she'd say, not knowing at all how I was going to react when she said it. I couldn't even begin to plan for something like that.

"I ... I knew it was you," she finally replied quietly. "When Connie told us that a man named Soldier was moving into town, I looked you up. I thought it might be a crazy coincidence, but then I saw you at the grocery store and ... the scar on your face, and ... I just knew."

She was too short to see as we walked toward our homes, but I was grinning so wide that my face fucking hurt.

"Why didn't you say anything?" I asked, afraid the stuff I was carrying would fall—my arms were shaking so much.

"Because I was ..." She sighed and shook her head. "I was scared."

That wiped the dumb grin right off my face. "Wait. You were scared of *me*?"

She stopped walking and turned to face me, shaking her head adamantly. "No, no, no! Soldier, I was never afraid of *you*. But I was afraid that if you knew I knew you from your life back there, you wouldn't want to know *me*. And Noah loves you, and I ..."

I raised an inquisitive brow at the abrupt halt to her words. "You what?"

She released a sigh as her eyes lifted to meet mine. "I really, really like having you around."

"I like being around too," I replied softly, staring down at her and holding on to my books and grocery bag for dear, sweet life.

I felt like a kid, carrying my stuff home from school, staring down at the prettiest girl in my class. It was a moment, a pivotal one, and I knew it despite never having a real moment before in my life. And that wasn't for a lack of experience with the opposite sex. I was far from inexperienced, far from a virgin. But my experience with girls had come with the territory of the things I used to do. They'd been with me for the status of being with me. They'd been with me for the connections, the things I could give them. Honestly, looking back, I wasn't sure any of those girls had ever truly liked me, and it had never occurred to me how fucking sad that was—until I was in *this* moment. Staring at Ray—*Rain*—while clutching my grocery bag and books and wondering if her hair was as soft and smooth as it looked.

"I just didn't want you to cut us off or … I don't know … regret being here or something."

I couldn't help but laugh, looking toward the sky and thinking about the things she didn't know. Embarrassing things. Things I never would've told her or anyone had this odd turn of events not happened.

"What's so funny?" Ray asked, a little defensive.

"Okay. I'm going to tell you something that's probably gonna sound weird, but hear me out."

She furrowed her brow and nodded. "Okay …"

"So …" I cleared my throat as the bag of groceries began to slip from my arm. I hoisted it back up as I thought about some of the letters I'd never sent but kept as a scrapbook of some kind. "You know what? Hold on. Stay right here."

I hurried past her toward my house as she nervously said, "Um, all right …"

I fumbled to hold on to the books and bag as I dug into my pocket for the keys. I had to be quick. I didn't want too much time to pass with her wondering what crazy shit was going on after she'd just dropped a bomb on me.

Holy shit. I can't believe this is actually happening right now, I thought as I dumped everything on the table and ran to my bedroom, where I knelt on the floor and dug a box out from beneath the bed.

In it was a stack of letters I had written to a girl who existed for the most part in my head, where I had imagined what incredible things she might've gone on to do after I rescued her from a violation I never would've forgiven myself for had I allowed it to happen under my watch. I pulled out those letters, holding them in my hands for the first time in months, unable to believe that the person I had written them to was standing right outside. I hesitated only a moment before climbing to my feet and running back through the front door, where I found her still waiting by her steps.

"Okay," I said, holding the letters tightly in my trembling hands. "So, when I was locked up, I had nobody. I-I mean, I had some friends inside, but from my life before, I had nobody. Not a single person gave a shit about me. Fuck, even my own mother only visited me twice in the entire time I was there."

Ray's face fell with a sweeping rush of sadness. "She only saw you twice … in nine *years*?"

"Yes," I replied simply, afraid that if I said anything more, the hurt and anger and everything else would overshadow what I needed to say.

"God, that's awful."

"Yeah, well, you never met my mother ... or ... I don't think so anyway ..." *Another time, man. Tell her what you need to say.* "Anyway, I had nobody to really talk to outside of the guys I knew at Wayward, is what I'm saying. No letters, no phone calls, nothing. And it sucked. It was lonely, and I hated it. I hated that ..." I looked away and stared at Eleven, sitting behind the screen door. Waiting for me to stop being a bumbling fool and feed him. "I *hated* that I had been such a fuckup that nobody wanted to stay in touch with me. I hated that I had hurt everybody who had once cared or that they were dead—or both.

"But then, one night, while I was lying in my bunk, I started thinking about this girl ..." I turned back to Ray, hardly able to believe that she was *her*. Unable to believe she was here, right now, looking back at me, all these years later. How the hell had I not noticed it before? "The one person I hadn't hurt at all. And I began to wonder what had happened to her, where she had gone, what she had done with her life ... I thought that maybe she might be the only person I had made a positive impact on and maybe she could be the only person to ever think of me and remember how good I was."

Ray's eyes held mine with an unexplained intensity and sadness as I clutched the bundle of rubber-banded letters. She stood there, frozen, clutching her book to her chest like she was afraid to let go, to do anything else but stare and wait with bated breath.

"So"—I held up the bundle in one hand—"I wrote letters to her. Whenever I had something to say or something happened, I would write these letters to Rain, thinking she'd never read them—but that was fine. She was just someone to talk to, you know, even if she only existed in my head. Like, uh ... an imaginary friend."

Ray's lips parted with a whispered exhale as she lifted the hand not holding her book and hesitantly reached out to take the bound letters from me. "You ... wrote these to *me*?"

I nodded, then chuckled through a rush of embarrassment. "I told you it was weird."

"No." She shook her head, looking at the top envelope, simply reading *Rain* in my shitty handwriting, "I ... I just can't believe you even remembered who I was. It was so long ago ..."

"Yeah, it was."

She lifted her eyes from the letters to look at me, her lips curved in an indecipherable smile. Then, she asked, "Would it be okay if I read these?"

It was surreal to accept that she was even holding them, let alone with an interest to read them, but I nodded. "Of course. Your name's on them, isn't it?"

Ray pulled in a deep breath and nodded before gesturing over her shoulder with the bundle in her hand. "I should probably ..."

"Yeah," I said, remembering that we both had lives to get back to. You know, a cat and a kid to feed.

Showers to take. Books to read. A pretty girl to think about.

"I'll, um ..." She took a step backward to her porch. "I'll see you tomorrow?"

"Tomorrow."

And the day after and the one after that ...

I hope.

She smiled, hugging both the letters and book to her chest. "Okay."

"Night, Ray."

"Good night, Soldier."

I reluctantly turned to head back into my house, where Eleven was already pacing and getting excited at the prospect of finally having dinner. I listened as Ray began her own ascent to her house, where Noah was undoubtedly waiting inside with his grandmother, as he did every other day after school. He was probably wondering what the hell was taking her so long, just as Eleven had been, and he might've even checked outside to see us talking. I felt a little guilty for not saying hi to him too, but—

"Hey, Soldier?"

I turned quickly before I could start to climb my rotten, warped steps and hurried over to stand at the bottom of her porch.

"Yeah?"

She stood just a foot before me, just about at eye-level, thanks to the steps giving her some extra height. Her breath hitched as she looked at me so closely, and mine did too. She looked different from this angle. I

mean, she was always pretty, but, man, head-on like this ·
…

I didn't think I'd ever seen anything more beautiful in my life.

"I never forgot you either."

"Oh, no?" The words propelled me forward until my toes hit her bottom step, standing now with my face just inches from hers.

She shook her head and wet her lips with the tip of her tongue. "How could I?"

I dared to lean forward, dared to brush my nose against hers, and—stupid me—I shuddered at the intimacy. It was humiliating, but, Christ, when the hell was the last time I'd been touched? Even hugs were rare, never mind … well, this.

"I can't believe it's *you*," I whispered, my heart in my throat and my hands itching to hold hers.

She smiled, dropping her eyes to my mouth. "I know. It feels so—"

Her front door opened, and then came a voice I didn't recognize. "Ray?"

Ray exhaled with a disgruntled sigh as she quickly took a step away, and I was disappointed, but I was also so elated that I almost didn't care.

Almost.

"Yeah, Mom," she answered without looking in her mother's direction. She kept her eyes on me as she grimaced with an unspoken apology.

I couldn't stop smiling.

"Are you ever coming inside, or do you live on the porch now?"

Ray rolled her eyes. "I'm coming in. Just give me a minute."

Her mom exhaled noisily. "Okay. Oh, and, you know, it's a little rude not to introduce me to your friend."

I peered around Ray to give her mother—a gray-haired woman, wearing an amused smirk—a wave. "Hi, I'm Soldier. I, uh … I live next door"—I gestured toward my little house—"over there."

She crossed her arms, never letting the smirk leave her face. "I know who you are." Given my reputation, I wasn't sure that was such a good thing until she added with a little teasing grin, "My daughter and grandson have made it their new hobby to talk about you."

"Oh," I replied, knowing damn well by the heat in my face that I was blushing like a fucking jackass.

But so was Ray.

"Thank you for that, Mom. So very much."

"Mmhmm," her mom replied cheerfully. "It was nice to finally meet you, Soldier. I'm Barbara, by the way."

"Nice to meet you too."

"Ray, I'll give you one more minute, but after that, I can't guarantee your son won't be the one to interrupt your little *moment*," she jabbed playfully before heading back inside and closing the door behind her.

Ray covered her face with her book and my letters to her, and I laughed under my breath, feeling suddenly like the teenager I had never been allowed to be.

"Oh my God," she groaned. "I'm sorry about that."

"It's fine. I like her."

She lowered the things in her hands and looked into my eyes with an unexpected desperation I thought I understood. That type of powerful, overwhelming emotion you didn't know what the hell to do with because it was just too ... everything. Too intense, too big, too consuming, too much for one person to deal with on their own.

Then, she said, "If I don't do this, it's going to drive me crazy all night."

I had no idea what exactly she was talking about, and still, I nodded and said, "Okay."

And the next thing I knew, she was stepping forward and pushing her mouth against mine in the simplest, most unromantic kiss of my damn life that lasted all of three seconds, in which the world and everything in it stood still and quiet.

Nobody had ever kissed me like that before, and, God, it was perfect.

She had stolen my breath in those seconds and zapped my heart into beating at the speed of light, and the moment she pulled her lips from mine, my entire body ached with the pain of already missing her.

Ray pressed her lips together as she took a deep breath, then smiled while walking backward to her door.

"Good night, Soldier," she said quietly, shyly, keeping her eyes locked with mine.

I didn't move a muscle, except to smile back. "Good night, Rain."

And it was only when she disappeared inside with her book and the letters I'd never thought she'd read that

I finally walked back home, where Eleven waited for me with unamused boredom written plainly on his face.

"Don't be jealous," I said, closing the door behind me and knowing I'd spend the rest of my life replaying that kiss in my mind.

CHAPTER
FIFTEEN

LETTERS: READ

D*ear Rain,*
My mom visited today for the first time. I've been locked up for six years. No letter, no phone call—she just showed up out of nowhere. Honestly, I think I had started to accept that she just didn't exist in my life anymore, like she was dead or something, and then the second I started to move on, there she was again. Like a cancer or some shit.

Can't believe I just related Mom to cancer. But let's be real here—that's exactly what she is, right? A fucking tumor that tries to kill me over and over and over again, and I wonder when I'll eventually just cut her out completely. I wonder if I ever could.

I wonder if you have a mom and if you like her. Or if she's a poisonous, soul-sucking leech, like mine.

Anyway, Mom showed up to tell me she has a boyfriend and a job. And you want to know how that felt? It felt like she was rubbing in how great her life is now that I'm not in it. Hell, she kinda said it herself. She looked happy even if she still looked like a sick fucking junkie. The last time I had seen Mom look happy was probably when I was, like, six or seven, when she was sober and back from one of her little "trips"—which I later realized was code for rehab.

Anyway, whatever. I don't give a shit anymore. One day, I'll be happy too. At least, I hope so. And I hope that when it happens, I'll be far away from her.

I hope I never fucking see her again.

And I think, most of all, I hope you're happy too.

Soldier

***

Dear Rain,

Why did your parents name you Rain?

My mom told me once that she named me Soldier because, once upon a time, she believed I'd save her life. It's such a cruel irony that I actually did save her sorry ass time and time again, and she never acknowledged it. Not once. Her self-absorption and addiction and whatever the hell else is wrong with her have left her so completely incapable of looking outside of herself that she can't see the sacrifices I've made for her. Which is why I don't think she could've picked a more appropriate name for me. Because my life has been one massive war of survival and sacrifice, yet somehow, I prevail.

193

What does that say about me? What does it say about her?

I'm thinking about Mom tonight, obviously. I wish I weren't. But that's my downfall too. She's my mom, and for every moment that I hate her, there's a moment in which I miss her and all the potential we had to have more than this dysfunctional, toxic bullshit of a relationship.

Anyway, I'm wondering why your parents named you Rain. Was it raining when you were born? Were they hippies? Did they make sweet, passionate love outside during a thunderstorm the night you were conceived?

I just laughed out loud and woke up the guy next to me. He's pissed. I should stop now.

Soldier

***

Dear Rain,

Today, they moved me from laundry duty to the kitchen again. I like the kitchen, so I'm cool with it. Laundry gave me too much time to think and get trapped inside my own head. You'd think I'd feel like that about cleaning, but I don't. Cleaning is relaxing. There's instant gratification for the work you've done. You can see your progress as it's happening. But laundry? Hell no. All I can do is load the machines and watch them spin while my mind plummets into places better left untouched. It's too monotonous, you know? Kitchen duty is better. I get to hang with a couple of the guys I like and eat as much of the food as I want.

Not that the food is great, but you get used to it.

Anyway, one of the guys on the kitchen crew asked about my scar, and I thought about you. It's a little crazy, isn't it? Of all the shit I've been through, the one thing that marked me for life was a direct result of saving you. And I'm glad for it. I'm glad for this scar. Because every time I look at it or touch it or someone asks about it, I get to remember all over again that I am capable of doing something good without it ending in someone else's pain. And if I tell myself that enough, maybe, one day, I'll start to believe it.

Soldier

P.S. Oh, and he thought my scar was pretty badass, like I'm some kind of gallant hero or something, and for once, I agreed.

***

"Are you a bad guy?" Noah asked me one weekend as I pulled the weeds from the small plot of dirt I had to my name.

I glanced over my shoulder and wiped the sweat from my brow. "Do *you* think I'm a bad guy?"

He dropped his gaze to the gravel beneath his feet and seemed to consider his own question for a moment. "I don't think so," he replied, although he sounded unsure. "But you were in jail, and my friend Greg says that only bad guys go to jail."

With a deep breath, I sat back on my heels and rested my hands on my knees. "Good guys go to jail too,

Noah," I said, choosing my words carefully, still not wanting to divulge too much information. "Unfortunately, sometimes, accidents happen, and even good guys have to pay for them."

"So, is that what happened with you? An accident?"

I still wasn't sure that his mother wanted me to talk about this stuff with him. But he was curious, and his questions were incessant, and trying to steer him away from them was exhausting.

"Yes," I said with a held sigh. "It was a horrible accident."

"So, like ... if it was just an accident, why did you have to go to jail?"

I released my breath and squinted up toward a sky that looked like it was about to pour at any second. "Because ... I made a decision—a really bad one—and I had to be punished for it."

I glanced over my shoulder at him again to watch the gears in his head turn. He was a smart kid, even in the things he didn't understand. He reminded me of myself in a way—except his mom was better.

His mom was more like Billy's. The kind I'd always wished I had.

"I know you're a good guy," he finally said. "But I think my dad's a bad one."

My eyes narrowed at him with suspicion. "Why do you say that?"

"Because he does bad things and they're not freakin' accidents."

There was no way I was getting more gardening done. Not with the sky looking like that and certainly not with Noah dropping bombshells out of nowhere.

So, I stood up, brushed my hands off on my jeans, and asked Noah if he was hungry because I was starving. He followed me into the house—Ray had lifted the restriction after realizing I wasn't in fact a creep—where I grabbed my T-shirt from the back of a chair Harry's wife had helped reupholster and pulled it on. Then, I went into the kitchen to make us a couple of bologna sandwiches while Noah hung out with Eleven.

"So," I said, taking out four slices of bread, "what do you mean, your dad does bad things?"

"Like ..." I glanced over my shoulder to watch as he pulled in a deep breath while his mouth twisted angrily. "Like when he hurts my mom. Crap like that."

The brace that had been on Ray's arm came to mind immediately, and I clenched my hand tighter around the butter knife as I slathered mayo onto the bread.

"He hurts your mom?"

"Yeah, sometimes."

"Does he hurt you?"

Noah didn't reply right away, and I took another glance over my shoulder to see him frozen with his hand resting on Eleven's back. I didn't want to push him or dig for information I wasn't privy to. The last thing I wanted was to make him uncomfortable. But I also wanted him to know he could tell me if he didn't feel safe, if he was scared. I wanted him to know that, as long as I was around, I'd do anything to protect them—him and his mom.

197

"Hey, it's okay. You—"

"He hurts me sometimes, yeah," he quietly confessed, every word coated in shame. "But he hurts Mom more."

Back when I had been a kid, sometimes, I'd hear my classmates making comments about my family. How old my grandparents were. How weird my mom was. Shit like that had mostly been innocent, looking back on it, but the implications hadn't been innocent at all. My skin would prickle and itch as every nerve ending in my body would scream at me to fight, to defend and protect.

That was how I felt right now, listening to Noah talk about his dad.

"Hurts her how?" I asked, bringing my gaze to the window above my sink to look out and watch Ray's house. As if the bogeyman in the big silver truck might show up at any moment.

"Mostly when he wants her to go in her room with him and she says she doesn't want to. Then, he gets, like … *really* mad." Eleven meowed at Noah's feet, but Noah was too focused on what he was saying to pay attention to the kitten that was starting to look a lot more like a cat these days. "He pushes her, and, um … I don't know. I don't really want to talk about this anymore."

"Yeah …" I cleared my throat of my anger and the urge to beg him to continue as I hurried to make the sandwiches. "It's okay, buddy. Don't worry about it. I'll just finish this, and we can eat, okay?"

***

198

Later that day, after the sandwiches were eaten and Noah got tired of playing with Eleven, I walked him back home. His house wasn't more than thirteen steps from mine, and he always insisted he could go alone, but I felt better, walking him back myself. You never knew with people these days. Especially ones who drove obnoxious pickup trucks.

Plus, walking him home meant seeing his mom.

He unlocked the door with the key he carried and headed inside, immediately shouting that he'd see me later as he ran to his room while I found Ray in the kitchen. She sat at the table, holding one of my letters in her hand, and I tried not to think too much about what she might be reading. It was fine that she was looking at them, fine that she was learning more about me, but something about being present while she read them ...

It made me want to run away and hide my head in shame.

"Hi." She looked up at me with a smile.

"Hey," I said, unable to stop myself from looking at her lips.

It had been days since she'd last kissed me, and I wanted to do it again. Hell, I wanted to do it a lot. But I wouldn't push it. Those things were always better when they happened exactly when they were meant to rather than forcing it along.

She lifted the letter she had been reading. "This is my fourth one," she said before allowing her smile to droop. "I'm so sorry you went through all of this."

I invited myself to sit down across from her. "It is what it is."

"You say that like it's so normal to be thrown in prison right after your best friend died in front of you and to not have anybody at all come visit you or even write …" She shielded her eyes with a hand and rubbed at her brow. "Nobody deserves that, Soldier. I mean, even freakin' … Charles Manson had people writing to him. He had visitors."

"Eh"—I shrugged—"if I were a celebrity criminal, random people would've written to me too."

She patted the letter lightly with her fingertips. "I should've written to you. I mean, I wish I had. I had heard about what happened, and I thought about it, but I …" She blew out a deep breath and closed her eyes, as if she couldn't bear to look at anything else. "I was going through my own stuff at the time, so I never, um … I never did … but I wish I had."

I shrugged again, more nonchalantly this time. "Seriously, it's fine."

Ray rolled her eyes at that, now looking as though she might even be annoyed with me for being so dismissive. "But it's *not*."

"Here's the thing, Ray," I said, folding my hands against her table. "It *has* to be fine because there's nothing anybody can do about what has already happened. The only thing any of us have any control over is what's happening *right now*, in this moment, and all we can do is our best to not let the bad shit happen again."

Ray studied me for a moment, her green eyes dancing as her lips turned into a little melancholy smile. "You are a remarkable man, you know that?"

I laughed awkwardly, shying away quickly to eye a cookie jar shaped like a cow.

One of its ears had been broken off.

Now, Ray had a twelve-year-old son. Things were bound to break at some point. But a twinge of intuition told me that cow had been broken in a way Noah had nothing to do with.

So, I turned from the cow to level Ray with a serious expression and said, "Speaking of remarkable men, why don't you tell me more about Noah's father?"

She swallowed and sat up a little straighter in her chair to favor the wrist no longer wearing a brace. It was a small tell but like I had already told her once before, if she wanted me to believe her stories, she would have to learn to act better than that.

"Did he do that to your wrist?" I asked point-blank, and she answered with wide, angry eyes and the opening and closing of her mouth. Like she wanted to say something, but didn't know what. So, I added, "Noah told me he hurts you."

She clenched her hand and slowly shook her head as her bottom lip began to quiver. "He wasn't supposed to say anything. I told him not to—"

"But I can't help you if I don't know," I interrupted, gentle but firm. "So, talk to me, Ray. Please."

Her gaze dragged slowly from her once-injured wrist to meet my eye for a fleeting moment, just long enough for me to witness the helplessness and despair she carried along with her, concealed from the rest of the world. I saw the hope she was desperate to feel, the prayer for salvation, but then, she abruptly looked away.

"There's nothing you can do anyway," she replied, no longer denying the truth. "And, really, it's not like there's anything *to* do. We don't even see him that often. He shows up every now and then, when it's convenient for him, and he—"

"Hurts you?"

She squeezed her eyes shut, and I thought she might finally say something. I thought she might even tell me everything. But instead, she stood suddenly from her chair with such force that it teetered on its legs. She turned to press her hands to the kitchen counter, hanging her head as her shoulders heaved with every anguished breath.

To contrast her brash rising, I stood slowly. "Ray," I said, my voice low as I approached with wary caution.

When I got no response, I laid a hand against her shoulder, engulfing her slender frame with my palm.

"Rain."

I spoke her given name with a stern edge, and she reluctantly looked over her shoulder to reveal the tears that glistened in her emerald eyes. The heart I owned had been locked away for so many years, but at the sight of her watery gaze, I listened as the door creaked open to that musty, old cellar, and I heard that telltale beating. Every thump a reminder that it was still somehow there, waiting for someone to hold it, to keep it safe.

The hand I held against her shoulder dared to move just a few centimeters over to her golden-brown hair, falling over her neck like a waterfall of honey. Touching its length for the first time after years of wondering, and you know what? It was even softer than I'd imagined.

"I know what to do with pain, Ray," I said, keeping my tone barely above a whisper. "Give yours to me. Let me carry it, so you don't have to anymore."

She turned against my touch, folding herself into the crook of my arm. It took everything in me not to wrap her into a tight embrace and protect her from the monster who'd hurt her wrist and whatever else I didn't know about. But I would know eventually. I would ensure she told me every last detail, and I would do whatever it took to make sure she never had to face him again.

"What would you do?" she asked, her eyes twinkling with tears and hope.

She lifted her palm, slowly bringing her fingertips to the side of my face, tracing the scar that ran from below my eye to disappear into my beard. The hairs at the back of my neck stood on end at her touch, featherlight and barely there, as I widened my stance and craned my neck to drop my forehead to hers.

She held my gaze and flattened her palm on my cheek, covering the evidence that I'd once protected her. Before I knew her name. Before I knew *her*. And she had to know now that there was nothing I wouldn't do. I'd mark my entire body if I had to. I'd lay down my life. I'd run to hell on my bare feet, harness the Devil, and force him to kneel in submission. All to be certain that the bogeyman she knew and feared never laid a hand on her or her son again.

But my tongue failed me now as she held me captive within her bejeweled eyes. I was rendered stupid and useless with the softness of her palm soothing the hardened, jagged edges of my heart, and all I could utter in reply was, "Everything."

Her mouth moved to mine as quickly as mine went to hers. A passionate rush of energy, forcing our bodies to converge in a frantic coupling of lips, opening on contact to coax tongues from their hiding places. I tasted her mouth, and she tasted mine, both of us savoring every moment with sharp inhales and choked whimpers. She hooked her arms around my neck, and I took my hands to her waist, digging my fingers into her flesh and biting her bottom lip to ward off the temptation to go further, to do more than just kiss.

"Soldier." My name was spoken breathlessly, almost as a sigh.

Nobody had ever uttered my name that way before. Nobody had ever said it as if it were the most cherished, most precious word to ever exist in the English language, and I wanted to wrap it up in a neat little bow to save for always.

I moved my lips to her jaw, then her neck, where I inhaled the scent of freshness and purity and warmth. A soothing blend that reminded me of childhood and sunshine and all the things I'd been missing for so long. I wrapped my arms around her, burying my nose in the crook of her neck as a consuming need to get lost in this emotion crashed against me. All of a sudden, all at once, she became everything I had lost and needed so desperately that I could hardly breathe, and now, with her in my arms, I released a deflating exhale, afraid to ever let her go again.

"Soldier," she repeated in a tone that matched her scent. Comforting and consoling. She weaved her fingers through my hair, cupping the back of my neck. "God ... why do I feel like I've needed this for so long?"

"I know I have," I replied, not giving a shit about how stupid I must look. Six foot seven and tucked around this woman who was well over a foot shorter.

She sighed into my shoulder. "I ... I need to tell you something."

The sound of her voice ...

It was reluctant and regretful, and that wasn't at all what I wanted to hear. Not when I was ready to bare my soul for her to steal and use at her will.

I swallowed in preparation as I stood up straight and took a step back, moving my hands from her waist to her shoulders. I didn't say anything; I just waited for what suddenly seemed like the end of the world to come tumbling down around me.

Life always did have a way of taking away the good things the very moment I'd gotten a taste.

Ray moved her hands to my chest and pressed them over my thundering heart, now more alive than ever. She stared ahead, watching every rise and fall of my chest, before asking, "Do you remember that night we first met?"

"Of course."

"You made me promise I would never go back to The Pit."

"I know."

"And I kept that promise"—she dragged her eyes from my chest to pin me with her tormented gaze—"but you forgot that I still lived in that town."

If she couldn't hear my heart before, there was no way she didn't now. My jaw clenched tightly against my grinding teeth as I looked down at her, immediately terrified of whatever was going to come next in this part of her life's story.

"I think it probably pissed them off—"

"Who's them?" I managed to mutter.

"Seth, his friends … you know, Levi—"

The sound that rumbled from deep within my chest rivaled a growl as I tore my eyes from hers to stare at the ceiling. "Fucking Levi …"

"Yeah, um … they didn't like you, Soldier."

"No shit."

"No," she said, harsh and frantic. "They *really* didn't like you. They didn't like you getting in the way, stealing their business, interfering with the stuff that didn't concern you, and when you stopped Seth from, um"—her breath shuddered—"doing what he was going to do …"

I could still hear her screams. I could still see her struggling against that tree. The look of panic and blind desperation in her eyes. The way she had feared me, even after I got her away from him, the way she thought I wanted her for myself. Like something to own and break.

I saw that fear alive in her eyes now. But it wasn't aimed at me despite the way she looked ahead at her hands against my chest.

"He knew where I lived, and he took what he wanted," she whispered.

And just like that, the girl I had saved became the girl I had failed.

Just another name to add to the list.

"No," I said, shaking my head. Not wanting to believe it was true.

I didn't want to hear what had happened, yet I wanted every last detail. I wanted her to pierce my skin with whatever torture had been inflicted on her. I wanted it stitched into my heart. I wanted it to be the end of me, just to keep it from being the end of her.

"It was just the one time," she was quick to say even with how much her hands shook against my shirt.

"Yeah, but it wasn't really, was it?" I sounded mad, but I hadn't meant to. My anger wasn't meant for her.

Her breath came in quivering huffs as she hesitated before quickly shaking her head.

Then, I uttered the words she didn't want to say, "And he's Noah's dad."

I hoped she'd say I was wrong. I hoped she'd tell me I'd misunderstood and that Noah was the son of someone bad, but not *that* kind of bad. But Ray couldn't give me that satisfaction because it would've been a lie.

Her teeth clamped down on her bottom lip, her fingers barely twitching against my chest, and my stomach bottomed out. The need to vomit rolled over me like a freight train, and I looked away, sucking in breath after breath, hoping to quell the rise of my fury before I destroyed something important.

"I thought I had saved you," I whispered, knowing how stupid and pathetic it sounded now.

God, what kind of idiot had I been to believe that I had somehow stopped every bad thing from happening in her life by protecting her once? Thirteen years. Thirteen fucking years had passed since that night, and while maybe my life had been a monotonous cycle of nothing much occurring for nearly ten of those years, hers hadn't. Shit had happened. Lots of it, apparently.

And it had been my fault.

Would things have been different if I had just stayed out of it? Would I have been able to live with myself if I'd just stood by and let it happen while I ignored her, like every other asshole there that night?

"Soldier, no," Ray said, reaching for my face with her hand, bringing my eyes back to hers. "You *did* save me. You were there for me that night when nobody else would even look. You were my hero. You showed me there were good guys in this world, and I never ever forgot about that. I never forgot *you*."

I stared into her eyes, unwilling to understand how this woman could have suffered so much hurt and still look at me with such hope. How was she not broken after all this time? And how could she continue to face that man time and time again? How could she face her son, the product of her continued torment?

God, shame on me.

"So, when he was last here, he"—I pinched my eyes shut, unable to believe I was about to speak the words— "hurt your wrist, and ..."

I remembered what Noah had said. That his dad would get mad when Ray refused to go to her bedroom with him.

I'm going to throw up.

She shook her head. "I wouldn't let him. That's why he got mad, and I told Noah to sit outside."

"Okay." God, no, it wasn't *okay*. But at least she'd fought him off. Not without paying a price, but ... she'd fought him off.

I struggled to steady my breath and heart as I said, "You won't see him again."

Ray gawked at the demand, as if I had some nerve. "Soldier, I can't just ... keep his son from him. H-how am I supposed to explain that to him?"

"You won't have to," I said, my fists clenching and unclenching. "If I see his big fucking truck roll up again, he'll deal with me."

"No!" she shouted, and that reaction startled me to narrow suspicious eyes at her. "No. Let me handle it. Please. I'll tell him I'm done with this shit and that I'll get a restraining order if he ever comes near us again. Just let me try."

Intuition told me not to agree, and it had nothing to do with not trusting her to try. No, what I didn't trust was Seth and his willingness to comply. The guy had been violating her for years. He had been acting out in violence for years. What the hell did she think was going to be different now?

But still, she was a grown woman, and I had to respect that.

"Fine." I relented hesitantly. "When will you see him again?"

Ray shrugged and wrapped her arms around her middle. "I never know. He comes around when he wants to. Sometimes, months go by before he shows his face, and other times, only days. It really depends, I guess, on what else he has going on."

My jaw clenched as the gears in my head squealed to life. What else *did* he have going on? This was Seth we were talking about, and I didn't know much about him, other than that he was Levi's buddy and what Ray had just told me.

"What does he do for a living?" I asked a little absentmindedly.

Ray's brow creased with uncertainty. "I … don't really know the details, to be honest. He doesn't tell me much. Just that he has to go on the road sometimes and …" She lifted her hands, then dropped them helplessly. "I really have no idea."

Levi's pals always helped him sell.

Without The Pit, where are they selling?

"Huh …" I nodded slowly, poking at my inner cheek with my tongue. "That's okay. Probably better you don't know."

"Why?"

I twisted my lips and shook my head while the gears continued to turn and turn and turn.

"Just a feeling I have."

CHAPTER

SIXTEEN

FIRST DATES & FIRST FLOWERS

"**W**ow."

I looked over my shoulder to see Ray standing on her porch in a fuzzy pink robe and matching slippers, a steaming cup of coffee clutched between her hands.

"What?" I asked, my lips lifting into a hesitant smile.

She studied me for a moment, wetting her lips with the tip of her tongue. "It's just not every day I get to stand outside on a beautiful spring day and see something that looks like"—she gestured toward me with the mug—"that."

I laughed, all too aware of the heat rising in my cheeks as I shook my head before returning my attention to the tiller in my hands, jabbing the blades into the ground, using my foot for leverage, and pressing on the handles to loosen the hardened soil. It was a small patch of land, roughly ten feet by ten feet, and the job of cultivating the soil would be done in no time. But it was hot for the beginning of May. The sun was beating down on me with its relentless rays, and even without my shirt, my back and brow glistened with sweat.

It was uncomfortable—I had never been a fan of the heat—but at least Ray seemed to be enjoying the show. And even if her compliments made me blush—I just wasn't used to being admired, I guessed—it was nice.

"Have I ever told you that you have really nice arms?" she asked, and I glanced over my shoulder again to watch her slowly take a sip from her mug, her eyes never diverting from me and my apparently *nice arms*.

"No, you've never mentioned that before," I said. Resigned to the fact that I wouldn't get much work done in her presence, I leaned against the tiller.

"Well, you do."

Nobody had ever complimented me the way she did. Lust-filled but otherwise pure. I sometimes wondered what to say while my tongue fumbled stupidly around the words, but today, I thought maybe I could test the waters of my own flirting ability a little.

"How nice would you say they are?"

"Like"—she tipped her head back and pursed her lips with consideration—"they're so nice that it is taking everything in me right now not to say *fuck this coffee* and enjoy you instead."

I had to look away and chuckle, unable to fight my stupid grin. This thing between us was new—only a couple of weeks old, give or take—and it had started off nice, easy, and comfortable. No pressure. Not to mention, I didn't want to push her into anything before she was ready. Especially knowing what I knew now about her life and history with the opposite sex. I wanted to keep everything on her terms. So, we flirted and kissed when the mood struck, exchanging little glances and soft touches every so often. And I was happy, genuinely content for maybe the first time in my life, and from what Ray repeatedly told me, she was too.

I wasn't sure Noah had caught on yet or if he thought his mom and I had started to just spend a little more time together. But whichever it was, he seemed content, too, and for that, I was even happier.

"What's the kid doing today?" I asked, turning my eyes back on the land to assess what I'd already accomplished.

Half of the yard had been tilled. Not bad for a little over an hour of work.

"Right now, checking out the new game my mom bought him." She walked down her steps and came to stand closer to my little yard. "Do you need help? I can send him over."

"No, I'm good." I grunted as I jabbed the blades into the next tough spot in the row I was working on. "Just thought he'd like to get his hands dirty if he wasn't doing anything else."

"I'll ask him."

She watched me through a couple more jabs of the tiller into the ground, sipping her coffee and keeping an arm wrapped tightly around her middle. There was something so normal about it, something that said we could have this all the time—maybe even forever—and I liked it a lot.

It was funny. For years, I'd never thought forever with another person could exist in my world. Yet there I was, envisioning her walking down the aisle in a premature daydream.

"Where did you learn to do this stuff?" she asked after another sip of coffee.

"What, dig in the dirt?"

She laughed. "No, I mean, gardening and … whatever it is you're doing right now."

"Well"—another grunt with another jab—"my grandfather had a huge garden that I helped him with. That's where I learned most of what I know"—jab, push, till—"and that continued while I was at Wayward."

"You gardened at Wayward?"

I nodded as I gritted my teeth for another stab of the blades through the dirt. "I did a lot of stuff there. Learned a lot. Most productive time of my life, to be honest. I probably wouldn't know how to survive right now if it wasn't for that place."

Ray softly bobbed her head, humming contemplatively. I didn't need to ask what she was thinking—I already knew.

How could a guy speak so fondly of prison?

How could I stoop so low to make out with him on a nearly nightly basis, knowing he's an ex-con?

"Anyway"—she cleared her throat—"I have laundry to do, but I'll let Noah know you asked for him to come outside and play."

I chuckled heartily, trying not to think too much about her abrupt change in subject. "Let me know if you need help with the laundry. I have a lot of experience with doing that too."

She smiled, looking up to my eyes fondly before stepping toward me and tipping her head back.

I bent to kiss her softly, barely brushing my lips against hers, as I thought, *This is nice. I could get used to it. I just hope I get to keep it for a while.*

***

"We should go on a date," she announced during her weekly shopping trip.

Noah wasn't with her today. I wondered if he was with her mom and was going to ask when she abruptly made a suggestion I hadn't expected but probably should've. I mean, that was what people who liked each other did, right? They went on dates. They made things official. They had dinner together and watched movies and ... other normal coupley things that I had never done before in my life.

"A date?" I asked, looking up from my sweeping and promptly smacking my head on the damn Produce sign.

Howard chuckled beneath his breath before wincing apologetically. "I'll move it, I promise."

He walked away, his laughter following him as he went, as I muttered, "He's full of shit. He's been saying he'll move that fuckin' thing for months."

"Yeah, a date," Ray replied while watching me rub my hand against the back of my head.

"Like"—my forehead crumpled with the thought—"what kind of date?"

I wished I didn't seem so stupid. And I hated that she knew it, too, as she laughed lightly at my expense and playfully rolled her eyes.

"You know, like, a normal date. Dinner, maybe go for a walk or go to the movies or something ..." She folded her arms against the handle of her shopping cart and shrugged like it all should've been obvious. "A normal date."

"I've never been on a date," I admitted point-blank, then quickly wondered what she would think of me, now knowing that at thirty-one, I hadn't done something most people did in their teens.

She cocked her head curiously, but didn't seem surprised. "Really?"

It was my turn to shrug. "Honestly, I've never really even had a girlfriend, so ..."

This time, she *was* surprised. "Wait. That night, um ... at The Pit ... I saw you with a girl. So, I thought ..."

I shook my head, both to respond and to remove the image of Tammi from my mind. "It wasn't like that. She, um ..." I glanced around me, making sure none of the other shoppers were within listening distance. "She wasn't a real girlfriend. I didn't like her much, and I'm pretty sure she only liked me for ... what I did, and, um ..."

Shame coiled up from the collar of my long-sleeved shirt and wrapped tightly around my neck. Thoughts of the things Tammi would do to me while stoned out of her mind off the pills I had given her filled my head. Memories of the things I'd do to her in exchange as thanks. It all felt like so long ago—a lifetime even—but the beads of sweat dotting my forehead made it all seem like yesterday.

How could I have ever been like that? That wasn't *me*. It was never who I wanted to be, so why the hell had I done it?

"It's okay. The past doesn't matter anymore," Ray said, as if reading my mind. "We'll go out on a proper date, and I'll show you how nice it is."

She said it with so much confidence and determination, and I wondered if it was for my benefit or hers.

***

Three days later, that Friday, Noah stayed at his grandparents' house, and I walked the thirteen steps it took to get from my stoop to Ray's porch. I held in my hand a bouquet of sunflowers I'd bought from the florist in town and knocked on her door. When she answered, wearing the prettiest white dress I had ever seen, I was glad I'd decided at the last minute to wear the shirt and pants I'd worn on Christmas with Harry's family.

"Look at you," she said softly, leaning against the door and smiling as she let her eyes wander from the top of my head all the way down to my feet.

"I could, but I think I'd rather look at you instead." I held out the flowers. "These are for you."

Her smile grew as she accepted them. "This might be your first date, but you're the first man to bring me flowers."

I chuffed and rolled my eyes to the ceiling. "Oh, come on."

She left the doorway to head into the kitchen, and I followed, closing the door behind me.

"I'm serious," she said, standing on her toes and stretching her arm to try and reach for a dusty vase on the top of her refrigerator.

I handed it to her before she could pull a muscle.

"Show-off." Her eyes teased while that smile never left her face.

She took the vase from me and laid the flowers on the counter before washing the murky blue glass and filling it with water. I waited patiently, standing by the fridge and watching her in that white dress with hundreds of flowers scattered all over. It held her curves in a way that made me jealous, and I had to will my dick to hold on to some self-control.

He had none. But if Ray noticed, she didn't let on as she put the flowers into the vase and turned to place them on the table.

"I have only ever dated one guy," she admitted, allowing her smile to droop a little as she arranged the big yellow blooms. "And he was never really romantic."

She was implying that I was, and I snorted. "I'm not sure I'd say I'm romantic either."

Ray's smile returned as she looked at the flowers, then at me, a new and different twinkle in her eyes. "You might not see it," she said, turning to head for the open door. "But I do."

I followed.

I thought I would follow her anywhere.

***

We could have taken her car to the restaurant, but we decided to walk instead.

I knew Ray was only a nickname, but strolling beside her, with the sun bringing light to the golden streaks in her golden-brown hair, an old, familiar tune rang through my head.

You are my sunshine, my only sunshine ...

It reminded me of my mother, but more than that, it reminded me of her. Of Ray. Of the streaks in her hair, as bright as the rays of sunlight casting shadows over the world around us.

Everyone waved to her as we passed. Everyone smiled. They looked at us with fondness, and I tried to imagine what they must've thought, seeing us together.

What does she see in him? She could do so much better. Why would she stoop so low?

But ... no, maybe not. Their smiles were too genuine, too adoring.

Look at them. Our little misfits, brought together by a kinder fate than what they'd been shown before. They'll make each other better; they already have.

Then, with a burst of confidence, I reached down and grabbed her hand in mine. Our difference in height made it a little awkward, but that quickly settled into something nicer as I interlaced our fingers and held tight while we continued to walk toward the restaurant.

I had never held a girl's hand like this before, and with a heart beating too loudly to notice if any of the onlookers gasped or snickered, I hoped she wouldn't let go. Her fingers felt nice between mine; her palm, soft and small, felt good against mine. Walking alongside her, like we were a real couple in a world that had somehow given me a second chance, felt comfortable and as warm as the sunlight. And, God, I prayed she wouldn't be bothered by my bravery and let go.

And I was happy to say, she never did.

***

When we got to the restaurant, we were seated toward the back. Momentarily, I questioned the hostess's motives with a narrowed glare. Was she trying to relax the other diners by secluding the felon? Did she herself not want a clear shot of me wielding my steak knife? But as she laid out menus on the table, she winked at Ray and told her it was the nicest table in the place.

"Way quieter and more romantic than over there," she said, bumping her shoulder against my date's. Then, she looked up at me, her smile beaming brighter than any light in the place. "Enjoy your dinner, guys."

Maybe it was time I stopped assuming everyone thought the worst of me.

"You're friends?" I asked as I pulled out Ray's chair—that was what guys on dates did, right?

She sat as she nodded. "She comes into the library a lot. She's studying to be a teacher."

I took my seat across from her and opened the menu. "What kind of teacher?"

"English, I think."

An image of Mrs. Henderson came to mind, clouding my view of the list of appetizers and drinks. She had been the only teacher I could remember liking, the only one I could recall caring. There might've been more in my youth, but that wasn't the time of my life when it mattered. I needed kindness then, I needed compassion, and she had given it to me—even if it had, at the time, fallen on deaf ears.

Then, I remembered that Ray had gone to the same school, so I asked, "Did you ever have Mrs. Henderson in high school?"

She smiled with instant recollection. "Oh my God, yes! Wow. Yeah … I haven't thought of her in forever. She was so sweet."

"She was," I agreed. "I had the dumbest crush on her. But I think part of that was because she was so nice to me when nobody else was."

Ray nodded somberly. Her menu still sat on the table in front of her, untouched. I had her undivided attention. It was nice to feel so important, and I wanted her to feel the same.

So, I put my menu down and said, "She's Harry's daughter. Have I ever told you about Harry?"

Ray and Harry had yet to be formally introduced, but I knew she had to have noticed the older guy coming around my place once or twice a week since I'd moved in. His visits were frequent, and I was sure I'd mentioned him enough that she would remember his name by now.

But she shook her head, to my surprise. "You've mentioned him a few times, but I don't think you've ever really told me about him."

"Well"—I picked up my menu again—"why don't we order some drinks and appetizers? Then, I'll tell you everything there is to know about Harry Fischer."

***

"So, tell me about the elusive Harry," she said after the waiter walked away with our drink and appetizer order. "Did you know him as a kid?"

I shook my head, folding my arms casually against the table. "Nope. I met him in prison."

She didn't even bat a lash. "Was he an inmate too?"

I smiled and chuckled at the thought of Harry doing anything bad enough to put him behind bars. "Nah. He's one of the officers at Wayward, and he kinda took me under his wing."

That took her aback a little. A line formed between her brows as they pinched with curiosity. "You actually made friends with an officer? Isn't that, like, frowned upon or something?"

"Eh … I mean"—I lifted a hand with my shrug—"there's appropriate relationships, but then there's inappropriate ones. Like, this guy I knew, Zero—"

"Not his real name, I'm assuming?"

"I never thought to ask. He was just always Zero."

She pressed her lips together, stifling a giggle, and nodded, gesturing for me to continue.

"Anyway, he was hooking up with one of the lady officers, and ..." I pinched my lips and shook my head. "Yeah, that was one of those inappropriate ones. We all pretended not to know, but, I mean, it's hard to ignore the people fucking in the dorm bathroom, you know? Not exactly the most private place on the planet."

Ray sniffed a laugh as she propped her chin in the palm of her hand. With a serene look on her face, she listened like I was telling her about cherished Sundays in my childhood or something. And I didn't care to wonder if that was weird or not. It was nice to be listened to. Like what I was saying mattered.

"Anyway, Harry became my inspiration to do even better. He's a good guy—the best really. I wouldn't be here if it wasn't for him."

"How did you meet?" she asked.

"Well, I mean, apart from me getting there and him being in charge of performing a very, *very* thorough search of my body?" I smirked and sniffed lightly at my own feeble attempt at making a joke, but she didn't laugh, and I quickly cleared my throat and shifted in my chair. "Um ... so, I had, of course, seen him around. I knew who he was, and he knew who I was ... but we never really talked. I didn't really talk much, you know? I was more focused on, like, keeping my head down and not pissing too many people off at first.

"But after a while, it was my birthday. And it was also the anniversary of Billy's death. And I, uh ..." I diverted my gaze toward a mounted deer head on the

223

wall and shrugged at its lifeless gaze. "I didn't handle it well, I guess. It was like … I'd always known what I had been arrested for, what I was convicted of, but it never really hit me until that particular day."

It was an awkward moment for the waiter to step in and bring our drinks with a muttered apology. After assuring us the appetizers would be out soon and he'd take our dinner order, he scurried away again. I figured he just didn't want to prolong his discomfort by hanging around longer, and I wondered if maybe this wasn't the time to talk about this.

Hell, maybe I shouldn't ever talk about it at all.

"So, what happened?" Ray asked, stirring the straw in her Coke.

I shook my head. "No, you … you don't want to know this shit. I shouldn't have—"

"Soldier," she cut me off gently, "I *do* want to know. I want to know everything about you."

It seemed unlikely that someone like her—beautiful in an understated and plain sort of way, innocent to the things I had done and seen—would care to know this shit, let alone sit here with me with the knowledge that there was a good chance she would kiss me later, as she had done every night for a couple of weeks now. Yet I had to eventually acknowledge that this was my reality, as surreal and good as it was, and Ray wanted to know about me.

So, with a little hesitation and a heavy exhale of anxiety, I picked up where I'd left off. "Okay, um … well, I had gotten into some shit with this random guy. I didn't really know him. He … I dunno … he had given me a *look* or something, so I made a stupid, nasty comment, and—in any case, I got thrown into the hole for a week, which was …"

It didn't take much thinking to put my mind back in that deafening, maddening cell of dark despair. The soul-crushing silence and solitude were, in itself, enough to drive a man toward insanity if he wasn't already there.

I shook the thought away and continued, "Anyway, I was in a bad place, and when I got out of there, it was worse. I thought more about Billy than I ever had, which is saying a lot, considering I thought about him pretty constantly, and it was driving me out of my mind. I felt like whatever I got in there, I deserved, so I was intentionally trying to mess stuff up for myself. Got into fights, got more time in solitary, and after a few months of that went by, Harry finally confronted me and asked what the hell I was doing. He told me he'd seen some real pieces of shit in that place and he had never thought of me as one, so it was about time I pulled my head out of my ass before I got myself more unnecessary time. So, I listened."

Ray rewarded me with a warm smile. "And the rest is history."

"The rest is history," I concluded as the waiter brought our appetizers.

***

Later, she asked, "When you were a kid, what did you dream your life would be?"

I told her very plainly, albeit depressingly, "I didn't dream of anything. I just hoped my grandparents would live forever, but they didn't."

A wave of melancholy washed over her as she slowly popped a piece of grilled chicken into her mouth.

Then, she asked, "Okay, one more for now. Who was your best friend, growing up?"

And I answered simply, "Billy."

That startled her, and I bit back the urge to confirm that, yes, I had inadvertently killed my best friend.

"I'm so sorry," she said instead of saying the obvious, and I appreciated her response so much more.

Nobody had ever been sorry before.

Nobody ever was for the villain.

"Okay, my turn." I rubbed my hands together, determined to make this at least somewhat interesting. "Um ... so, why did you move to River Canyon?"

The steady connection of her green eyes was suddenly broken as she dropped her gaze to the plates of stuffed mushrooms and crab cakes. The hard, heavy swallows, shifting the muscles in her throat, told me I had made a mistake by asking. She clearly didn't want to talk about it, and I made the safe assumption that it had something to do with Seth and his pals over in our old stomping grounds.

"The same reason as you," she finally replied after a few long moments of silence, bringing her gaze, now shrouded in pain and sadness, back to mine. "A fresh start."

***

Dinner was filled with food I wished I'd never tasted, only for the fact that I knew I would miss it every other night I couldn't have it. The conversation between us flowed freely and easily, pieced together by lingering looks and flighty, sometimes-nervous laughter. It felt good to see that our connection surpassed the physical and wasn't just through Noah, his infectious personality, and a brief but impactful meeting in our past.

Somewhere around the time dessert was brought to the table, I realized that, wow, this was real. Like, this—me, in a nice restaurant, with a pretty woman who genuinely liked me—was *happening*. And I would go home afterward to my own place—one I was growing prouder of by the day—to hopefully dream of this night and pray that it would happen again.

Ray extended her foot, resting it beside mine beneath the table, as she dived into the fudge brownie sundae we'd decided to share, and out of nowhere, a wave of bittersweet sorrow came over me, joining the awe I couldn't shake, as I hoped Gramma and Grampa could see me now. I hoped they were proud that, despite it all, I'd still managed to find myself here, knowing the goodness in me had come from them and them alone.

"So, I have another question," Ray said before bringing the loaded spoon to her mouth.

My eyes focused on her lips wrapping around the metal utensil, pursing and pulling. A drop of hot fudge remained in the corner of her mouth, and I salivated at the thought of licking it away. To taste the chocolate mingling with the taste of her.

I swallowed repeatedly at the lust bubbling deep in my gut and lower, cleared my throat, and grabbed my own spoon. "Yeah?"

Her cheeks reddened as she hesitated. "Okay, I ..." She laughed and shook her head, laying a hand against her face. "God, I don't even know how to ask this ..."

As my spoon dug into the mountain of ice cream and brownie, I shrugged. "Come on. I'm an open book. Ask me anything."

She blew out a breath. "Okay, okay, okay, um ..." She inhaled, closing her eyes, then opened them to pierce me with an apologetic gaze. "Have you ever ... been with anyone before?"

Fucking hell. I didn't mean to laugh at the question, but with my mouth wrapped around the spoon, I snorted through my nose and chuckled from deep in my chest. Ray was instantly embarrassed, groaning and covering her eyes as she tried to suppress her grin and shook her head.

"I'm sorry. It was dumb."

"No"—I laid my spoon on the plate and quelled my laughter—"it's not dumb. I just ... I wasn't expecting it."

Then, I folded my hands and emptied my lungs. "Yes," I replied simply.

Still embarrassed, she cleared her throat and gave her head a rapid shake before grabbing her spoon hastily. "I mean, obviously. God, I don't know why I even asked. I don't know why I even thought—"

"I mean, I was pretty young when I was arrested, so I could see why you'd think I hadn't," I offered weakly, trying to make her feel less silly. "Not a kid, but ..." I shrugged half-heartedly. "The thing is, if I'm being honest … I don't feel like anything counted then. Like, before."

She dipped her spoon into the sundae as her eyes once again met mine. "No?"

I shook my head. "That's what I was saying to you earlier, about girlfriends and whatever. None of it actually meant something to them or … to me." Shit. Being honest was hard, and that was evident in the tightness in my chest and the rapid thrum of my heart. "I mean"—I cleared my throat, trying to relieve my discomfort in the conversation—"I lost my virginity to a girl who didn't have the cash for pills, and being an idiot, I said okay. Because, in my head, it was better to get rid of them than to have them lying around for Diane to take. And I never, um …" My gaze dropped from hers—so sad and pitying—to stare at the melting ice cream. "I never did that again. I mean, had sex in exchange for pills. It felt … wrong and dirty and …"

I stopped myself then. Because hadn't it all felt dirty? Whether it was that one time in exchange for two pills or in a dirty fast-food restaurant restroom with a very high Tammi for the sake of simply having sex, wasn't it all self-deprecating and disgusting? I wasn't proud of any of it. None of it was the behavior of a good person—a good *man*—and maybe that was why I felt that none of it had counted. Not now. Not for the person I was today.

"I've only ever been with Seth."

A pang of hurt and sympathy struck my heart like a lightning bolt at Ray's own admission. I brought my eyes back to hers, and she offered a weak smile.

"When was the last time?" I asked, not sure why I even cared to know while dying to know more than just that.

Had I known her already? Had it happened right next door from me, when I was only thirteen steps away and capable of stopping him?

My stomach churned with a warning.

"Um ..."

She pulled her lips between her teeth, and I realized abruptly that maybe she didn't want to talk about this at all. God, what kind of asshole asked a woman to relive those memories? Why hadn't I thought of that from the start?

"I'm sorry," I said, feeling it was my turn to apologize, but she shook her head.

"No, it's okay. It's just that I don't honestly remember. It's been a while, I think, and anytime it happened, I dunno. I usually just ... blocked it out."

I had told her I'd gladly carry her pain. I hadn't been lying about that. But, man, it was a heavy load, and I hung my head under its weight. Wishing I could do something to erase it all and start fresh.

"It hasn't always been completely terrible. We actually sorta dated for a while after I found out I was pregnant. He had apologized and said he'd try to be better," she added, as if that made it all okay. "But ... it's never been particularly good either."

Rage could be powerful. It could be enough to make a man kill, and for the right reasons, I thought it could be justified. I could kill Seth, and I knew it would be justified. Maybe not in the eyes of the law, but I didn't need it to be. Not when, in my heart and mind, I knew it would be right to rid the world of another vile man.

But I also knew I wouldn't do it, as nice as it was to think about bashing his head against a brick wall. No, I wouldn't do it because, for once, I felt I had too much to lose.

I reached out with a hand—so much bigger than hers—and laid it over her arm.

"Then, anything with him doesn't count either," I said in nearly a whisper.

She rewarded me with a smile, genuine and sweet, and I prayed if we ever found ourselves in bed together—if ever she was ready—it would count.

CHAPTER

SEVENTEEN

SALVATION & REDEMPTION

"So, on a scale from one to ten, how much do you like it here?" Ray asked as we walked down Main Street after dinner.

My belly was stuffed, my heart was full, and my hand held tight to hers. Our difference in height, shown in the reflection of the shop and restaurant windows, was almost comical, and I had to stop myself from laughing a couple of times. And as funny as it was to see her—so small—next to a giant like me, it also felt good. To know I could be the power she'd been missing for so long. Her protector and strength.

"Oh, I'd give it a solid eleven."

I glanced toward Patrick's brother, Ryan Kinney, the local pet groomer and tattoo artist, walking across the street with his wife and their kids. The group of them could give the Addams Family a run for their money, yet nobody in town seemed to bat a lash.

I could relate.

The locals had been skeptical of my presence initially, and I couldn't say I was friends with everyone—especially Mrs. Montgomery, the cranky old lady who liked to bust my balls at work whenever she tottered in. But now, I could walk around town without a single one of them staring warily, and I knew that came down to me and the solid reputation I had been building for myself.

It was a good feeling.

"Wow, an eleven, huh? That's impressive."

"Why? What about you?"

"Oh"—Ray wrapped her other arm around mine—"I wouldn't wanna live anywhere else—that's for sure. And I love being at the library. Being surrounded by books is my happy place."

I glanced at her with curiosity. "You know, I've never thought to ask what books you like to read. I've seen you read those mushy romance novels"—she poked at my side for teasing her, and I laughed, brushing her hand away—"but what else do you like?"

"Oh God, everything," she answered, laughing easily and pulsing her hand around mine. "There's nothing I don't enjoy; I just have to be in the mood. Like, sometimes, I go on a crime thriller kick, and other times, I can't get enough of horror. A few years ago, I couldn't stop reading memoirs and travel journals. Like ..." She laughed again, shaking her head. "I don't even know why. I just couldn't get enough of reading about places I'd never been to."

"Well, that's the cool thing about books, right? Like, you don't have to leave the house to be transported somewhere else." I smiled down at her, and although it felt a little sad, I hoped she couldn't tell. "I mean, that's why I started reading anyway."

My mind traveled back to my life after the loss of both my grandparents. Poverty had been new and unfamiliar, a terrifying adventure I had never thought I'd ever have to embark on. On one horrible day, when Mom had forgotten to give me a few bucks for lunch, I'd sat in the cafeteria, hungry and angry and too ashamed to say anything to one of the teachers or lunch aids. I glanced at a kid I barely knew, saw him reading a book with a boy wizard wearing round glasses on the cover, and asked if it was any good. He insisted it was the greatest shit he'd ever read in his life, and I made the split decision to ditch the rest of my pointless lunch period to check out *Harry Potter and the Sorcerer's Stone* from the school library.

My tumble down the Hogwarts rabbit hole was swift and welcome, and a love for reading had been born. And believe me, the healthy escape was far more embraced than the hole in my belly, and it was one that I'd taken with me, clinging to every book I got my hands on like a poor man held tight to his last penny.

I couldn't begin to imagine what my life would be like without books. Where would I be now had I not had those fictional friends to hold my hand and imagination captive? What would I have done differently if I'd always been fully submerged in the tumultuous, awful reality of my life?

"Why did I start reading?" Ray contemplated with a thoughtful hum, then sucked in a deep breath as we turned down the street leading to our community of tiny houses. "I think, at first, it was just the thrill of doing it. My sister is older—"

"I didn't know you had a sister," I interrupted, startled to learn something new about this woman I was certain I could no longer live without.

I'd always wanted a sibling. I had always wanted that sibling to be Billy if I could have my way. How different would my life have been if that had been the case? Would his mother have hated me so much, so effortlessly, now if she had been my mother too?

God, it was silly how easily the thought of Billy's mom could make me want to cry.

I cleared my throat and blinked my eyes, focusing my attention on the pretty lady beside me.

"Yep. Just one. Stormy. She lives up in—"

Oh God. I couldn't stop myself from huffing out a laugh. "Wow."

I hoped I hadn't offended her, and I was glad when she laughed along with me.

"Oh, I know. Thanks, Mom and Dad, right? And to answer the question about my name, the one you wrote in your letter—"

I sucked in a deep breath at the reminder that she had read them at all.

"My parents thought they were super cool, naming their kids after their favorite type of weather"—she

235

laughed and rolled her eyes at her parents' expense—"and coincidentally, we were both born when it was raining. They said it was good luck or something—I don't know. Personally, I've always thought it was dumb. But *anyway*, Stormy lives up in Salem now, so I don't see her as often as I'd like. She's three years older than me, and back when she started reading, I was so jealous and made her teach me. I would read everything I could get my hands on; it didn't matter what it was.

"But then I guess it turned into this fascination with the idea that these people—you know, authors, writers—they could take the same twenty-six letters and turn them into something completely different from what was already out there. Like, at this point, I don't believe anything is one hundred percent original, but even still, no two books will be exactly the same. That's just amazing to me. It's like magic."

There was a sense of childlike wonder in her tone as she talked. It was adorable and endearing, and I thought I could listen to her talk forever.

"You should write a book," I suggested, smiling down at her.

"*Me?*" Her voice was shrill and amused as her hand squeezed affectionately around mine. "Oh God, I can't. I don't have that kind of talent or creativity. But I do love to read what others write, and I love to do my part in getting their work into other people's hands."

I pressed the hand she wasn't holding to my chest. "Well, I, for one, am eternally grateful for your service."

A comfortable quiet encircled us as we walked down the narrow road through our little neighborhood of small houses and smaller yards toward our respective homes. The night was pleasant—warm enough to be without heavier clothes, cool enough to enjoy it. It was my second favorite kind of weather—first being the rain— and to be sharing it with Ray made the night that much sweeter.

I don't want this to end, I caught myself thinking as we neared her house. But of course, it would, but at least I'd have the memories to keep me company through the night. Memories with her were always better than being haunted by the nightmares of my past.

"It's really hot, you know," Ray said, breaking the silence with her melodic voice.

My brow pinched with curiosity. "What is?"

"That you read."

We stopped at the bottom of her porch steps, and I immediately recalled the time she had first kissed me only a few weeks earlier.

"Oh, you think so, huh?" I asked, turning to stand parallel to her. "I always thought it was kinda nerdy."

"Oh, no way." She looked up at me, her eyes glittering with mirth and unmistakable flirtation. Her hand left mine to trace a line from my wrist to my elbow and back. "Men who read are usually smart and sensitive—"

"Oh, right, absolutely." I nodded, struggling to bite back a teasing grin. "Like this guy I knew, Wolf. He was a big reader like me. Really liked the classics especially. Super-sensitive dude. Like, this one time, he caught this other guy crying on the phone, and he just"—I flicked my wrist for emphasis—"whipped the dude in the throat with the book he was reading. Told him to shut the fuck up and stop acting like a pussy. I mean, super-*super*-sensitive guy."

"Oh my God."

Ray's resounding giggles permeated the air around us as she took her hand from my arm to give my chest a playful smack. I didn't want to go home yet, and this moment felt too much like the end, so in a bold move, I captured that hand once again in mine and held it firmly against my chest, directly above my heart.

Can she feel it? I wondered. *Can she tell how hard it's beating for her?*

Her laughter faded into a whispered gasp as her eyes, illuminated by a single streetlamp and the sconce hanging beside her door, lingered on her fingertips resting against my chest. They moved a little, feeling the ungiving muscle and bone, and she swallowed before parting her lips.

Kiss her, my mind demanded. *You've done it before, so do it now. Fucking kiss her.*

But my hesitation was juvenile, and I could only chalk it up to the inexperience of knowing something genuine. Did she *want* to be kissed? Did she want me to make a move? Why hadn't I been granted the gift of clairvoyance so I wouldn't have to deal with questions like these? And how fucking stupid was it that I didn't have the answers to them at thirty-one years old?

If only she'd do something else, if only she'd give me a sign …

And then, as if she were the clairvoyant one, her hand slid from mine, moving upward to rest on my shoulder. Fingertips dancing against my neck and into my hairline, applying just a little pressure and urging me down to her waiting lips.

Message received.

I mimicked the movement by placing my hand against her neck, my fingers in her silken hair. I took a step closer to minimize the gap between us, and on the slow descent of my lips to hers, we both smiled simultaneously.

It began like a spring breeze—gentle and warm—but quickly escalated to the strength of a summer storm. Hands wrapped in hair as mouths opened with a gasping invitation. Hot, wet tongues delved and tasted and explored, desperately reaching for places kept south of the border, concealed within my jeans and under her dress. My erection was quickly raging, pressed hard to the center of her belly, aching for more than just the friction of cloth.

"Soldier," Ray panted, breaking the kiss long enough to release my name.

I answered with a moan, moving my hand from her hair to just outside her breast, to hold the underside of its fullness against the web between my thumb and forefinger.

"Is this okay?" I asked, knowing it was a tentative move.

I was prepared to back away from her if she so much as flinched. But she responded by arching her back and groaning into my mouth.

"Yes," she replied, and I took that as my cue to glide my thumb across the heavy flesh. Stroking, rolling, pinching as my mouth left hers to move downward to her neck.

Ray's hands held to my head, combing her fingers through my hair as she gasped wordlessly.

"Noah is with my mom," she said, as if I wasn't already aware.

"I know," I muttered, my mouth open against her neck, licking and sucking. Tasting and marking.

"Come inside?"

It was a request as much as it was a demand, and I stopped abruptly, lifting my head from her neck to search her eyes.

"Are you sure?"

She was a grown woman, capable of making her own decisions. But pain ran deep, and trauma embedded itself even deeper. My concern was with her comfort more than it was with anything else. I cared for her, not just her body, and I didn't want to take another step further without knowing for certain that she was okay— if that was at all possible, and if not, I would respect that too.

But Ray held my gaze and nodded. "I would tell you if I wasn't," she assured me as one hand moved from my hair to seek the evidence of my want and need for her.

She gripped me through my pants, stealing a groan from my lungs. *Fuck*, it had been so long since something other than my own hand had touched my dick, and while time had an odd way of making it not seem to matter after a while, it fucking mattered now. My hunger for her grew until I was all at once starving.

So, I nodded, prying my lips away from her neck. "You'd better unlock that door fast," I teased. "Or we're not making it off the porch."

"Not sure the neighbors would like that all that much," she teased right back, taking my hand and moving up the stairs backward.

"The neighbors would understand." My eyes never left hers. The spell she had over me was so great, so powerful.

She laughed, leading me toward the door. "The neighbors would call the cops."

"Yeah, maybe, but only because they'd be jealous." Carnal intent took control as I pressed her back to the door, caging her in with my arms and pressing the strength of my dick against her once again. I lowered my mouth to her ear, smelling her hair and tasting her skin, before adding, "And I'd happily let Officer Kinney slap the cuffs on me to hear you scream my name loud enough for them to hear."

She shuddered, releasing a hot breath against my cheek. "I think I'd rather have you to myself all night than let you sleep at the police station with Patrick."

"Then, like I said, you'd better open that damn door."

I was quick to capture her lips once more before backing away, reluctantly giving her the space to find her keys in her bag and unlock the front door. I leaned against the doorframe, unable to keep my eyes off her. Unable to believe that this was the same girl I'd protected years ago. The same girl I'd held close to my heart and written letters to for all those years I was held from society. It had to all mean something, right? It had to mean *something* that I would find myself here, that we would allow our feelings to grow until they reached this turbulent, pivotal point in which I could hardly look at her without wanting to explode.

It was always meant to be her.

The thought struck swiftly, kicking my heart with an intuitive truth that took my filthy, dirty mind and flipped it upside down, to bring forth that sensitive guy she believed I was because of my books and love of reading. But it was the truth, wasn't it?

Ray and I ... Rain and Soldier ...

We were always meant to be. And if it couldn't have happened that one night when we were teenagers, then fate had seen to it to bring us back together in adulthood, to take our trauma and grief and hardship and somehow, someway, make it better.

She pushed the door open and met my eyes as she took my hand to bring me inside. "What?" she asked, smiling as the house enveloped us in its hushed darkness. "Why are you looking at me like that?"

"Like what?" I asked, pushing the door shut and locking it behind me.

"Like you're seeing me for the first time all over again," she replied, wrapping both hands around one of mine, taking me down the hallway to a room I'd never been to before.

"Maybe I am."

The hallway was too dark. I could no longer make out her features or expression, but I felt her. I felt her hands; I felt her presence. I felt the warmth and need charging through the sliver of space that separated us on the short walk to her room, where she pushed the door open and released me from her grasp. A shred of light came in through the window, silhouetting her figure in its gentle glow as she wasted no time in sliding her hands over her breasts and belly and thighs to grip the hem in her grasp and pull it up and over her head.

"What do you see now?" she asked, her voice low and husky, as she stepped out of her heels and moved deliberately toward the bed in nothing but her bra and panties.

My heart hammered wildly—a pathetically nervous reminder that it had been ages since I'd been with a woman. That this was my first time alone in one's bedroom. That this was the only time I'd ever felt something for someone I was about to sleep with. And thank God it had to be her. Thank God it was Rain.

"What do I see?" I parroted, entering the room and stalking toward her as my fingers painstakingly undid the buttons of my shirt.

She nodded as she met the mattress and stepped onto it, resting on her knees.

"I see my hope," I answered, letting the shirt drop to the floor. "I see my dreams." I undid my pants and pushed them down low on my hips. "I see my salvation and redemption."

My hands reached for her, and hers, for me, and I framed her face with my palms. We lay together, and I worried I'd crush her beneath my weight, but she didn't protest. Instead, she welcomed me, opening her thighs wide and inviting my hips to nestle comfortably against hers. Calling me home to her warmth.

I found her gaze as I pressed deeper, firmer, harder against her, stopped from entering only by a couple of scraps of flimsy cloth. I was certain the closeness was torture, but then, fuck, if I were to eventually find myself in Hell, maybe torture wouldn't be so bad.

"I see the stars," I continued, rolling against her gently, moving like the spilling waves against Connecticut's rocky shore. "I see the way they pierce the darkness with light, making the night beautiful when it would otherwise be haunting and terrible."

Her lips parted with a hushed sob, and her hands moved between our bodies to free my weighted erection and graze her fingertips along its length. I hung my head, hiding the humiliation of my shivering impatience. To feel her touching me now reminded me of when I had been young—horny and inexperienced and too fucking eager for my own good. I was going to embarrass myself—I knew it—and I wasn't proud of it. But, holy fuck, if she kept touching me like that—gripping and moving her hand just right—I was going to blow before I could get inside her.

"Look at me," she whispered, pulling her soft panties to the side and guiding my body to the entrance of hers.

Shame be damned, I did as she'd commanded. My eyes found hers in the hazy dark, and I sank into the wet, hot apex of her thighs in a movement so devastatingly slow that all I could do was hold my breath to keep the moment from ending too soon.

"Oh my God," I groaned, my voice choked and my chest tight.

"Are you okay?"

She lifted her hands to frame my face, and I couldn't help but grunt a strangled laugh.

"I should be asking you that."

I knew what intimacy was like for her. How awful and deranged her toxic relationship with sex had been. I should've been more attentive. I should have been more present.

So, I found my voice and asked, "Are *you* okay?"

Fuck, I was light-headed. I lowered my forehead to hers, remaining still and just settling. Finding my breath. Calming my heart. Getting used to her body and what it was to be with her in completion.

"I'm fine," she said as if she was surprised, letting her hands roam the length of my chest. "I'm more than fine. I'm … God, you feel so good."

"You're sure?"

"I've never been more sure of anything in my life."

Her hips rose, pulling me in further, and I responded by moving against her. Finding a gentle rhythm with gritted teeth and a prayer that I could just hold on for a while longer.

"Fucking hell," I gasped as that prayer went ignored and unanswered.

It was building too quickly, even as slow as we were moving. My breath hitched; my muscles tensed. I tried to still our bodies for just a moment, just to let the urgency die, but Ray shook her head.

"It's okay," she whispered, stroking her hands over my neck and chest. "Just let it go."

And as if she alone commanded the functions of my body, I did in a way that was simultaneously beautiful and so fucking powerful that I gasped on a cry that would've been mortifying had I the capacity to think beyond how it felt to be with her, inside her, one with her in every meaning of the word. And if that were to be the only time it would happen, I absolutely would've felt like an asshole for lasting all of three minutes. But as I collapsed beside her, shuddering and panting and relishing in the beauty of being fucking alive, I knew without a doubt in my mind that this was the first time of many. I'd get my chance to make it up to her, and, dammit, I would.

"What do you see now?" she asked softly, brushing the hair off my forehead. Not at all perturbed by my embarrassing impression of a pubescent boy.

"Fuck, Ray," I murmured, only half awake and barely able to pry my lids apart. But I did, opening my eyes to gaze into hers, and I smiled sheepishly. "Right now ... I see everything."

***

There were things I used to dream about. Having a wife, having a house, having a family—things that seemed more likely to be a forever fantasy than to ever become my reality, especially when I'd spent such a sizable chunk of my life locked up. Everything behind those concrete walls seemed far-fetched and impossible, but, man, I would dream, and I'd wonder what kind of husband I would be. What kind of dad.

I liked to imagine I'd be like Grampa—full of unconditional love and never-ending devotion for the people in his life. He never had a lot of money to express that love and devotion though, so he showed me in other ways. Taking me fishing. Reading me stories before bed. Making me a good, filling breakfast every chance he had. Those were the things I loved about him, and those were the things I missed the most.

And that was what I thought about now, the morning after Ray and I'd had sex for the first time, as I made her a big breakfast of scrambled eggs, bacon, and home fries. The pans on the stove sizzled, adding an extra note to the music playing from the speaker wirelessly connected to her phone, and I remembered mornings just like this from my youth. Except in those memories, it was Grampa doing the cooking, wearing nothing but his pajama pants on a warm spring day, while Gramma sat at the table, watching him with undying adoration and singing along to the songs she played.

"It's nice to be waited on for once," Ray commented, her chin propped up in the palm of her hand.

Elvis's "Can't Help Falling in Love" began to play as I glanced over my shoulder.

"Well, get used to it," I replied with a grin.

"Oh, I will. Especially if you insist on doing it shirtless. That's even more appreciated."

I turned off the stove; loaded our plates with fresh, hot food; and brought them to the table. Ray couldn't have looked happier at the sight of a meal she hadn't had to cook, and I made a silent vow to cook for her more often. Or, hell, all the time, if she'd let me.

Steam billowed from both our plates, the food too hot to eat, and with Elvis encouraging me to do something else I remembered Grampa doing with Gramma, I scooped Ray's hand in mine and pulled her from the table.

Then, we danced. And I knew I wasn't good at it— I'd never danced with a girl before, unless you counted Gramma—but that didn't matter when she smiled at me and I sang those infamous words to her, and we were both so wrapped up in the moment that neither of us heard the front door opening.

"Hey, honey, we're—"

"Hey, Mom! I'm—"

Two voices began to speak at once, and both stopped abruptly at the sight of Ray and me dancing in her kitchen. She spun away from me quickly, startled by the intrusion, then clapped her hands to her chest and laughed, beside herself.

"Oh my God, you guys scared me!" she exclaimed as Noah and Ray's mother walked warily toward us.

Noah's eyes were on me the whole time. A look of betrayal heavy in his darkened gaze.

"What are you guys doing?" he asked accusingly, putting his hands on the back of Ray's chair and eyeing the plates of food.

"We were actually about to sit down and eat," his mom replied, acting like the moment wasn't heavy with suspicion.

I cleared my throat, suddenly self-conscious of not having a shirt on. It wasn't like Noah hadn't seen me shirtless before—I had no shame, and it was my preference when doing work on the house or yard—but right now, in this setting … I might as well have been naked.

"Would you guys like any? There's some left on the stove," I said, gesturing toward the pans.

"I'd love some. It smells great in here," Ray's mom said with a smile that was growing more aware by the second. "But first, Ray, can I talk to you for a minute?"

The tone of her voice said this was a conversation meant to be had alone, and with the quickly shot glances in my direction, I had a feeling I knew what—or who—it would be about.

Ray threw an apologetic look in my direction before ushering her mother down the hall to the bedroom I had just spent the night in. But the thing about our houses— hers and mine—was, they weren't very big, and the soundproofing wasn't the most efficient. And although she and her mother whispered, in the quiet enveloping the rest of the house, I could easily make out bits and pieces of their hushed conversation.

"… sure … this?"

"… don't … worry … good person."

"I … know … you're right … but … prison … past."

I rolled my lips between my teeth, staring at the plates of food growing colder by the second on the table. Then, I noticed Noah with his hands still clamped on the back of the chair. The kid wasn't a toddler, nor was he an idiot. He knew what was going on, and if I was going to stay in his good graces—and, dammit, I wanted to—I had to smooth things over. Make sure he was okay. Get his blessing or some shit.

"Hey."

He hardly lifted his gaze to mine. "What?" The bite in his tone nearly made me flinch.

"I think they're talking about me," I whispered, keeping my voice low.

Noah barely nodded. "Yeah."

"Good things, I hope."

He shrugged. "Maybe."

Stop beating around the damn bush. "Hey, um … I hope you're okay with …" I threw a hand toward the hallway. "You know … your mom and me. I just"—I took that hand and gripped the back of my neck with it—"I like her a lot. And we … I don't know if you know this, but we kinda go way back, and—"

Noah shut me up by abruptly lifting his head and meeting my gaze. "Why wouldn't I be okay with you dating my mom?"

"I … well, um … I don't really know. I just thought—"

"You should've told me," he spat out, shining light on the depth of his betrayal. "It wouldn't have made me mad. I dunno why you didn't just *tell* me."

I imagined the situation from his point of view. Walking in on your friend, shirtless and slow dancing with your mother. It wasn't that he didn't give us his blessing. It was that he hated being left in the dark.

"I'm sorry, buddy."

"Whatever," he grumbled, dropping his glare back to the table. "You probably never wanted to be my friend anyway. You just wanted Mom."

"Hey." I pushed off the counter and hurried to drop into the chair beside where he stood. I looked ahead at him and his downcast gaze. "Look at me for a second."

He could only flick his eyes in my direction before looking away again. Maybe I should've put on a shirt before deciding to talk to him.

"Even if your mom wasn't in the picture, I would still be your friend. You understand me?"

"Yeah, right."

"I'm serious right now, Noah. You were the first person in this town to really see me for who I am, and I will never forget that."

He shrugged and rolled his eyes away.

"Man, you're the coolest kid I've ever known, and you're my best pal. Nothing's changing that, okay?"

Seconds ticked by, and Noah remained stone-faced. Ray and her mom finally emerged from her room, announcing happily that they were ready to eat. But instead of doing the gentlemanly thing and making Ray's mother a plate, I continued to watch Noah, waiting for his response.

Had I really fucked this up so bad, simply by being with his mom? I wouldn't take back a second of last night, not for anything. But was it so impossible to have both his friendship and Ray's affection? Was I too greedy to expect that I could?

He eyed me warily, studying my every move. Defensive and aware. His eyes flicked toward his

251

mother, already beginning to casually eat, like nothing out of the ordinary was going on. He swallowed, and I realized he was shaking. His hands trembled in fists at his sides, and another revelation hit me. One I knew well.

He's scared. He's afraid he can't protect her.

Noah had never known his mother to be with a man who didn't hurt her. He had witnessed it probably more times than I could even imagine. God, I couldn't even pretend to know what that kid must've seen—but I had seen my own share of shit regarding my own mother. I had felt helpless more times than I could count, I had felt desperate and hopeless, constantly trying to find ways to make it better, and the last thing in the world I wanted to do was make him feel the same way.

"Are you guys gonna eat?" Ray asked, digging into her scrambled eggs before volleying her eyes between Noah and me. Then, she scowled. "What's going on? Noah, what's wrong?"

Noah shook his head. "Nothing." Then, he hurried toward the couch and dropped onto it like a sack of potatoes. Crossing his arms and scowling toward the blank TV screen.

Ray stared at her son, stunned and taken aback. "What the heck? Noah, what's—"

"I got this," I interrupted gently, holding up a finger to ask for a second alone as I followed Noah into the adjacent living room.

He didn't even look at me as I approached and crouched in front of him.

"I'm not gonna hurt her," I said quietly, hoping Ray or her mother couldn't hear in that little house without adequate soundproofing. This was between us. "And I'm not gonna hurt you either."

He lifted his worried gaze to mine. "You swear?"

I laid a hand over my heart. "Buddy, you and your mom are the best things to happen to my life in a very, very long time—hell, maybe ever. And I swear I would rather die than hurt either of you."

He tightened his arms to his chest and loosened the scowl on his face, making way for the panic and worry. "Good, 'cause I-I don't think I could actually beat you up, but I'd try."

It was my turn to scowl. "You try to fight for your mom?"

His head jittered in a nod. "Sometimes," he muttered.

Judging from the shame touching his downturned eyes and lips, I'd say he wasn't very good at it.

"How 'bout I teach you how to kick my ass?" I asked, fighting the urge to clench my own fists. "Just in case."

Noah's face was quick to shift from helpless to hopeful in a matter of seconds as his gaze jolted back to mine. "You'd do that?"

"I told you I'd do anything to keep you guys safe, didn't I? And if that means teaching you to knock me on my ass, then you got it," I replied, standing up and offering him my hand. "But let's eat first."

CHAPTER

EIGHTEEN

UPWARD SPIRAL

If someone were to analyze my life from the very start, they'd probably say I had been destined for failure. That no matter how hard my grandparents had tried, things were inevitably going to go south for me, given the circumstances with my mother and the shit she got herself into.

A self-fulfilling prophecy, they'd say when I started tumbling down that dark and twisted path of selling drugs.

And I thought, if I hadn't ended up in prison, they probably would've been right. Because no matter how good my intentions and heart might have been, that road I was on never would've taken me anywhere good. Hell, if I hadn't been locked up, there was a good chance I would've been dead by now, killed in a deal gone wrong or some shit like that. I never would've been given the chance for redemption. I never would've met Harry, I never would've gotten a job at The Fisch Market, and I never would've met Ray again or her son.

Needless to say, my downward spiral had officially been turned around the moment entered that barb wired fence. And right now, thanks to my second chance in River Canyon, life was definitely on an upswing.

A couple of nights a week, after I came home from the grocery store and did some work on the house, Noah would come over to hang out for a while, and I would teach him how to defend himself. I had no professional training, and I definitely had the advantage of size on my side. But while I couldn't guarantee he wouldn't get his ass kicked in a fight, I was confident he'd at least get in a couple of decent shots—or make a solid attempt at trying.

Most weeknights, I ate dinner with Ray and Noah. Sometimes, Ray cooked, and sometimes, I did. A couple of times, Noah even took a stab at throwing a meal together. Afterward, we would watch a movie or play a board game together before Noah showered and went to bed while Ray and I made out on the couch.

On the weekends, Noah went to his grandparents' house, and Ray and I went on our dates. Eating dinner, going for walks, having sex that very quickly began to feel like making love, and sleeping in each other's arms until the sun came up.

Routine had settled in—a good one—and it struck me one day, as I walked into the grocery store to discover that Howard had finally moved the Produce sign, that life was truly, without a doubt, good.

Finally.

"Where did they put the canned beets?" Helen Kinney, mother to Officer Kinney, muttered to herself that same day, wandering down the aisle pushing a cart. "They were right over here a couple of weeks ago. So, where did—"

I looked up from mopping up a box of shattered sauce jars and pointed to the left. "Oh, all canned vegetables were moved to aisle four."

She turned and offered a grateful smile. "Thank you so much, Soldier," she said in her melodic Irish accent. "Why'd they have to go and move everythin' around?"

I shrugged and leaned against the mop handle. "To make your life a little more difficult, obviously," I teased.

She laughed lightheartedly. "Certainly feels that way!"

Then, with a wave of her hand, she was off, heading toward aisle four. I got back to my mopping as Mrs. Greta Montgomery tottered down the aisle I was working on.

Now, Mrs. Montgomery was a tough cookie. She was older than sand and bore the resemblance of a turtle with a hunched back, which only made her short stature even shorter. She was also a cranky old woman who didn't lower her guard easily to newcomers. She didn't trust me, and she made no secret of that by how she pointed her sour expression in my direction.

"I hope you're changing the water in that bucket," she said, jabbing a knobby finger toward the bucket at my feet. "If there's one thing I hate at the church, it's when they mop the floor with dirty water."

I was certain there were a thousand things she hated more, but I wasn't about to say so. I'd won plenty of fights in my time, but I wasn't sure I could win against her.

"I'll be changing it as soon as I'm done cleaning up this mess," I promised, giving her my biggest grin.

"What's the point of mopping if you're just going to use dirty water? Might as well not clean at all."

"Couldn't agree more."

"I feel the same way about that Facebook," she went on, moving along and pushing the cart past me. "What's the point of yammering away on there when you can just call someone?"

I shrugged. "I don't have Facebook, so I couldn't say."

She stopped to glance at me with studious eyes. "You're not on the World Wide Web?"

I stifled a snort as I lifted one shoulder in another shrug. "Not really."

"How do you talk to people then?"

"I call or text all the people I care to talk to," I replied. "Although, to be honest with you, most of the people I want to keep in touch with live here anyway, so …"

"What about family?"

"Don't have family."

She scoffed, shaking her head. "Everyone has family."

"I don't. My grandparents are dead, no aunts or uncles or cousins."

Her scowl might've softened just a little as she asked, "What about your parents? Siblings?"

I pulled in a deep breath before replying, "I never knew my father, I'm better off not knowing my mom, and I'm an only child."

"Hmm." She looked away, studying her bony fingers clutching the handle of the cart. "Everyone deserves family."

I nodded. "I agree. But they weren't a part of the plan for me, I guess."

She huffed another contemplative sound as she nodded. Then, she stared right into my eyes and asked, "Do you like banana bread?"

The unexpected question left me taken aback as I nodded. "Yeah, I do. Haven't had it in a long time, but—"

"Stop by my house later if you'd like some. I just baked a few loaves."

And just like that, she was wandering off again and leaving me to finish the mopping. I couldn't help but smile to myself, feeling like I'd finally made some headway with the old crone, when she stopped abruptly and turned around.

"And remember what I said about mopping with dirty water!"

I snorted and lifted my mouth in a lopsided grin. "I have a feeling you'll never let me forget."

***

"Soldier!" Howard greeted me as I headed back inside after helping Marjorie Bush load her car with her grocery bags.

"Yeah?"

"You wanna come into my office for a second?"

There was a long list of things I'd prefer to do over spending any time in Howard's office. The guy was nice enough—I mean, he had offered me a job, experience unknown, and I couldn't forget that—but, man, his office always smelled like onions and egg salad, and having any kind of conversation with him was about as exciting as watching the hands of a clock tick away the hours. But he was my boss, and he knew I wouldn't say no, onion stench and all, so I nodded.

"Yeah, sure. Hold on a sec," I said before hurrying over to purple-haired Kylie, wife of local music legend Devin O'Leary, who was having one hell of a time trying to reach a sack of flour off the top shelf.

I grabbed it for her, no problem, and she returned the favor with a grateful smile.

"I was ready to climb the shelves." She laughed, her cheeks pinking beneath the warm overhead lights. "Shopping always sucks when Devin's not around."

Devin was a couple of inches shorter than me at six-five, which was nothing to scoff at. The one time I had the pleasure of meeting the guy, he'd laughed good-naturedly before graciously handing over the title of Tallest Guy in Town.

"You don't have to climb anything. Just yell for me, and I'll be there," I replied, already taking a step backward to head in the direction of Howard's office.

"Thanks, Soldier."

Kylie lifted her hand in a slight wave, and I turned with a nod of my head, then hurried toward the door at the back of the store, already open and waiting for my arrival.

Howard was sitting at his desk and gestured to the chair across from his. "Come. Sit."

Now, I hadn't held down many jobs in my life—not including neighborhood drug dealer, of course. But the ones I'd had, I was good at, and I'd never gotten fired from any of them. Grampa had taught me to work hard, to treat even the most demoralizing jobs as a privilege, and to be the best at whatever my title happened to be. That was the exact work ethic I'd applied to my months at The Fisch Market, and I wasn't lying when I said it was my favorite job I had ever had.

But right now, it sure as hell felt like I was being fired.

"Should I close the door?" I asked warily, entering the small room and hesitating beside the offered chair.

He swished a dismissive hand through the air and shook his head. "No, no, that won't be necessary. Please, sit. Do you like Tootsie Rolls?"

"Um …" I slowly lowered my ass into the uncomfortable chair. "Sure. They're okay."

"Ah, I love Tootsie Rolls." He opened a desk drawer and pulled out a bag of the chocolate-flavored candy.

"My wife tells me I'm going to rot my teeth out of my head, but, boy, I can't quit."

"Sir, of all the bad habits you could have, bingeing on Tootsie Rolls is definitely one of the better ones."

He pursed his lips to blowfish proportions as he slowly nodded and unwrapped a piece of his personal kryptonite. Then, after he popped it into his mouth, he clasped his hands on the desk and leaned forward.

Shit. I had never gotten fired before, but he definitely looked like a guy about to do some firing.

I glanced toward the open door to watch Tess O'Dell stroll by with her daughters, and I wondered if Howard wanted to humiliate me by canning my ass in front of all these people I'd grown to like a lot.

"Soldier …"

Fuck. Here we go.

I took a deep breath, gathered my dignity, and faced him like a man.

"When Harry asked me to do him a favor and give you a job, I had no idea what to expect or if I was going to regret my decision. He swore I wouldn't, but"—he lifted one shoulder in a shrug—"you can understand why I was skeptical."

I cleared my throat of all foreboding and replied, "I'm glad you took a chance on me." Maybe sucking up would spare me my job.

"So am I."

Wait. What?

"Harry neglected to tell me that you're one of the hardest-working guys on this planet—or at least that I've seen. You go above and beyond, performing tasks you're not being paid for, getting to know the customers, building relationships with them …" He grabbed another Tootsie Roll and began to twist off its wrapper. "You're a rare find, Soldier."

"Thank you, sir," I answered, still unsure of what he was getting at.

"Harry told me you got your GED and a degree in business."

I swallowed, nodding. "I did, yeah."

"What do you say we do something with that degree?" His eyes met mine as the candy flew into his mouth.

I tipped my head curiously, still unsure of where this conversation was going. "What did you have in mind?"

"I'd like you to fill the position of assistant manager."

I wasn't sure I had heard him correctly. Christy Scott had just walked by the door with her excited young son, so it was possible the words had somehow gotten muddled in the noise.

"Wait. I'm sorry, what did you say?"

Howard smiled fondly, like I was the most adorable thing he'd ever seen—and I knew that wasn't true when he had a picture of his cute grandkids sitting right in front of me. "How would you like to be assistant manager?"

The words weren't computing. The possibility that, after only a handful of months, I'd be offered such a prestigious position at his store seemed unlikely, given the circumstances of my situation. In my head, the guy wasn't even supposed to *like* me, let alone hand me a job like that so soon, and I kept expecting for him to laugh, tell me he was just pulling my leg, and proceed to down the rest of those Tootsie Rolls while I slunk back to my broom and dustpan.

But he didn't.

Well, except for the Tootsie Roll part.

He unwrapped another.

I cleared my throat. "Are you sure about this?"

He nodded adamantly. "I wouldn't be asking if I wasn't."

My heart was frantically beating, threatening to explode with every slam against my chest. "What would I have to do?"

Howard unwrapped another Tootsie Roll and popped it into his mouth. "Oh, we'll go over it, but don't worry. I know without a doubt that it's nothing you can't handle."

Disbelief forced a laugh from my chest as I shook my head and inhaled the stale scent of eggs and onions.

"Can I still sweep the floor?" I asked.

Howard's laughter joined mine as he said, "I didn't expect you'd still want to, but, Soldier, if it makes you happy ... sure. You can still sweep the floor."

***

On my break, I burst through the door of The Fisch Market like a kid busted out of the building on the last day of school and hurried down to the library. Ray was manning the front counter, helping to check out a mother and her young daughter, when I walked through the door.

"Hey!" she greeted me with a grin until I pushed through the swinging counter-height door to bend and wrap my arms around her waist and bury my face against her neck. "Soldier …" She laughed with a touch of embarrassment, scanning another book and placing it in the woman's cloth bag. "You're not supposed to be back here."

"I know. I'm sorry," I muttered against her neck before inhaling her fresh floral scent and letting go. I hurried back to the other side of the door, where I belonged, and said, "I got promoted."

Her eyes widened at the announcement. "Oh my God, really?"

I nodded, struggling to keep the need to bounce around bottled up tight. "You're looking at the new assistant manager."

The woman—I thought she might've worked at the bakery—turned to me with a fond smile. "Congratulations, Soldier!" she cheered before taking her bag of books in one hand and the hand of her little girl in the other.

I thanked her before they had a chance to walk away, and then it was just Ray and me. Her eyes were on me, reflecting more pride than I'd ever seen in my damn life.

"We have to celebrate," she declared, and that was how we found ourselves at the diner that night.

It was rare for us to go out to eat during the week and even rarer for Noah to accompany us on a school night. But exceptions had to be made, and it was a special occasion.

"So, you aren't gonna clean the store anymore?" Noah asked as he brought his burger to his mouth.

I shook my head and swallowed a bite of my grilled cheese. "No, I'm still cleaning the store. But that's by choice."

He wrinkled his nose and stared at me like I'd lost my mind. "You *like* to clean?"

"I actually do."

He glanced at his mom, who glanced back at him and said, "I know. He's out of his mind."

I laughed before taking another bite of my sandwich. It was hard for people to understand how I could enjoy cleaning. I mean, I got it—why would anyone *like* to handle dirt and grime, especially when it wasn't their own? And believe me, there wasn't much about scrubbing a filthy bathroom I could call desirable. But the results were, and that was exactly the point.

When I mopped and swept and polished the dirtiness away, I could stand back and admire the beauty that had always been hidden underneath. Sure, sometimes, there wasn't much I could do to give a dirty space a brand-new shine. The floor was stained, the carpet was sometimes worn and mottled, but, hey, weren't we all? And did that mean we didn't deserve to be fresh and renewed every now and then? Of course not.

"It's rewarding," I said, giving them the abridged version. "And cathartic."

"It's a *chore*," Ray countered, her eyes dancing with flirtation. Her smile teasing.

I plucked a fry from her plate and pointed it at her. "Well, someone's gotta do it"—I popped it into my mouth and grinned as I jabbed my thumb at my chest—"and that someone might as well be me."

"You enjoy yourself." She snorted, her eyes twinkling with jest. "And while you're at it, would you clean my bathroom? Because I freakin' *hate* doing that."

"Baby, I'd clean your whole damn house if you asked me to."

Noah's eyes widened with hope and desperation. "Wait, wait, wait … does that mean I don't have to vacuum or do dishes anymore?"

I shrugged, eyeing Ray with a raised brow and a smirk. "Hey, if your mom says it's okay …"

He grabbed at his mother's arm and tugged at her shirt. "Mom, do I still get an allowance if Soldier does all my chores?"

Ray glowered at me with a threat that said, *You're sleeping alone tonight,* as she replied, "Nobody is doing your chores for you, Noah."

He pouted as she brushed him off and nudged her chin toward his burger.

"Now, finish up. We have to get back home soon. Don't forget that you have school in the morning."

With a grumble, he took a begrudging bite. I polished off the rest of my plate while keeping my eyes on them both. A bolt of awe struck my heart as Ray bumped her elbow against Noah's ribs, and when he glanced at her, she smiled adoringly, and he couldn't help but smile back.

This little mother-son duo was incredible. They had been through war. They had seen things I couldn't fathom, experienced things I wouldn't wish on anybody, and yet they remained strong and ironclad. Weathering every storm that came at them, unwilling to succumb to the damage. They had done it together, proving they didn't need anyone else, and yet, somehow, they saw me as worthy of being included.

Out of the corner of my eye, I saw Officer Kinney approaching as his brood left through the front door. He smiled and waved when he saw he'd gotten my attention, then offered his hand for me to shake.

"Patrick," I said, accepting the gesture.

"Soldier." He waved at Ray and Noah. "Hey, guys. Sorry to interrupt your dinner. I just wanted to give my congratulations on the job upgrade."

"Thank you," I said, grateful for his acknowledgment and friendship. "Word gets around fast, huh?"

He chuckled at that. "Small towns. You know how it goes."

"I do." I nodded fondly.

"Ya know …" He hesitated as his face took on a somber expression, biting his lip and slipping his hands into his front pockets. "I'll be honest. I wasn't sure what to expect of ya when ya moved in. I liked ya enough after we met, but …" He shrugged and offered an apologetic grimace.

"I get it, man," I said, unsure of where he was going with this.

"Given your past and family history, I'm sure ya understand."

Family history?

I smiled as the gears in my head creaked to life while not wanting to dig too deep into the past with Noah present. "It's cool, man. You and I are all good—you know that."

"Anyway, I just wanted to say, you've been a great addition to this town. And I'm not just sayin' that as ... ya know ... Mr. Cop. I say that as a *friend*. We're lucky to have ya. I truly mean that."

I was aware of the stigma of a man getting publicly emotional, especially in the presence of another man. But the clenching of my throat couldn't be fought as I nodded and said, "Thanks, Patrick. But honestly"—my eyes flitted between Ray and her son—"I think I'm the lucky one here."

***

Ray didn't actually make me sleep alone that night. Instead, after sending Noah to bed, we made out on the couch before moving into her bedroom, where she locked the door and rode my body with her head thrown back and her nails piercing my chest. And when we were both sated and exhausted, she tucked herself beneath my arm and curled up against my body and asked if I'd stay.

I had never stayed over with Noah in the house.

"Are you sure? What about—"

She yawned, nuzzling her cheek against my chest. "He knows we sleep together, Soldier. He's not oblivious."

"No, I know. But—"

"If *you're* uncomfortable, that's okay. But don't leave to protect Noah from something he's already aware of.

And honestly, we both feel better when you're here anyway."

I furrowed my brow, staring into the darkness as my arm tightened around her small body. "He said that?"

Her head softly bobbed against my chest. "We talked about it the other day. You make us feel safe."

She didn't need to clarify who they felt safe from. *Seth.* Their personal bogeyman. And if I made them feel better about him forever lurking in the shadows, unknowing when he'd come back—if he *ever* came back—then I'd be hard-pressed to ever let her sleep alone again.

The house was still as Ray's breathing softened. She drifted off toward slumber, and I closed my eyes to follow her into our dreams. But Seth lingered in my head—threatening me with nightmares and silent sinister promises to be back one day—and then there was Officer Kinney's voice …

"Your past and family history …"
What the hell was he referring to?

I knew my personal history. I was the only one in my family with a record. Gramma and Grampa had worked so diligently to keep my mother clean in the eyes of the law even if her body wasn't clean of the drugs and booze. They had hidden her wrongdoings, they had protected her, and while some might've judged them for what they'd done, I knew it had all come out of a place of love—for their daughter and also for me.

But then what the hell had Patrick meant by that? Surely, I would know if my mom had been arrested or incarcerated at some point—right?

The easiest thing would be to ask Officer Kinney—I knew that. But I also didn't want the discussion to be opened to other things I didn't care to talk about, things that didn't matter—or so I thought.

And why bother when I already had the World Wide Web at my fingertips?

Thanks again, Harry.

Carefully, I lifted my arm from Ray's body and reached for the nightstand to grab my phone. After opening the web browser, I typed in my mother's name: *Diane Mason.*

Millions upon millions of results popped up. Too many to weed through.

I refined my search: *Diane Mason, Connecticut.*

The first several listings were for obituaries. Another was a lawyer's office, and another was a real estate agency. But then there was the eighth listing down, and that one snagged my attention.

An article titled, "Man Dies of Fentanyl Overdose, Friend Arrested for Murder."

Murder. I swallowed as my brows drew together. *This* was what people found when searching my family name. Sure, the article was dated back to the day after Billy's death, and nobody knew then that I'd only be convicted of manslaughter. But still, the word triggered a nauseous reaction in my gut, and Billy's mom suddenly came to mind.

Does she still believe I'm a murderer? Even all these years later?

Of course she does. I took her only child away from her.

Ray slept soundly beside me as I pinched the bridge of my nose, fighting the urge to cry.

We had all made our choices. We had all made stupid, life-altering mistakes. I understood this now, but that didn't quell the constant ache in my heart. I'd gotten used to it after all this time; it had become a part of who I was. But every now and then, it made itself known, rising above the noise in my head and the good I'd found in life.

I never stopped hating that relentless, nagging pain. I never stopped feeling I deserved it.

Enough. Keep reading.

Air filled my lungs, and I pushed past thoughts of Billy and his heartbroken mother. I skimmed the brief account of Billy's untimely demise and my arrest on the side of the road that February night over a decade ago, looking for my mother's name. I read past the comments from Billy's dad, a firsthand account from a witness, and then there it was.

I sat up in bed as I read, *Soldier's mother, Diane Mason—no stranger to being in trouble with the law— had no comment to make at this time.*

"What the hell?" I muttered to myself, staring at the words as if I could will them with my mind to offer more info.

My fingers thrust into my hair as my earlier questions were multiplied. What trouble? What had she done? I mean, shit ... my mother had been taking her share of drugs for at least as long as I'd been alive and had lost more jobs than I could count. But I had never known her to break the law, and, yeah, okay, thinking about it now, I could see the absurdity in that mindset. Her habitual drug use was in itself against the fucking law. But Patrick Kinney and this reporter from nearly a decade ago wouldn't have known about that or anything else unless she had a record. A record I knew nothing about.

I could just ask him, I thought. *But ... God, I don't want to talk to him about this shit. He just told me how much he liked having me around. I don't want to make him regret that by divulging more info than I need to.*

I tossed my phone to the bed and dragged the palm of my hand over my face as I considered whatever options I had that didn't involve going to the police.

Then, Ray stirred against my side. "Hey, what's wrong?"

I laid my hand against her hip. "Nothing. Don't worry about it."

"It doesn't seem like nothing."

Grinding the heel of my palm against my eye, I replied, "I'm just thinking about something Patrick said."

"What did he say?" She snuggled closer, turning her head to kiss my chest.

As I ran my fingers through her hair, I brought light to the questionable comment about my family history and told her about the article I'd found, insinuating my mother had a dirtier record than I was aware of. Ray was sleepy, but she listened, nodding her head softly every now and then to let me know she was still awake.

And then, when I was finished, she suggested in a raspy voice, "The library."

"Oh, shit." I didn't know why I hadn't thought of checking the library before. "There might be something in the archives."

"If there was any kind of incident—" She yawned, which only reminded me of how tired I also was, and I yawned myself as she continued, "There might be an article somewhere."

"Huh …" I slowly nodded. "Yeah, I think I'll spend some time in there tomorrow after work."

Ray hummed contentedly. "Good thing I'm the brains and you're the brawn."

"Hey"—I laughed, jostling her as I lay back down— "are you calling me stupid?"

"Not at all, Brawny," she teased, tucking herself back inside my embrace. "Now"—she laid a finger over my lips—"shush and go to sleep with me."

I kissed the tip of her finger and nestled my chin against her shoulder. Then, before anything else had the chance to keep me awake, I fell soundly asleep to the hush of her breathing.

CHAPTER

NINETEEN

DAVID

My first day as assistant manager was a lot like any other day. Except my name tag read a different title, and when I walked into work, Howard told me I could roll my sleeves up if I'd like.

"You're sure?" I asked, startled by the abrupt change in tune, even as I was already shoving my long sleeves up toward my elbows.

"Soldier, it's nearly eighty degrees out there today, and it's only going to get hotter. Wear a T-shirt tomorrow."

He didn't even bat an eye at the tattoos blanketing my arms—random works of both decent and amateurish art I'd acquired before and during prison—and I couldn't tell if he never truly gave a crap about them or if he'd just gotten used to the idea. Either way, I was grateful to finally cool off, even as his wife came walking into the store, surprised to find me showing off my ink.

"Has Howard seen this yet?" Mayor Fischer asked, scowling until her face looked like a pug's.

"Yeah, he just gave me the okay," I said, hauling a box of canned peas onto my shoulder and heading in the direction of aisle four.

Connie followed. "Well, you do know that if anyone finds your … *artwork* offensive, you will have to cover up again. You understand this, yes? As assistant manager, you have a certain image to uphold, and if you cannot or refuse—"

"Mayor," I interjected lightly, turning to face her, "I understand."

Her lips pursed until they resembled a prune as she studied me with wary eyes. Then, she nodded once. "Glad to hear it." With that, she turned on her heel and walked away like a woman on a mission—as always.

And then the morning dragged by, even as I kept busy sweeping the floor and stocking the shelves and helping Mrs. Montgomery read the labels on four different boxes of salted crackers. All I could think about was getting down to the library on my lunch break and searching through the newspaper articles on file, hoping I could find any clue about my mother's history. Wild scenarios filled my head as the time passed, everything from bank robbery to arson to money laundering to grand theft auto, even if none of them made sense.

But then again, not much did.

Because how had I not known? How had I not had any kind of inkling that she might have a police record?

Suddenly, everything—my life, my history, my family—felt like a lie before I even knew what the lie might be, and as soon as the clock chimed lunchtime, I told Howard that I might be a little longer than usual and I'd work later if need be to make up for it.

"Whatever you need to do," he said with a friendly smile before I ran out the door and headed down the street to the library to find my girlfriend and whatever secrets lurked in my family's past.

***

Ray loomed over my shoulder as I searched through archives and the internet on one of the library's computers. She held a cup of coffee in hand and took a sip before offering it to me.

"Thanks," I muttered, keeping my eyes on the screen as I gulped it down, then winced at how sweet she liked it to be. There had to be an entire bag of sugar in that mug. "Jesus, your teeth are gonna rot out of your head."

She giggled, taking the cup back and clutching it right to her chest, protecting it as a mother would her child. "That's what my mom always says."

"Yeah, well, she's not wrong." I sucked at my teeth. "I feel like my whole mouth was just sandblasted."

"Oh, stop. It's not that bad."

"Sure … if you don't mind chewing your coffee." I shot a teasing glance over my shoulder.

Ray only laughed before taking a hearty sip and humming with dramatic satisfaction.

Shaking my head, I returned my attention to the computer screen and scrolled through the articles for anything related to a woman named Diane Mason. Anything mentioning drugs. Anything that might point me in the right direction. And even though a lot came up in the search, none of it had anything to do with my mother, and my time was running out before I had to get back to the store.

"Like finding a needle in a haystack," I grumbled as Ray took a seat on my lap. I wrapped my arm around her and sighed, pressing my cheek to her shoulder. "I should've come by later when I had more time."

She frowned sympathetically. "I didn't think it would be so—wait, what's that?"

"What's what?"

Ray pointed at the screen. "Right there."

"*Man dies in accident. Woman arrested on the scene,*" I muttered, reading the headline, then scrolled down further to see a picture of—you guessed it—my mother. "Well, holy shit, this has to be it."

"Your mom is gorgeous," Ray said, gawking at the picture of a much younger version of Diane Mason, one I used to know. The one I'd called Mommy, the one I'd once thought walked on water. "God, you look so much like her."

"Fantastic," I grumbled bitterly, frowning as I read.

A twenty-four-year-old man was killed in a car accident yesterday at the corner of Lake and Shaw. Police say David Stratton was driving the car when it lost control and struck a tree. Also in the car was his

277

girlfriend, Diane Mason (24), who survived the accident but sustained minor injuries. Controlled substances were found in the vehicle following the crash, and Mason was arrested at the scene. Hours later, she was released from police custody after no drugs were found in her system. Legal action will not be pursued.

"Wow," Ray uttered quietly once we were both finished reading. "Her boyfriend was killed. That's so sad."

"Yeah ..."

I tried to resist feeling any kind of empathy toward my mother, but it was hard as I looked at the grainy picture of the totaled car after the wreck that had taken the life of her significant other. She had suffered a major loss, and I hadn't known about it until now. Was that what had sent her down a path of destruction? Could grief have been the culprit?

I sucked in a breath of heavy air, allowing that familiar ache to gnaw away at my heart again, until their ages and the date on the article sank in.

"I was six," I said, thinking out loud. "This was right before Christmas. My grandparents told me she had just gone on one of her little trips, which I eventually assumed meant rehab. But ..." I wiped a hand over my mouth and shook my head. "She'd been in an accident, arrested, and then ..."

"Maybe she went to rehab after that," Ray offered, shrugging.

"Yeah, probably. But she was in a freakin' fatal car crash." I scoffed incredulously. "How the hell did they not say anything to me? I mean, why—"

"You were a *little kid*, Soldier. Maybe ... maybe they didn't want you to be afraid. You said they always protected you from the stuff she was up to, so obviously, they wanted to protect you from this too."

I knew she was right. God, logic told me that she was. Hadn't I been saying it all along? But this newfound knowledge, the reality that my mother had been in a fatal accident when I was six years old, made the thought of simple protection seem so far-fetched and absurd and ... fuck, it was so *cruel*.

What if she had died? Would Gramma and Grampa have even told me?

Of course they would've, I told myself, pressing my white-knuckled fist to my mouth. *Don't be stupid. You know they would've said something if she had died.*

Yeah, but how can you be sure of that now, knowing this? You don't even know how long she was in the hospital. You don't even know what her injuries were. You didn't even know about—

"Stratton," I blurted out too loudly, earning myself a couple of questionable looks from others in the library.

"Huh?" Ray narrowed her eyes at the screen as I sat up higher and pointed at his name.

"Her boyfriend was David *Stratton*. Holy shit."

"I'm not following."

"Hold on." My heart hammered wildly in my chest as I opened up a new browser window and searched his name.

The accident had happened so many years ago, so I wasn't sure anything would come up, but there it was. An obituary for David Murphy Stratton.

Survived by his parents, grandparents, aunts, uncles, cousin, and a younger brother.

"Levi," I said conclusively, jabbing my finger at the screen before thrusting that hand into my hair. "Oh my fucking God. He had to be Levi's brother."

Ray was speechless as she stared at the screen, clutching her coffee mug and sitting still as stone on my lap. Her head began to shake from side to side, disbelief settling in to keep the truth from infiltrating her mind.

"No," she insisted. "That's … Soldier, no, that's …"

But she wouldn't say it was impossible because, clearly, it wasn't. My mother had been involved with Levi's brother, David, who died in a car accident when I was six, and now, my mother was with Levi—or at least the last time I had checked.

"That's so fucked up," I muttered, wiping my palm over my mouth.

"What?"

"She's fucking her dead boyfriend's brother."

"Your mom is *with* Levi?"

I nodded with nausea in my gut and confusion in my head. "The night I got out of prison, I walked in on them going at it on the couch."

Ray's eyes widened as she sucked in a deep breath and shook her head. "Wow … I mean, maybe they're not related. Maybe they're … God, I don't even know."

"Yeah," I murmured, unsure of what to make of all this new information myself. Unsure if there was anything to make of it at all. "Look, I gotta get back to work. Can you do me a favor though?"

Together, we stood from the chair, and she looked up at me, nodding. "Of course. What's up?"

"If you get a chance, find whatever you can about David Stratton. Print it out and bring it home."

***

But as it turned out, there wasn't much to find about David Stratton, other than a couple of brief articles mentioning an arrest here and there for drug possession. He had done time, but how much, I wasn't sure. All I knew was, the guy had had a record, and he had died twenty-five years ago. My mother had been in the car with him, she'd witnessed her boyfriend's death, and now, she was involved with his drug-peddling brother.

It probably meant nothing, I realized, but the wheels in my brain wouldn't stop turning. Conspiracy theories and irrational conclusions kept me from enjoying the dinner I was sharing with Ray and Noah. They chatted about his school day and if he had homework and what they were going to do that weekend. I heard it all, but I couldn't will myself to engage when all I could think about was the night Billy had died and how Levi had smiled as I was being driven away.

What if Levi's problem with me had less to do with me stealing his business and more to do with—

"… Soldier come too?"

The sound of my name pulled me from a thought that already felt wrong and asinine. Noah was looking at

281

me, curious and hopeful, and I bounced my gaze between him and his mom.

"What?" I asked sheepishly, picking up the fork to start eating the meal they'd already finished.

"Um"—Ray rolled her lips between her teeth and eyed me warily—"we were planning on spending Saturday with my family—"

"Do you wanna come?" Noah nearly bounced out of his chair with the question.

I shrugged as I shoveled a heaping forkful of lasagna to my mouth. "Sure. Why not?"

Noah was instantly thrilled while Ray, on the other hand, pursed her lips and eyed me with irritation. Like I'd said the wrong thing.

"I just figured you had stuff to do," she said, her voice coming out in a hurried huff. "And I mean, I didn't expect you'd really *want* to head all the way back to our hometown. Because, you know, my parents still live there."

Her eyes rounded with a message, and I was receiving it loud and clear. She was scared of what would happen if I went back there, and—dare I say it—she was probably worried about us being seen together.

But whatever she was afraid of, I wouldn't let it intimidate me. I wanted to meet her family. I wanted this to feel like the real deal—the realest deal of all—and if that meant rolling into my old stomping grounds with a big *fuck you* sign taped to my forehead for anyone who had a problem with me to see, then so be it.

I was living my life now, and I wouldn't allow the past to control me. Not anymore.

***

Stormy was as inconspicuously beautiful as her sister, but while Ray radiated sunshine, her sister was the physical embodiment of her name with hair blacker than night and a wardrobe to match. Her exterior was that of stone, adorned with black-and-gray tattoos and more piercings than I could count, and her eyes watched me with hardened skepticism. Honestly, I couldn't blame her one bit—even if their parents both seemed to accept me with open arms.

"So, Soldier," Stormy began, folding her arms against the table and ignoring the pizza on her plate, "how long exactly were you locked up?"

"Just a little less than ten years," I answered without hesitation before taking a bite full of pepperoni, sauce, and cheese.

Her thin, tattooed brows lowered with suspicion and guarded curiosity. "You were behind bars for a freakin' *third* of your life? How does that not royally screw someone up?"

"Oh my God, Stormy!" Ray exclaimed from beside me, turning her attention to her older sister. "What the hell is wrong with you?"

Stormy shrugged. "And I'm over here, wondering how you've never considered you could be sleeping with a psychopath."

Noah was quick to come to my defense with a, "Soldier is *not* a friggin' psychopath," as his mother and

283

grandparents all gawked at the big-mouthed goth sitting across from me.

But I didn't react in the way I knew she was looking for. If she was trying to shake me, I wasn't going to let her.

Chris, their father, who had only just met me that morning, let his hand fall to the table with a resounding *thunk*. "Stormy, knock it off right now. Soldier is a guest in this—"

"It's fine, sir," I cut him off, holding up a palm to stop him from continuing to scold his daughter, who I felt had every right to come to her sister's defense. I turned to Stormy with the same stern glare that she held on me, but instead of cold and bitter, mine was—I hoped—warm and assuring. "I promise I've passed my psych evaluations. So, no, I'm not a psychopath."

She slowly lifted the slice of pizza from off the plate, never taking her eyes off me. "Right. That's exactly what a psychopath would say."

"Yeah, probably," I agreed with a resigned nod. "But would a psychopath offer to show you those records? Because I could get my hands on them, if you—"

"Oh my God!" Ray swatted my arm with the back of her hand. "You're not showing her anything. She's just being stupid."

Before anyone else could say anything, Barbara, Ray's mother, put a cork in the conversation by asking her daughters how work was going in their respective fields. Stormy worked at a tattoo shop up in Salem as the resident body piercer, and I snagged the opportunity to warm her up by asking if she could get me any kind of discount.

She snorted at the question and gestured toward the old, faded tattoos on my arms. "Why? You wanna cover some of that crap up? Or do you just need someone to put some new holes into your body?"

I laughed. "Both."

She pursed her lips, continuing to study me with that ice-cold stare, before nodding. "We could probably work something out, if you wanted to take the trip up to Massachusetts."

Ray smiled at her sister's hesitant turn toward more friendly territory. "Maybe we could take a long weekend up there soon." She curled her arm around my bicep. "I mean, if you can get the time off work ..."

"Yeah, I'm sure Howard wouldn't mind giving me a weekend off. I haven't called out of work since I started."

Stormy was slow to smile, but there it was, daring to peek through her rock-solid exterior. "Let me know, and I'll talk to the artists at my shop. I'm sure Blake or Cee could squeeze you in somewhere if you give me enough of a heads-up."

The mood was lightened then when it was determined that the three of us would take a little road trip up north to visit Stormy—something Ray had apparently never done in the years since her sister had moved away from Connecticut. I assumed it had something to do with her being a single mother needing to work a full-time job with little downtime to do things like take vacations and visit her big sister—until I walked out of the house after dinner to stare out toward the cemetery across the street.

Stormy followed. "Hey."

I turned to look down at her, startled by how short she actually was when her toughened demeanor had the ability to look me straight dead in the eye.

"Oh, hey."

She crossed her arms over her chest and leaned against one of the wooden posts holding the roof over our heads. "Look, I'm sorry for being such a bitch."

"It's cool."

"No, it's really not, but okay." She chuffed and turned her attention to the headstones behind a wrought iron fence. "My sister doesn't have the best luck with men. I don't know how much she's told you, but—"

"I know enough," I muttered through a jaw that immediately pulsed with anger and hatred toward a guy I knew wasn't far from where I stood.

Where are you now, Seth?

Are you with Levi? What about Mom?

Do you know I'm right here, practically in your backyard?

I dare you ... I dare any of you to show up and ruin this shit I have now. I fucking dare you.

Stormy grunted and nodded. "Yeah, so you understand why I was a little skeptical when she announced she was bringing home an ex-con to meet the family."

"I absolutely do."

"And here's the other thing." She repositioned her combat boots against the wooden floor. Crossing one leg over the other, locking her arms tighter against her body. "I remember when that guy died. I remember when they arrested you. I was *there*. Rain wasn't, but I *was*. I saw it all happen."

My lips rolled between my teeth as I nodded slowly. It made sense. Stormy was around my age, and if you had grown up in this shithole of a town back in the day, you had either hung out at The Pit—may it rest in Hell— or you hadn't gone anywhere at all.

"I got out of here that summer," she explained. "After what happened, I knew I had to leave, or I never would. So ..." She cleared her throat, as if to wipe away the past that would never truly leave any of us alone. "Anyway, when she told me she was spending time with you, you can see why I wasn't happy about it. Like, I had told her to take Noah and get the hell out of here, and she *did*, but then she goes and starts spending time with the freakin' guy who killed—"

My eyes darted toward hers, and she dropped her apologetic gaze to the porch floor.

"Sorry," she quickly injected. "I know it wasn't on purpose. It's just ... there's fucking ... fucking *Seth*, and now ... *you* ..."

"Hey," I said, not intending to sound harsh and menacing, but I did. Because ... well, I guessed I didn't particularly appreciate being lumped together with a piece of shit who had to force himself on someone to get what he wanted. And when I had Stormy's attention, I added, "I am *not* him."

"No," she replied, nodding as her triple-pierced bottom lip was clamped between her teeth. "I wasn't sure about that before, even after Rain told me what you had done for her ... you know, back then ..." Her gaze volleyed toward my scar, then back to my eyes. "But now, after actually meeting you, I see now."

"See what?"

She cocked her head and stared at me like the answer was obvious before she replied, "That you might not have killed someone intentionally back then, but for her ... you would in a heartbeat."

***

Stormy was intense, and being in her presence was soul-sucking even if I did appreciate her company—especially after getting the conversation on the front porch out of the way. So, after a little time passed, filled with more conversation and dessert, I told Ray I needed to get some more air and thought I'd take a walk across the street to the cemetery. She offered to go with me and admitted she had enjoyed hanging out there when she was younger.

"The dead can't hurt anyone," she said with a melancholy smile.

But even though I rarely turned down her company, I did then. Because truthfully, there was someone—an old friend—I wanted to see, and I didn't want anyone else to witness my collapse, in the event it happened while in *his* presence.

So, I walked across the street alone and remembered that night years ago when I'd dropped her off just a few houses down. I remembered thinking she was so young—"*She's a fucking kid, you asshole.*" Funny how a gap of a few years could matter so much when you were that young. Funny how it didn't matter now. Funny how I couldn't stomach the thought of wanting her then, but wanting her now filled more moments in my day than I could count.

But thoughts and images of want and desire vanished the second I passed through that wrought iron gate and into the cemetery I hadn't visited since shortly after my grandmother's death. I had wanted to see my grandparents' graves when I was younger, but the shame of what I'd been doing prevented me from stepping onto the hallowed ground. The fear of facing their disapproving ghosts had kept me away, and now, I walked past the row I knew they lay in and quietly apologized for not stopping.

"I've already seen you guys before," I told them, as if they might be listening. "And I'll come back. I just have to do this first, okay? I just …"

The truth was, I didn't know where I was going. I hadn't thought to check the directory or ask anyone who might know. But I wandered, scanning the names on the headstones quickly as I passed. Hoping I'd stumble upon the one I was looking for before it got too dark to see without a flashlight—and there was no way in hell I was walking through a cemetery at night.

I could handle a lot of shit, but the thought of being alone and surrounded by dead people creeped me the fuck out.

A half hour quickly passed, and as I turned down another row of graves, I was growing more aware of the setting sun and the need to head back when my eyes fell on an unexpected ghost I should've been more prepared to encounter. But the way we both stopped in our tracks, the way those eyes widened with startled recognition when they landed on mine, and the way that hand pressed against a heart I was surprised to find still beating after all these years ...

I didn't think I could've been prepared for that.

I didn't think I could've ever been prepared for the way my own heart skipped a thousand beats and my eyes stung and burned with a roaring stampede of desperate emotion as I urged my feet to not fucking run to her like a little boy would after being lost for too long.

"Soldier?" Billy's mom asked, surprised, stepping toward me with apprehension.

She hates you.

Don't forget, she hates you.

Don't forget, she wished you were dead instead.

I wouldn't allow my feet to move as I stood there, frozen, at the start of the dirt path. "H-hey," I stammered like an idiot. "Sorry, I-I ..."

I didn't want her knowing I was looking for her son's grave. I didn't want her to be aware that I was about to desecrate his resting place with my presence, knowing damn well she'd never want me within fifteen thousand feet of it when I was the reason he wasn't here right now and living his life.

So, instead of admitting the truth, I said, "I, um ... I was just going for a walk ..."

You really are a fucking idiot.

"Sorry," I hurriedly repeated before turning around with my hands stuffed into my pockets, ready to run the hell away and get back to Ray's parents' house before someone else from the past could jump up and haunt me.

But Billy's mom called after me, stopping me in my tracks once again, "Soldier, no, wait."

I didn't want to turn around and look at the woman I used to wish could've been my mom instead. I didn't want to see that hatred I still remembered so vividly from my sentencing over a decade ago. But I listened to her footsteps approach softly through the dirt as I braced myself for the inevitable backlash, the *how dare you* and *who the hell do you think you are*. I decided to let it happen though. I decided she deserved to give it to me one more time without being surrounded by court officers and a pitying judge. It was the least I could do after the heartache she'd suffered.

But then she asked, "How ... how are you?" Which was so much different than the verbal beating I'd been expecting.

"What?" I dared to glance over my shoulder.

Billy's mom could barely smile with her trembling lips, but she did. "How have you been? I ... I heard you had gotten out, and I w-was hoping I'd see you around, but ..."

What? I could hardly believe the things I was hearing, the things she was saying. How the hell was it possible that this woman, who had hated me so much then, could smile at me now? What tripped-up, screwed-up, fucked-up rabbit hole had I fallen into when I passed through that wrought iron gate?

"Um ... I'm o-okay, I guess. I—"

This felt too wrong. It felt awful and backward to be standing there, feet away from where Billy's corpse was buried, talking to his mother like she hadn't once wished I could trade places with him.

I pulled one hand from my pocket to pinch the bridge of my nose. "I'm sorry. I just ... I don't know what to even s—"

"I'm s-so sorry," she gasped, forcing out a sob and quickly covering her mouth with her palm. "Oh *God*, Soldier, I'm so sorry."

The tears came faster than I could react as Billy's mom crumpled before me. Crying and sobbing into her hands and wailing like a wounded animal. My heart pleaded with my arms to hold her while my brain reminded me relentlessly of the things she'd once said, and I couldn't find the strength to touch her the way I wanted to.

Instead, I pulled a wrinkled napkin from my pocket and handed it to her as I said, "You have no reason to be sorry."

She accepted it, not questioning if it had been used or not, and replied, "Y-yes, I do." She dabbed at her eyes and wiped her sodden face. "I knew you needed me. I-I knew you were alone, and I a-a-abandoned you."

My stomach churned as she spoke the words, as I remembered exactly the way it had felt to be left by her, and still, I shrugged like it didn't matter. "It's okay. I-I deserved—"

"Don't." She pointed a finger at my face, her expression now one of stern sincerity. "Do not say you deserved to ... to ..." She twisted her lips, like she could

292

hardly stand to spit out the words. "To be shunned a-and hated and spoken to like you meant nothing. Because you had meant *the world* to me."

Anguish pressed against my chest, forcing a gasp from my throat. "It-it's in the past." I shook my head, chasing away every emotion that threatened to take control.

"I want you to know I meant nothing I said," she continued, stuffing the used napkin into her pocket. "I was angry and hurt and heartbroken, but I *never* hated you. Who I hated was myself for never realizing that my son had a problem, and I hated God for taking him away, and I hated your goddamn mother for putting you in such an awful, desperate situation ..." She touched her fingers to her forehead and inhaled deeply, shaking her head a little. "I'm sorry. I shouldn't have said that."

I brushed it off with a shrug. "It's fine. She's dead to me."

She winced momentarily at the harshness in my words before continuing, "Anyway"—she dropped her hand back to her side as her eyes met mine—"I hated so much back then, Soldier, but I never ever, ever *truly* hated you. And I never ever, *ever* should've said what I did."

A breeze blew through the cemetery, lifting stray hairs off my neck and taking a decade's worth of pain with it. I let Billy's mom hug me tight, and I hugged her back and squeezed my eyes shut as she smoothed her hands over my hair and soothed my aching heart with the gentleness I had missed for so long.

Then, after a few minutes, she gripped my biceps and took a step back, wearing a smile I'd never thought I'd see again.

"You came to see Billy, didn't you?"

I nodded. "Yeah. I never really got the chance, so …"

"Come on. I'll take you to him."

She held tight to my arm as we walked down the path I'd found her on. We stopped at a black marble headstone, inlaid with his picture and inscribed with his full name, birth date, and the date of his death.

My birthday.

The day I had met Officer Sam Lewis and was stuffed into the back of his patrol car.

It was weird to see that date written out, permanently etched into a slab of stone. It was weird to know his casket had been lowered feet below where I stood. It was like I knew he had died—fuck, I'd been there, for crying out loud—but I hadn't fully accepted it until I saw the place where he was buried. And now, it was suddenly real, and I knew with a sobering certainty that this hadn't all been some screwed up nightmare.

Billy's mom must've felt my knees threaten to give out because she gripped my arm tighter and said, "Here, sit down."

We turned to take a seat on a nearby bench, just diagonal from the shiny black gravestone. I couldn't take my eyes off of it, even when I was desperate to not look. I just couldn't turn away.

"I've had all these years to get used to him being gone, and I still sometimes expect him to just walk through the door, like he's been playing some horrible joke on me all this time," Billy's mom said quietly, as if she could read my mind.

"It's just surreal," I replied, not knowing what else to say.

"It is."

Moments passed with me staring at my childhood best friend's name carved into a slab of marble and his mother sitting beside me. I wanted to say something to break the silence while not knowing what there even was to say, and I was grateful when she finally spoke.

"I wanted to come see you," she admitted. "I thought about it so many times, but I didn't know if you'd want to see me or ... I don't know. I guess I was just scared."

She didn't clarify what she had been scared of, and she didn't need to. There were a thousand things that would've been valid.

"But I'm glad you're here," she continued. "I'm glad we had this."

Her hand patted my arm, and this moment felt like a true goodbye. I knew that the second I left this place, I would likely never see her again, and I was acutely aware of the racing of my heart. That desperate, frantic feeling of needing to hold on, to do something to keep her from leaving again even if it was on a happier note.

But I said nothing as we stood and hugged again.

"You've been taking care of yourself, I hope," she said, holding me tighter than before.

"I have."

"Good. That's good. I'm happy to hear it."

"What about you?" I asked.

"I have my good days and bad," she admitted, almost apologetically. "Mostly good lately."

I nodded. "I get it."

We walked each other to the gate and were about to part ways as she wished me a safe trip to wherever I was living and a good life and to not be a stranger if I ever happened to be in the area again. Then, I turned, ready to head back across the street, where I knew my girlfriend and her son would be waiting, when I was struck hard with another reason to make her stay.

"Wait." I turned on my heel and stopped her from walking to the parking lot. "Can I ask you a question?"

Billy's mom was startled as she nodded. "Of course. What is it?"

"What do you know about David Stratton?"

Her lips parted at the sound of his name, and her eyes widened with obvious recognition. She swallowed and raised her chin before dropping it in a slight nod. Eagerness ate away at me, knowing with certainty that she had more info than I'd already gotten from the library, and I was two seconds away from demanding she spill every last bean she had.

But instead, she pulled her phone out of her bag and asked, "Where are you living now?"

"Uh …" I hesitated, unsure of if I should utter the name out loud, in the event that anybody might be listening. But I realized we were alone, apart from the dead, and they couldn't talk. "River Canyon."

"Let's meet for coffee soon," she said before taking down my number. "Then, I'll tell you everything I know about David Stratton."

CHAPTER

TWENTY

A SEA OF SAUCE & PARANOIA

"So, then Jay showed me this really cool game he has, called Super Mario Odyssey."

I nodded absentmindedly and continued to push the broom as Noah trailed behind me, talking a mile a minute about his time he'd spent at a friend's house after school.

Ray had said he'd be okay, walking home by himself after hanging out at his friend's house. But it would be dark, and there was a bogeyman lurking in the shadows. We never knew if or when he would strike again. Noah's friend's house wasn't far from The Fisch Market, and so I'd made the suggestion for him to stop by after hanging with his friend. I said I could keep him company on the walk home, and of course, Ray had been cool with it. I was more than glad to have him chill with me for a while—I always was—but as it turned out, my head wasn't in the greatest place.

Come to think of it, it hadn't been ever since I'd run into Billy's mom.

And it wasn't that I hadn't enjoyed seeing her and making peace with that part of my past. We had both needed it desperately, and it was good that fate had allowed it to happen. But we had agreed to meet for coffee at Black & Brewed, and she had promised to tell me everything she knew about the man my mother had watched die. The possibilities felt endless. I knew she had to know something of substance because otherwise, why would she want to take the time to come all the way here just to say, *Hey, sorry, but you're shit out of luck*?

My nerves couldn't handle the anticipation and anxiety.

"… friggin' listening to me?"

I realized I had, at some point, gotten so tangled up in my thoughts that I stopped pushing the broom, and Noah was now standing beside me. I glanced at him to read his annoyed expression and quickly offered an apologetic smile.

"Yeah, I am. Sorry."

Noah wasn't an idiot though. "No, you're not," he grumbled, rolling his eyes.

I pushed my hair out of my face and huffed a sigh. "Noah, seriously, I'm sorry. I'm just distracted, so—"

"Why? Are you pissed at Mom?"

"What?" I narrowed my eyes, taken aback. "No, why would you think I'm pissed off at her?"

"Because my dad gets really distracted and annoyed when he's pissed off."

Every now and then, the reminder that Seth could father this cool, amazing kid barreled against my chest like a raging elephant. I was able to forget most of the time, but on those rare occasions, I had to bite my tongue from declaring to the world that Noah deserved better than that piece of shit. He deserved the best.

He deserves me.

"Well, I'm not," I said, keeping a stillness in my voice. "I'm just thinking about an old friend's mom. I saw her a few days ago when we were at your grandparents' house."

Noah's features contorted with his immediate understanding. "Ohh, that lady we saw you with?"

"Right."

He nodded, accepting the offered information. "Did you see your friend too?"

"Sort of ... well, not really." I resumed my cleaning, an image of Billy's black marble headstone flashing through my mind. "He died a long time ago."

"Oh ..." Noah dropped his darkened gaze to the floor I'd just swept. "So, um ... why were you thinking about your friend's mom?"

"Because I'm going to see her tomorrow." I swallowed, keeping my eyes ahead at the Produce sign I used to repeatedly smack my head against.

"Why?"

"Because ..." I sucked in a massive breath of air, puffing my chest out until I couldn't take any more in. "She just wants to tell me some stuff ... about, uh, my friend. And … I guess I'm just nervous about it … because I don't know what she's going to say."

Noah nodded, brow furrowed and eyes squinted. I knew he didn't quite understand what I was saying and didn't know what to say in reply.

So, I cleared my throat and said, "Anyway, what were you saying before? Something about Mario?"

He perked up immediately, welcoming the change in subject, and I forced my attention to remain on him while I finished closing up the shop. Then, with the doors locked and the keys in my pocket, we headed home.

As we walked, we passed by other neighbors and people I'd started to consider friends, all who waved and greeted us with friendly grins. None of them looked at me as a villain anymore—not even grouchy old Mrs. Montgomery, whose mouth even twitched into something resembling a smile every now and then. And it irked me all of a sudden that I was allowing Billy's mom—someone from my dark, dirty past—to infiltrate this happy, sunshiny bubble I had created for myself. She didn't fit into this place, whatever she was going to tell me wouldn't fit either, and, God, what the fuck had I been thinking, even mentioning David in her presence?

"Do you like video games?" Noah asked as we turned toward our neighborhood.

"I do. I haven't played them in a long time, but I used to play a lot when I was a kid."

"Why don't you play anymore?"

I shrugged. "I just don't really have anything to play on. I don't even have a TV or—"

"Why not?"

"Why what?"

Noah walked along the edge of the curb as we turned the corner, then kicked his feet through a puddle leftover from last night's rain. I smiled at the childlike innocence he still managed to hold on to, even at twelve years old and after withstanding the abuse his father had put him and his mother through.

It was a good thing that he could still be like this even if only sometimes. Carefree. Happy. It was likely a survival mechanism—I knew that—but it was good. I just hoped he could hold on to it longer than I had.

"Why don't you have a TV?" He hopped back onto the curb and continued to stroll beside me.

"I don't know. I guess I'm too busy reading to think about it. And when I'm not reading, I'm hanging out with you guys, and you already have a TV."

It was a valid point even if my attention was more on Ray than it was on whatever was playing.

"Yeah, but if you had a TV, then I could come over and play video games with you."

With narrowed eyes, I glared at him as we turned onto Daffodil Lane. "Why can't I just play video games at your house?"

Noah rolled his eyes and grumbled, "Well, you never have before."

I barked with a laugh that rang through the night. "Dude, you've never asked!"

"Yeah, well …" He chuffed and shrugged begrudgingly. "You're always too busy with my mom."

I quelled my laughter when I saw the hurt flash across his face and heard the rejection in his voice. Noah had been, first and foremost, my friend, and it hadn't occurred to me that since I'd started seeing his mom as something more than, well, his mom, I might've also, in turn, put our friendship on the back burner. Sure, I'd taken the time to teach him some self-defense, and I had dinner with him and Ray most nights. But we rarely took time for us nowadays, and that was my fault.

"So, hey, maybe I *should* get a TV," I said as we approached our respective houses. "And you can bring your Switch over for us to play."

"You'd have to get a controller too," he pointed out, immediately perking up. "That way, we can play together."

"You wanna come with me to pick them out?"

Noah grinned as he walked backward up the porch steps. "Yeah, sure! When do you wanna go?"

"This weekend?"

His face lit up like the lamp hanging from the porch ceiling. Relief and contentment wrapped themselves around me, only to unravel quickly when Noah pushed the door open without needing his key.

We entered the house to find Ray standing in the kitchen and washing dishes, her back to the door.

"Hey, Mom!"

"Hi!" she called happily without even a glance over her shoulder. "How was—"

I thrust a hand toward the door as Noah pushed it shut. "You left this unlocked?"

"What?" Ray turned off the faucet and grabbed a towel to dry her hands with. She looked over to see my impatient expression and hand, still gesturing toward the door. "Oh, yeah. I figured you guys were coming—"

"But you didn't *know*."

Her lips pressed into a terse line as her hands stilled within the towel. She swallowed before addressing the boy frozen at my side. "Hey, honey, go get in the shower, okay? You can tell me about your night after."

From the corner of my eye, I saw him turn toward me, then back to her before nodding. But I didn't look at him. I stared at his mother with only one thing on my mind.

What if it hadn't been us?

Noah left us alone, and once I heard the bathroom door close behind him, I took a few steps toward Ray, slowly closing the gap between us.

"Ray, you can't be like that," I said, keeping my voice down. The last thing I wanted was to freak Noah out. But, *shit* ...

"Like *what*?" She was exasperated, laughing incredulously and shaking her head. "I knew you guys were coming back, so I unlocked the door. What's the big deal?"

"The big deal is that Seth is out there, and you have no idea when—"

"He's not coming back."

I scoffed. "Oh, he's not, huh?"

She wet her lips and dropped her gaze to the towel in her hands. "No."

"How do you know that? Is he dead?"

Her jaw shifted as she shook her head. "No, but ..."

"Then, you can't assume that he's not coming back. And you don't know when that's going to happen, if it does, and if I'm not here—"

"Jesus, Soldier." She rolled her eyes back to mine. "You're being freakin' ridiculous."

"Am I though?"

She laughed again, unraveling her hands and letting the towel hang limp as she walked toward me. "Yes." She outstretched her arms, and I met her halfway, bending at the waist to wrap my arms around her hips for hers to wrap around my neck. "I told him to stay away, and he will. It's been months."

"Oh, so you think he's going to just start listening to you now?"

"Yes," she replied, stern and serious. "I told him I'd call the cops if he ever came back, and the last thing he wants is to be arrested again."

She pressed her body to mine as her lips touched my cheek, then my neck. "You're sweet for being so worried though."

"*Someone* has to worry about you," I muttered, burying my nose in her hair and taking a deep breath. "And Noah."

"We're fine," she assured me as her fingers tangled in my hair and curled to grip the back of my neck. "As long as you're here, I know we're fine. And if I'm not worried, you shouldn't be either."

Resignation didn't come easily, but I pretended as I sighed and nodded. The bathroom door opened, telling us that Noah was done in the shower. Ray released me from her grasp and kissed my lips before heading in the direction of his room.

I helped myself to some dinner and sat at the table as the sickening churn of foreboding made itself at home in my gut. The fork poked around at the ravioli, blazing trails through a sea of sauce, while I thought about Ray and her willingness to trust despite the hell she'd been through. How could my presence alone give her so much confidence in that asshole staying gone?

"He must've been exhausted," Ray said, breaking through my thoughts. "He told me about his time at Jay's house and could barely keep his eyes open."

I glanced up to watch her approach. "Yeah, he had a good time," I agreed, nodding. Then, I held her gaze firmly in a proverbial grasp and said, "Ray, please do me a favor and promise you'll keep that door locked whenever you're here."

Her eyes filled with an exhausted disdain toward my paranoia, but neither of us could prove whether it was simply unfounded worry or a premonition. So, she relented with a reluctant nod.

"Okay. I promise."

"Thank you."

"I'll get you a key, so you can let yourself in when you want."

She said it like it was as obvious as the sky being blue, but the impact of the statement struck my heart with warmth. It said, *You belong here.* It said, *I'm in this for the long haul.*

And as I abandoned my ravioli to kiss her and pick her up and take her to bed, I found I'd not only forgotten about the door—now closed and secured with the lock—but also my nerves over seeing Billy's mom.

But after we made love and Ray fell asleep and I had to head back home to feed Eleven, the worry was back in full swing to control my brain for the rest of the night, leaving me unable to sleep or focus on my book. And all I could think was, *Man, I really wish I had that TV now.*

CHAPTER

TWENTY-ONE

A GOOD MAN

Billy's mom was already sitting at a table in the middle of Black & Brewed when I arrived at River Canyon's only coffee shop. Rearranging the napkins on the table, crossing one leg over the other and back again, she was fidgeting uneasily, and I was the anxious creep, watching her discreetly from the big picture window at the front of the shop.

I was already worried about this meeting. The paranoia of what she might say had kept me up all night, and I had dragged my feet through the workday in tense anticipation over facing her again. But now, seeing that she was just as nervous, with her foot jittering as it dangled over her right knee, I wasn't sure I wanted to go inside at all. I could text her and apologize, lie and say something else had come up. I could carry on with my life, never spending another moment in her presence, and

I'd probably be okay with that. Only probably though, but the odds were good. We had left things at a happy place the last time we saw each other, so why push my luck?

With my mind made up, I began to back away from the window, ready to retreat home, where it was safe and secure. Eleven needed to eat, I needed to shower, Ray would be home soon, and she'd be making dinner. Yes, it was a good plan. It was a comfortable plan ...

But David Stratton. What about that? Don't you want to know what Billy's mom has to say about him?

"Fucking hell," I muttered through gritted teeth just as Officer Kinney's heavily tattooed brother, Ryan, walked by.

"Ya all right?" he asked, raising a brow at my clenched fists and stiff jaw.

"Yeah, sorry." I ran my fingers through my hair, hoping I looked presentable enough. "It's just been a long day."

"I hear ya." He clapped a hand against my shoulder. "Hope it gets better."

"Thanks." I mustered a half-hearted smile as he walked away, and when he was out of earshot, I muttered, "Unlikely."

No, no, no ...

I gave my head a quick shake and uncurled my fists. Why was I being like this? I had absolutely no idea what Billy's mom had to say. I knew she wanted to do it here, away from the town our lives had both changed in, but that didn't really mean anything, did it? Maybe it was simply that she didn't want the risk of someone who had known him—Levi maybe—to get wind of her gossip, which was understandable, wasn't it?

So, with the assuredness that this was going to be in fact fine, I propelled my feet forward before I could talk myself out of it again. The door pushed open easily to greet me with the music of River Canyon's famous Devin O'Leary and the Blue Existence, and there was Billy's mom, springing to her feet to greet me.

"Soldier, hi." Her hands lifted as I approached, and I let her press her palms to my cheeks. "You look tired. Are you okay?"

God ... her compassionate soul wrapped around mine like a rediscovered old blanket, and I fought the urge to close my eyes and weep under its comfort.

How starved I had been for maternal affection. I'd never noticed until being in her presence again, and I remembered all over again how desperately I'd wished she could've been my mom instead.

"I didn't get much sleep last night, but I'm okay."

"You're sure? Are you sick?"

No, just terrified.

"Really, I'm okay," I repeated with a reassuring smile. "Thanks for coming all the way out here."

She returned the smile and let it linger on her lips for a moment or two as she studied my appearance, a veil of nostalgia and sadness falling over her gaze. I swallowed, strangely uncomfortable now under her studious stare. I smiled uneasily, glancing away toward purple-haired Kylie behind the counter, when Billy's mom began to speak.

310

"Some days, it's easy to forget he ever existed outside of a dream, just to get by, and it feels like he was never really mine," she admitted, her voice nothing but a whisper below the sound of John Mayer, now playing over the speakers. "But somehow, seeing you and remembering you two as little boys, I know he was real. Because if you can exist in those memories and now here, in the real world, then … I know he must've existed at one point too. I just wish I could have seen him like this, like … like you." She swallowed as her eyes drowned. "All grown up …"

My throat was choked with an uncomfortable emotion, and I glanced back at her with pleading eyes. "Mrs. Port—"

"Please, call me Laura."

Then, she laughed, brushing away her grief-driven confession. She sat and gestured toward the chair across from hers.

"This place is lovely," Laura commented, lifting her hand and gaze to address the shop and its exposed beams and dark woodwork. "Really, the whole town is. I honestly don't think I've ever been out this way before, but it's very nice. Quaint."

I carefully sat, unable to take my eyes off of her. It was still so strange to be in contact with her after all this time, without the presence of my friend or the hostility I'd once known. I kept expecting for it to end, as if her true demeanor was just lying low, like a snake in the grass, waiting for the opportunity to strike.

Her eyes came back to mine. "Do you like it here?"

"I do. It was a little rough at first. People were kinda scared of me, I think ..." I laughed awkwardly, glancing toward the purple-haired woman behind the counter. "But it's gotten better."

"Good." Laura nodded. "Did you just come from work?"

I glanced down at the apron I'd forgotten to take off. "Oh ..." A chuckle rumbled through my chest as I reached around my back to untie it. "Yeah."

"What's The Fisch Market?"

"Local grocery store." I took the apron off and draped it over the back of the chair. "I'm the assistant manager."

Her eyes widened. "Oh, wow. Good for you," she said, clearly taken aback. "So, you're doing well for yourself here, I take it. And ... so soon after ..." She swallowed, not wanting to say the words I knew were hanging on the tip of her tongue.

"Yeah ..." I laughed uneasily. "I kinda got lucky for the first time in my life, so ..."

There was that smile again. Affectionate. Compassionate. "Good for you, Soldier. Really, I'm so happy things are going well for you."

"Thank you."

A thought popped into my head. That she and my mother still lived in the same town, that they might be in contact. That Laura might actually be here to fish for information—had I already revealed too much?

"What's wrong?" She must've noticed my sudden shift toward apprehension.

"Um …" I cleared my throat and glanced around the coffee shop—not at all busy and quiet, save for music in the air. "My mother doesn't know where I am, and I, uh … I really want to keep it that way."

"Soldier, I don't have any contact with her at all."

My eyes met hers with a gentle warning. "But in case you ever do, I want her knowing nothing. Not where I am, not where I work. I don't want her knowing you've seen me at all."

Her brows pinched with concern as she nodded softly. "I understand, and you have my word. Really, I haven't spoken to her in …" She inhaled deeply before shrugging with her exhale. "God, it must have been … five years, maybe six. I think the last time was when I saw her at my doctor's office. She was the secretary there, and …"

My interest was suddenly piqued, and I remembered that first visit from my mother while I had been at Wayward. She'd told me she had gotten a job at a doctor's office, one she seemed proud of.

"Never mind," Laura said, waving her hand dismissively. "It's nothing—"

"Wait. Did she say something?" I interrupted. Because as much as I wanted nothing to do with my mother, my desperation to put these discombobulated pieces together couldn't be thwarted.

"Um …" She pinned her lips between her teeth as her brow remained crumpled with contemplation. "Well, she said hello, like we had always been great friends or something, and, uh … she asked how I was doing, and I didn't know what to say to that because ... well, what could I say really?"

She lifted her eyes to mine and curled the corner of her mouth in an apologetic smile. Like she was sorry for not wanting to talk to the mother of the guy who had inadvertently taken her son from her.

"Anyway, what I really remember is that she asked if I had seen you." She swallowed and folded her hands on the table, interlocking her fingers and gripping them tight. "Which I found odd. Not just because of the nature of the situation, but that she ... she was whispering, like she didn't want anybody to know that she was asking. And when I told her no, she nodded and said, 'Good.'"

I narrowed my eyes with questions I knew she wouldn't have the answers to. "Good? Why the hell would she care if I was seeing you or not?"

Billy's mom shrugged. "Maybe because ... I don't know because ..." She was hesitating, and I looked at her expectantly, encouraging her to continue. So, she sighed and dropped her gaze as she concluded, "You didn't deserve it?" She said it like a question. Like she wasn't sure of it herself.

"Yeah," I muttered, wiping a hand over my beard and pinching my chin thoughtfully. "Maybe."

"Anyway, she doesn't work there anymore, I don't think. I only saw her the one time, and that was so long ago."

"Yeah, well, that's par for the course."

The conversation lulled, and I cleared my throat before offering to buy us both a drink. She gratefully accepted before asking if I'd like money, but I declined.

The least I could do was buy the woman a freakin' cup of coffee for driving all the way here.

So, I ordered and waited for Kylie to make our drinks. Billy's mom stayed at the table, and I turned from the espresso bar to glance at her. To drive home that this was real, that she was here, and we were ... what? Rekindling seemed extreme, but she clearly cared for me, and that had to mean something, didn't it?

My phone rang, and I pulled it out to see Ray's face light up the screen. With a smile I couldn't contain, I answered as Kylie handed the two drinks to me.

"Hey."

"Hey, Brawny. Are you here for dinner tonight?"

"Um ... I'm not sure. I'm at Black & Brewed now, and we're just sitting down with coffee," I admitted. I had told Ray I was meeting Billy's mom—Laura—and she was more than supportive, but I'd neglected to tell her what time I'd be seeing her.

"Oh! I'm sorry. I should've texted. I didn't realize," Ray quickly replied. "Sorry."

Her constant need to apologize profusely for little things like calling me at inopportune moments made me grit my teeth, knowing what had instilled those insecurities and fears in her.

"You're fine," I assured her, placing both cups on the table.

Laura mouthed, *Thank you*, before eyeing the phone pinned between my ear and shoulder curiously.

I asked Ray, "What are you cooking?"

"Noah really wanted meatloaf, so it's in the oven now."

"Oh, damn." I took my seat and gripped the paper cup of coffee. "You know I love your meatloaf."

Ray giggled, as if meatloaf were a code word for something else. "So, should I save you some?"

"Yeah, I'll be over later."

"Okay." There was a smile in her voice, and that made me smile too. "You have your key?"

"Yes, ma'am," I said, thinking about the spare key she had given me that morning before we both left for work.

"Okay. I'll see you later. Good luck with your friend's mom."

"Thanks."

Then, she was gone, and with a smile I couldn't help and warmth surrounding my pulsing heart, I tucked the phone away. My eyes lifted to find Laura watching me with a knowing glint in her eye as she brought her cup to her lips.

"Sorry," I said needlessly, gesturing to my pocketed phone. "That was my girlfriend."

"I figured," she jabbed playfully over the brim of the cup. "She makes you blush."

"What?" I rubbed my palm against my cheek. "Nah … it's—"

"It's *cute*," she said, finishing my sentence with a teasing grin.

Then, she sighed, resting her chin in her hand and staring across the table at me with a wistful, melancholy look in her eyes. I didn't know what to make of it, just as I hadn't known what to do with her reactions back in the cemetery or the sad confession she'd made just minutes before. So, I shifted in my seat and smiled uncomfortably before bringing my coffee to my lips and taking a long pull.

Then, she dropped her hand to the table and gripped her cup as she said, "I remember this one time, years ago, when I dropped Billy off at your grandparents' house. Your mother was God knows where. I watched you boys run upstairs to your room, and I said to your grandmother, 'Do you ever wonder what's going to happen to him?' And I … I don't know why I said it. It was probably an awful thing to say, and I probably should've kept it to myself, but I always worried about you, and I know your grandparents did too.

"Anyway, your grandmother said, 'As long as I'm around, he'll have the best damn life I can give him, and I just have to hope that'll be enough to carry him through when I'm gone.' And I was just thinking about that—about how she'd be happy to see you now, to know that whatever she and your grandfather had done was truly enough."

My throat constricted around a toughened ball of emotion. I hadn't expected her to drop emotional bombs like these. I hadn't expected her to mention Gramma and Grampa. God, I could talk about my mother forever without shedding a tear, but bring Gramma and Grampa into the conversation, and I could easily turn into a blubbering baby. But then she'd had to mention them being proud of me now, after everything …

Fuck, it was laughable, honestly.

"I don't …" I cleared my throat and shook my head. "I don't think they'd think too highly of me, personally …"

"No." She shook her head, keeping her gaze soft. "Some horrible mistakes were made, yes, but you were never lost to them, Soldier, and that's what matters. That's what made you who you are today; that's why you are where you are now. You said it was luck before, but, no, there's nothing lucky about it. It comes down to you and your good heart and soul and nothing more than that. And that … that was your grandparents, and it was obviously enough. More than enough even. They would be so proud of you, and I am too."

***

"Something that's important to remember," Laura said as she lifted the apple fritter she'd been tempted by to her mouth, "is that your mother and I aren't the same age. She's six or seven years younger than me, so we didn't exactly run in the same social circles."

I couldn't help but huff a bitter laugh. "I highly doubt you'd have hung out with the same people as Diane anyway."

Laura winced after taking a bite, her eyes full of apology. I knew she had spent years in cahoots with my grandparents, on a mission to protect me from the inevitable turmoil my mother would have on my life. I also knew she had felt like a failure, just as Mrs. Henderson had, when none of them were to blame.

Nobody was. Just me, my choices, and those made by my mother.

"In any case," she continued after swallowing, "I would see her around town, but I didn't really get to know her until you and Billy became friends in preschool."

"And that's how you knew David?" I asked, eager to know more about this man I'd never heard of.

She studied the golden-brown crumbles on top of the fritter as she nodded thoughtfully. "Yeah," she said, drawing the word out. "David was ... well, I *heard* David was a good kid, growing up. I have no idea if that was true or not—again, I didn't really know him well, personally—but from what I heard around town and from your grandparents, he had started life as a good kid. But your mother had a habit of getting in trouble, and David developed a habit of always being around her ..."

That was interesting. I had assumed it'd been the other way around. I had expected to find out that my mother had been the good one, destined for greatness, thanks to my grandparents, until she got wrapped up with the wrong crowd. To hear that she had been the troublemaker from the start was all at once startling and yet ... not.

"I was my grandparents' second chance," I muttered almost to myself, staring at my second cup of coffee, half full and cooling in the air-conditioning.

Laura hummed a contemplative sound. "I think so. I know they blamed themselves for your mother, and when you came along, they thought you'd be her saving grace. Honestly, I think she thought so too—"

"She always used to say I was supposed to save her," I told her, my glare hardening on the coffee cup. "So, I did, and that's why we're here."

Laura nodded somberly, not needing me to elaborate as she went on. "Well, the truth was, it was everyone that needed saving from your mother, and I believe you saved your grandparents. You saved them from the guilt; you gave them someone to love them back for everything they did. But, unfortunately for David, nobody was there to save him. He had been arrested a couple of times, I think—"

"Yes." I nodded, staring off toward a shelf full of antique books. "I found a few articles about his arrests. Public intoxication, graffiti—nothing too crazy, and from what I read, he hadn't done any time, other than a few overnights in—"

"His father was a cop," Laura informed me, her stare pinning me to the spot.

Well, that made me sit up taller.

"Wait. What?"

She nodded, exaggerating the movement of her head to her chest. "Matthew Stratton was a cop."

"Shit. That explains a lot," I murmured, thinking of Levi and the shit he had managed to get away with.

"Yep," she agreed, and somehow, I knew we were referring to the same thing. "And that night, when your mother and David got into the accident, David's father made sure she was let off the hook despite the car being full of her drugs."

"Nothing was found in her system," I said, reciting only what I'd read.

320

Laura shrugged with a doubtful expression on her face. "Yeah, that's what they said, but knowing your mother …"

Gramma and Grampa must have known she'd been wasted that night. God, of course she had been—how could I, her fucking son, have believed any different? And really, what was the likelihood that her boyfriend, sitting behind the wheel, had been intoxicated and not her?

"Do you think my grandparents knew?" I asked, wondering too much how far they'd been willing to go to protect their daughter.

Laura released a heavy breath and closed her eyes. "Soldier, I believe your grandparents had a lot of hope that she would one day shake those demons off her back, and I believe they went to some pretty great lengths to try and give her as many chances as they could to make that recovery possible."

I could only imagine what she was implying, and those images filtering through my mind brought my fists to clench against the table. Laura laid one of her hands over one of those fists and squeezed her fingers around it.

"I don't judge them for any of it. As a mother of someone who had his own demons, I can tell you with certainty that I would've done anything to keep him safe had I been aware of what he was doing. Even if that meant watching him destroy everything else around him."

Maybe it's good he's dead, I caught myself thinking, and I quickly shook my head, chasing the thought away.

Because who the hell was I to judge? I had led my best friend to his death. I had protected my mother too. I had thrown ten years of my life away for her. How was that any different from my grandparents doing ... whatever it was they'd done or Billy's mother swearing she would've gone to the same lengths for him if she'd had the chance?

We were all just heartbroken people, trying to keep the ones we loved from succumbing to their inevitable doom.

"I'm sorry I never told you about the stuff he was doing," I quietly said.

Laura shook her head and replied, "You were kids. I can't hold a child responsible for remaining loyal to his friend, whether it was right or not."

She was a lot more forgiving than I thought I would've been in her position, and to me, that was astounding.

"So, Levi Stratton ..." I found myself saying, needing a change in subject. "He's David's brother, isn't he?"

Laura nodded solemnly.

"The last time I saw my mom, she was with him."

"I know." She poked at the fritter, now sitting on the table, only half eaten and nearly forgotten. "If you're going to ask me about that, I told you, I really don't—"

"No, I know. I'm just ..." I groaned, scrubbing my palms over my cheeks and beard. "I guess I'm just connecting the dots."

"I understand, and I can't say I blame you. But don't let your curiosity get the better of you, okay? In the long run, none of it matters. Separate yourself from it. You're here now, living a good life, and you know you're better off."

I hadn't needed her to say it to know she was right. But I appreciated it anyway, and I expressed that gratitude with a nod.

But then a question I'd been wondering since I had known of David demanded to be asked. I knew I wouldn't be happy until I got it out there, so I went for it.

"One more question before I get to my girlfriend's meatloaf," I said, swallowing in preparation. "Was David my father?"

Laura sucked in a deep breath, her somber gaze taking me in before she lifted one shoulder in a weary shrug. "I don't know that anybody really knows," she admitted. "Well, except for your mother, David, and maybe your grandparents and members of David's family …"

"But?" I asked, almost hopeful in the way I put that little word out there.

"But … you know how tall your mother is and how tall your grandparents were, and, well …" She shrugged again. "David had to have been at least six foot five."

CHAPTER

TWENTY-TWO

JUST LIKE HIM

She had said it didn't matter if David was my father or not, and I'd told her she was right. But that night, after I ate the meatloaf Ray had saved for me and then went home to feed Eleven, I couldn't get the thought of him out of my head.

David Stratton, six foot five—tall, just like me. Dead at twenty-four—not much older than I'd been when Billy died.

Lying in bed, with Eleven curled up at my side, I pulled up the old article regarding the crash that had taken David's life. I looked at his face in black and white. I studied the grainy structure of his nose, his cheekbones. The ridge of his brow and the curve of his smile. Just to try and see how many features we shared, if we shared any at all, but, fuck, the picture was so small and fuzzy, so it was hard to make anything out.

He probably wasn't your dad.

Shit ... but what if he was?

I climbed out of bed, mind racing and heart hammering, and dropped to the floor to do a vigorous stream of push-ups in an attempt to clear my brain. Eleven watched me curiously as I counted aloud, the way one might count sheep.

"One ... two ... three ..."

Did he know about me?

"Four ... five ... six ..."

Did Gramma and Grampa know about him?

"Seven ... eight ... nine ..."

Did he ever meet me and I just don't remember it?

"Ten ... eleven ..."

Did he care?

"Fuck."

I pushed off the floor and onto my knees, thrusting my hands into the strands of my hair, still damp from the shower. My mind was never going to stop with the questions, and I knew it, but what the hell was I supposed to do about it? The guy was dead. He'd been dead for twenty-five years.

But his girlfriend is still alive.

No. I shook my head furiously. *Don't even go there.*

But she would have answers.

"*Fuck*," I groaned, stretching the word out until I had no breath left while sliding my hands over my face and beard.

The last thing I wanted was to contact my mother. She had made it very clear she wanted nothing to do with me, and I'd made it just as clear that I was making a clean break from her toxicity once and for all—and I had. My life was good. My life was exactly what I'd always dreamed it could be, and the last thing I wanted to do was jeopardize it by seeing Diane Mason.

But I hadn't planned on this, had I?

***

At work the next day, after even less sleep than I'd gotten the night before, I made the reluctant decision to see my mother one last time—and this time, I meant it; it *would* be the last. But I knew damn well I wasn't going to rest without at least asking her the questions I had endlessly parading through my head.

But I also knew I couldn't ask Ray to accompany me.

Levi might be there, and even if he wasn't, Diane might tell him.

I couldn't have him know Ray and I were connected because he would run to Seth. I couldn't risk Seth coming back—even though, chances were, he'd eventually come back anyway. But I had to let that happen of his own accord and not out of revenge for me.

So, on my lunch break, I called the next person—the only one—I could think of.

"Soldier!" Harry answered on the first ring. "How the hell are ya, son? How long's it been? Two days?"

I chuckled. Harry and I talked a lot.

"I'm good. How are you?"

"Can't complain. Vacation has been nice. Relaxing."

"Good for you, man. What have you been doing?"

326

"Ah, just some stuff around the house. Painting the deck, fixing the steps ... you know."

I snorted. "I gotta be honest with you, Harry ... that sounds like a really shitty vacation."

He laughed with me. "Hey, at least I'm getting Sarah off my back about this stuff. Happy wife, happy life. Remember that."

I couldn't help but smile at the implication that I might actually have a wife one day.

Shit ... would Ray say yes right now if I asked her to marry me?

We hadn't even exchanged *I love you*s yet, but ... something in my gut told me she actually might accept my proposal ... if I asked, I mean. Which I wouldn't. Not yet. But ...

Shit.

I had to give my head a little shake to remind myself that wasn't what I was calling about. Then, I said, "Hey, so, Harry, I, uh ... I was wondering if you could maybe give me a ride somewhere."

"Yeah, sure. Where did you have in mind?"

He had agreed before even knowing the destination.

Harry was, as I'd said before, a good friend.

"My mom's place."

It was then that he hesitated before saying, "Soldier ... son ... do I have to remind you how things went last time? I understand she's your mother, and I get that it's hard, letting go, but—"

"No, it's not that. I don't want to try and fix shit with her."

"Then, what is it?"

I'd purposely kept the private investigation I'd been conducting to myself to avoid his scrutiny. He knew nothing, and in order for him to agree, he needed the truth. So, in as few words as possible, I told him about the things I'd recently discovered about my mother—the car accident and the boyfriend who had died. I mentioned that I'd met with Billy's mom to talk about it, and that she'd implied the man could've been my dad, and that I wasn't sure I'd be able to rest again until I knew my mom's side of the story.

"I don't know, Soldier ..." Harry sounded uncomfortable and unsure. "You realize you don't know that she'll actually give you the answers you're looking for, right?"

"I know. But if I don't at least try, I'm gonna go crazy. I can't stop thinking about this shit."

Harry, to my relief, understood, and the next day, he played hooky from his household chores—I mean, vacation—to pick me up from my house while Ray was at work and Noah was at school.

I didn't like hiding the excursion from them. But I knew Ray would've had something to say about it. I knew she would've tried to stop me—or worse, she'd have insisted on coming. It was best to tell her after the fact, and I told Harry just that when he asked why I hadn't asked my girlfriend to give me a ride instead.

He eyed me with wary skepticism from across the car. "So ... are you *trying* to piss her off by keeping secrets or ..."

"I'm trying to protect her," I countered. "She doesn't need to get wrapped up in this shit any more than she already is."

That was half of the truth.

The other half had everything to do with Seth and my insistence that he never see Ray and me together. But not even Ray's mother knew about the ongoing situation with Seth, and I didn't feel it was my place to tell Harry.

"You can't protect everyone, you know," Harry replied, eyeing me like there was something more on his mind, but wouldn't say it.

"No," I agreed. "But I can protect her ... and Noah."

"You must really like her, huh?"

He spoke to me the way I imagined Grampa would've had we made it to the point of girlfriends and relationships. And I couldn't help but wonder if David Stratton would've spoken to me that way, too, had he been given the chance to be my father. Had he been allowed to live.

"Something like that," I muttered, looking out the window and wondering if Ray maybe felt the same way about me—something like *like*, but ... more.

***

"You want me to come up with you?"

Harry pulled into a spot in the parking lot adjacent to the building. It had only been months since I'd been there last, but, man ... the grass was longer, the weeds were bowing against the sidewalk, and the paint had chipped more off the windowpanes and front door.

Where the hell was the landlord? At what point had he stopped giving a shit about keeping the place maintained? And why? I knew the guy had been old when I was a kid, and that would only make him older now—if he was even still alive. It was possible that he just couldn't handle the responsibility anymore. But how had nobody in this place stepped up to the plate? How did nobody have any sense of pride in the place they lived in—even if it was a shitty hole-in-the-wall?

Anger and disappointment tugged at the corners of my mouth as my eyes drifted toward my mother's dirty, dingy window. "Nah," I muttered, answering Harry's question. "I got this."

"You sure? Because, Soldier, if you need me—"

"Harry," I interrupted, turning to face him, "you being here is enough. Just wait for me, okay? That's all I'm asking."

He responded with a gentle nod. "You got it, buddy. And, listen, if you *do* need me—"

"I know. You're right here." I patted his shoulder, filled with so much gratitude for this unlikely friend. So thankful to have him in my life, helping me and being there when nobody else was. "Thank you."

He forced a smile, deepening the lines on his face. Reminding me that he was much older now than he had been when I first met him years ago.

With a deep breath, I left the car and headed for the main entrance of the apartment complex. The place had always lacked in any semblance of security. Since we'd moved in, the main door had never been locked, and there weren't any functioning security cameras on the grounds. So, I wasn't surprised to find it unlocked now, but the fact that the knob no longer turned or clicked shut was disheartening.

"What the fuck?" I muttered, entering the hall and surveying my surroundings.

The overhead bulb, hanging just above the doorway, flickered in response as I walked toward the staircase, stepping over shreds of debris, empty cigarette packs, and the occasional plastic bag. The stairs creaked beneath my feet, and the banister rocked under my grip. Zoning would have a field day in this place, if they gave half a shit. The whole building would likely be condemned, and all of these people—whoever was left—would have to find somewhere else to squirrel away their drugs and whatever else they were up to.

Nothing good—that was for damn sure. Nobody in this building was ever up to anything good.

Three floors up, I found myself at my mother's door. I stared ahead at the slab of steel and its chipped-paint facade, realizing in the matter of a millisecond that I was scared to knock.

Would she answer? Would Levi? And what the hell would I even say? I mean, *shit*! It had felt so important to be here, to see her, to confront her about the past, and I'd gone over the words a thousand times on the two-hour-long ride while Harry tapped along to some classic rock and told me about his new power washer. But now, facing the worn and weathered door I'd once passed through hundreds of times, my mind was a clean, blank slate.

Go back down, get in Harry's car, and get the hell out of here.

But what about getting answers? Harry would ask if I talked to her. What the fuck would I say?

Tell him nobody was home. Tell him it—

Voices came from the other side of the door. Muffled words, spoken in harsh tones. One of them was my mom—I knew that—but who were the others? There was one—no, two men with her. They spoke brashly, heatedly, as they came closer. Were they fighting, arguing? I couldn't tell, but they were heading toward the kitchen, nearer to where I stood, and when I heard the locks being undone, I bolted. Hurried away toward the stairs, ready to leave.

"Where the hell are you going?" I heard a man say as the door creaked open.

It was Levi.

Afraid he had seen me, I glanced toward the apartment door, only to see not him, but my mother with her ratty, old purse slung over her shoulder.

"I'm going to get some cigarettes. You have a problem with that?" she snapped, her voice rough and hoarse.

"Grab a few six-packs too," he called just as she closed the door behind her.

My mother began to walk in my direction, her eyes on her hands as they rifled through her purse. "A few six-packs ... yeah, okay, 'cause I wanna deal with your drunk asses all—"

Her sunken gaze lifted to see me, standing two steps down into the stairwell. She froze, nearly dropping her purse from off her shoulder.

"Hi, Diane."

"W-w-what …" She swallowed and blinked rapidly, then licked her dry, cracked lips. "What are you doing here?"

As if I'd forgotten entirely about my fear of seeing her, I leaned against the wall and tucked my hands inside my jeans pockets. "I came to ask you a couple of questions."

Her nostrils flared as her eyes widened … with what? It wasn't anger or irritation. No, there was something else there.

Fear.

She's afraid.

Of what? Me?

"You shouldn't be here," she said, her voice trembling and hushed. "You need to get the hell out of here."

"Not until I talk to you."

She huffed, taking a peek over her shoulder toward the door, then gestured with a frantic hand down the stairs. "Go. Go downstairs. Get outside."

My brows pinched as I eyed her warily. "Are you going to talk to me?"

She clenched her jaw. "I said, *go.*"

With a roll of my eyes, I did as she'd asked, descending the three floors two steps at a time with her hurrying behind me, her flip-flops slapping all the way. I barreled through the entry hallway, beneath the flickering bulb, to burst through the front door that no longer closed. The warm breeze hit me, and I was grateful for the fresh air as I turned around on my heel to face the woman I'd once been foolish enough to hold on a pedestal.

"I'm not letting you leave until you talk to me," I said, keeping my voice low and menacing.

But she was already walking away in the other direction, digging out a pack of cigarettes from her bag.

"*Diane*," I growled through gritted teeth. "Stop—"

She shot a hardened look over her shoulder. "Will you keep your goddamn voice down? Get over here."

A cigarette was pulled from the pack and placed between her lips as she led me to the other side of the building. We were secluded by a cluster of trees, but I had a clear view of Harry, sitting in his car. My escape route.

She flicked her lighter and set the flame to the end of the cigarette. "You want one?" she asked, holding the pack out to me.

I glared at the four remaining cigarettes with raised suspicion as if they might be laced with arsenic or cyanide. But reason quickly told me she'd had no idea I was coming, so she'd have no reason to poison her pack with anything and risk losing her precious smokes. So, despite not having smoked since high school, I accepted her offer, slid one out, and held it between my lips.

"Now, you can't say I never gave you anything," she said with a condescending curl of her lips as I took the lighter and lit up.

I snorted and rolled my eyes to the clear, happy sky as I filled my lungs with smoke. Then, I sputtered through an exhale and coughed, pinching the cigarette between two fingers and pulling it from my mouth.

"Yeah, thanks for the cancer," I choked out.

The side of her mouth twitched, and I thought she might actually give me a real smile.

But before she could give herself the chance, she cleared her throat and asked, "What did you want to say to me? And keep it down. I don't know who's listening, and—"

"Who do you think is listening?" I watched her skeptically.

Was she really that scared, or had she completely lost her mind?

She squinted her eyes in the sunlight as she stared up at me. "I think you already know."

And with that, understanding cleared the suspicion from my mind, and I slowly shook my head. "What the hell did you get yourself into, Diane?"

"Nothing I wasn't already into," she countered with a defeated shrug and a puff of her cigarette. "What did you have to say to me?"

I wanted to ask her more about Levi. How long she'd been involved with him, if he was living with her, if she was working with him or simply keeping his bed warm. But my time with her was limited, and my focus had to be the reason I'd come.

"Was David Stratton my father?"

Her eyes widened at the unexpected question, and her startled gaze met mine. "H-how do you know that name?"

"I read an article."

She blew out her held breath, cigarette smoke permeated the space between us, and she shook her head. "I don't know."

"You don't know what?"

"I don't know if he was your father." She shrugged like it all meant nothing and lifted the cigarette back to her mouth.

"How do you not know?"

"What do you mean, how do I not know? Soldier, do you even know how many guys I was fucking when I got knocked up?"

I didn't want to cringe at her language. I wasn't a child, and I knew damn well my mother had *fucked* more than her fair share of men. But she was still my mother, and the idea of her *fucking* anyone made me recoil a little.

"But the article said he was your boyfriend."

She pursed her lips and slowly nodded at the cigarette as an unexpected wave of sadness clouded her eyes. "Yeah ... he was."

"And wasn't he ..." I hesitated, clearing my throat and questioning how much I should actually say. I didn't want to allude to talking to Billy's mom. I didn't want to get anyone else into trouble. "Wasn't he tall? I ... I saw a picture, and ..."

She slowly exhaled. "He was."

"So"—I waved the forgotten cigarette in my hand, trying to put the pieces together—"isn't it possible that he—"

"Jesus Christ, Soldier," she hissed impatiently. "It doesn't fucking matter, okay? Why the hell do you even want to know? Knowing won't change anything, okay? It'll just make shit worse."

"I ... I don't know," I answered stupidly. "I guess I just want to know—"

"What? You were hoping both of your parents weren't pieces of shit?"

That wasn't at all what I had wanted to say, and I winced. "I've never called you a piece of shit, Diane."

She wagged the burning end of the cigarette at me, ash falling to my feet. "You didn't need to say it. I can see it in your eyes. I can hear it in your voice every time you call me by my name. *Diane*," she mocked, her nose wrinkling with disgust. "I know you hate me, kiddo, and that's fine. Whatever I gotta do to keep you the fuck away from here. But"—she shook her head, chuckling with something like bitterness—"you just keep coming back, don't you?"

I opened my mouth to reply, to ask what she was talking about, when the sound of a door slamming shut echoed through the air. Her eyes widened, the way they had upstairs, immediately full of fear and worry, as she looked over her shoulder. Staying still. Staying quiet. Listening.

I tried to glance through the trees and see what she was looking for. "What are you—"

337

She whipped her head around to stare at me. "You need to get the hell away from here. Do you understand me? And *stay* the fuck away. I don't want to ever see you back here."

"What—"

"I mean it." She spoke through clenched teeth, her voice quaking and her hands shaking. "Go. Live your life. That's all you've ever wanted, right? To get away from here? Now, you got it. So, *go*."

I thought about mentioning that I had wanted to take her with me all those years ago. That I had saved all of that money so that we could start over somewhere else— somewhere better—*together*. But what would be the point now?

So, I reached out and gripped her shoulder, startled by how frail and bony it was. "What are you afraid of? What—"

She thrust her hands against my chest. The impact did nothing but send a message. "Soldier, *leave*. Get in that car over there before anyone sees you and *go*."

"Okay." I stomped the cigarette out with the heel of my boot on the concrete surrounding the perimeter of the building. Then, I pulled a pen from my pocket. "But I'm giving you my number."

"Oh, Jesus fucking Christ ..." She sounded shrill as she pulled at the dry strands of her hair. "You can't—"

"You don't have to call me," I said, scribbling the digits onto an old receipt I had on me. "But if you need help, if you need me ... if you need *anything* ... I'm here. Okay?"

"What I *need* is for you to go—"

"Mom." I took her hand and stuffed the crumpled slip of paper into her clammy palm. "I'm *here*."

Her chest rose and fell with every heavy breath. Her eyes stared into mine, misting with tears, as her lips pinched around every protest she kept locked inside her mouth.

Neither of us spoke in those few seconds of shared air, but everything she felt was spoken in her eyes. Her regret. Her failure. Her abundance of apologies. I could feel every single one as the realization that this would truly be the last time I saw my mother pierced my heart.

"I have to get some cigarettes and a few six-packs," she announced quietly.

I nodded, too acutely aware of the pain and anguish tugging at my nerves. "Okay."

She hung her head and turned around, ready to walk away, when she abruptly stopped. She pulled in a deep breath before spinning on her heel, dropping her purse, and allowing her arms to fly up and around my shoulders. I bent at the waist, pulling her in for a tight hug—maybe the realest, truest embrace we'd ever shared in my entire life.

"You know," she said, speaking against my shoulder, "I always hoped he was your father. I always hoped you'd be more like him."

I said nothing as she pulled away and wiped her eyes, taking a step back and picking her purse up from the ground. She held her head higher and held the strap tight as she plastered a fake smile on her face.

"You are, Soldier. Like him, I mean." She nodded as she continued moving backward, leaving the shelter of the trees. "You're a good man, and he was, too."

Then, she was gone, hurrying away before I could utter another word.

My eyes burned with impending tears, and my lungs deflated with a sigh. I shook off her abrupt departure before taking a step in the direction of Harry's car.

But then something caught my eye.

Something bright against the ground of soil and dead grass. A piece of paper maybe.

This wasn't here before, I thought as I bent to pick it up. I would've noticed when I had stomped out the cigarette. *It must've fallen out of her bag when she dropped it.*

At first glance, I saw it was a handwritten prescription, and I thought of running after her to give it back. But then, after giving it a better look, I saw it was for oxycodone … written in my mother's handwriting.

The doctor's name printed on the top was Dr. Erin House, OB/GYN, and I thought about what Laura had said.

"… I saw her at my doctor's office. She was the secretary there, and …"

"Holy fuck, Mom," I muttered, crumpling the stolen paper and stuffing it into my pocket. "What the fuck are you doing?"

Or better yet … who was she doing it for—herself … or the guy in her apartment?

CHAPTER
TWENTY-THREE

BIG EMPTY

"… in the chocolate flavor?"

I gave my head a quick shake before focusing my attention on Mrs. Montgomery, holding up a container of dietary fiber chews.

"I'm sorry," I said before clearing my throat. "What was that?"

Her scowl deepened. The woman looked like a toad. "What, do you have cotton in your ears?"

"Mrs. Montgomery, I'm sorry. I just …" I swallowed to chase away the thoughts of my mother and the prescription she'd written out for herself. "I'm kinda having a tough week, but—"

"*Life* is tough. Get used to it," she snapped.

"Oh, believe me, I'm more than used to it," I fired back, a harsh bite in my tone.

The old woman studied me with a hardened glare. Our relationship was hot and cold. Some days, I could get a little hint of a smile from her while, others, I was lucky if she even looked me in the eye when she spoke to me. I was always polite though. Always kind and willing to take her sharp and heated comments, for the sake of my reputation in town and my job. But today, I was tired. Mentally and physically exhausted. And I couldn't find it in me to be anything but.

She held my gaze with an iron grip, her mouth twitching with irritability and whatever snappy comeback she had waiting. But then she surprised me by thrusting the container toward my face—as close as she could get with her short arms and four-foot-nine stature—and said, "These. Do you have them in chocolate?"

I slowly took the container from her while cocking a brow and narrowing one eye, wondering what the hell had kept her from firing back at me. "Um, give me a sec while I check the stockroom."

"Fine. I'll wait here."

I hurried for the door at the back of the store, where I searched the rows of boxes, bags, and towers of cans until I found what she was looking for. I grabbed a box of twelve containers of chocolate dietary fiber chews to restock the shelf and hurried back to where Mrs. Montgomery was still waiting.

"Here you go," I said, pulling out my box cutter and slicing through the tape. I pulled out a container and handed it over. "Chocolate."

"Hmph."

She dropped it into her cart and turned to walk away, but then she stopped. She glanced over her shoulder and looked up at me.

"Whatever's on your mind, it won't last forever. And before you know it, it'll be just another memory."

My lips rolled between my teeth as I let what she had said sink in, and then I nodded. "I know. But that doesn't help what's going on in the present though."

"No. But you might want to think before you let it affect your life. Ask yourself … does this matter? Does this serve me to care? And if the answer is no"—she reached out and tapped my aproned chest with a knobby finger—"then you might want to reconsider the next time you ignore your friends for something that doesn't belong in your head in the first place."

I sniffed and felt the corner of my mouth lift in a reluctant smile. "Mrs. Montgomery … are you saying you're my friend?"

She clicked her tongue and began to push the cart away. "Don't go making assumptions, Mr. Mason. They'll only make an ass out of you."

Howard appeared by my side as she disappeared down the next aisle, and I said, "That old bat just called me her friend."

"Well, yeah," he replied as he wiped his hands against his apron, "she speaks very highly of you."

I guffawed at that. "Get out of here, man. That woman hates me."

He shook his head. "Actually, she was the one who suggested I make you assistant manager in the first place."

I stared at the man like he'd sprouted a second head. "No, she didn't."

He nodded. "Yep. She knew I needed more help around here, and she mentioned what a trustworthy, hard worker you are."

"Wow." I glanced toward the direction the old woman had walked away in. "Who knew?"

I grabbed the broom and resumed my therapeutic sweeping of the floor. Heeding Mrs. Montgomery's warning and forcing my mind to think of anything but my mother. Ray. Noah. Eleven. The upcoming weekend and our plans to buy a TV. Howard lingered, watching the bristles scrape against the bleached wood floorboards with crossed arms and a gentle bob of his head. As if I needed his approval. As if I needed to know if I was doing a good job or not.

Then, he said, "So … listen, Soldier …"

With those words spoken, the broom froze, and my arms stilled. Nobody said those words without dropping a bomb immediately after.

"What's up?" I asked, all of a sudden terrified I might lose my job without any reason to be terrified at all.

"Connie and I were talking the other day. She needs some help with the Fourth of July festival. The ladies who work with her, Christy and Rosie—you've met them, right?"

I nodded. There weren't many people I hadn't met at this point. Especially working in such a central hub like the local grocery store.

"Well, they have most of it covered, but there's some stuff—hanging the banners, stringing some of the lights, things like that—that they need a little more help with, and since you have the height, I thought you might be willing to lend a hand."

God, this guy needed to work on his conversation starters.

My nerves settled as I nodded. "Yeah, absolutely. You didn't even need to ask, man. You know I'm always down to help."

"Well, I just didn't know if you had things going on with that girlfriend of yours."

"It's all good, man. You just let me know whenever you need me, and I'll be there."

***

"So, you're not just making friends, but you're also becoming a fixture in town," Ray said on the way to Harold's, the local department store.

I chuckled from the passenger seat of her old car. "I guess so."

She reached over and laced her fingers with mine. "I'm glad they're finally seeing what I see," she replied softly.

"And what exactly is it that you see?" My mouth curled into a teasing smile as I gripped her hand tightly, never ceasing to be amazed at how right it felt in mine.

Her cheeks were florid in the morning sunshine streaming through the open window. "My sweet, gentle giant." Her voice was quiet against the warm air rushing into the car, but Noah heard her from the backseat, and he groaned in agony.

I bit back laughter as I glanced over my shoulder. "What's up, buddy? You feel okay?"

"No," he muttered, rolling his eyes to meet mine. "You guys are gonna make me puke."

"Well, aim it out the window, okay?" Ray replied, grinning into the rearview mirror at her son.

"Nah. I'm gonna aim it at you," Noah said, jabbing his finger at my shoulder. Laughter heavy in his tone.

"Hey"—I chuckled and shook my head—"I don't handle puke well, man. You throw up on me, and I'm gonna do it, too, and I'll definitely make sure to do it right back at ya."

Noah groaned with disgust between bursts of giggles. "Mom's car's gonna be so gross."

"Right? Can you imagine what that's gonna smell like? Jesus ... especially in this heat ..."

"Okay"—Ray feigned a gag from beside me—"can you guys stop with the puke talk, please?"

Noah let loose a victorious chuckle, like he'd won and gotten the best of his mother.

Ray rolled her eyes toward me, her lips quirked into a smirk, as if to say, *What am I going to do about that kid?*

There was an adoration in her eyes I never stopped admiring. The love she held for her son, her devotion to him. It amazed and fascinated me ... and it made me jealous. Jealous of a kid more than half my age. Because he had been born under one of the worst circumstances imaginable. Some mothers would've hated him, resented

346

him, held their trauma against him … and it would've been understood. Hell, my mother had resented me for less.

But not Ray.

She had this ability—this *gift*—to separate the child from the circumstances in which she'd had him. She could separate Noah from the bastard who had given him to her. She was the strongest, most beautiful person I'd ever known—inside and out. And while I didn't believe anybody on this planet was perfect … she came really, really close.

"What?" she asked, squinting her eyes at me for a moment before turning them back on the road.

"Huh?"

"Why are you looking at me like that?"

I snorted as I willed my heart to calm down. "Like what?"

"I dunno …" She smirked, her brows pinched with confusion. "You're just looking at me funny."

Am I?

Forcing a chuckle, I tore my gaze away and shook my head as I busied myself with the radio buttons. But while I searched absentmindedly for a new song to listen to, I wondered how exactly I'd been looking at her. What kind of look was it … apart from funny? And what did it mean? Would I even know?

Most days, it was effortless to go with the natural flow of this relationship. It was easy to navigate. But every now and then, the truth that I didn't know how to be a boyfriend hit me with the force of a thousand bricks, and I wished Grampa were alive so I could get his advice.

Maybe I should call Harry, I thought stupidly as I settled on a station playing an old Seether song.

"They used to be one of my favorite bands," Ray said, making small talk. Probably intentionally to steer the topic away from funny looks and the question of what they meant.

"Oh, yeah?"

She nodded. "I used to think I was such a badass, listening to them and Breaking Benjamin and ..." She tipped her head contemplatively before snapping her fingers and pointing at me. "Oh! You know who I used to love too? Staind. They were amazing."

"All of them were pretty good," I agreed.

"What music did you listen to when you were younger?"

I didn't like talking much about when I had been younger, especially with her. But music had the potential to be harmless—unless talking about the memories tied to particular songs. Like Stone Temple Pilots' "Big Empty." It would forever take me back to the side of the road, watching as Billy's body was stuffed into a black bag.

"Um, I listened to the usual stuff," I told her. "Like this"—I gestured toward the speaker—"or, you know, like you said, Breaking Benjamin, Staind, Marilyn Manson ..."

"Well, of course. Because you *were* a badass," she jabbed, reaching over to poke me in the side while her lips stretched into a teasing grin.

But I didn't smile back.

So much for safe.

"I wasn't a badass, Ray," I argued, furrowing my brow. "I was *bad*. There's a difference."

"You weren't *that* bad." Her voice was quiet, hushed. Barely audible above Shaun Morgan's gruff, surly vocals.

"No, I was pretty fucking bad." I mean, I had sold drugs to high school kids, for crying out loud.

"You might've done bad things," she countered in a whisper, "but you were still a good person. I knew bad people, Soldier, and you weren't it. Not to me."

I couldn't argue that, so I didn't.

Instead, I cleared my throat and said, "Anyway, um … but mostly, I listened to the stuff my grandparents' liked."

Ray smiled. "Like what?"

"Oh, um … The Beatles and Van Morrison … Eric Clapton, Elton John, Tom Petty …"

"Oh, Grandpa likes Tom Petty," Noah chimed in from the backseat. "Right, Mom?"

Ray's eyes met the rearview mirror. "He does. Tom Petty's one of his favorites."

"It's, like, the soundtrack of my childhood," I continued, thinking about those days on the dock, fishing with Grampa, or cooking in the kitchen with Gramma. The good days. The days of my childhood worth remembering and holding on to.

"I wish I could've met your grandparents," Ray mused thoughtfully as she turned the car into Harold's parking lot.

"Yeah," I replied as the old but familiar sting of grief struck swift and hard. "Me too."

***

That afternoon, after going shopping and grabbing lunch, Noah and I carried the sixty-five-inch flat screen from Ray's car and up the steps to my house.

Ray, meanwhile, had gone back to her place to get dinner started. She was making white chicken chili—a meal that had quickly become a favorite of mine.

"Watch that," I reminded Noah as he stepped over the rotted plank of wood. "I really need to fix that shit."

"I can help," he said as I fished my keys from my pocket while struggling to steady the underside of the big box on my forearm.

"I'll let you know when I get around to it."

The door now unlocked, I pushed it open to Eleven's welcoming meows. Noah and I carried the television to the couch, where we propped it against the cushions until we were ready to put it up. It was already late, and we were both tired and hungry, but I told him he could help me put it up the next day.

"Can I feed Eleven?" he asked, wiping the sweat off his palms onto his khaki shorts.

"Yeah, sure. I'm just gonna jump in the shower real quick."

After I'd spent so much time in Ray's hot car and hoisting around a heavy TV, the sweat stains beneath my pits were gnarly, and I could only imagine what the rest of me looked like … never mind the smell.

Later, after showering and putting on a fresh pair of clothes, I wandered into the hall, only to find Noah across the way in my bedroom, standing in the open doorway of my closet. My brow furrowed as I crossed the threshold. He wasn't one to snoop—or at least, he never had before.

"Hey, buddy," I said slowly, making him aware of my presence. "Uh … whatcha doing?"

Startled, he turned on his heel. "O-oh! Um … sorry. I, um …" He swallowed and pointed to Eleven, sitting at his feet, licking his front paw. "Eleven ran in here, and I went after him, so, uh …"

"It's cool," I said, dropping the towel in the hamper by the door. "Well, you wanna head back to—"

"What is that?"

"Huh?"

"That."

Noah pointed to the top shelf of the closet. I followed with my eyes and spotted the only thing I had left of my childhood, then smiled.

"That, my friend, is a tackle box," I said, raking my wet hair back against my head. "My grampa used to take me fishing a lot in the summer, and that's what he'd bring with us."

Noah's stare turned melancholy as he nodded. "I've never been fishing."

"No?"

He shook his head.

"Well, we're gonna have to change that. Maybe when school's out, you and I can go down to the water and see what kinda fish are out there."

His smile lit up his whole face. "Really? You'd wanna do that?"

"Absolutely. I mean, as long as your mom is cool with it."

That was all it took for him to take off running past Eleven, down the hall, and out the door, where I was sure he hopped over the rotted wooden step and up his porch stairs. I chuckled to myself as I bent over to pet Eleven between the ears, picturing Noah bursting through the door and begging his mom to let him go fishing, as if we were going right now, at six o'clock in the evening.

He reminded me of … well, me.

Running up the stairs to my room after Grampa had announced we were heading down to the dock for the day. Throwing on whatever clothes I could find, not caring if they were dirty or clean or even the right size.

I glanced at the old red box and smiled through the bittersweet ache. Because, as much as I missed the man who had raised me, it had been decades since I'd felt this close to him. And somehow, the idea of taking that old tackle box out to the water felt an awful lot like bringing him back to life.

CHAPTER

TWENTY-FOUR

THE BOGEYMAN RETURNS

I woke with a gruff sigh to a room still dark and a small, lithe hand running slow, lazy circuits along the waistband of my pants. My lips quirked into a half-dazed smile as my eyes closed to the softness of her fingertips, dipping playfully beneath the elastic.

"What are you doing?" I asked in a sleepy, teasing tone.

Ray's lips pressed to my shoulder as her hand traveled lower. "Waking you up, obviously."

I smirked toward the ceiling. "But it's Sunday."

"Yes"—she kissed across my chest, her fingertips grazing the base of my quick arousal—"it is."

"I sleep in on Sundays."

"Oh, so sorry." Her hand was quick to leave my pants as she propped herself up on her elbow, looking down into my eyes with a feigned expression of apology. "Should I let you go back to sleep then?"

I snorted, rolling over and flipping her onto her back. "Well, I'm already up now. Might as well do something about it ..."

"Are you sure? I mean, it only takes you, like, two seconds to fall asleep, so if you *really* want to sleep in ..."

She accentuated the pout of her full bottom lip as my hand rounded her hip to dip between her open thighs, finding she'd already taken off her underwear. I groaned, sliding my fingers over her smooth, slick, delicate skin, and she bit her lip.

A sound not unlike a growl scraped along my throat as one finger easily slipped inside.

"God, how the hell are you already so wet?"

The lip trapped between her teeth was released then, followed by a hushed gasp. "I woke up like this," she admitted.

I lifted one side of my mouth in a smile as I worked that finger slowly. Moving in, moving out. "Oh, yeah?"

She nodded lazily, already sated and drifting toward bliss. "I had a dream."

My head dropped to kiss her collarbone, her neck, her ear. "A dream, huh?"

Ray writhed beneath my body, half covering hers, and she spread her legs further. "Yeah ..."

"About what?" I tasted her earlobe, drawing it into my mouth.

"Oh God," she moaned, elongating her neck, granting me better access. "It was about ... about you."

354

"Yeah? And what about me?"

Her laugh was breathy and exasperated. "Come on, Soldier ... you know ..."

I added another finger and nipped at her neck. "Was I eating a sandwich?"

That made her giggle as she turned her head and brought her hand up to cup my bearded cheek.

"You definitely weren't eating a sandwich."

I lifted my head to find her gaze with mine. I smiled when I saw her looking up at me with a monumental amount of affection. So much that I had to remind my heart to keep beating for her. Always for her.

"Was I ... was I riding my bike?"

She shook her head, giggling again past her bitten lip. "No ... but you were definitely riding something."

"Was *I* riding something"—I raised one brow and widened my grin—"or were you?"

Ray's elated smile filled the darkened room with sunshine as she laughed and pulled my mouth to hers.

"Both," she whispered before capturing my lips in a kiss that forced the breath from my lungs.

In a flurry of tangled tongues and lips, we moved in the hazy glow of the rising sun, barely peeking through the blinds on her window. Her shirt was lifted and thrown to the floor, and my pajama pants met the same fate shortly after. I rolled to my back, giving her the freedom to take back the reins, and she did. Straddling my lap, guiding my throbbing, single-minded dick to the one and only place it ever wanted to be.

"Fuck," I hissed through clenched teeth as her body joined mine and sank lower, taking me deeper. "Jesus, Ray."

She answered with a muffled hum, smiling as if she were dreaming, and then she began to move. Rocking against me like the waves sloshing against the shore, lulling me toward the edge with her steady rhythm, before drawing me under to drown in a euphoric sea.

"Sol ... Soldier," she gasped, clawing at my chest and clinging tight to whatever she could grab. "I'm ... I'm going to ..."

"Yes," I urged, encircling her waist with my greedy hands. "Let me feel it, baby. *God ...*"

Ray had given me so much in the months since we'd gotten together.

The promise of good, home-cooked meals every night; the chance to be a positive role model for her son; another form of transportation; a warm body to sleep with every night we were able. And the realization that sex and orgasm could be anything more than a simple means to an end.

With every gift offered, I accepted and fell deeper into everything I felt for her, and the quick descent only continued as we collided in a chorus of quiet moans and gasps and heavy breathing. Our foreheads kissed, our eyes locked, and our hearts hammered with every pulse given and taken until there was nothing left to do but collapse in a heap of sweat and elation.

"Okay, I can go back to sleep now," I muttered, wrapping my arms around her bare shoulders and holding her tight.

"Mmhmm," she muttered with a nod, smiling against my chest. "We could probably get a solid hour or two in before we have to get up."

I stroked my thumb against her cheek. "I like the way you think."

The seconds ticked by to remind me I was still exhausted, and before I knew it, my limbs had grown heavy, and my breathing had slowed. I was moments away from comfortable sleep when my thumb grazed over a new wetness against her cheek, and I frowned.

"Hey," I whispered, my voice rough and groggy. "Why are you crying?"

Ray released a shaky breath and swallowed. "I just … I really like you."

My heart ached just beneath her ear as I replied, "I really like you too."

"No." She sniffled. "I mean, I *really* like you, Soldier."

I furrowed my brow, uncertain if I had said anything different or misunderstood. "Okay … and I really—"

She scrambled to lift onto her elbow, and I opened my eyes to stare into the watery green abyss of hers. God, how the hell could she look so sad, so worried, when we had just shared the most incredible, intense orgasm of my life?

"I have never liked someone as much as I like you … *ever*," she said, and I began to wonder if she intended to say a word other than *like*. "I have never had something as good as this before."

I gently nodded. "Neither have I," I whispered as my eyes searched hers for the things she wasn't saying, unsure of why I was whispering at all.

"And I'm just so"—her tears startled me by falling harder, faster, as her hand flattened to my chest—"*so* scared of losing it."

"Ray ..." I shook my head, lifting my hand to collect her tears in my palm. "I'm not going anywhere, okay? I have nowhere else to go, and even if I did, I'd only want to be here. With you. And Noah. Okay? So, don't ever worry about that."

She squeezed her eyes shut, pushing more tears between her lashes as she nodded rapidly. "I-I know. I b-believe you, but ..." She shuddered with a quiet sob. "I'm just s-s-so worried, and I can't st-stop worrying, and ... and I d-don't know w-w-why."

"You're worried because you think, just because you've never been allowed to have something this good before, that means you should never be allowed to."

She sniffled again and nodded.

"But, baby, don't you think it's possible that, after losing so much and so often, it's about time you won? Because I do." I laid my hand over hers, pressing her fingertips over my frantic heart. "It's about fucking time I won, Ray, and if I get to win, then you do too. Okay?"

She pulled in a deep breath, quelling her sobs as she nodded. "Okay," she whispered. "If you win, I win."

She calmed. Laying her head back against my chest and drifting quickly toward sleep with my thumb stroking her cheek and my fingers running through her hair. Her body grew heavy against mine as her breathing evened out, and I knew she was asleep. Maybe to dream about me again. Maybe to dream about whatever had spiked her fears enough to make her cry. But wherever she went, she didn't take me with her, and for that extra hour I could've been sleeping, I stared at the sunlight streaking across the ceiling. Wondering if it was really, truly, honestly possible for me to win at all or if I was always ever destined to lose.

***

"So, what video games did you play when you were a kid?"

"Oh, uh … hand me that screwdriver over there."

Noah reached with his free hand and grabbed the Phillips head from a nearby shelf.

Once it was in my palm, I tightened the mounting bracket to the wall and continued, "I liked a lot of games. You know … Super Mario Bros., Tetris, uh … Legend of Zelda …"

"What about, like, Sonic the Hedgehog?"

I shook my head. "Sonic was Sega, and I only had a Nintendo and Super Nintendo. One of my old friends …" I took my hands from the metal now attached to the wall, and Noah followed suit. "He had a Sega Genesis, so I'd play sometimes when I was over at his place."

"Your friend that died?"

Man, kids were funny. Their lack of filters, their uninhibited honesty … it was refreshing and startling, all at once.

"Nah," I said, shaking my head. "Different friend."

"Oh … what happened to him?"

I shrugged. "Who knows? He moved when we were in the fourth grade."

Noah nodded like this all meant something to him as I screwed the mounting plate to the back of the TV. And then, together, we hoisted it up and brought it to the wall. I could've asked one of the other guys in town to help me out, and maybe I should've, just to be safe. But this felt like a Noah and me thing, and I wanted to keep it that way. To make that memory, so years from now, we could say, *Hey, remember that time we fumbled like idiots to get that TV on the wall? Yeah, that was fun.*

I hoped I still knew him then.

"Okay, let's get 'er up," I said. "Ready?"

Noah nodded, and on the count of three, we had the thing up from the couch and in our arms. I held most of the weight while Noah did his part to steady it. Twice, I asked if he was okay, and despite his lips being rolled tightly between his teeth and his face being the color of a fucking tomato, he nodded. We hung it up easily enough, and with a lung-emptying exhale, Noah stood back to admire our handiwork.

"Good job," I said, lending my hand for a high five.

"Now, we just gotta get you a Switch."

He grinned up at me, waggling his brows, and I responded with a laugh.

"One step at a time, pal. We—"

The moment was fractured by the cracking sound of splintering wood coming from somewhere outside. Noah and I both turned our heads so fast that my neck popped in places I hadn't known it could.

360

"What was that?" Noah asked in an urgent, hushed voice.

I was already moving to the door. "I don't—"

That was when she screamed.

"Mom!" Noah shouted, sprinting the twenty feet from the living room to the door, where I stopped him, my hand against his shoulder.

"Stay. Here," I warned him while my heart resounded like a bass drum in my ears.

Noah's panicked eyes, already flooding with tears, met mine as I opened the front door. Then, before I could warn him again to stop, he ran.

"Fucking hell," I gritted through clenched teeth, and I took off after him.

Thirteen steps from my stoop to her porch. Up the stairs. Through the broken front door, splayed wood and splinters everywhere. Past a knocked-over chair and a broken lamp. I searched for Ray, but I couldn't find her at first. All I saw, all I could focus on, was a man, standing near her kitchen table.

Seth.

The bogeyman had returned.

Through the sound of whooshing blood pumping past my eardrums, I could hear Noah.

"Get away from her! Get off! Asshole, *get off of her!*"

Noah lunged at his back, and I yelled for him, "Noah!" His name tore through my throat as Seth wrestled with him, pulling at the skinny boy's arms around his neck.

That was when I saw Ray. Bent over the kitchen table, her dress torn. A small pool of blood puddling beneath her face.

A soul-rendering rage overcame my body at the sight of her shaking. Frozen. Eyes squeezed shut. I had no idea where on her head the blood was coming from—it didn't matter. Just seconds after entering the house, I stormed forward, eyes on nobody but the piece of shit who had dared to infiltrate the happy bubble we had built for ourselves.

"You little bastard," Seth growled, unlocking Noah's arms from around his neck and throwing the kid onto the floor easily. "I'll teach you not to fuck with me."

He raised his clenched fist and crouched, ready to strike Noah's face, but he didn't get the chance. My arm was around his neck, his back to my chest. I lifted him away, his feet barely scraping the carpet as I pulled him backward toward the door. He gasped and sputtered. Choking, clawing at my arm with frantic fingers.

Kill him, kill him, kill him, kill him, kill him kill him kill him, a voice in my head chanted as my arm tightened around his throat.

Seth's strength was waning. He was about to lose consciousness.

Just a little longer. Just a little tighter, and he'll never come for them again. He'll never come back.

"Mom!"

Noah's voice pierced the red fog, and my eyes dodged toward the table where I'd last seen Ray. But she wasn't there now. She was on the floor, cowering against the kitchen cabinets. Smeared blood coated her cheek, her nose, her lips, down her chin and onto her chest—a dark contrast to the pallor of her colorless skin. She was in shock, and Noah was beside her, wrapping his arms around her and calling her name. Thinking about nothing but making sure she was okay.

"Noah, call 911!" I shouted, drawing his attention to me.

His stare was on me now, immediately blank, as though he couldn't understand what I was saying.

"Call 9—*fuck*!"

I'd been too distracted. I'd put my guard down. Seth slipped from my grip, holding on to my arm and getting the upper hand. Noah screamed as my arm was pulled behind my back, my body thrust against the wall beside the door.

"And who the fuck are you, huh?" Seth growled, pressing his forearm to the back of my neck. "I'm gonna teach you to mind your own fucking business, asshole."

"The hell you are," I replied, my voice muffled against the wall, before kicking my foot back, knocking Seth's leg out from under him.

He cursed and released me from his hold, falling to the floor as I turned. I gave him a second to look up at me, to see my face, to allow the recognition to settle in, if it were to come at all. And, of course, it did.

"Ho-ly shit," he uttered, a giddy, fascinated smile stretching his ugly features. "Soldier Mason. So, this is where you ended up, huh? You're the new guy next door."

I said nothing as he rose to his feet, the top of his head reaching my chin. He sneered up into my eyes and pointed at the scar stretching the length of my left cheek.

"That's a nice little souvenir you got there," he said, nodding at his handiwork. "Too bad it wasn't a fucking hole in the head."

My expression was unmoving as I said in a flat monotone, "Get the fuck out of here before I kill you."

He barked a sinister laugh. "You don't have it in you to kill me, Mason."

But he turned and pointed at Noah, beside his mother, clutching a phone in his hand. "Let's go, boy."

Noah shook his head.

"Noah!" Seth roared, making the kid jump and quiver. "You're going to listen to me right now. Get your ass outside. We're getting the fuck out of—"

"You don't have to go anywhere with him, Noah," I interjected, locking eyes with the scared boy, who now looked years younger than he was. "He's not going to hurt you."

Seth looked over his shoulder, narrowed eyes scanning my face. "Who the fuck do you think you are?" he asked, voice low in an attempt to threaten me. "That's my *son*. I can tell him to do whatever the fuck I want." He looked back at the boy. "Noah! Get the fuck outside!"

"N-no," Noah replied, shaking his head. "I'm not going."

Seth's pride was evidently wounded at his son's protest.

The man looked back at me with a blend of malice and disgust, then asked, "You just can't get the fuck out of my way, can you?"

"Not as long as you keep showing up."

He snorted a wicked chuckle. "And they're afraid of me?" He shook his head, continuing to laugh. "Do they know you're a murderer? Does she know"—he pointed behind himself at Ray—"that she's fucking a murderer? And she's scared of *me*?"

"Your time is up," I told him, flexing my fists at my sides. "Get the fuck out now."

"You *are* fucking her, right?" he asked, still trying to ruffle my feathers, even as he headed for the broken door. "How does it feel, Soldier? Knowing you're just getting my sloppy seconds?"

As he stood in the open doorway, I spun to snatch his arm, twisting it around his back and feeling the telltale sensation of a bone snapping. Seth yelped, sounding like an injured dog, as I brought my mouth to his ear.

"If you ever come back here, I promise you, I will end your fucking life."

"Not if I end yours first," he challenged, his voice strained under the weight of his pain.

I released his arm, shoving him toward the steps and hoping he'd fall. But no such luck. He slithered his way down, like the fucking snake he was, clutching his fractured arm to his chest.

When I was sure he wasn't turning around, I went to Ray.

Noah sat beside her. "I-I didn't call the cops," he admitted, clutching the phone. "I d-didn't want them to take you away."

I could only stare at him as my hands were held out, frozen, ready to tend to his mother. "Noah, they wouldn't take me away."

"But ..." Shame filled his eyes with tears. "He ... he said that you ... you ... that you're a-a-a ..."

He couldn't say it, what he had heard come from his father's mouth. That I had killed someone. He couldn't admit out loud the possibility that it might be the truth.

"That's not something you have to worry about, okay? You don't ever have to worry about me. You worry about your mom and yourself. That's it. And if I tell you to call 911, that's what you do. You understand?"

He was crying as he nodded. "I-I-I'm sorry."

This kid, who I had known for six months of my life, thought he'd done the right thing by protecting me.

For once, someone had looked out for me, and I couldn't be mad at him for that.

"It's okay, buddy," I said as I reached out to lay my hand over his head. "Now, do me a favor. Get a wet washcloth and an ice pack from the freezer. Then, call 911."

***

Her nose had been broken. Her cheek had been bruised. Seth hadn't gotten the chance to do much more than

366

that—thank Christ—but it was her mind that was wounded most of all.

Officer Kinney sat with us in an emergency room bay, asking questions about the break-in and if we knew the guy who had broken in. I let Ray do the talking, unsure of what she would say.

I was ready to blow a fuse when she claimed to not know the intruder. But instead of saying anything, I walked away as she spoke to him while the on-call doctor tended to her wounds, angry with myself for not killing Seth when I'd had the chance. Angry with her for not doing something to protect herself and her son.

Officer Kinney passed me on the way out, nodding his chin in my direction.

"I understand ya feel helpless," he said.

You have no fucking idea, dude.

"Things like this …" He shook his head. "They just don't happen here, so to see it happen now … it's unsettling. And I'm sorry ya had to walk in to see what ya saw. I can't imagine."

"Yeah," I said on an exhale, crossing my arms over my chest tightly.

He hesitated, eyeing the pad of paper in his hand before looking back at me, uncertainty in his gaze. "Are ya sure ya didn't recognize him?"

Fucking hell, Ray.

My gut told me to tell him the truth. To tell him I knew exactly who it was. That this was my chance to bring the proverbial hammer down on that son of a bitch's head. But my heart said I had to talk to Ray first. I had to know what was going on in her mind, why she hadn't told him herself. And then I'd make a choice.

"Yeah," I muttered. "I'm pretty sure."

Patrick nodded slowly, sending his gaze downward toward the floor. "I gotta be honest with ya ..." He lifted his eyes again, his half-hearted, lopsided smile full of apology. "I almost thought he might've been connected to your past."

I couldn't help but huff a sardonic chuckle because that Officer Patrick Kinney was a smart guy for such a small-town cop who had very likely never seen the type of shit I'd experienced.

But I couldn't tell him that, so I just shook my head and said, "When I have something to tell you, man ... I'll let you know."

Whether he could read between those lines or not, I wasn't sure. He just flattened his lips into a tight line and nodded slowly.

"All right," he relented. "I already said this to Ray, and I'm sure I don't need to say it to you, but I'm going to anyway. If you see something"—he clapped a hand over my shoulder—"say something. Ya have my number."

"Yep."

"All right." He nudged his chin in the direction of the ER bay where Ray was waiting, shaken up and hurt. "Go take care of her."

"I will," I promised before turning around and heading back inside.

***

I convinced Ray to come stay at my place—at least until we knew she and Noah were safe. Ray—wearing a nasal cast and claiming she was fine when, obviously, she wasn't—made a joke about using the incident as an excuse for them to move in with me, and I shut her down with a hardened look as she quietly carried some of her clothes into my bedroom.

"I'm not laughing, Ray," I said, keeping my voice down to prevent Noah from hearing me.

He was busying himself in the living room, setting up his Switch on my new TV.

His TV had been broken in the fight.

"Well, if you can't laugh at life, then you're just letting the bad guys win," she muttered beneath her breath.

But they are *winning. Doesn't she see that?*

I shook my head and slowly closed the door, letting it click shut before speaking again. "Why didn't you tell Patrick the truth?"

Ray wouldn't look at me as she carefully placed her clothes into the drawer I'd cleaned out for her. "You know why."

"No, I really don't. Goddammit, Ray. You could've gotten him arrested. He could be sitting in a fucking jail cell right now with a restraining order against him, but you *let him go*." I shook my head and sat down on the bed, clapping my hands against my thighs and feeling helpless. "*Why*? Why the hell would you do that?"

She was silent, staring into the open drawer at the shirts she'd just placed inside. Jesus … I knew I couldn't begin to know what it was like to be her. To be a victim in this way. To be hurt repeatedly, physically … mentally. To be used and broken. I couldn't begin to understand what it was like for her, and I wouldn't pretend to. But what I wanted was to help. To protect her, to save her. And how the hell was I supposed to do that when she wouldn't try to protect herself?

"You were going to kill him," she finally whispered.

"Yes." I nodded to her back.

"You weren't going to think twice. You were just going to do it."

"Yes."

She turned around then, revealing her tearful eyes to me for the second time that day. "And the cops would've arrested you. They would've taken you away from me."

My heart dropped to the bottom of my stomach as I blinked and turned away. "They could've said it was self-defense. It could've—"

"Okay. Maybe. But then what? Even if Seth wasn't around anymore, you don't think word would've gotten back to his friends? You don't think Levi wouldn't find out? God, Soldier, why do you think I've never said something before?"

My jaw shifted. "I—"

"Because I've *always* been scared of what would happen to us. And now, with you …" She huffed and ran a hand over her face. "You didn't want them knowing where you were, but guess what. They do now. And if you weren't here? *Nobody* would be here to keep us safe."

I was flabbergasted and stunned. Because, fuck, she had a point. It wasn't a great one. I still felt she should've pressed charges and gotten a restraining order, but I understood now why she hadn't.

It wasn't just that she was afraid of what might happen to her.

She was afraid of what might happen to *me*.

"Ray …" I smoothed my hand over my hair and shook my head. "Rain … I—"

"I love you," she said abruptly, sure and sincere. "That's what I wanted to say this morning when I only told you I really liked you. I *love* you, Soldier. I love you more than I've ever loved anyone else … apart from Noah. And I love that you would've committed the worst crime in the world to protect us. I love that you want to see him go away and never ever, ever come back. I love you so much for that and for everything else you've done for us. But I need you here more than I need him gone."

My mouth was dry with the revelation of her words passing round and round and round in my head.

I love you, I love you, I love you.

When the fuck was the last time someone had told me they loved me?

It was so long ago that I couldn't remember who had said it or when. And now, I didn't know what to do, what to *say*. How to appropriately react without making a complete ass of myself.

"Um …" I cleared my throat and rubbed at a random spot above my eyebrow. "Wow. I …"

"I don't need you to say it back," she said, cutting me off. "I just want you to understand why I keep avoiding the police. Because I'm scared of what steps Seth will take next, never mind what his friends would do if he were thrown in jail."

I had to laugh at that while my heart begged me to find a way to tell her how I felt too.

"You know, maybe they wouldn't care," I said, a feeble attempt at lightening the mood. "They might even be thrilled to get rid of that hotheaded asshole."

"Maybe," she said, quietly turning back to the open drawer to finish putting away her things. "But I don't think I care to find out."

CHAPTER
TWENTY-FIVE

GRAMPA'S SECRET

If someone had told me ten years ago that I would one day be living with a girlfriend and acting as a father to her son, I would've laughed in their face and told them they were insane.

Because what woman in her right mind would look at me—a six-foot-seven felon with a scarred face and shitty tattoos—and think, *Yeah, that's the guy I wanna build a home with?*

Yet there I was. Flipping burgers and turning hot dogs on a hot day in June with Noah at my side while Ray plucked a few stray weeds from the garden full of baby cucumber, strawberry, and of course, tomato plants. A neighbor from the community—a younger woman named Julia—rode by on her bike and waved, wishing us a good night, and we waved back, wearing smiles and smacking at the mosquitoes that relentlessly bit at whatever skin they could stick themselves into. Like a real, normal family.

Despite the lingering threat of the bogeyman hanging over our heads, it was starting to feel like we actually were.

"So, your birthday's coming up," I said to Noah as he flipped a burger, just as I'd shown him.

"Yeah," he said with a shrug. Like it wasn't a big deal that he was turning thirteen.

All things considered, he was still somewhat better off than I had been when I was thirteen. And that, to me, was a big deal.

"What do you wanna do?"

He glanced up at me like I had lost all my marbles somewhere. "What do you mean?"

"How do you wanna celebrate?"

Noah wrinkled his nose and scratched at a fresh mosquito bite. "I dunno …"

"I mean, do you wanna have a party or something? Or do you just wanna chill out with us and have dinner? Or …"

He sniffed a laugh. "Whatever. I dunno."

Since the attack in the house next door, Noah had been quiet, more reserved. I knew he was confused about his mom's choices to not press charges. I knew he was scared. But with the way he'd been hanging around me the past few weeks since that day, even to the point of coming to work with me every day he didn't have school, I also knew he felt better when I was around.

I was even starting to feel a little grateful that I hadn't snapped that asshole's neck.

But while I respected that Noah had to handle things in his own way—which included seeing a therapist once a week—I was worried that kid I'd met all those months ago would be lost in his head somewhere. I was worried he'd fade away, just as I had. Forced to harden to accommodate for the circumstances he had been born into. And I needed him to know he didn't have to. If he had any choice in that, he didn't have to do a damn thing as long as I was around.

"Well, I mean, we could go fishing, if you want to," I suggested, reminding him of something he'd wanted to do badly before the attack.

A small glimmer of excitement sparked in his eye as he looked up at me. "Yeah, maybe we could do that."

"That would be fun."

He nodded. "And, I mean, if you want to, maybe we could have pizza or something. Like, on my birthday."

"So, you don't wanna go fishing on your birthday?"

"Well, we can, but ..." He shrugged and turned a sizzling hot dog. "I kinda like the idea of having a party too."

"Yeah," I said, catching his mom's eye and the small, affectionate smile that had begun to form on her beautiful face, "I do too."

***

And so, despite the dark Seth-shaped cloud that hung over our heads, we threw together a little impromptu birthday party for Noah. We invited his grandparents and aunt Stormy, Harry and his wife, and a few kids from

Noah's class. It wasn't a big gathering of people, but they all fit perfectly in the place we now called home.

Noah was running around the yard with his buddies and their Nerf guns as Harry and I looked on with cold cans of soda in hand. My old friend glanced up at me with a smile on his face, one that reminded me too much of Grampa's.

"What?" I chuckled uncomfortably, diverting my gaze to the can in my hand.

"I'm just thinking," he replied, looking away to take a sip from his drink.

"Careful, old man. Don't wanna hurt yourself."

Harry chuckled gently, shaking his head. "I'm just proud of you, is all."

"Harry, man," I groaned sardonically. "You're not allowed to get all sappy on me now. I gotta pick up the pizzas in a few minutes. I can't be walking in there, looking like I've been crying it out over here."

"No, no, no. I want you to look around for a second," he said, turning to face me. "You have a beautiful girlfriend, who is, for reasons I can't figure out, absolutely crazy about you."

I snorted, glancing in the direction of Ray, laughing with her sister and mother. "Thanks. You really know how to make a guy feel good about himself."

He chuckled, laying a hand against my arm. "You have that kid over there, who looks at you like you're his entire world. You have this place, which"—he turned to glance at the trailer that was looking pretty damn good these days—"if I can remind you, looked like a literal pile of crap when you first moved in.

"You did all this," he said, nodding with approval and satisfaction and a bunch of other good shit I couldn't put my finger on. "You defeated the odds, son. I can safely say, looking at this life you've built for yourself, you've actually won."

A grin tugged at my lips as my mind went to a conversation Ray and I'd had recently.

"If you win, I win."

But the thought of that morning—lazy sex and worried tears—reminded me of our last day spent in her house. It reminded me of why they were *really* here, sleeping in my rooms and eating dinner in my kitchen instead of theirs. She loved me—I knew that—but that wasn't why we'd forged a life under the same roof.

It was because of the bogeymen.

And no matter what happy life we managed to find for ourselves here—with birthday parties and barbecues and gardens full of homegrown vegetables—it would never feel permanent or real, like it was truly ours, until that bogeyman was gone.

Or we were.

***

"So, what are you guys gonna do? Just go down to the Sound and see what you can catch?" Ray was amused, sitting cross-legged on the bed we now called ours as I pulled the tackle box down from the top shelf of the closet.

I chuckled. "Pretty much. Howard is dropping off a couple of rods in the morning for us to use until we get our own."

She watched me drop the heavy metal box onto the bed, tipping her head and putting on that smile I now understood to mean she was thinking about how lucky she was—for whatever reason. "You know, I never would've pegged you for a fisherman."

"Well"—I unlatched the two clasps with a metallic *click*—"I'm not really. It's just something I did with Grampa in the summer. He was really the fisherman, but I"—the lid creaked open to reveal the bobbers, hooks, and lines I hadn't seen in decades—"went along for the ride."

The air left my lungs as I stared at all of those things, these little cheap trinkets—some of them rusted, but I'd never have the heart to throw them out—that would mean nothing to anybody else but me. Every single one of them seemed to awaken another core memory, and I held each one up to tell Ray all about it.

"This one," I said, holding up a big, barbed four-pronged hook, "went right through the skin over my kneecap when I was nine."

Ray grimaced.

I held up a wooden egg bobber. "Grampa convinced me when I was, like, five that these were actual eggs laid by waterfowl."

"Oh my God," she said with a gentle laugh. "That's so cute."

"Yeah, I was adorable," I joked as I picked up a round bright-green bobber. One that was never meant to be dropped into any body of water.

My throat tightened as I turned it over in my hands, and when Ray asked me what it was, I coughed and pushed my lips to smile.

"I made this for him for Father's Day when I was …" I filled my chest with air, trying to remember. Wishing I could call Grampa up and ask. "God, I had to have been three, maybe four years old. I had made it out of clay or Play-Doh or something in preschool, and all I remember is Gramma telling me how proud of it I was. Rumor has it, I couldn't wait to give it to him, so he got it a few days before Father's Day."

A harsh reminder of the cruelties of time smacked against my heart, harder with every beat, that my grandfather wasn't here now. To see me pass on this torch, this pastime we had shared. He'd never gotten the chance to see me as a father to someone—biological or chosen—and, man, that hurt. It hurt so much that I had to clear my throat a few times and busy my hands, dropping the little fake bobber back into the box and lifting the tray out to find another treasure. One that struck harder, deeper.

"Ah fuck," I muttered, lifting the old picture out. "I didn't even know he kept this in here."

Honestly, I had never looked beneath the tray at all. He'd always said I didn't have to, that everything I needed was right at the top, and he'd never been wrong. But now, looking at the picture of my grandfather as a somewhat younger man, holding me as a toddler, I wondered what else might be tucked inside.

"Can I see?" Ray asked gently, holding out her hand.

I passed the picture to her, which warranted an instant smile.

"Oh my God," she cooed, touching its surface. "You were the cutest little kid."

"What the hell happened, right?" I offered a teasing grin to hide the emotions that were relentlessly threatening to sweep me away.

"Nah," she said, still staring at the sweet moment between Grampa and me, forever frozen in time. "You just graduated from cute to hot somewhere along the way."

Sniffing a chuckle, I pulled out an old greeting card—an anniversary card from Gramma—and a picture of the three of us from my First Communion. Then, just as I was about to make a comment about how he had nothing of my mother hidden in his box of treasures, something else caught my eye. Something beneath one last memento—a picture of our old dog, Sully.

"What ... the *fuck* ..." I dropped the pictures and card on the bed as I carefully lifted out the pistol.

Ray's smile was quick to fall from her face. "Soldier, is that a gun?"

Of course, she knew it was a gun. I was holding it right in front of her face, turning it over in my hands.

And still, I nodded slowly and said, "Yeah."

"No way. No." She shook her head adamantly. "I'm sorry. I know it was your grandfather's. But there is no way I feel comfortable with that thing being in the same house with my son. At least not without it being locked up and hidden somewhere."

"I didn't even know this was in here," I admitted sheepishly, not knowing the first thing about what to do with the damn thing. "I didn't know Grampa had a gun."

God, was it even legal?

Why did he have it at all?

"Well, um, can we get rid of it?" Ray was wringing her hands in the bottom of my T-shirt she had taken to sleep in.

"Yeah," I promised, my resolve firm. "I'll just put it back in the closet until I figure out what to do with it. I'll talk to Patrick."

"*Please* hide it," she begged me, and I satisfied her by concealing it in a bundle of spare sheets.

But even though neither of us said as much, we both knew there was no way we'd forget it was there until it was gone.

CHAPTER
TWENTY-SIX

MURDER OF ONE

A long time ago, back in the 1600s, some people had believed that the number of crows in a murder could determine their fate.

One meant death or a catastrophic event—something of that nature; two meant joy, good things; three or four decided whether someone would have a girl or boy ... and so on.

It was something I had read in a book from the Wayward library, and I remembered thinking then that it was nutty. That people had once known so little about life and science and just the way things worked altogether that they felt they needed to look to the birds in a freakin' tree to know what the hell was going on when Jacob or some shit had come down with a killer case of consumption.

But now, as Noah and I walked down to the shore, with our tackle box and rods in tow, I looked to the single crow that seemed to be following us, and I started to wonder …

What if they were onto something?

"That bird is freaking me out," Noah mentioned without knowing what was going through my head.

"You and me both."

"You should give it some food. Maybe it'll go away."

I shook my head, glancing at the grim black bird. "Feeding it will just make it want more."

"Well, I mean, it obviously wants *something*," Noah said, rolling his eyes up at me.

Yeah. My soul.

I cringed inwardly at the thought and shook it away. I was being irrational and ridiculous, and I knew it. But I had woken up with the eerie sense that something was about to go wrong, and no matter what I did, I could not get rid of it. It was the same foreboding I'd had for months, sneaking up when I least expected it. But this was different. It was powerful and consuming, needling away at my brain, and that crow wasn't helping.

However, as we turned off Main Street and onto Oak toward the beach, we did get rid of that damn bird. And I tried to take that as a good sign.

***

"All right, buddy. So, what you wanna do is reel in your line until it's hanging about a foot or so." I demonstrated and then gestured for him to do the same.

Noah slowly cranked the reel until he did as I'd instructed. "Like this?"

"Yep. Perfect. Now, pull back your arm like this, then quickly sweep the rod forward." I did just as I'd said as Noah watched intently, eyes widening as the fishing line sailed through the air and into the water fifteen feet away. "Now, don't forget to release the reel button, too, or it won't go anywhere."

He nodded, and then, with determination set heavy in his eyes, he mimicked my movements and dropped his lure just a couple feet closer than mine.

"How's that?" he asked with a triumphant smirk.

I held tight to the rod as I clapped him on the back. "I'd say pretty freakin' good. I mean, for your first try."

"Next time, mine will be farther than yours."

"Yeah, I'd like to see you try," I chided, bumping my elbow against his arm.

It was a gorgeous July day on the water. The sun was just hidden enough within the clouds to keep the day warm while not blinding us beneath its rays. Very few people crowded the shore, thanks to it being midday on a Tuesday, while everyone else was still at work.

I had taken off my shirt once we arrived, and Noah had done the same. It was too hot not to. But now, I was regretting it as the eyes of a couple of housewives wrangling their young kids stared in my direction. Their mouths moved in whispers to each other, their eyes peering over the frames of their sunglasses. I pretended not to notice, but Noah was less skilled in the art of subtlety, and he made no secret of his annoyed glances in their direction.

"They know Mom's your girlfriend," he grumbled.

"They don't care about that. It doesn't matter to them as long as they just look."

"It does matter though, right?"

I shrugged, then nodded. "I mean, *I* think so. But some people have different ideas of what's okay and what isn't."

"Well, I don't think it's okay."

"And that's why you'll get all the ladies one day. They like good guys."

We stood there in a nearly comfortable silence, watching our lures bob in the distance. But I could hear the wheels in Noah's head turning. I could see his brow furrowed with thought, and after a minute of watching him gnaw at his bottom lip, I finally asked what was on his mind.

He hesitated, twisting his lips to the side and cocking his head. Then, finally, he asked, "Are you *really* a good guy?"

A laugh barked past my lips. "Dude, if you have to ask, I'm doing something wrong."

He shook his head and groaned. "No, you know what I mean. I always thought you were, but ..."

I turned my head to look at him, stunned by this sudden confession. "But what?"

"But ..." He sighed, his breath coming out with a tremor. "My dad ... h-he *knew* you."

It had been weeks since Seth had broken into Ray's house. Noah had been more reserved than usual, quieter and rigid. But I had assumed it was because of the things he'd seen. I'd never once questioned how he might've taken what he'd heard from his father's lips.

How could I have been so stupid?

"*How* does he know you?"

I had always assumed that, if my relationship with Noah continued, I'd eventually have to answer these questions. But I had never anticipated when or how he would ask, and so I'd never prepared myself to answer.

Part of me wanted to tell him to talk to his mom. To get whatever answers she was comfortable giving him. But then another part—a louder, more incessant part— told me to be honest with him. That hearing it from me would be better for him, as well as me, so I took a deep breath and went with it.

"I grew up in the same town as your parents," I said. "I mean, I think you already knew that about your mom, but your dad was there too."

Noah nodded softly, focusing on his lure bobbing in the water. Waiting for a fish to bite. "Were you friends?"

"No." I shook my head, unable to fight my bitter chuckle. "Definitely not friends."

"I figured."

"Yeah, we, uh … we didn't get along well."

"Did you get into a fight?"

I chortled at that as I nodded. "We did actually." Then, I turned to face him, pointing at the scar on my cheek. "Your dad gave me this quite a few years back."

Noah's lips actually quirked into a half smile. "So, *that's* where you got that scar."

I tipped my head with curiosity, and Noah's smile broadened.

"That was one of the first things I asked you, remember? I asked you if you got your scar in jail."

I laughed, reaching out to grip his shoulder and give him a playful little shake. "That's right. I forgot about that."

His grin faded as his eyes dropped to my hand. Then, he said in a small, quiet voice, "My dad said you're a murderer."

There it was. The question I had dreaded the most. The one I'd been avoiding.

"He did," I replied, holding steady to the rod and my composure.

"Why would he say that?"

"Because"—I sucked in the scent of the beach and exhaled—"I killed someone, Noah."

"*What?*" He was shrill, shocked, and—fuck me—scared, and I wondered how he'd managed to live in this town all these months without hearing someone say something about my past.

"Listen to me," I said, meeting his gaze. "I'm not a murderer. It wasn't intentional. But someone died because of something I had done a long time ago, and that's why I was in prison."

The fear seemed to dissipate from his eyes as the tension left his shoulders, and I was filled with relief. But he was still clearly uneasy about what I'd told him, and who could blame him? Death wasn't an easy concept for anybody to understand or accept, especially not a kid who had yet to experience a loss of that caliber. To stand beside someone you knew—someone *close*—who had ended someone else's life was an even more difficult thing to come to terms with, and I couldn't expect him to take it in stride.

"We don't have to talk about it anymore," I told him, filling the air with something other than the seagulls above and those ladies' muffled whispers. "But if you want to, if you have questions or whatever, I want you to know you can ask me."

Noah nodded, keeping his eyes on the pole in his hands. "Well ... who died?"

"My best friend, Billy," I told him. "Remember that friend I tell you about sometimes? The one who passed away?"

He nodded.

"Well, that's the friend. We had known each other for a really long time."

"Oh ... were you sad when he died?"

I didn't mean to scoff, but the question seemed as absurd as the audacity of those women. Openly staring at a guy who was clearly trying to enjoy a nice day with a kid who could've been his son.

"Of course I was sad," I said, incredulous. "He was my best friend, Noah. I didn't *want* him to die. It was a horrible accident—that's all."

"But then why did you go to jail?"

"Because his death happened as a result of something stupid *I* had done," I tried to explain without wanting to divulge that I'd been making money as a part-time drug dealer. "And because I had made that stupid mistake, I had to pay the price for it, so I did."

"Oh," he repeated, nodding with a little more acceptance than before. "So ... you're *really* not a bad guy."

"No. Definitely not a bad guy." Then, I pursed my lips and looked up to a sky of fluffy clouds. "Well, at least, I don't think so anyway. But I guess, if you ask around, you might find someone who thinks I am. I mean, the jury's still out on Mrs. Montgomery ..."

"Yeah, right." Noah laughed, rolling his eyes in my direction. "Mrs. Montgomery loves you. She stopped by the library the other day and told Mom that if she were younger, she wouldn't be able to keep her hands off of you."

I barked with a laugh, staring at Noah. "She did *not* say that."

"Oh, yeah, she *definitely* did. She also said you have a nice butt."

"That old perv." I chuckled heartily, still unsure of what to make of that old woman.

My laughter faded as we stared off into the distance, watching the lures out in the water, bobbing against the surface, not catching a damn thing. It was the gamble you took when you went fishing—a lesson I'd learned years ago. Sometimes, you came away with nothing but a nice day outside. Other times, the day itself was hideous, but you brought home enough fish to feed your family for a couple of weeks.

The last time I'd been fishing, we had caught a cooler's worth of bass. But they were all been shamefully forgotten as we planned a funeral and settled into a new normal of not having Grampa around. Gramma eventually told me to toss that old cooler in the dumpster by the school. Just to spare me the added trauma of scooping out two-week-old dead fish.

Believe me, it had been appreciated.

"Man, I think this is gonna be a bust," I muttered, shaking my head with disappointment. "It's still early, but—"

"Do you love my mom?"

I coughed at the sudden inquisition. "Um … well …"

"Because she says she loves you, but I don't hear you say it back to her."

There was a protective quality in his tone. Like the way a father would question a man's intentions with his daughter. And that was exactly what Noah was doing—figuring out what the hell I wanted from his mom. And who could really blame him? His mom didn't have the greatest experience with men, and he wanted to make sure I wasn't looking to be just another asshole, using her and leaving once I had my fill—which was far from the truth.

I glanced at him, wearing an apologetic, embarrassed expression. "Can I be honest with you?"

"Sure."

"I haven't said it back because I'm not sure I know what it feels like to love someone in the first place," I admitted, feeling like an idiot, even as I threw the words out into the universe. "Like, I wanna be sure before I go making declarations like that, you know what I mean?"

He hummed contemplatively, nodding his head like he understood. And, hey, for all I knew, maybe he did.

"I think love is when someone is more important in your heart than you are," he said, speaking like a guy who did in fact know more on the topic than me.

"Huh," I said, nodding. "That makes sense. You know, you're pretty smart."

He shrugged nonchalantly, then asked, "So, do you think you love her?"

"Well, I mean, I would do anything for her—and you. So, I guess that makes her pretty important."

"And do you think about her all the time? Because, like, this girl in my class—Beth … I know I love her because I think about her almost every minute of every freakin' day."

I turned with narrowed eyes. "Wait. You have a girlfriend?"

He sighed, a little forlorn, and shook his head. "She's not my girlfriend."

"But you want her to be?"

"Maybe. I don't know." He groaned exhaustedly. "Stop changing the subject. Do you think about Mom all the time?"

I swallowed. "Every minute of every freakin' day."

"Well, there you go."

I shifted my jaw, looking toward the horizon as an overwhelming urge came over me to walk down to the library and burst through the doors while declaring that I had apparently fallen in love for the first time in my life and I had needed a thirteen-year-old to make me realize it.

"Wow," I uttered, full of clarity and awe.

"You should tell her."

"Yeah …" I nodded, my stare blank and my heart hammering. "I think you're right."

"Then, you should get married so that you can be my dad."

And there it was.

That was what this was truly all about.

He had felt betrayed by the knowledge of my crimes and couldn't stomach the idea of wanting a cold-blooded killer for a father figure. He needed the confirmation that I wasn't in fact a homicidal psychopath. He needed to know I was a good guy—for him and his mom. He'd needed to know I loved her, that I was doing right by her, and that I would do right by him too. To fill a void he'd had since the day he had been born.

Hell, I guessed, in a way, I knew the feeling.

And that was exactly why I knew I would do my damnedest to be the guy his biological father never would be. The type of guy Noah—and his mother—deserved.

"Buddy, I don't need to get married to be your dad. If you want me, you have me. There doesn't have to be more to it than that."

It was a moment. Noah glanced at me, and I, at him, and I could tell he wanted to hug me as much as I wanted to hug him. But it was in that second that his line pulled taut, and he turned away quickly as he gasped.

"I think I got one!" he shouted, his face lighting up brighter than the sun poking through the clouds.

My pride matched his as I stabbed the sand with my fishing pole before giving him my entire focus. I helped him reel in a porgy—the first of three fish we would catch that day—and I knew he was going to remember that moment for the rest of his life, just as I remembered all the moments on the water with my grandfather. And I was glad it was me who got to be a part of it.

***

"Hey!" Ray said, coming through the door after a long day at the library. "Smells like fish in here!"

Noah jumped up from beside me on the couch, our game of Mario Kart forgotten as he ran to his mom. "We caught three fish," he announced hurriedly. "And then we walked home, and Soldier taught me how to skin and gut a fish, and we cut it up and made dinner."

She looked over her son's head and met my eye with a smile and every bit of the love she had for me.

How the hell had I not realized I felt the same when I looked at her?

"Sounds like you guys had a good day."

Noah nodded, clearly proud of himself. "It was freakin' awesome."

She dropped her purse beside the door and wrapped her arm around Noah's shoulders to kiss his cheek—until she leaned in close and scrunched her nose with disgust. "Oh God, kid, you stink!"

He pulled his shirt up and gave it a whiff. "Yeah, I smell like fish guts."

"Lovely," Ray grumbled, giving him a playful shove. "You'd better get in the shower before we eat."

He rolled his eyes but agreed with a muttered, "Okay." Then, he trudged his way down the hall to the bathroom, leaving us alone.

Ray approached slowly in her work clothes. A tight knee-length skirt. A formfitting sleeveless shirt. Modest black heels with just enough height to get me excited. I loved her in shorts and T-shirts, and there was something so attractive about her in my shirts. But this version of her … the librarian …

This was Sexy Ray. The Ray that screamed to be called Rain while on her knees in front of me.

"And what about you?" she asked, hips swaying. "Did *you* shower yet?"

My eyes were hooded as they met hers. "Yes, ma'am," I replied before groaning at the warmth of her body pressed to mine.

One hand molded to her hip while the other slid up the length of her side to grip the back of her slender neck. Her lips curved into a relaxed smile as my fingers toyed with the curled ends of her hair hanging from her ponytail.

"Good," she appraised, flattening her hands on my chest before tipping her head up, offering her mouth.

I kissed her softly, not intending to deepen the moment until she parted her lips with a silent plea for my tongue. It was unexpected when her desire for intimacy had been understandably hesitant at best since Seth's attack weeks earlier. I hadn't pushed for more than she was willing to offer, hadn't even hinted at wanting more, but I couldn't deny that I was grateful now as her hands slowly grazed the length of my shirt to hook her fingers through my belt loops, tugging my hips closer to her belly.

"I've missed you," she whispered against my lips, and whether that was to mean specifically today or the weeks since our world had been shaken, I wasn't sure.

My hand on her neck slid around to graze my thumb across her cheekbone. Her smile widened as she looked into my eyes, and the words dangled at the tip of my tongue. Those three words I hadn't uttered since my grandparents had died decades ago. Three little words I'd never thought I'd utter again. I wanted her to know. I wanted there to be no more time passed between now and her hearing the truth of my feelings for her.

"Here," I said, nudging my head toward the couch. "Come over here with me."

We sat together. Ray insisted on sitting in my lap, her fingers stroking the lengths of my hair. It was almost as if she needed to touch me, the contact necessary, and I found it nice. Relaxing. Every touch a reassurance of the truth in what we had between us.

"What's up?" she asked, her brows coming together with a look of trepidation.

"Something happened today," I began, wrapping one arm around her waist and laying my other hand against her thigh.

The worry lines on her forehead deepened. "Okay …"

"I told Noah why I was at Wayward."

It was a point-blank statement, and judging by the look on her face, it wasn't one she'd expected. In fact, she didn't look happy at all as her gaze fell to her lap and her jaw shifted with obvious irritability.

"Soldier … you had no right—"

"I know I should've run it by you first, and I'm sorry I didn't," I quickly interjected, already jumping into fight-or-flight mode to keep her from getting mad. To keep her from leaving. "But he had asked, and I thought it would be better to just … lay it out and be honest instead of making him even more suspicious."

"But why was he even suspicious at all?" Her eyes met mine, accusation heavy in her glare.

"Because he wanted to know why Seth had called me a murderer."

Her eyes softened, and her shoulders slumped. "Oh …" She brushed a strand of hair from her face. "Oh God, that poor kid …"

"Yeah, so I guess he's just been trying to work this out in his head for the past few weeks, and today, he finally confronted me about it."

She reluctantly nodded. "What did he say when you told him?"

"Well, he was a little shaken up at first, but after I explained it a little—while leaving out the dirty details, of course—he was okay."

"So, he's fine with it?" She eyed me skeptically, and I laughed in response.

"Well, I don't know if I'd say he's *fine* with it, but … he gets it. And he's fine with *me*, and honestly, I really can't ask for more than that. But"—I forced a lighthearted chuckle—"I guess his therapist is gonna get an earful about this now."

It was meant to be a joke, but, man, I was just on a roll today because Ray didn't laugh. Instead, she turned away as her eyes filled with tears and her bottom lip wriggled ferociously.

Quickly, I pressed my palms to her cheeks, cradling her face in my hands as I turned her gaze back to mine. "Hey, what's wrong?"

She bit her lip, a feeble attempt to keep her tears from falling, before she just gave up the fight altogether. "He probably thinks so poorly of me."

My brows pinched as I shook my head. "What? No, baby. Of course he doesn't. Why would you think that?"

"Because I really know how to pick 'em," she said, attempting to smile at her own poor excuse of a joke. "We all know his father is a piece of fucking garbage, but to add insult to injury, the first and only man I ever allow myself to fall in love with is an ex-con, convicted of"—she threw a gesture toward the ceiling and her eyes followed—"fucking manslaughter."

"*And* possession of a controlled substance." The corner of my mouth lifted in an apologetic smile while my heart begged to admit that she was the first and only woman I'd fallen in love with too.

A watery laugh pushed past her lips. "Oh, of course, silly me. How could I forget?"

"Baby, Noah doesn't think anything badly about you," I assured her, tracing the curvature of her face with my fingertips. "All he cares about is that you're safe and happy. That's it. And he believes that, as long as you're with me, you are."

She looked into my eyes, her tears drying sticky on her cheeks, as she nodded. "I know I am," she whispered, wrapping her hands around my wrists.

"And he is too," I assured her, feeling like a broken record while knowing I could never tell her enough.

I would tell her as much and as often as she needed.

The timer pierced the moment, letting us both know that dinner was ready, and she reluctantly left my lap with a feathery brush of her lips against my cheek. As I took the baked sea bass out of the oven, Ray went to change into something more comfortable—much to my chagrin. Then, when she returned minutes later, I was setting the table, instantly smiling at the sight of her in my T-shirt with her hair piled high on her head.

Librarian Ray might be the sexier of her personalities, but this Ray … comfortable, real, and relaxed …

This one surpassed the fantasy.

This one felt the most like mine. The one that best suited me.

"You're giving me that look again," she said, sidling up beside me to help set the table.

"What look?" I lifted the corner of my mouth in a teasing smile.

"The look you give me when I think you're going to finally tell me how you feel, but then you find something else to distract yourself with. Which is fine. I understand, and it doesn't change anything between us. But … that's the look. And I know that because I know I look at you the same way."

I couldn't stop my chuckle from rumbling gently through my chest. How she had me pegged so accurately, it blew my mind.

My heart rattled against my ribs, hammering frantically with an uncertain panic that I knew was absurd.

"Ray," I said, watching as she busied herself with placing the three plates at each of the chairs.

"I'm not trying to guilt you, Soldier. That's not the type of relationship we have. We do things at our own pace; I love that we're able to do that. You'll say what you need to say in your own time. I just—"

"I love you."

The final plate slipped from her hand to drop at Noah's spot at the table as she turned to face me, her lips parted and her eyes already welling up with fresh tears. "What?"

With those words now out in the universe, my chest puffed with a new confidence, a sense of freedom, as I gripped her shoulders in my hands and said, "I love you," enunciating every word and enjoying the way each one felt on my tongue.

Ray clapped a hand over her mouth as she laughed through the tears. "I don't know why I'm so surprised. I already knew … I mean, I *thought* I knew, and—"

"What are you guys doing?" Noah entered the room, eyeing us with the sass of a surly teenager.

"I love your mom," I declared proudly, and he met my eye with a knowing twitch of his lips.

"About time," he muttered as he dropped into his chair.

"And I love you too, Noah."

His eyes were quick to flit toward mine, distracted from the casserole dish of baked fish and vegetables. It pained me to witness his confusion, as if he still couldn't understand that my commitment to his mother extended to him as well. He swallowed, licking his lips through the hesitation, then nodded without saying a word.

Ray held her hands to my cheeks, and I pressed a kiss to her lips.

"Thank you," she whispered on an exhale.

"Don't thank me for what I'd be doing anyway," I replied before kissing her once more.

We sat down together, ready to enjoy the meal Noah had caught earlier in the day. And as they helped themselves and smiled at each other while we headed into this new chapter of our relationship, I took a moment to quietly look at them. To allow the realization that, in some way, we had become a family to settle in. I loved these people. I had chosen them, the way I'd once chosen Billy's mom to be mine, but this time, they'd chosen me too.

This is my favorite day, I found myself thinking. *This is the best day of my freakin' life.*

And little did I know then, it would be the last good day we'd have together in this chapter of my life.

But it really was … a very, very good day.

CHAPTER

TWENTY-SEVEN

NO MORE SUNSHINE

hat is that? I thought the moment I was
shaken abruptly from a comfortable, restful
sleep, my arm around Ray's waist and her
back pressed to my chest. *Is someone playing music?*

I opened one eye just a crack, only to be greeted by
the darkness of night.

What time is it?

*Does it fucking matter? It's obviously too early—or
late—for someone to be playing that shit.*

But the music continued to play.

With an angry grumble, I pulled a pillow over my
head, ignoring the irritating sound and closing my eyes
again. My nose found Ray's hair and the springtime
flowers and lavender she kept there, and I smiled to
myself despite the noise.

I love her, I love her, I love her, I thought, allowing the truest of truths to resound louder than the offending noise penetrating my ear drums despite the pillow.

I love her, I love her, I love her.

And how lucky I am to be given that chance.

How lucky we both are to be given each other.

I love her, I love her, I love her, I love …

Then, with a smile, I fell back to sleep before the music stopped.

***

"Brawny, get up. Your alarm keeps going off."

I didn't know if it was her voice or her finger poking me in the ribs, stomach, and crook of my neck that woke me up first, but I did eventually open my eyes from beneath the pillow over my head.

When the hell did that get there?

I pulled it off and yawned. Only then did I open my eyes to Ray, already showered and dressed in her library attire.

"Fantasy librarian Ray," I muttered groggily, and she glanced over her shoulder with an amused smile, mid-lipstick application.

"What?"

"This is the fantasy version of you."

"Oh?" She snorted, turning back to the mirror. "Are pencil skirts and ugly blouses part of this fantasy of yours?"

I chuckled a gruff laugh, then cleared my throat of the lingering sleep while pulling myself up to sit in bed.

"When I was a kid, I had it bad for one of my teachers—I think I told you about that. Mrs. Henderson, remember? She always dressed like that. You know, put together and nice and all, but also, like, every teenage boy's wet dream."

I watched her reflection shift from startled to amused in a matter of seconds. She laughed as she twisted off the top of her lip gloss.

"So, she set the precedent for every other woman for the rest of your life."

"I guess." I laughed with her as I reached for my phone on the nightstand. "It still blows my mind that she ended up being Harry's daughter. She was the nicest person to me in school, and he was the nicest ..."

What the fuck? I thought as I stared at the notifications on the screen.

"What is it?" Ray asked, caution and worry in her tone.

My heart slammed against the wall of my chest as I stared at the four missed calls from early this morning. The last one had come in around four thirty a.m. Three new voice mails. All from my mother.

"My mom called," I said, my voice barely above a whisper. "Jesus, why would she call? What does she want ..."

I was already shaking as I stared at her name in my voice mail inbox, terrified of what she might have called about. Yes, I'd given her the number. I had been insistent that she call if something came up, if she needed me for anything. But had it been stupid of me to assume she never would?

Now, staring at those three messages waiting to be heard, I wanted to yell at her and say the gesture had been nothing more than a Band-Aid to keep my guilt from taking over. She wasn't actually supposed to use it. She was supposed to throw the damn number away, lose it, like she did everything else.

My hands were shaking so much that I thought I'd drop the phone.

How did she still have this type of control over me?

"Soldier," Ray said, her gentle voice slicing through the shroud of panic and fear as she laid her hand against my bare shoulder.

"She left me voice mails." I presented the phone to her.

"You want me to play them?" she guessed, and I nodded, planting my elbows against my knees and covering my face with my hands.

And then my mother's frantic, trembling, whispered voice filled the room.

"H-h-hey ... I wasn't going to call because"—she cackled maniacally—"because the last thing you probably want in your life is to hear from your old j-j-junkie mom. But ... but, Soldier, um ... um ... if you get this ... um ... call me, okay? Call me. I-I-I-I need to tell you some things. Okay? Call me."

"You know ... um ... I-I-I never wanted things to b-be like this, you know? That night you were born ... I thought you'd change things. I *wanted* you to change things. I wanted y-you to save me, and I think ... I think that's where I fucked up, isn't it? Th-that I-I-I-I put so, so, *so* much on a fucking *baby*, and I never put a fucking

404

thing on *me*. I never tried to save *myself*, and that's my fault, okay? I've spent a long time trying to own that, and th-that's what I'm doing now. Owning it. I fucked up. I fucked *you* up. I fucked David up, and your grandparents, and … and … everything. But that's on m-me, okay? It's all on me. O-okay … b-bye."

"W-when you were a baby, I used to sing that song … what the fuck was it called—oh, right. 'You Are My Sunshine.' D-do you remember it? Do you remember me singing that to you? Those were the best, best, best moments of my life. *You* are the best thing to happen to me, and y-y-you know, Soldier … I never thanked you. Y-you know … for e-everything, so … th-thank you. Thank you, baby. Everything I've done has been for you. Not at first, but … now … o-o-okay, um … um … I-I love you …"

The final recording of her manic, emotional voice faded into hushed static until there was nothing but the sound of my frantic heart.

Ray and I were quiet and still, holding our breath, as if we were scared to let new air slip into the room. Mutually scared of something neither of us was quite sure of.

Then, with a shaking hand, Ray put the phone back on the nightstand.

"Soldier …"

"Ray"—I shook my head—"please don't."

She sat down in front of me on the bed. "I just—"

"*Rain*."

My voice cracked heatedly through the hush of hers, and startled, she looked at me, clamping her lips shut.

405

Immediately apologetic for saying something at all. For thinking she'd even know what to say about a situation she knew nothing about. But I wasn't supposed to make her feel like that, and I scrubbed my hands against my face, inhaling deeply until my lungs couldn't hold anything more. Then, I dropped them down to my lap, already feeling exhausted after a full night of sleep.

"I'm sorry."

Ray shook her head, her brows pulled together with sympathy. "No, don't apologize. You're angry and confused—"

"I'm not confused," I interrupted, shaking my head. "There's nothing to be confused about."

Ray looked doubtful. Unconvinced. "But ... why would she say all of that now? Why did she ..." She shuddered, and I was sure she thought I hadn't seen it, but I had. "God, why did she sound like that? She sounded so ... *scared*."

I didn't want to be impatient with her. There were things she didn't know about, things she had no reason to understand, and that wasn't her fault. So, when I responded, I urged the anger and stress I only felt when it came to my mother to stay out of my tone.

"Ray, she sounded like that because she had probably popped too many pills and was having a bad trip."

Disappointment seeped into my veins as I spoke the words out loud, and then I felt like an idiot for being disappointed at all. What the hell had I expected from my mother? Had I really thought that, one day, she'd clean herself up and get better? Had I really thought that she might have a change of heart?

No, I didn't think I'd truly believed it would happen, but I'd be a liar to say I had stopped hoping.

I didn't think anybody ever truly stopped hoping. Even for the things they knew to be impossible.

"Do you really think that's all it was?" Ray whispered, her hesitancy obvious. "Because, Soldier, I don't know. She just ... she sounded really—"

"What? Desperate? Anxious? Terrified?"

Ray picked at her cuticles and nodded reluctantly.

"Yeah, I know. That's how she always sounds when she's on some heavy shit."

Ray's eyes met mine with more skepticism than I appreciated. "Are you sure?"

"Am I sure?" I snapped, throwing the blanket off and climbing out of bed with enough haste that I nearly tripped over my own stupid feet. "I think I'm pretty fucking sure, Ray. More so than you are." I glanced over my shoulder on my way to the closet. "No offense."

"Okay."

She's just trying to help. She's just trying to make sense of this with me.

I gripped the top of the doorframe, squeezed my eyes shut, and pushed out a breath. Then, I turned around to face her, still sitting on the bed where I'd left her.

"You don't know my mother the way I do," I said, my voice quiet and gravelly. "And I can understand wanting to believe that she'd say that stuff for a reason other than being stoned out of her mind. I get wanting to believe that she might actually love—" My voice cracked beneath the heaving weight of a pulsing need to cry, and I cleared my throat, pinching my nose and willing those feelings away. "She's incapable of loving anything, Ray. That's how she is, how she's always been."

Ray barely nodded, could hardly look at me. Couldn't even blink without letting one rogue tear slip over her cheek. At first, I thought that tear was evidence of pain I had inflicted, and I hated it. I hated myself for speaking harshly, for snapping and bringing forth memories of her past.

But then, when she got to her feet, squeezed her eyes shut, and propelled forward until her arms were around my waist and her cheek was pressed to my chest, I realized she wasn't upset with me at all.

She was upset *for* me.

"I'm so sorry," she whispered, pressing her lips to my skin.

I touched my chin to the top of her head and held her body to mine. "Don't be."

"Well, I am anyway."

She squeezed my waist, and my hands flattened on her back, pressing her to me closer, harder. Wishing I possessed the ability to make her atoms fuse with mine.

"How much time do you have before work?" I asked, hating that she had to leave at all.

She lifted her arm from my waist to check her watch. "About an hour."

I tipped my head so that my lips touched her hair. "Okay. I'm jumping in the shower really quick, and then I'm making breakfast."

She smiled against my chest. "I'll wake Noah up."

408

I watched her leave the room as my mother's voice lingered in my head. *"I love you,"* she had said for the first time maybe ever, and, God, how I wanted to believe it.

But, like I had told Ray, I wasn't sure Diane Mason was capable of loving anything—apart from her little pink pills. And I had to convince myself that was okay; I'd been convincing myself of that for most of my life.

And besides, as long as I had the love of Ray, I didn't need my mom.

I'd never really had her to begin with.

***

The eggs sizzled in the pan as the bread hung out in the toaster, getting ready to pop up and scare the shit out of me at any moment.

Ray sat at the table with Noah, having a conversation about him helping her at the library for the next couple of days until his grandparents got back from their trip to the Poconos.

Eleven played with the dangling ends of my shoelaces, startling every few seconds when the bacon crackled and popped.

Nothing was out of the ordinary. Everything was good. Everything seemed exactly as it should. Yet a cloud of foreboding hung over my head, the same one that had brought that single crow to accompany us on our walk to the beach just the day before. An eerie feeling of unease, the notion that something was about to go wrong …

Maybe things are simply too good, I considered just as the toast popped up, making me gasp and jump.

Ray laughed. "Every single time."

"Motherfucker," I muttered, chuckling lightly as I grabbed the four slices of toast and popped two more in.

That's what it is. I'm just not used to things being this good.

But Seth is out there. Levi is too. And those calls from Mom ...

I had told Ray those calls were nothing. I had told her she was just obviously having a bad high. But ... what if I'd been too quick to dismiss Ray's concerns? What if I was wrong and something had—

The sound of a car door closing tore my attention away from the eggs and bacon. I looked up through the kitchen window to find a car parked outside my house, one I didn't recognize.

Then came the footsteps, crunching over the gravel path to the steps.

"Ray, keep an eye on the food," I said, already on my way to the door.

My stomach somersaulted with every nauseating flop as I wondered who was showing up at my door at eight o'clock in the morning on a Wednesday.

I opened the door before the visitors could knock, and when I did, my eyes met those of a ghost from the past.

"Soldier Mason?"

I swallowed at my dry throat before I could convince my tongue and lips to reply.

"Officer Sam Lewis."

The man wasn't dressed in the uniform I remembered, and there were more lines etched into his otherwise baby-like face. But he was the same man I remembered from over a decade ago—there was no doubt about that. But why he was standing at my door now, I couldn't begin to imagine.

"You remember me," he stated with a reluctant curl to one side of his mouth.

"I could never forget the guy who slapped the cuffs on right before he stuffed me into the back of his squad car."

Officer Sam chuckled, a hint of sadness in the sound. "No, I guess not."

My eyes left him to survey the man standing beside him. A little younger, a little thinner. Not nearly as friendly-looking as Officer Sam.

"What can I do for you guys?"

Officer Sam tipped his head, casting his gaze behind me, then offered a small smile to Ray ... or maybe it was Noah.

"Um, this is my partner, Detective Miller," he said, addressing the man beside him. "I was hoping we could maybe come in and chat for a few minutes."

I glanced at Detective Miller, who was already staring right back at me with a glare I was sure he thought was menacing. "Sure ... as long as you don't mind watching me eat my breakfast."

"Not at all," Officer Sam said.

"Great."

I opened the door fully, allowing the two men inside. They wiped their feet respectfully against the mat, then followed me to the table, where Ray was suspiciously watching as she laid the full plates on the table.

"Soldier?" Her eyes volleyed from me to the officers behind me. "What's going on?"

"Ray, this is my old friend, Officer Sam Lewis—"

"Actually, it's, uh … it's Detective Sam Lewis now," he quietly interjected with a smile, one I returned.

"Hey, good for you, man. Congratulations."

He laughed easily, concealing the unmistakable glint of dread in his eyes. "Thanks."

I sat down as I said to both her and Noah—who, I noticed, hadn't spoken a word since I'd opened the door—"*Detective* Lewis and his partner, Detective Miller, came by to chat while we eat." I tried not to let it show that my nerves were warning me against eating altogether. "Detectives, this is my girlfriend, Ray, and her son, Noah."

"Ma'am," Detective Miller greeted, speaking for the first time since they'd arrived and nodding his chin toward Ray.

"Nice to meet you, Ray," Detective Sam said before offering his hand to Noah. "How're you doing, pal?"

Noah glanced at me, his eyes full of suspicion and uncertainty, but I nodded my assurance. Letting him know that he could trust these guys. That, no matter why they were here, they meant him and his mother no harm.

Noah accepted his hand, and they shook.

"I'm okay," he replied in the small voice he used when he was worried. Scared.

"Good," Detective Sam said as his partner left the table to wander around the living room.

412

I watched him as he surveyed the space. What was he looking for? Or better yet, why the hell were they here in the first place?

Detective Sam cleared his throat and moved his hands to his waist, hooking his thumbs into his pants pockets. "I'm sorry to disturb you all," he said, and I knew this was it.

This was the moment when he was going to announce why they were paying me a visit, and I pushed myself toward a heavier air of nonchalance as I reached for the pepper shaker.

"And I'm sorry I didn't make enough for you guys to have some," I said, shoveling a forkful of scrambled eggs into my mouth, only stopping to add, "But I can't say I was expecting you, so ..."

Detective Sam stood there over the table, no less of a black cloud in the moment than Seth and his friend Levi, while Detective Miller over there made himself comfortable. Sitting on the couch, petting my damn cat.

The little traitor nudged into the detective's palm, and I fought the urge to roll my eyes.

"No, it's ... it's fine," Detective Sam said, gesturing for us to continue eating.

"Cool." I swallowed my eggs and lifted a slice of buttered toast to my lips, wishing my fucking hands would stop shaking. "So, what'd you guys wanna chat about?"

Ray's wide eyes darted toward mine. "Um, should we ..."

She was already starting to rise from the table when I lifted my hand, stopping her.

413

"No, it's okay. Finish eating. Whatever they have to say, they can say it with you guys here." I glanced toward Detective Sam. "Right?"

He was hesitant to nod, but still, he did. "Well, um …" He cleared his throat, pulling a pad of paper and pen from the breast pocket of his button-down shirt. "Soldier, can you tell us when the last time you saw Diane Mason was?"

The toast was already being lowered back to my plate when it slipped from my fingers altogether as the sound of my mother's manic voice mails echoed through my brain.

"Diane Mason?" I parroted as Detective Miller rose from the couch to wander over to the table.

"Yeah. You *do* know her, right?" he asked, narrowing his eyes with a sneer of his lips. "She *is* your mother, correct?"

Ah, so this guy likes playing the bad cop. Got it.

"Yeah, but …" My elbow dropped to the table as my palm cradled my forehead. "I … no, I, uh … I haven't seen her in a little over a month."

"She called this morning though," Ray added for me, holding her own with more strength in her tone than I thought I could muster in my pinkie at the moment.

Detective Sam's head nodded gently as he began to scribble on his pad. "Around what time?"

"Um …" Ray grabbed my phone from the table and punched in the passcode before navigating toward the call logs. "She called three times at three seventeen, three forty-two, and four twenty-one."

"And, Soldier, where were you?" Detective Miller's voice was full of accusations.

My eyes met his as I dropped my hand to the table with a heavy *thunk*, rattling the silverware. Noah's bewildered eyes shot toward me while mine stared ahead at the detective, who was waiting for my response.

"I was *here*," I said. He raised a single brow and stared for one second too long, and I scoffed, shaking my head incredulously. "Seriously, man? Do you really think she'd be calling me if I was *with her*?"

"Hey." Detective Sam's voice drew my eyes away from his partner's. His smile was apologetic, and I appreciated it. "We're just doing our job, Soldier. You know that."

Ray laid her hand over mine as I pulled my lips between my teeth and blew out a heavy breath, calming the rapid beat of my heart and the tremors in my limbs.

Then, after I mustered enough calm to speak civilly, I said, "I was sleeping in my bed. I woke up because I'd heard something, didn't register what it was, and went back to sleep. It wasn't until I woke up again that I realized she had called."

More scribbles of pen against paper, more nods.

"Are you ever going to tell me what this is about?" I demanded as Detective Sam continued to write.

Detective Miller went to the plate then, almost like he'd been waiting for this moment since they'd arrived.

A surprising look of sympathy fell over his face, then, "Your mother's body was found this morning."

What?

No.

415

No, no, no.

"Oh my God," Ray uttered, holding her hand over her mouth, as Noah eyes volleyed quickly between me and her, not knowing what to say or do.

Ray went to wrap the hand lying over mine around my fingers, but I pulled away as I pushed my chair back and rose quickly to my feet. Rushing to the sink, gripping the lip of the countertop, I ground my teeth together. Clamping my jaw shut. Shaking my head and wondering if I had heard him correctly.

"Noah," Ray whispered from behind me, "come on."

"But, Mom—"

"No, baby, let's go."

She came to stand beside me, laying her hand gently against my back. I didn't look at her. Couldn't move my eyes from the spot I stared at.

But still, she said, "I'm going to the library, and I'm taking Noah with me."

I nodded.

"If you need me, I will leave work, okay? Just call, and I'll be here."

I nodded again.

She pressed her lips to my back and whispered, "I'm so sorry."

Then, she bid the detectives farewell and left the house with her son trailing reluctantly behind her.

When the door closed behind them and I knew we were alone, I asked, "How?"

"We believe it was an overdose," Detective Sam replied, his voice rough. "I'm sorry, Soldier."

416

I ignored his sympathies, tamped down my emotions, and spun from the sink to cross my arms over my chest. "Where did you find her?"

He hesitated. His eyes fell to the pad of paper, and his throat moved with his slow, hard swallow. "That's not—"

"*Where?*"

Detective Miller straightened his back and eyed me with curiosity as he answered, "Just outside the high school."

I lifted my chin slowly, standing tall, as a whole new sense of awareness and terror steamrolled over where I stood. Detective Sam met my glare with the same understanding, one Detective Miller seemed oblivious to. Memories of a night that still haunted my nightmares rushed back. That patch of cold dirt on the side of the road, just in front of the high school I'd dropped out of. Billy's lifeless body. The tears on my face, drying fast in the cold night air, and Levi's grin as an officer drove me away.

I would bet anything that my mother's body had been found on that very same patch of dirt.

I would bet anything that she had been put there.

"It wasn't an accident," I stated bluntly.

Detective Sam shook his head, following my train of thought. "No. I don't believe it was."

Detective Miller cocked his head, eyeing me coolly, and I bet he thought he was real hot shit with that badge hanging from his belt.

"You wanna come with us down to the station?" he asked, tipping his head back as he spoke.

417

"Am I a suspect?"

He pursed his lips, studying me through suspicious eyes, then asked, "Should you be?"

"What do you think?" I challenged, not caring for a second that this man was in a higher position of authority than I, a convicted felon, ever would be.

Detective Miller's glare was as cold and steely as that badge. But a moment later, he shook his head. "I think you're a little kid in a big man's body, who just found out his mom was murdered, and you wanna help us figure out who might be responsible."

That was all it took for me to push away from the counter and grab my phone from the table before following the two detectives out the door and to their car.

***

Stepping into a room they usually used for interrogation, Sam—who had insisted I call them both by their first names—brought a paper cup of the shittiest coffee I had ever had in my life. It wasn't unlike the coffee he'd given me a lifetime ago, but somehow, this time, it tasted worse.

Maybe because, this time, I wasn't cuffed to a bench, waiting to be locked up.

Or maybe it was that, this time, I really was on the side of the good guys.

When we'd first gotten to the station, he had asked if I wanted to formally identify my mother's body even though it wasn't necessary. Her fingerprints had already been processed, not to mention the ID they'd conveniently found in her pocket. But Sam thought I might like to see her for closure or something like that.

But I declined.

"Thanks for the offer, man, but I think I can live without that experience," I'd said, and he'd replied with a melancholy chuckle.

Now, we sat in the cold, sterile room, three cups of shitty coffee between us. Sam looked at me from across the table with his friendly puppy-dog eyes while Josh— Detective Miller—wore the face of someone ready to kick some serious ass.

I was quickly finding that my initial assessment of him being a dick had been wrong. The guy was tough, but he just wanted to do his job ... and do it well. In fact, I found I liked him quite a bit.

"Soldier, I understand your mom might not have been the greatest person, but ... she was still your mother, and I'm sorry. This has to be difficult," Sam said, offering his condolences for the third time since he'd come to my door that morning.

"Honestly, I'm surprised it didn't happen sooner," I replied with a shrug.

Man, was that ever the truth ... and I was using it to keep my emotions from running away with what I had left of my composure.

"So, can you tell us anything about the people your mom knew? Anybody she was enemies with?" Josh asked, tapping the end of his pen against the pad of paper in front of him.

I turned the cup slowly in my hands and nodded my head, not quite meeting his stony eyes. "There's one guy

419

you wanna look at. Levi Stratton," I said, the image of my mother fucking him on her couch vivid in my mind.

"Levi Stratton?" Josh repeated, readying his pen.

"Yeah. He sells drugs around town—or at least, he did. I can't honestly tell you what he does now. But back in the day, he and I sort of, uh … competed with each other for business."

Sam narrowed his eyes, leaning further against the table. "He sold drugs to kids too?"

I nodded. "That was a big part of his clientele, yeah, although he probably found business elsewhere too. Anyway, uh, when I was released, I first went to my mom's place and found her with Levi. They were, uh … *together*."

Josh nodded as he wrote everything down. "Do you think they could've been working with each other?"

I chewed the inside of my cheek as I thought about it, and then I lifted a finger from the cup and wagged it at the detectives. I furrowed my brow, remembering something I'd forgotten. Something I'd found when I last saw my mother alive.

"Actually, the last time I met with her—"

"Your mother?" Sam clarified, and I nodded.

"Yeah. She dropped her bag when she was leaving, and something fell out. It was a handwritten prescription for oxy. You know, like, torn from one of those pads doctors have. But it was in her handwriting."

Sam leaned back in his chair, a look of interest blanketing his features. "Isn't that interesting, considering that we found a prescription pad on her when her body was found?"

"She wouldn't have carried that around," I muttered, thinking out loud.

"No, I'm inclined to agree with you," Josh replied, still scribbling.

"So, Levi Stratton," Sam repeated, drumming his fingers against the table. "Anything else you can tell us about him before we bring him in?"

"Yeah. He's her dead ex-boyfriend's brother," I said, bringing the cup of coffee to my lips.

I eyed the two detectives from over the brim as both pairs of eyes lit with intrigue. Josh scribbled onto his pad while Sam typed something into his phone, and all I could think to say, to break the silence, was, "You know, you guys really need to invest in some better coffee. I mean, for fuck's sake, I drank better shit in prison."

***

The detectives offered to give me a ride home, but I told them I'd get a cab and left the station with a couple of handshakes and the promise that Levi Stratton was finally going down.

Then, I called Harry and asked him, once again, for a ride.

He found me across the street from the high school, just as he'd found me all those months before. It was risky for me now to be sitting out in the open like this.

What if Levi saw me? What about Seth?

But, to put it simply, fuck them. They were the last things on my mind as I stared across at that sacred patch of dirt. The last place my best friend had been alive. The last place my mother had lain—well, apart from the morgue. I stared at it and the permanent tire tracks marring its surface, and I wondered what else it had seen. How many overdoses? How many drunken girls and guys? How many car accidents? The amount of memories it held, the things it knew, the things it had seen ...

Fuck, if it could talk, what would it say right now? *Jesus, fuck, this guy again?*

Harry got out of his car and wandered over, wearing the uniform I knew well.

"You're making this a habit now," he commented, standing above me with his hands on his waist. "What's going on?"

"My mom died," I replied simply, only glancing at him for a moment before looking back at the spot across the street.

Harry blew out a deep breath, then groaned. "Ah, son ..." His weary, old bones lowered to sit beside me, his arm wrapping around my hunched shoulders. "I'm so sorry."

"Yeah," I muttered quietly, rubbing a hand beneath my nose. "Me too."

I didn't make him linger with me for long. I rose to my feet after another few seconds passed, and I held out a hand to help him up. Then, I asked if he could take me home, and he didn't say no. He never would.

We chatted along the way about everything but my mother. He asked me about Ray, and I told him I loved her. I asked him about Mrs. Henderson, and he told me she was expecting her third—and supposedly final—

child. We talked about the upcoming fall and the holidays it held, and he asked if I wanted to do something with his family for Thanksgiving and Christmas. I told him I'd love to, but I'd have to run it by the lady of the house.

"Ah, I guess you do have your own family to think about now, huh?" he said, flashing me a smile I couldn't refuse.

"Yeah," I replied just as we pulled up to 1111 Daffodil Lane. "I guess I do."

I said goodbye, and he once again said he was sorry. I told him I was tired of people being sorry for me, and he got out of the car to give me a hug.

"Then, how about I just tell you that I love you and I'm here whenever you need me?"

I blinked back the tears I had been fighting off all damn day. "Love you too, Harry."

He clapped his hand against my back, then pulled away. "All right. Get in there and be with your family. Be in touch though, okay?"

"You know it."

Then, I watched him drive away, staring at the taillights as he drove down the street and then turned out of sight. An ache wrapped itself around my heart, choking the breath from my lungs and making me wish I hadn't let him leave at all.

Why do I feel like I won't see him again? I laughed, beside myself, shaking my head and wiping a hand over my eyes. *It's been a long fucking day. I'm tired, I'm hungry, and that's all it is.*

I headed up the broken steps and unlocked the door, and inside, I found Ray, Noah, and Eleven on the couch, playing the Nintendo Switch. They both turned with a start at the sound of me entering, and then they were on their feet, rushing over to bombard me with hugs and headbutts against my ankles and questions about the day I didn't feel like answering.

"I just want to cook dinner and go to bed," I told them, heading for the kitchen.

"Oh, I thought we could just order a pizza," Ray suggested.

"Nah." I opened a cabinet and pulled out a box of pasta. "I don't mind cooking."

"Are you sure?"

I flashed an exasperated look over my shoulder. "Ray, if I didn't want to, I wouldn't suggest it."

She barely bobbed her head in a nod as her cautious eyes danced over my face. "Okay."

In silence, I went through the motions of getting out a jar of sauce, a pot to boil water, and another smaller pot to heat the sauce. I opened the jar, dumped it into the pot, and put it on the stove to simmer. I dug through the spice rack, added a dash of this and a dash of that to liven the sauce up a bit. I filled the pot with water and put it on to boil. All while a tidal wave of memories hit. One by one, each punching me in the gut harder than the last.

Mom talking to me on the phone from rehab on Christmas.

Mom waking me up on my eighth birthday.

Mom coming to the hospital to hold my hand while my face was stitched up.

And in every one, she sang to me.

"You are my sunshine ..."

I stared into the pot, watching all the tiny bubbles collect along the bottom, then fizzle out to make way for new ones. And I thought about her last moments.

"You are my sunshine ..."

Had she known she was dying? Had she been scared?

"You are my sunshine ..."

No, of course she'd been scared. And of course she knew something was happening ... or at the very least, she knew something was going to happen. She had called.

Jesus, she had *called*, and I hadn't answered. I had fucking woken up, I had heard the phone, and I had fallen back to sleep instead of answering.

"You are my sunshine ..."

God, why hadn't I just fucking answered?

"You're gonna save me, right, baby?"

My lungs stuttered as I pulled in a jagged breath of air. I reached up to grip my hair in clenched fists, desperately fighting against the memories and that goddamn stupid fucking song that I wished so badly I could forget while being so, so, so incredibly sad that she hadn't thought to sing it to me one more time. Just one more fucking time.

"You are my sunshine ... you are my sunshine ... you are my sunshine ... "

"You're gonna save me, right, baby?"

"Fucking bitch," I found myself saying, drowning the sound of her voice from my head with the sound of my own. "You goddamn fucking bitch."

"Soldier?" Ray called from the couch, cautious and hesitant.

But I ignored her.

"Fuck you," I muttered through gritted teeth, clutching my hair and staring into the bubbling pot. "God, fuck you for doing this to me."

Every twist of ill fate that had struck my life was directly related to her. And nearly every single one had been because of the pressure she'd put on me to protect her. To *save* her. To rescue her from the demons she'd created for herself. And all she could give me in return was *this*. Abandonment. Guilt. An ache so deep, so heavy, that I had to force the air in and out of my lungs just to keep them working.

I didn't deserve this. I never deserved any of it.

I never deserved *her*.

My body reacted before I could think as my hand wrapped around the empty jar on the counter and threw it against the wall. Glass shattered, and the remainder of the sauce inside splattered against the wall and onto the floor, making another mess that Diane Mason would never clean up.

"You are my sunshine ..."

My chest constricted violently as a sob worked its way past my lips, and my body doubled over. Crumpling to the floor in front of the stove and the pot of bubbling water.

"Noah, go to your room," Ray ordered with urgency as she hurried into the kitchen.

"But, Mom—"

"Listen to me and go to your room now." She enunciated every word as she reached over me, turning the stove off before dropping to her knees.

Noah begrudgingly did as he had been told as Ray wrapped her arms around me, pulling my body against hers.

Then, I cried.

I cried because nothing I had done was good enough.

I cried because I had failed.

I cried because she'd never possessed the ability to love me enough to get herself out of the shit she was in.

And finally, I cried because she was gone and there was nothing I could do to save her from that, nothing I could've done to stop it from happening in the first place. Because, for the first time ever, I had put myself first.

***

"Jesus Christ," I croaked, my voice scraping against my raw and gravelly throat. "I feel like such an asshole."

Ray was on her knees, gingerly picking up pieces of glass, when she turned to me abruptly, startled. "Why would you feel like an asshole?"

I shook my head and wiped a hand against my face, sticky from the deluge of tears. "Because I fucking lost it for a little while there. I didn't mean to. I just ... I dunno ... it just happened."

427

"Brawny," Ray replied in a soft, soothing tone, standing to dump the broken shards of jar into the garbage. "Your mother died. She was *killed*. You're allowed to lose it."

"But I'm not allowed to scare you guys," I argued as I got the sponge from the sink to wipe the splattered sauce from the wall and floor. "There's no excuse for that."

She came to stand with me, wrapping her hand around my wrist to stop me from walking away. "You didn't *scare* us," she insisted, firm and sincere. "We were *worried* about you. We *are* worried. There's a difference."

She took the sponge from me and cupped her other hand against my jaw, pinning me to the spot with her affectionate gaze. "I'll clean this up. You go talk to Noah. Let him see you're okay."

I was ready to protest. The last thing I wanted was to face him when I'd already promised a dozen times to never hurt them. But it didn't take long to realize Ray was right. If I ran, if I avoided him, it would only make me look like the coward I'd claimed not to be.

So, with my head hanging and my heart in more pain than I'd thought imaginable, I trudged down the hall to his room, where I knocked on the door.

"Yeah?" he called from inside, and I entered to find him on his bed, lying on his stomach and reading a book.

Ray had told me once that Noah had always hated reading until he met me. Seeing him with a book now, reading without persuasion, made me smile—even if just a little.

"Hey," I said, closing the door gently behind me.

"Oh, hi." He scrambled to sit up and stuffed a scrap of toilet paper between the pages to hold his spot. "Are you okay?"

No fear was reflected in his eyes. No anger or hesitancy. Just concern and worry.

"Um ..." I scratched at the back of my head, not sure how to answer. But honesty felt like the best option, so with a sigh, I sat at the edge of his bed and rested my elbows against my knees. "Not really. But ... I'm a little better, I guess."

Noah pulled his knees to his chest, wrapping his arms around them. "I'm really sorry your mom died," he muttered quietly, almost awkwardly. Almost as though he didn't know if it was the right thing to say.

"Thanks, buddy."

"Did someone kill her?"

Dropping my gaze to my hands hanging between my knees, I barely nodded. "Yeah, we think so."

It was a lot for anybody of any age to make sense of and process, let alone a kid who'd never known death in his short thirteen years. And it would figure that, as soon as I had entered their lives, I'd bring with me the black angel of death on my shoulder.

But, I reminded myself, *you also brought them the protection and strength they had lacked before. And that counts for something. It* has *to.*

"Do you know who did it?" Noah asked, his brows pinching as he tried to work through the tragic and disturbing truth that someone could be capable of intentionally taking another person's life. That someone could *want* to.

"I have an idea," I confirmed while keeping the secret of exactly who to myself.

Had Noah met Levi during his visits with his dad? Had he met my mother? What kind of stuff had this kid seen?

No. I couldn't allow myself to go there. I would never ask. We would never talk about it—unless he wanted to. Wondering about it now would only give my imagination the freedom to run wild, and nothing good could come of that.

"I hope the cops get the bad guys," Noah said, resting his chin on his knees.

"So do I."

"But ..." His eyes met mine with mature sincerity, our souls connecting. "If they don't ... you will, right? You'll get them?"

The booming beat of my heart resounded through my aching head as I suddenly became aware of what Noah had built me up to in his mind.

I was his hero. Superman. A godlike entity most boys envisioned their father being.

I'd never had one of those. I had Grampa, and I'd loved him fiercely, but I'd always seen him for what he was—an old man. My devotions had lain elsewhere—with my mother and the never-ending need to protect her from her own demons.

But I had become for Noah the thing I'd never had, and I wasn't about to take off that mask now.

"If they ever dare to come here," I said, holding his gaze with the strength of my own, "I'll get them."

For you, Ray, and Mom ... I swear to God, I'll get them.

CHAPTER

TWENTY-EIGHT

BETWEEN THE RAINDROPS

D etective Sam Lewis called me the morning after my mother's body was found.

I was at work, unloading a delivery of produce, when the call came through, and I didn't waste a second before answering.

"Give me a minute," I told Howard. "This is important."

He waved me off with a sympathetic, understanding nod. "Do what you have to do."

The moment I'd walked into work, I had apologized for not showing up yesterday. He'd been aware that there was a family emergency, thanks to Ray and the phone call she'd made on her way to work, but it hadn't been until after I came in that morning that he was aware my mother had died.

He wouldn't, however, know that she'd been murdered.

I wanted to avoid the questions. At least for the time being. The last thing I needed was for everyone in town to once again look at me with accusing eyes and questioning glances, wondering if my past had found itself on my mother's doorstep. Not realizing that it was *her* life that had ultimately stained *mine*.

I hurried into the storeroom, away from anybody who might be listening, and answered the call before Detective Lewis could hang up.

"Hey, Sam," I said on a held breath. "How's it going?"

"Well, I call, bearing good news," he said, giving me the response I'd been hoping for. "We got Levi."

My brow furrowed with instant suspicion. "Wow, that was quick."

"He knew we were coming. I mean, believe it or not, he was just hanging out at your mom's place. Said he lived there."

I nodded toward a stack of canned soups. "Yeah, I just … I don't know. I guess I expected him to run or something."

"Nope. And actually, he seemed exhausted. You know, almost relieved. It was strange. But, hey, what matters is, we have him. He confessed to lacing her drugs with fentanyl with the intention of killing her, and he agreed to give up the name of another guy he worked with. Someone he said was also involved."

My glare on the soup cans hardened as my brow furrowed. "Seth."

433

"You know him?"

"Unfortunately."

Sam grunted a contemplative sound, and I wondered what he was thinking, knowing it was unlikely that he'd share it with me.

Instead, he said, "Levi asked to talk to you."

My jaw clenched, and my fist flexed. "Why?"

"I don't know. All he said was, there was some stuff he wanted to talk to you about."

"Well, you can tell him to shove that right up his ass," I replied without hesitation.

Sam offered a humorless chuckle. "That's what I thought you'd say. Anyway, Soldier, I just wanted to give you the update. Either I or Detective Miller will call you with any other developments, all right?"

"Yep," I muttered, nodding. "Thanks, Sam."

"Of course. Talk to you soon."

He ended the call, and I stuffed my phone back into my pocket. I should've gotten back to work right away, knowing Howard was currently lifting those heavy boxes by himself when he probably shouldn't, but I didn't move from where I stood. Instead, I lowered slowly to sit on whatever was behind me—a stack of boxes containing mayonnaise, apparently—and stared ahead at the chicken noodle and tomato basil.

Levi had been arrested, and I hadn't been there to grin like a fucking maniac as the cops drove him away.

I hoped someone had though. I hoped someone had been there, thanking God that the piece of shit had finally, finally, *finally* gotten what was coming to him after too many years of slipping under the law's radar.

But Seth …

I tried to imagine the motive for Levi, and while I was only guessing, I suspected it likely had something to do with the death of his brother. Revenge perhaps. However, knowing Seth had been involved somehow—according to Levi—set a different tone. That changed things, and suddenly, that revenge seemed an awful lot like a message.

One directed at me.

"What are you up to?" I muttered to the minestrone, wiping a hand over my mouth and down my bearded chin.

But the minestrone couldn't answer for Seth. None of the soups could, and neither could I. But all I hoped was that the cops got their hands on him before he got *his* hands on anyone else.

***

I didn't feel like cooking, and neither did Ray. So, we asked Noah what he felt like eating, and after thinking about it for a few minutes, he told us he really wanted a cheeseburger from Dick's Diner. And while we didn't often make a habit of eating out, we thought a night outside of the house might help to brighten our collective mood, as dark and gray as the sky overhead.

"A storm is coming," I commented on our walk to the diner.

Luckily, our neighborhood wasn't far from Main Street. If the skies decided to open up on our way back, we wouldn't have far to go.

"Helen said we were getting some nasty weather this weekend," Ray replied, looking toward the black sky with a fearful grimace.

"Guess we can't go fishing then," Noah grumbled, kicking his feet along the sidewalk.

"Well, we'll see how bad it is." I wrapped my arm around his shoulders and pulled him against my side. "Otherwise, you can help me paint your room."

"At your house?"

"Yeah," I said, lifting one side of my mouth in a half smile. "Maybe we can head down to the store, and you can pick the color."

"I guess that's a good idea." He nodded, lifting his feet off the sidewalk a little higher now. "I mean, since we still can't live in our house and everything."

On the other side of me, Ray wrapped her arms around mine, hugging it against her chest as she pressed her cheek to my bicep. "Actually, I was thinking … maybe we should just fix our place up and ask Connie to help us sell it."

I raised a curious brow. "Oh, yeah?"

Noah looked around me to glare at his mom. "Why? Where are we gonna live then?"

"I think we're pretty comfortable where we are, don't you think?" she asked him, bringing her eyes up to meet mine.

Although she and Noah had been living at my place for several weeks now, it had never been discussed if it was a permanent change or just one we'd live with until it felt safe for them to go home. And considering the recent developments in the situation with Levi and Seth,

I thought I'd made the accurate assumption in thinking that, once they were both locked up, things would go back to the way they had been. I would be disappointed—I loved sharing my space with them, and so did Eleven—but I, of course, would respect Ray's decision to do whatever she thought was best for her and her son.

But hearing this now, that she wanted to stay with me, made my heart feel lighter than it had in days—weeks maybe.

"You mean, stay with Soldier?" he asked.

Ray nodded before saying, "Yeah. As long as you're okay with that … and Soldier's okay with it too, of course."

Noah was slow to nod, and his smile was even slower to grow. But when it did, he looked like a kid on Christmas as he beamed bright enough to light up the blackened sky.

"Yeah," he said as he slid his arm around my waist, "I think that's a good idea."

I pulled him tighter to my side, my smile matching his. "I do too."

***

We had a quiet and comfortable but fast dinner as we listened to the low, growling rumbles of thunder in the distance. The ominous clouds let loose the moment we stepped out of the diner, and we laughed as we ran through the rapidly multiplying raindrops, racing each

437

other home until Ray and I were breathless and panting and Noah was more than ready to keep going.

"Jeez, you guys are old," he chided before running the rest of the way down Daffodil Lane.

I took Ray's hand, interlocking our fingers, and tipped my head back to feel the rain patter against my face.

"You look happy," Ray commented quietly.

I smiled as we strolled. "I *am* happy."

She smiled, but her eyes held a little doubt. But it was true. Even despite my mother's death and the lone bogeyman still lurking in the shadows, I was truly, undoubtedly happy.

"I love you," Ray whispered, squeezing my hand.

We passed beneath a lamppost, the light illuminating the hundreds of raindrops as they fell to wet the ground at our feet. I stopped us from walking and tugged at her hand, pulling her against me. She laughed loudly, elated as she pressed her hands to my soaked T-shirt, the fabric plastered to my skin.

"I love you too, Rain," I said, my throat clenching around the words as they were spoken. "And it's because of *you* that I am happy. It's because of you that I love my life. Things that I never thought could ever be possible have been turned into a reality because you're in my life. And I know you thank me for everything all the time, but right now, I'm thanking you. For opening your mind and giving me a chance when everyone else was reluctant, for loving me, and for giving me a life I never thought I could have. I could never thank you enough for that. Because I've finally won."

438

Even in the rain, I could see the watering of her eyes as she swallowed. "If you win, I win, Soldier, and I'd say we both got very, very lucky," she whispered, moving her hands up from my sodden shirt to grasp my face between her palms.

She lured me down to her open, waiting lips to kiss me deeply, passionately between the raindrops beneath a lamppost on Daffodil Lane. Her hands pushed into my hair as mine tangled within hers, our mouths opening wider and deepening the dance of our tongues.

I will miss this so much, I thought, immediately shaken by the mere act of thinking it at all, and it worked its way down from my brain to my heart, settling in to cause an ache the kiss couldn't touch, let alone erase.

Ray pulled back, leaving me instantly lonely and longing for more. But her eyes met mine with a promise.

"I think we need to get inside and take care of this," she said, dragging her fingers slowly from my shoulder, down my chest, across my navel, and right along my bulging erection, straining painfully against the zipper of my jeans.

I groaned, instantly desperate for her touch the second she took it away. "Only if I get to take care of you first," I said as I grasped her hand and led her home, desperate to seek refuge from the warning bells residing only in my mind.

***

My hips rolled beneath her as I held on to her waist, staring into eyes that held every little thing I'd ever found important. Her fingers clung to my chest, piercing the skin with the crescent-moon shape of her nails. Her lips fell open; her jaw trembled. Her gaze flooded with a plea for release, and I would be damned to deny her.

My hand slid around her waist, resting on her thigh as my thumb pressed between her legs. Circling. Grinding. Moving with purpose and tantalizing persuasion.

Ray's eyes fluttered, threatening to slam shut at the cusp of her orgasm, but I stopped her with a tightened grip on her thigh.

"Don't close your eyes and disappear," I whispered in a low, husky voice. "Stay with me. Let me have this. Let me watch."

Her head jittered something of a nod. "Brawny, I'm not going anywhere."

The statement was multifaceted, and I held on to it with every bit of strength I had as my thumb worked and our hips came together and apart, together and apart, until her body tensed and she came undone. She strained to keep her eyes on mine, to not throw her head back and bite her lip, the way she always did. For a moment, I thought it was cruel to not let her, to not release her from my hold. But I needed to see the way her eyes hooded and deepened with euphoric lust at the moment of climax, to witness her passion for me in this fraction of time. To know without any inkling of doubt that I'd put that there and that no other man would ever do for her what I had.

I needed it.

No, my *soul* needed it.

And when she settled, her limbs loose and her jaw slack, I pulled her to me. She pressed her cheek to my chest and gasped for air, stroking her fingers over my skin and listening to the beat of my heart as it slammed against my rib cage. Every thump another promise to belong to her for as long as it could pump the blood through my veins and forever after that.

"You know"—I stroked my fingers through her hair and down her shoulder—"I think what makes me the saddest about my mom is that she never knew what this felt like."

Ray held her breath as she asked, "What what feels like?"

"To love someone as completely and thoroughly as I love you," I replied, closing my eyes and gliding my fingertips over the ridges of her spine. The slopes of her sides. The curve of her breasts. Everything. All of it. Every inch I could reach.

"You don't know that she didn't. Maybe she loved your dad like that."

"No." I shook my head against the pillow. "She didn't even love herself, Ray. There's no way she loved my dad—and sure as hell not the way I love you. But ..." I pulled in a deep breath, expanding my chest and letting it out fully, allowing my lips to smile on my exhale. Even as the tears filled my eyes. "I like to think she would be happy to know I have this, you know? She knew all I wanted was to get out, and I did. And that was her doing because if she had let me come home, I would've stayed. I would've hung around, and who the fuck knows what would've happened from there? Hell, I'd probably be back in prison by now, for all I know. But she … she's the one who told me to leave, so I did, and how crazy is that? That I wouldn't have been here—I wouldn't have been with *you*—had she just let me stay."

The tears slipped from my eyes and onto the pillow beneath my head, but still, I smiled. Because after everything, after all I'd done for that woman to protect her, thinking it was all for nothing, it had taken her death for me to realize that she had done the same for me.

She had saved me.

"Because she loved you, Soldier," Ray replied, and I realized she was crying too. "Maybe she didn't know how to show it, or maybe she just couldn't, but … she did. I don't need to have met her to know that. You were her sunshine."

I nodded, the pain in my chest coalescing with all the love I felt for the woman in my arms and the woman no longer here. "Yeah"—I kissed the top of her head—"and now, you're mine."

CHAPTER

TWENTY-NINE

FINAL SHOWDOWN

Ray had fallen asleep beside me, lulled by the pelting rain and booming thunder, while I could only lie awake, staring at the ceiling. Every now and then, the dark room was illuminated by a strobe of flickering lightning, only to be followed by another crash from overhead.

How she could sleep through God's wicked wrath, I had no idea. But it wasn't the storm that kept me awake.

The incessant tugging in my gut was entirely to blame for that. The little something whispering in my ear, the nagging derived from somewhere deep within my soul. It was relentless, and I could only spend so long tossing and turning before I just had to give up altogether.

I carefully climbed out of bed and made a successful escape without waking the woman who held my heart.

Quietly, I left the room, only to be greeted by a gentle *tap, tap, tap, tapping* coming from the direction of the living room. Every hair on my body stood on end as I froze just outside my bedroom door. The adrenaline stampeded through my veins in a powerful rush, and I steadied my nerves as I slowly, stealthily made my way down the hall.

But when I reached the living room, my lungs emptied instantly at the sight of Noah, sitting on the couch with his Nintendo Switch in hand. He jumped at the sight of me, then relaxed with a nervous burst of laughter.

"You couldn't sleep either, huh?" I asked, crossing the room to drop onto the couch beside him.

He shook his head. "I don't like the thunder."

"I didn't know you were scared of thunderstorms."

"I'm not *scared*," he grumbled defensively, not tearing his eyes from the screen. "I just don't like them."

I nodded understandingly. "Yeah, I get that. I used to hate the snow 'cause it reminded me of the night my friend died. It didn't scare me or anything. It just … you know, brought back bad memories."

Noah glanced at me for a brief second. "Thunder makes me think of yelling."

I lifted one side of my mouth in a sympathetic smile. "Yeah, I can understand that."

He didn't bother returning the smile as he looked back to his game just as another roll of thunder cracked directly above the house. Noah flinched, leaning closer to my side and shivering through the anxiety and fear. He quickly moved away, not wanting his pride to be more wounded than it already was. I wished I could've told him to curl up beside me if it made him feel better. I didn't care if he was thirteen or a growing boy or what. The kid was scared, and primal instinct told me to protect him, to make it better. But I didn't.

Instead, I asked, "What are you playing?"

"Mario Kart."

I lifted my hands in an exasperated shrug. "And you didn't ask if I wanted to play? What the hell, man?!"

He reluctantly grinned and got up to grab the other controller, then connected the console to the TV.

We played for a while, making sure to be quiet when we cheered and goaded each other so as not to wake his mother. But the fun and distraction helped calm his nerves, even as the storm rolled over our little town, and that, in turn, made me feel better. Even the horrible nagging in my gut had started to dull a little.

But forty minutes after I started playing, during a tense trip down Rainbow Road, Noah looked to me with widened eyes, a strange look on his face as he allowed Toad to run straight off the track.

"Do you hear that?"

My brows pinched as I paused the game and looked at him curiously. "Do I hear wha—"

But then I heard it. An engine rumbling in the near distance. Loud and obnoxious, coming closer by the second.

I knew that sound, and so did he.

"Noah." I dropped the controller to the coffee table and grabbed the remote, turning the TV off and shrouding the room in darkness. "Get to your room."

He sprang to his feet, ready to move, but still, he protested. "Wait. I—"

The truck rolled closer and closer.

"*Now*. Go. Get your shoes on."

He was running down the hall. "What? Why?"

I was on his tail and thinking quickly as he stuffed his feet into his shoes, questioning me all the while.

There were two windows in his room. One that faced the front of the house, one to the side and hidden from the street. I glanced out the front-facing window as Seth's big, loud pickup truck rolled to the curb, running over the Belgian blocks I'd laid around the garden in the spring. I watched him get out of the truck and saw the coal-black metal gleaming in his hand, glimmering in the downpour.

Breathe.

Breathe.

Don't panic.

I reluctantly tore my stare from the window and saw Noah standing beside me, his frightened expression aimed where mine had just been.

"I-is that a gun?"

"Look at me." I took his shoulders in my hands.

He was trembling, shaking his head involuntarily. "Soldier, w-why does he have a gun?"

I glanced out the window, praying we had time, and saw Seth climbing the porch steps to the empty house next door.

He thinks they're in there.

It was obvious when I saw the gun in his hand, but it was even clearer now.

Seth was here for one reason, and it wasn't to talk.

"Noah. Listen to me right now."

He looked at me then, his eyes rounded with fear and too petrified to cry, even as his bottom lip quivered.

"You're going to climb through the window, you're going to stay hidden and get away from the house, and when you turn the corner, you're going to run. Do you know the way to the police station from here?"

He nodded frantically.

"Good. You're going to take my phone, and when you get to the next street, you're going to call 911. Okay? Keep running. Run as fast as you possibly can and get to the cops. Do you understand?"

I pushed at the window at the side of the house, finding it stuck. I cursed loudly, then grabbed Noah's baseball bat. Terrified Seth would hear the shattering glass, I winced as I swung, just as a crack of thunder crashed overhead.

"Thank you," I caught myself saying out loud—to who exactly, I had no idea.

As I pulled the blanket from Noah's bed and used it to push away the jagged shards of glass jutting out from the window frame, I said, "Noah, tell me you understand."

"I understand."

"What are you going to do? Tell me."

"Uh-uh … stay hidden until I get to the end o-of the street, c-c-call 911, then run."

I grabbed his shoulders, guiding him to the window. "And where are you running to?"

"The police."

447

"Good. O—"

My words were cut off by a loud crash coming from next door. I turned to look out the other window, knowing Seth would be coming any minute.

"You have to go," I hurried to say, draping the blanket over the bottom of the window frame. "I'm going to help you out, and you're going to drop down. Ready?"

He could barely nod as the tears began to stream down his face. He threw his arms around my waist, holding on for sweet life.

"I love you," he cried. "I-I didn't say it before, but I do. I-I love you."

"I love you too, buddy." A blinding pain seared through my chest as I took his wrists in my hands, knowing I had to get him away from me while wanting to hold on tighter than I'd held anything before.

"N-no, y-you come too," he begged, his sobs growing stronger. "G-get Mom. We … w-we can—"

"We don't have time," I told him gently, prying his arms from around me and stuffing my phone into his hand. "Come on, buddy. Take a deep breath. You gotta do this for me, okay? Go get help."

I didn't wait for his response as I maneuvered him toward the window, easing him out into the downpour.

My hands were under his arms, ready to let him go when he said quietly, "You're gonna save Mom, right? You're not going to let him—"

"*Nothing* is going to happen to your mom," I whispered, meaning every word. "Now, remember what I said, and *go*."

He dropped to the wet grass and held tight to the wall of the house, crouching in the shadows, and I nodded to myself, knowing he had this. He was going to be okay.

I couldn't spare the time to continue watching him. With the bat in hand, I hurried to the room next door and shook Ray awake before running to the closet.

"Soldier?" she asked, her voice groggy. "What ... what are you doing?"

"You have to wake up," I instructed, digging through the sheets on the top shelf and finding Grampa's gun.

"What? Why? What's wrong? Is it No—"

"Seth's here."

And as if the psychopath could hear me utter his name, I heard his thunderous footsteps clomping against the porch next door.

He was coming.

Ray bolted upright in bed. "*What*?"

"Seth is here," I repeated, checking the barrel to find the chamber loaded.

Thanks, Grampa.

"Oh my God, Noah!" Her voice was shrill, and I urged her to be quiet.

"Keep your voice down," I ordered, whispering as I hurried to her side. "Noah is fine. I got him out. He's going to be okay."

Please, God, let him be okay.

Without another word, I hauled her out of the bed and positioned her in the corner, wedged between the dresser and nightstand. I pulled her down to crouch against the wall and pressed the gun to her palm.

"Take this." I positioned her hands around the grip.

At the feel of the cool metal in her grasp, her breath quickened with the rapid ascent of her panic. "*What*? N-no, Soldier. I-I can't. I-I d-don't—"

"He has a gun, Ray."

"Oh God, oh God, oh God, oh God, oh God ..." She trembled violently.

"Ray. Take a deep breath. Try to calm down."

"You t-take this!" she hissed in a loud whisper through the tears streaming down her face. "I-I-I c-can't ..."

"No." I shook my head. "I'm a convicted felon on probation. If I fire a gun and I happen to get out of this shit alive, I'm done. And I'm not going back to prison. I'm with you, or I'm nowhere at all, okay? So, you're going to sit here, and you're not going to leave this room."

The crack of splintering wood came from outside, and I stood, peering through the window. Seth had begun to climb the stairs, only to be stalled by the crumbling of the step I had never fixed.

"Holy shit," I uttered in a breathless whisper, unable to wrap my head around the coincidence.

You don't have time for this. Move.

"I'm going to lock the door," I told her, moving backward away from the window, watching as Seth struggled to free his leg. "You do not open it, no matter what you hear. And if someone comes in, you shoot. Do you understand?"

"Soldier, I-I can't do this—"

"Tell me you understand, Ray." I grabbed the baseball bat from beside the closet door.

"O-oh God," she sobbed, struggling to regain control of her breathing.

"Tell me, baby."

She sputtered on another sob before forcing one, two slow, controlled breaths. I couldn't see her from where I stood. That was a good thing, as far as Seth and his murderous intentions went. But I wished I could see her. I wished my eyes could find hers to show her the startling calm I felt. To show her I wasn't afraid, and if I wasn't afraid, there was no reason for her to be.

"Rain."

She pulled in a deep breath through her nose, and then she said, "I-I understand."

"Okay." I nodded to the darkness and held the doorknob in my hand, flicking the lock. "Remember, stay in here. No matter what you hear."

I began to close the door behind me when she said, "Soldier, wait."

"Yeah?"

A resounding bang came from the direction of the front door. The sound of splintering wood followed.

He was trying to get in.

It wouldn't be long now.

"I-I love you. I love you s-so much."

My composure had been held; my guard had been up. But at the sound of her voice professing her feelings in the dark, the broken sound of her heart fracturing under the weight of her fear, it was almost enough to

451

make me falter. To make me second-guess my decision to hold him off for as long as I could before the cops could reach us.

"I love you too," I said as another loud crack broke through the night and the front door swung open.

I shut the door before she could say anything more.

Seth's heavy footsteps moved slowly through the dark living room as I made my way down the hallway, alerting him of my presence the moment I entered the open space between the kitchen and living room, where he stood.

Lightning flickered through the windows to illuminate his wicked smile. "Soldier."

"Seth."

It felt like a showdown from an old Western movie. The sides of good and evil facing off with only several feet of space between them. Neither of us moved from our positions as my grip tightened around the bat and his fingers flexed around the pistol in his hand.

"Where's my son and Rain?"

"Is that *really* who you came for?" I inquired doubtfully.

His chuckle was humorless as he tipped his head back to face the ceiling. "Well, yeah, I did come for them. But if you're asking if I'm here for you too"—he nodded, dropping his chin to look at me again—"then the answer is yes."

My jaw pulsed. "Your *beef* is with me, not them."

He nodded. "Yeah. Yeah, it is. And do you know why?"

"Tell me, please."

He held the gun up, pointing it directly at my chest, and even as my heart sped up, I didn't let him know it.

"Because you have been a pain in my fucking ass your entire fucking life," he said, raising his voice. "David—you know about him now, right? Diane told us you did. He was a goddamn idiot for getting involved with your whore of a mother, and when he knocked her up, he became so ... so"—his jaw clenched, and his head shook—"*consumed* by the idea of getting you back and being a dad. But your fucking mom, man ... she wouldn't give him that. She *refused*, but he sure as shit died trying. Did she tell you that too?"

She hadn't mentioned that. The information was all news to me. News that I might've taken to heart under different circumstances.

"Why do you even care?" I asked, shrugging. "Why does it even matter to you?"

"Because he was my cousin!"

He dropped his gun-holding arm and shook his head, turning away. It was an opening. I could've rushed him, taken him down. But I didn't. I couldn't risk a slip of his finger on the trigger. I couldn't risk letting down my guard before the cops were at least within earshot.

"His parents raised me. He was like my fucking *brother*, and when he died, shit fell apart. My aunt and uncle lost their goddamn minds, and Levi was so fucking *obsessed* with getting back at your piece-of-shit mother. But he always wanted to keep your ass out of it. He always said you were just a kid, and I went along with that, even after they hauled your ass away, but ..."

453

He turned back to me, shaking his head. "You just couldn't leave shit alone, could you? And you just kept coming back, over and over and over again, like a goddamn cockroach. No matter how many times we thought you were gone, there you were. And then you ruined everything."

"How the hell did I ruin anything for you, Seth?"

He barked a bitter laugh, tapping the barrel of the gun against his thigh. "Are you serious? Come on, asshole! Of all places, you ended up here, next door to the bitch and my kid. Then, you just *had* to swoop in and get to them. You *had* to be the fucking hero."

"As if you wanted them." I snickered, shaking my head.

Seth lifted the gun and aimed it at me again. "Don't you fucking tell me what I did or did not want. That's not up to you to decide.

"And anyway, I got the fuck over that. I let it go. But you ... you couldn't just *stop*. You had to go back to your little mommy. You had to ask questions, give her your fucking number—oh, she told us *all* about that. And we had a good thing going with her, too, Levi and me. She did her job, fucked us—"

"You fucked her too?" I couldn't help but ask, my nose wrinkling with disgust.

"Yeah, and she didn't fight it like that little bitch, wherever she is. Your mom, she was good for something—I'll give her that. But then she saw you, and she lost that goddamn script, and we knew—we just *knew* you had it. We could only guess what you were gonna do with it or who you were gonna tell. She fucked up, so—"

"So you killed her." My hands tensed around the bat, holding on so tight that they ached.

Seth nodded, an air of pride emanating from his apologetic grin. "Had to, man. Should've done it a long time ago, to be honest, but Levi kept finding reasons not to." He shrugged, as if to say, *What can ya do?* "And the thing—the *real* kicker—is ... we would've stopped there. You would've gotten the message, and that would've been the end of it. But ..." He blew out a breath and shrugged before raising the gun once more. "You just *had* to go ahead and give the cops Levi's name."

"You would've done the same thing," I argued, shaking my head as I stared down the blackened barrel of the gun. "You can't blame me for that."

Seth slowly nodded his head. "No, I guess not. I guess I should be more pissed that Levi gave me up—family shouldn't stab each other in the back like that. But"—he shrugged again, this time with more nonchalance—"he's the one behind bars now, and ... well, you're not.

"So, listen, this is what's going to happen. You're going to tell me where that little shit and his mother are," he demanded, his eyes cold and devoid of any moral soul. "Then, you're going to watch me kill them before I kill you. Simple, right?"

"Or you could just kill me and be done with it," I offered, desperate to buy more time.

Where the hell are the cops?
Did Noah even make it there?

455

"Tempting, but, no, sorry. Eye for an eye, man. You took everything away from me, so you're gonna watch as I take everything from you. Now, let's go." He took his first steps, moving toward me.

I shook my head. "Then, you'll have to get through me to get to them," I said, backing up to block the hallway entrance.

Seth pursed his lips and nodded. "Okay."

He aimed low and fired.

A blinding pain seared through my thigh, spreading down my leg and up into my hip. I gasped against the urgent need to grant my leg the permission to buckle and give out from beneath me as I held tight to Noah's bat and my resolve, raising it up higher and swallowing the bile that threatened to corrode my throat.

"Who the hell brings a bat to a gunfight?" Seth asked, chuckling good-naturedly as he walked closer. "I mean, seriously, man, you could've been a little more prepared."

"Or maybe it's just that I'm not a coward." I tipped my head, staring into the frozen abyss of his eyes, coal black in the night. "Is that what you are, Seth? Are you such a pussy coward that you'd rather stand over there and shoot me than look me directly in the eyes when you take my life? 'Cause I dunno, man. I think, personally, I'd rather wrap my hands around your goddamn neck and stare at you until you couldn't look back."

It was a risk to talk to a man holding a gun that way, especially when that man had shown up at our door with nothing but murder on his mind. I knew I was playing with fire, but I had to buy time. That was all I was doing, just buying us some more time until the cops got here. Then, they'd haul him off to lock him away for a long time, and we could finally be free to go on with our lives without wondering if the bogeyman was lurking around every corner.

Maybe we could get married.

Maybe we could have another kid.

Maybe, one day, we could even have enough money to buy a place in River Canyon's historic neighborhood. One of those pretty, old houses with a white picket fence and a big yard. Plenty of room for a dog, a swing set, and gardening.

Those were nice thoughts. But they were nothing but the pipe dreams of a man wishing desperately he had the time left to make them happen.

The dare was enough to make Seth's jaw clench as he took the remaining steps to close the distance between us. I swung hard but too low, catching him in the arm and setting my injured leg off-balance. It knocked him back a couple of steps as he hissed through the pain, but he didn't waver.

"All right, asshole," he said through gritted teeth as I tried to steady myself and hoist the bat up high again, "how's this for being a coward?"

And before I could think, before I could react, before I could imagine another perfect scenario in a perfect life I'd never have, his cold, dead eyes met mine as he charged forward, pressed the open barrel of the gun to my abdomen, and fired.

The next few minutes felt surreal as the rain pummeled against the roof and the bat slipped from my hand to the floor.

I gasped for air and pressed my hands to my gut, aware that he had shot me. Aware that I was bleeding as gushing warmth seeped through my shirt and between my fingers. Aware that my breath was leaving my lungs now in short, shallow bursts ... yet I felt nothing.

Seth stared into my eyes as I reached a hand out, grappling for his shirt. Trying to hold on until I couldn't stand any longer.

"Now, I'm just gonna wait right here," he sneered, keeping his gaze pinned to mine as my knees buckled, "and I'm gonna stare into your fucking eyes until you're no longer looking back."

Somewhere in the distance were sirens—a whole chorus of them—and I coughed, the taste of copper heavy in my mouth.

Then, I smiled.

Good job, buddy.

"The fuck are you smiling about?" Seth growled, clenching my shirt in his tightened grasp.

"Be-because ..." I wheezed, lying there on the floor and wishing so badly I could trade places with the man looking down at me. "I won."

He cocked his head, fury raging in his eyes. "How the fuck do you figure?"

I thought of Rain. I thought of Noah.

I thought of the short amount of time we had shared together. The happiness I had experienced. The freedom I'd had the chance to know. The love and the family.

And I thought about how they'd get to go on with their lives without ever having to be afraid of this man again.

"Because th-they're still here."

CHAPTER
THIRTY

RAIN

Growing up, I'd found it impossible to not notice Soldier Mason.

He wasn't popular in the way a celebrity worked their way up the social ladder until every household in America knew their name. In fact, he wasn't particularly popular at all, especially within the crowd drawn to The Pit.

Soldier was known by simply existing.

He was kind. He was startlingly attractive as a kid and undoubtedly gorgeous as he ventured into adulthood. He was generous. He was helpful with an unrelenting hero complex. And each one of these characteristics had lent itself to an existence that touched every single person who ever came in contact with him.

So, yeah, it was impossible to not notice him, and I'd never forget the first time he'd noticed me.

460

It was a mundane Wednesday, and I was grocery shopping with my mom after school. I was a kid, only twelve or so, unable to reach a bottle of extra virgin olive oil from the top shelf. I grew exceedingly frustrated with every attempt to reach that last bottle, shoved all the way to the back, and I was afraid I'd have to return to my mom empty-handed—until the impossibly tall boy reached over my head and grabbed it without breaking a sweat.

"Here," he said, lowering it down in front of my eyes.

I glanced over my shoulder, mouth open like one of the goldfish Stormy had won at the carnival a few months back.

"Thank you," I whispered, surprised I'd been able to find my voice at all—he was so good-looking.

And, oh my God, was he ever. His face looked like it belonged in one of my teen magazines, right alongside the other pubescent heartthrobs of our time, with his wavy, dark hair, enviable bone structure, and honey-colored eyes. And he stood taller than even my dad, who I had previously been convinced was the tallest and strongest man I'd ever known, but there, in aisle eleven, I wasn't so sure anymore.

I also wasn't sure about that new feeling building and swelling and warming the region of my lower belly at the sight of his smile.

"Yeah, no problem," he replied. "Have a good day, all right?"

461

And that was it. That was the first time I'd truly met Soldier Mason, the first time he'd brightened my day and made me question my emotions.

And he'd had no idea.

Now, I sat in a chair in the hospital waiting room, wearing a clean pair of sweatpants and a T-shirt Patrick Kinney's wife, Kinsey, had dropped off for me at the emergency room. My son was beside me, his heavy head pressed against my shoulder once he finally—somehow—found sleep after living through the nightmarish ordeal at 1111 Daffodil Lane.

On the other side of me was Harry, who had come as soon as I texted—and how I'd managed to string together coherent words—"*Soldier's been shot and it doesn't look good*"—I couldn't tell you. I guessed I'd just done what I'd always done before—whatever had to be done.

Then, there was Patrick, sitting on the other side of Noah. Neither man spoke while Noah slept, and so I was left to think about that time—the first time I'd truly made Soldier Mason's acquaintance. And I wondered how I'd be able to go on living without ever getting the chance to tell him about it.

What if I never got to tell him I had actually written to him? Two times, I had written letters to him during his time in prison, only to think twice and throw them out, feeling stupid for entertaining the thought that he'd even want to hear from me.

God, why hadn't I told him already?

What if I never had the chance to admit that from the moment he had saved me that first time in The Pit, I would pray to him, the way one might pray to their god?

462

I would pray for him to come back, to make things right again. To prove once again that some men were good and decent and deserving of good and decent things themselves.

What if I never ever got the chance to tell him I'd loved him long before I spoke the words out loud? What if I never got the chance to say those words again?

God, I hated my brain right now. I hated that I couldn't stop the train of my thoughts, that I had no control over the panic and worry that surrounded the string his life held on to.

My eyes squeezed shut, and my heart jolted violently as I remembered those last moments before the police had arrived ...

POP!

The first gunshot rang through the house, snapping violently against my eardrums.

My gasp was loud—too loud—and I clapped a hand over my mouth, allowing myself a wail of terror behind my palm.

The cat jumped from off the bed and scurried underneath, cowering and staring at me through his glowing yellow eyes. Looking at me for comfort, but he wouldn't find any from me.

"W-what was that?" I whispered to Eleven, my voice shrill, but of course, the question went unanswered.

My heart rattled against its cage and reverberated through my bones. I wanted to jump up and run. I wanted to leave the room and make sure Soldier was okay.

All I could think was, Soldier, Soldier, Soldier, *his name on an endless, frenzied loop.*

But he had ordered me to stay here, to keep quiet and remain hidden, while he went out to confront the angry, awful, hateful man I had once—so, so, so many years ago—desired.

Before the years of abuse, apologies, and assault.

Before the fear of what would happen to me and my son if I dared to go to the police.

But now, the man I loved more than I had ever loved myself was out there. Fighting that evil man. Looking down the barrel of Seth's gun. Being braver than I'd ever been in my entire life.

All to save me after he'd already saved my son.

"What ..." I gasped, searching for air as my hands shook around the gun. "W-what if he's dead?"

God, God, oh God ... I couldn't breathe. I couldn't think. I couldn't face a world without Soldier. Not anymore. Not again. What would I do? How would I go on?

Jesus, how would I live, knowing he'd sacrificed himself for the sake of my survival?

How could anybody love me so much?

POP!

I jolted backward, wedging deeper into the corner of the room.

My eyes stared toward the door, my mind and body reaching a whole new level of fear I'd never touched before.

Soldier. Oh God, Soldier.

Then, I was on my feet, and I was running. I knew he had said not to unlock the door. I knew he had said not to leave. But, oh my God, I couldn't let him do this alone.

I couldn't let him die alone.

God, God, God, please don't let him die.

My fingers flicked the lock, and I bolted out the door, running down the hallway, gun held tight within my hands.

An animalistic sound erupted from my body at the sight of Seth in the living room, hovering over Soldier's crumpled frame.

He looked up in time as I raised the gun, aiming it right at his cold, soulless gaze, pinned right on me.

And then, without a second thought ...

I fired.

It was then that I'd witnessed the death of two men, just moments before the police and paramedics arrived.

The man I loved and the man who had taken him from me.

I clutched Soldier's hand as he slipped away. I told him I loved him so many times, but not nearly enough, and I stared into his eyes and begged a god I wasn't sure was listening anymore to bring him back to me, to not take him away, to just make him better and not allow him to leave.

Seth, on the other hand, had died alone, and while the paramedics were able to bring back the tiniest shred of Soldier's life—enough to warrant hope—there hadn't been much they could do about the bullets in Seth's heart.

Now, Soldier was in surgery. Had been for hours, and it had been about that long since we'd received any kind of update. The looks on the doctors' faces told me I was foolish to hope, silly to pray, and delusional to believe he might survive, but, dammit, what else could I do?

This wasn't supposed to be like this. He was only supposed to save my life that one final time before the cops hauled Seth away, leaving us with the freedom to finally live our lives together in peace. It wasn't meant to end like this. He wasn't supposed to die. I had saved him. After he had saved my life three times, I had finally saved his, and he wasn't supposed to fucking die.

I sharply inhaled through my nose, still halfway plugged from the bouts of tears I'd shed earlier, and then I covered my eyes with my hand and cried some more.

Harry laid his big, comforting palm against my leg. "I know, honey," he said, his voice gravelly and holding his own deep sorrow.

"I-I can't live without him." There was no air to be found in this room, and I gulped on nothing, finding it hard to breathe. "I can't—I can't do this ..."

He said nothing. He only nodded with tearful understanding and left that hand on my thigh.

My parents arrived a few minutes later, both of them rushing into the waiting room and bringing a new wave of tears to my eyes.

"Oh, Rain. Oh God, sweetheart."

Mom rushed to me first while Dad shook Harry's hand, then Patrick's, all of them making quick introductions.

"Are you hurt?" Mom held my face in her hands, looking me over as I tried to shake my head.

"I'm fine," I told her, but I wasn't, was I?

Maybe I hadn't been physically hurt—dear God, imagine what would've happened had Soldier not been there—but emotionally? Mentally? It was a wonder I could hold myself upright. Considering all I'd been through, after all those years … it was a miracle I could function at all.

"After everything that has happened, honey"— Mom's eyes met mine, her irises blurred by her own tears—"nobody would blame you if you fell apart. You're *allowed* to not be okay."

The strained splintering of her voice settled in my throat, forming a hard, sticky ball of emotion that threatened to choke me to death.

There was always someone who needed me to keep it together.

So, I cleared my throat, ignored the pain searing through my heart, and turned from her pain-stricken eyes. "I'll be fine," I told her while knowing damn well that, as soon as I got in the shower, I'd allow myself the ten minutes to let my pieces fall and scatter before I needed to get up and put them back together again.

It was what I did.

It was what I'd always done.

Noah stirred against my shoulder, nuzzling against me the way he'd done as a baby, before lifting his head abruptly and surveying the room through eyes that were immediately wide and free of lingering sleep.

"Where's Soldier?"

This poor boy. The things he'd witnessed. The things he'd been exposed to when I tried so hard to protect him, to do the right thing. Now, I just felt like I had failed.

God, I had failed everyone I loved.

With a hard swallow against that sticky ball, now back with a vengeance, I said, "Baby, he's still in sur—"

Through the corner of my eye, I watched a man in scrubs enter the waiting area. Harry was the first to spring to his feet, and I followed, a sickening pang of panic striking my stomach with every shuddering beat of my heart.

Noah was at my side, my parents and Patrick standing close by, as I asked, "How is he?"

The doctor cast his gaze from one pair of eyes to another, addressing us all with a look of somber regret that obliterated my soul a little more with every passing second.

And with every one, somehow knowing what he was about to say, I thought about those last moments I'd had with Soldier.

Those minutes that I knew would surely haunt my dreams and everything in between for years to come—hell, maybe even forever. The seconds before the paramedics had come and brought him back and taken him away. The ones in which I'd held his hand, aware of the blood leaving his body and pooling around us both. Swallowing us into a black hole, where maybe we could both live together—one in which no harm could reach us, no pain or suffering. And I'd told him I loved him. I'd told him over and over and over again because if that was the last thing he ever got to hear, he deserved to know

468

that. As hated as he might've been to some, he was, at the end of it all, loved.

He would always be loved.

My resolve to keep it together was already crumbling by the time the doctor brought his eyes back to mine. My knees locked, my hands holding tight to Harry and Noah.

"*How is he?*" I repeated, wishing this man would just get on with it and tell us what we already knew.

He swallowed and offered an apologetic smile. One that said news like this never got easier to deliver, no matter how many times he'd had to be the messenger.

"I'm sorry," he said, holding my gaze. "I'm afraid it doesn't look good."

Soldier had saved my life three times before I saved his once. And as the bricks holding my walls together were crushed, settling as dust on the floor of that waiting room, I knew it hadn't been enough.

CHAPTER
THIRTY-ONE

TIME TO GO

SOLDIER

At eleven, I had developed a crippling fear of dying after witnessing my grandfather collapse on the sidewalk in front of our house, only to, a couple of years later, watch my grandmother lose her quick and sudden battle with cancer.

My denial was strong—an impenetrable tower in the center of my mind and everything I did—and I got by on the belief that if I simply wanted it hard enough, I alone could avoid death.

I fought hard for myself. I fought harder for my mother. And I survived—we both did—just as I'd believed I would, despite the obstacles that had come our way. I had made sure of it.

But when I was twenty-one, sitting on the side of the road and watching my best friend take his last breath, any fear of dying I'd had disappeared. The realness of mortality was driven home, toppling that tower over with a single blow, and I was overcome by a simple acceptance that death was just an inescapable part of life. Somehow, I'd found a sense of strange comfort in watching Billy die. Almost as though if he could do it, so could I.

And I held to that tightly throughout the rest of my life. That, if I were to meet the end of my life at any given moment, I would do it fighting until I couldn't fight anymore. I would accept my fate with dignity, and then the transition would be simple. Easy-peasy—just as it had been for Billy.

Because like I said, if he could do it, so could I.

But at thirty-one, I realized that the difference between Billy and me was that he'd believed there was nothing in his life worth living for. Leaving this life and taking that step into whatever came next had come so easily for him because, hell, whatever it was had to be better than what he had been doing here, right?

But leaving Ray wasn't easy.

Although she had told me repeatedly that she loved me, that she always would, it couldn't bring me the comfort I needed to settle into the acceptance I'd thought I had. Because acceptance meant giving up, and giving up meant to give in.

I didn't give in. I held on to every last shred of my life, just to get one more glimpse of her bright emerald eyes. Not until I wasn't given a choice, and then …

Nothingness.

That was the first time I had died. Before they brought me back and Ray was gone. She'd been replaced by strange voices, strange faces, strange hands, strange sounds. Muttered words of encouragement and reassurance that they had me and I should stay with them and I had to hang in there. As if I had a say in the matter.

But I asked them about Ray in words I thought made sense, and the strangers assured me she was fine, she was safe, and that was all that had ever mattered. It was all I needed.

And I died a second death, knowing now that if I couldn't be with her, if my body wouldn't allow it, I wouldn't be anywhere at all.

And somehow, as the clock struck eleven eleven, I accepted it.

***

I didn't know where I was, yet I didn't feel lost.

Encircled by blinding light and a warmth similar to standing on a dock in the middle of the summer, I was met by a presence I knew. One that knew my name, called me buddy, and said it was good to see me again.

Grampa.

He was there with me. I knew it. I felt him all around me, an embrace of comfort and light, but I saw nothing.

"Where are you?" I asked, calm and without fear, searching the white for a face, a hand … anything to see or feel.

"My boy." *Gramma.* "Oh, my sweet little man."

472

I laughed like they were playing a game of hide-and-seek. I laughed because there was nothing little about me at all.

"I can't see you guys!"

"We're right here, buddy." Grampa's voice swirled around me, squeezing and soothing, just like one of his hugs.

Somewhere in the distance, a dog barked.

Sully.

"I've missed you," I said, on the verge of tears now. "I wish you could've met them ... I wish you could've seen—"

"We did, honey."

I searched for their eyes in the light, praying for a glimpse, for proof, for anything to tell me they were really there and I wasn't trapped in some horrible purgatory, to be haunted forever by the voices of the people I'd loved and lost and missed. But I found nothing. Not even my own hands, held in front of my face. Nothing but light and sound.

"Hey, man." Another voice now. One that struck a deeper chord and left me choking on the threshold of despair.

"Oh God, Billy."

He laughed that nasally laugh I had almost forgotten the sound of. "What did you freakin' do, man? You seriously went and got yourself shot?"

Oh, that's right. That's what happened.

"Yeah ..." I felt for my body and the blood. My hands met with the firm mass of my stomach, but not the

473

hot stickiness of the blood that had poured from me before.

"Always have to be the hero, don't you?"

I spun in a circle, desperate to look him in the eyes. "I didn't save you though."

"Man, how were you gonna save me when I wouldn't save myself?"

"But I'm sorry, Billy. I could've done something or told someone—"

"I know that, man. We were both stupid kids, doing stupid shit. But we're good, you and me. We always have been."

I continued moving, floating along on a sea of nothing through a world of blinding light.

"What is this?" I asked Billy or Gramma or Grampa—anybody who would answer. "Why can't I see anything? Where are—"

My words were halted by a faint, familiar tune, someone singing in the distance.

"*You are my sunshine ...*"

I closed my eyes to the lyrics, allowing every word to encircle my heart with a comfort I hadn't known since I had been a little boy, unburdened by a truth that would eventually destroy my innocence.

"*My only sunshine ...*"

The voice was closer now, and the place where I knew my chest should be ached with longing as I desperately wished for a time when I could climb into her bed, curl up beside her, and not care about where she'd been or what she'd been doing.

"*You make me happy when skies are gray ...*"

I remembered her arms around me. Remembered her scent, her voice, her youthful smile before addiction had the chance to swallow her whole. She was beautiful, I realized. God, I hadn't acknowledged that in so long, but, man, she was. The second prettiest lady I had ever known.

"You'll never know, dear, how much I love you ..."

That voice was even closer, nearly beside me, and I feared the moment I'd open my eyes and not see her there. I wanted to look at her face, to know that she was as okay as I was now. I wanted—no, I *needed* to know for sure that she had been saved if not in the last life, then in this new one, full of happiness and love.

But what if she wasn't there?

Would I be able to handle the crushing grief of losing her yet again?

"Please don't take my sunshine away ..."

That familiar sensation of no longer being alone swept over me, and somehow, I knew it was her.

But I couldn't bring myself to open my eyes.

"Mom?"

"Hey, baby."

Her voice was as crisp and clear as a November day, and the scent of spiced apples enveloped me, tugging at the edges of my mouth to curl my lips into a melancholy smile.

Yet I still couldn't open my eyes.

"Are you better now?" I asked her.

"So much," she replied, and I could hear her smile.

I bet it looked exactly the way I remembered it as a little boy.

"I want to look at you, Mom. I need to—"

"Oh, baby, I know." Her hand, soft and warm, barely touched my jaw, and I shuddered with a desperate sob. "But if you saw me, if you saw any of us ... you would never leave."

"Leave?" I croaked. God, why did this hurt so much? Why did I feel any pain at all? Wasn't this supposed to be Heaven—a paradise in which no man knew hurt or sorrow or any of those awful earthly emotions and aches? "But—"

"You're not supposed to be here yet, Soldier. It's time to go."

I shook my head, frustrated without understanding. "I don't get—"

"It's not for you to understand, baby. Not yet."

Panic folded itself around me as an energetic pull tugged at my being. Yanking an invisible chain, forcing me away from her and this place.

"Mommy"—my voice broke as I laid my hand over hers—"I don't wanna go."

It didn't seem fair. It didn't feel right. I had fought so hard for so much of my life, to regain this version of her, and the thought of giving it up now felt like the cruelest punishment of all.

"You were always my sunshine, baby. But it's time for you to be hers. There's nobody left to save. I'm okay now—we all are. Now, go live your life."

A violent pull of the chain sent me backward toward an unknown, and I begged my eyelids to open, just to catch a glimpse of my mother before she was gone once again. Just a peek. Just a reminder before I was left to embark on my journey without her.

I tried, and I tried, but to no avail until, finally, my lids slowly peeled back to stare out into the bright white of the warm light shining from all directions. And then, slowly, my vision adjusted, and I was greeted by the face of an angel.

Ray, I thought as I took my first breath in the next chapter of my life.

It was eleven eleven.

EPILOGUE

TWO WEEKS AT A TIME

There had once been a man named Soldier Mason, who was told since the day he had been born that he would be a hero and a savior, and he took it to heart. He proceeded to live life in the gray areas between black and white, doing what he knew was wrong to keep his heart on the edge of what was right, never once faltering to make good on the promises he had made to protect others at all costs.

And that was what he had done—until the night he died twice. Until he was set free and pulled back to this world to begin the third chapter of his life, unburdened by the brand he had worn since the first time he had entered the world.

My knees jounced beneath the table now as I thought about that man.

I hardly noticed him now when I looked in the mirror. Every once in a while, I'd catch a glimpse of residual hurt in his eyes or a hint of the past flashing across the scars he carried. But I was far from the man I had been before my reunion with Rain, before that night I saved her life one last time and she, in turn, saved mine.

The Soldier Mason I knew now was a friend, a husband, and a father of two. He was a homeowner and a member of the River Canyon town board. He was a hard worker at the local grocery store and grateful to call himself a partner in the business. He was a proud man, content and satisfied. But most of all, and most importantly, he was good.

This place didn't feel like somewhere a good man would go though, yet it felt necessary. The thought of coming had kept me awake too many nights. Ray had finally convinced me to just go and get it out of my system one night after we wrangled our two-year-old son into his bed—with little help from his big brother, who thought watching Miles outrun both of us was the funniest thing on the planet.

"If it becomes too much, you can just leave, and if not, you stay and get out of it what you need," she had said a week ago while lying on our couch, too exhausted to do anything but wrap her arm around my waist. "But either way, you should go. I think you need to."

And I'd thought, at the time, she was right.

Now, I wasn't so sure.

This felt too much like stepping into the past, and in some delusional way, I was beginning to worry I'd start degenerating the longer I sat there.

Then, the door opened, and I lifted my head to watch as another ghost sat in front of me. The guard he came in with fastened the handcuffs to the table while I stared ahead, unable to tear my eyes away from the last living member of my family.

Levi Stratton.

"You have an hour," the guard said, addressing us both before turning to me. "If you finish earlier, just bang on the door."

I nodded. "Thanks."

He left with a curt bob of his head and closed the heavy door behind him, leaving Levi and me alone for the first time in our lives.

How I had never noticed before that we had the same eyes and nose, I had no idea. I guessed I'd just never thought to look.

He leaned back in his chair, studying me as I studied him. Taking each other in for the first time, apart from outside influences. There was nobody to impress. Nobody to fight—that part was over; it had been for four years.

"So," he finally said, breaking the silence while steepling his hands on the table.

"So, I guess you're my uncle."

Levi actually barked a laugh. "Sorry to break it to ya."

I tipped my head and shrugged. "It is what it is. Can't choose who we're related to."

He nodded slowly, as if to agree. "I heard you died."

I held up two fingers. "Twice actually."

He leaned back in his chair, turning down the corners of his mouth. "Impressive. But it figures a big motherfucker like you would have nine lives." He

480

twisted his lips and dropped his gaze to the table. "More than I can say for Seth."

There wasn't any bitterness or anger in the statement. Only a residual, lingering sadness that I knew all too well.

"I'm sorry," I told him. Not to apologize for my wife or what she had done to save our lives four years ago. But to offer my condolences for a loss I assumed to be great.

Levi brought his gaze back to mine and lifted his chin in acknowledgment of the subtle olive branch. "Hey, eye for an eye, right? I supplied the shit that killed your best friend; your woman killed mine. And besides"—he shrugged and shook his head—"I can't say the asshole didn't have it coming. Something was bound to get him eventually."

Hearing the confession come from his lips that he was the one who had given my mom the drugs that would end Billy's life stirred something inside me that had been sleeping dormant for the past few years. I had learned better to live with the grief and sadness while carrying on with life as a husband and dad—a good one, one I would've wanted for myself. But that guy had been left at home, and the Soldier Mason of the past fought to keep his hands to himself.

"You wanted to kill my mom," I accused, knowing the statement to be true.

And Levi didn't even try to deny it. "Yeah, I did. Or at least, that was the plan anyway."

He sat up straighter and shifted on his chair, making himself more comfortable.

"You gotta understand something, man. This was never supposed to be my life. We had it good for a long time. I mean, even in that shithole of a town, my family was okay. We had money. My parents had decent jobs. We had a nice house. But David met your mom and went all stupid over her even though my folks more or less threatened him with his life not to see her ..." He chuckled sadly before saying, "I guess that isn't really that funny.

"Anyway, I hated that bitch for what she did to him—well, to all of us, really, but mostly him. He loved her. Would've given her the freakin' world if he could, and then he knocked her up, and ... I dunno. We were all hoping that would be what turned shit around. Like, if David was gonna insist on being with Diane, then maybe having a kid would—"

"Save them?" I lifted a corner of my mouth in a sardonic half smile. One I knew he wouldn't understand.

But he nodded, surprised to find I had gotten what he was implying. "Yeah. Exactly. But, of course, that's not what happened. She kept the baby—*you*—from him for who the hell really knows why. I don't think any of us really got it. Maybe ... I dunno. Maybe she was scared my parents would fight your grandparents for custody or some shit. Only God knows what was going through that bitch's head. But it fuckin' ruined my brother, man. He wanted you so bad."

My heart ached a little for the father I'd never had a chance to know. The one who had wanted me more than my mother ever did. I wanted to know about him. What he had been like, who he had been, how much of him I could find in myself—all of the things I had never cared much to know until I learned that my father had a name.

David Stratton.

"Then, after he died, my dad …" Levi's eyes clouded with his own sadness and pain—something I recognized deeply. "He hated your mom, yet he went to hell and back, trying to protect her from herself—for *you*. But the stress and depression over burying my brother drove him to a massive heart attack. Killed him"—he snapped his fingers—"just like that, right in front of me."

My lips fell open with a gasp I kept concealed. Giving him the space to continue his confession. One I wanted, but hadn't even had to ask for.

It was like he needed to tell it as much as I needed to listen.

"Mom went a few months later. Pneumonia. And what the hell was I supposed to do, huh? It was just Seth and me at that point. David had already fucked up his reputation by the time he died, so I figured I'd follow in his footsteps 'cause what else did I have?"

I answered then, "You could've gotten a *job*, man. You could've done better for yourself."

His face hardened, turning his features to stone. "Oh, hey, pot. It's me, kettle. I'd shake your hand if I wasn't chained to this fucking table." He rattled the cuffs to further prove his point.

"We all made our fucking choices," he continued. "We knew what we were doing, but we did what we had to do. Simple as that. I'm not judging you, but you sure as fuck had better not judge me."

I twisted my lips, thinking about that for a moment, only to realize he was right. Maybe in the beginning, I hadn't understood the tragic magnitude of what I was doing, back when I was naive and young. But eventually when I was older—wiser—I knew. I just couldn't stop, not until I had been forced to.

"Fair enough," I conceded with a bow of my chin.

He relaxed again, just a little. "I'm not proud of the shit I did or what happened to Billy—fucking kid didn't have that coming. But nothing we can do about it now. You're just lucky you got out when you did. Seth would've gotten to you before he got to your mom."

"What?" I let my mouth fall open, shocked by the sudden revelation. "I thought—"

Levi's eyes softened just a little. "I didn't kill your mom, man. Back in the day, I'd hated her, yeah. She had driven my brother crazy, she had killed him, and I had wanted her as cold and dead as he was … but …" He sucked in a deep breath, then said on his exhale, "I, uh … I dunno … when you were locked up, we … we hooked up, and, uh, I guess I sorta grew to love her."

He licked his lips and kept his eyes on the chains holding him down. Hiding the sorrow he held in his heart, and I realized then that someone had actually loved my mom in the end. The warmth of knowing someone had cared for her—in whatever dysfunctional, fucked up way—brought a relief I hadn't known I needed, and I struggled not to tear up from the gratitude coursing through my bones.

"Anyway"—Levi cleared his throat and swallowed hard—"Seth pumped her with those fucking pills, and I helped him cover it up after the fact."

I shook my head, disbelieving. "But I—I told the cops—"

"You told them what you thought you knew." He looked up at me and lifted the side of his mouth as he shrugged. "So, I took the rap."

"But Seth ..." I slouched against the chair and held my hand to my forehead. "He said you turned him in."

He nodded slowly, giving me the space to let the truth swallow me up and leave me feeling hollow. "For dealing, man. Not murder."

"Jesus Christ, Levi." I glanced toward the door, shaking my head. "Why didn't you—"

"We're all protecting someone, Soldier. But some of us don't get to win."

We were more alike than I ever could have imagined. Once upon a time, the Soldier I used to be never would've admitted to our similarities or the parallel paths we had walked unknowingly. But the man I was now hung his head, wishing I had known before. Wishing we could've been there for each other instead of warring over—what? A beef we never truly had?

It felt stupid now. Juvenile and petty.

The guard opened the door abruptly. "All right, time's up."

I acknowledged him with a nod. "Can we just have another minute?"

He took a moment to consider it and then sighed. "I'll give you five, but wrap it up, okay?"

He closed the door behind him, and Levi nudged his temple toward the door. "Charlie and I are tight, but don't tell anyone I told you that."

I could only smile, remembering what that had been like. Befriending Harry and not wanting anyone to know until it just didn't seem to matter anymore. And now, we were inseparable, like father and son. He had been my best man at my and Ray's wedding, and we had made him our youngest son's godfather. I loved him the way I had loved Grampa, and if Grampa were still alive, I knew without a doubt he'd love Harry too.

Levi eyed me expectantly, waiting for whatever it was I wanted to say, whatever had driven me to ask Charlie for another minute.

"There's still a lot I wanna ask you," I said, studying my tattooed hands, folded tightly on the table.

Levi hesitated before nodding. "Well, I guess you could write to me if you really wanted to."

"Yeah, I could," I said, considering the idea, "or, you know, I could just come back."

He didn't answer right away. He could only watch me with cautious suspicion, eyes narrowed and mouth pressed shut. I could understand why he'd assume my motives were malicious, maybe thinking I had all intentions of seeking my own revenge on him for what he had done. The crimes he had committed. The murder he had taken the blame for.

But … I didn't know. Call me crazy—and, hey, maybe I was—but didn't we all deserve a little forgiveness for our sins? And if Levi was my only chance at getting to know the father I had been denied,

486

then I didn't see any reason why I couldn't find it in my heart to forgive him just a little for his—even if I would never ever forget.

I mean, even Charles Manson had visitors in prison.

He laughed through his nose, shaking his head and eyeing me with disbelief. "You'd actually wanna visit me again?"

"If you don't mind."

"No, I mean … it's cool. I just … I dunno. I guess I figured I'd be dead to you as soon as you walked out of that door."

I slowly stood up, shaking my head. "We're each other's last living relative, man. Might as well get to know each other."

He didn't reply. He just stared ahead at the empty chair across from his as his features softened around the edges.

I wondered for a moment if anyone had come to see him at all in the last four years. Maybe Tammi. Maybe some other specter from the past. But I knew I was kidding myself. Nobody had come to see Levi in four years. Nobody cared if he was alive or dead.

As the guard opened the door, I clapped a hand against Levi's shoulder. He didn't meet my gaze.

"I'll see you in two weeks?"

I kept my eyes on him and watched as one side of his mouth slowly lifted.

"Yeah," he replied gruffly, nodding. "Two weeks."

Then, with a squeeze of my hand around his shoulder, I nodded to the guard and made my way through the door. Through the hall, through the detectors, and out the main entrance to head back to my car. I got in and started the engine with a quick glance toward the pictures I kept clipped to the visor. Grampa holding me as a toddler. Gramma and Grampa sitting with me on a Christmas Day when I was a little kid. Billy and me on our bikes. Ray and me on a date at the diner. Noah and me on the dock. Ray, Noah, and me with the smallest member of our family, Miles, on the day he was born.

And as Wayward's gray stone exterior faded to nothing behind me, I drove toward two kids who needed me, and a wife who loved me, and a town that had shown me the forgiveness I needed, and a house in historic River Canyon that I knew Grampa would've been proud to know I called mine.

And so was I.

I was proud to call it all mine.

If you or someone you know is suffering from substance abuse, there are people out there who want to help.

Don't wait until rock bottom.

Don't wait until it's too late.

SAMHSA

(Substance Abuse and Mental Health Services Administration)

1-800-662-HELP (4357)

ACKNOWLEDGMENTS

Well, before I can mention anybody else, I *need* to give the most special of shout-outs to my sister and best friend, Karen. Because if you hadn't come along with the name Soldier, this guy would've been Garrett. We are *all* grateful for your naming services, but especially me. I'm always grateful for that, and I'm always grateful for the time we spend brainstorming. Most of my stories wouldn't exist without that—especially this one. I owe you lots of Dunkin' iced lattes for that and everything else.

Now that I've gotten that out of the way, I have to give a shout-out to my family—my parents, husband, my son Jude, and my other sister—and other best friend—Kelly. Without your patience, support, help, encouragement, and pride, I never would be able to accomplish everything that I have accomplished. I say it a lot, but I don't think any of you truly understand how much everything you do has impacted my transition and growth into this author life. Thank you all for that. So much.

Next, there's the beta readers and friends who have read this thing before anyone else—Jo, Melanie, Leanne,

Erin, and Jessica. You guys. I knew while writing Soldier's story that this thing was special, but, man … it wasn't until you read it and told me yourself that I realized I wasn't just a crazy author infatuated with a fictional man born in my own mind. You made me believe that this truly was special, that I wasn't delusional, that something happened to me during the writing of this story, and that I had grown. Thank you all for the endless amount of support and constant words of encouragement and praise. Without you all there to stroke my ego, I probably wouldn't be as confident as I am, and that is truly appreciated.

Then, there's Jovana, editor extraordinaire. Your tears are my victory, and I say that in the most loving way possible. My nerves go haywire every time I send a book your way, and every single time, you reassure me all over again that I'm doing the right thing with my life. You are a gift and a treasure, and I am forever grateful to have found you.

To my brand-new PA, Jessica. At the time of writing this, we have only been together for a week or so, but you have already made my life infinitely easier. I don't even think I realized how much I needed you until you were in my life. Thank you so much for all your help, all you've done, and all of your copious amounts of support and encouraging words. I already feel spoiled, and I don't know what I'd do at this point without you. Well, no, I'd probably be going even more crazy … but you're keeping that from happening.

MURPHY RAE. MY MURPH. Oh my God. My love for you is intense. Every single time I present a new book for you to cover, I just know it's going to be epic. And this one? What a freakin' trip. You were inspired, you were taken over, you neglected everything else, and you created a masterpiece. Just like all the others, but, dude … this is next level and we both know it. I'm so glad to know you. I'm so glad you want to work with me.

Then, there's Team Dearie and the Dearies. My cheerleaders. All of you people who believe in me and cheer me on and look forward to every single release like I'm someone. You blow my mind every day. Thank you.

And finally, to you, Dear Reader … God, you. You, you, you. After feeling like I was losing for so long in this life, it is because of *you* that I have finally won. And I continue to win, as long as you're in my corner, reading these books and loving the people I make up in my mind. Thank you for that. Thank you forever.

About the Author

Kelsey Kingsley is a legally blind gal, living in New York with her husband, her son, and a black-and-white cat named Ethel. She really loves doughnuts, tea, and Edgar Allan Poe.

She believes there is a song for every situation.

She has a potty mouth and doesn't eat cheese.

Holly Freakin' Hughes

Daisies and Devin

The Life We Wanted

Tell Me Goodnight

Forget the Stars

Warrior Blue

The Life We Have

Scars & Silver Linings

A Circle of Crows

Where We Went Wrong

Hoping for Hemingway

32 Rowan Blvd

The Girl in the Front Row

The Hero in Her Story

Saving Rain

The Kinney Brothers